W9-ADB-938

GREENCASTLE
and the Denizens
of the Sacred Crypt

Books by Lloyd Kropp

THE DRIFT

WHO IS MARY STARK?

ONE HUNDRED TIMES TO CHINA

GREENCASTLE and the Denizens of the Sacred Crypt

| a novel by |

LLOYD KROPP

FREUNDLICH BOOKS
New York

Library of Congress Cataloging-in-Publication Data

Kropp, Lloyd.
Greencastle.
I. Title.
PS3561.R6G73 1986 813'.54 86-2180
ISBN 0-88191-037-6

Published by Freundlich Books
(A division of Lawrence Freundlich Publications, Inc.)
212 Fifth Avenue
New York, N.Y. 10010

Distributed to the trade by Kampmann & Co., Inc.
9 East 40th Street
New York, N.Y. 10016

Manufactured in the United States of America

10 9 8 7 6 5 4 3 2 1

Any writer who writes about a sensitive and slightly confused sixteen-year-old boy who keeps slipping in and out of the so-called real world will almost certainly draw upon his own experiences. Novelists will often deny this, but novelists are all liars, which probably has something to do with why they take up the writing trade in the first place.

Greencastle bears some resemblance to the town where I lived when I was in junior high school. The main character sometimes expresses opinions I remember from my own adolescence. The events, however, are almost entirely imaginary. The characters are also imaginary, although three or four of them are composites from real people I knew at various times and places. My parents, for example, are nothing like Roger Cornell's parents, and (thank God) I never had a teacher who was anything like Emma Leibolt.

However, the seasons and feelings of childhood are real. And Playground Joe is real. I have only changed him a little, and given him an epithet.

LLOYD KROPP

Angel of air and light and dreams,
this book is for you. Now, here,
all at once in the garden of the evening.

And for Stephen and Alex.

And very much for Tim Hillmer.

Contents

1 Playground Joe Loves the Sky

Nobody ever won a game of anything from Harry Fisher. That was something he wrote down years later, hoping it would turn into a cautionary tale he could tell his children. Something about the tragedy of having to win every time. Or perhaps it was only that Harry was too careful about limiting himself to places where he was sure of winning. Perhaps he outsmarted himself along with everyone else.

Harry was a genius. He had suspected that much the first time he had met him. Harry was never distracted by things other boys were distracted by. He never forgot anything, except by choice. He had this knack of reducing any problem to its absolute forms and necessities and then spreading all the parts out in front of him. Life, for Harry, was a series of moves.

He and Harry Fisher and Dennis Kirk and Frank Aldonotti had been lads together during the early 1950s. The world, as usual, was full of danger and uncertainty. During the summer and fall of 1951, the Korean War had come to a standstill at places called Heartbreak Ridge and Porkchop Hill, and the peace negotiations at Kaesong had gone nowhere. Another war was destroying French Indochina. The stability of the

Middle East and the world petroleum market were threatened by a mad Iranian who cut off all oil from his own country to the West, got sick, and then conducted his fierce negotiations from a hospital bed. China had been overrun by the Communist Horde, and Russia made threatening noises everywhere. The king of Egypt, a man of inexhaustible sexual energy, was murdering his own people and emptying his country's treasury. Shirley Temple was divorced.

Still, it seemed to him that America was a good place to live and that this was a good time to be alive. The wars were terrible, but far away and trapped in small places. The threat of Communism was frightening, but it gave a sharp and beautiful definition to the American way of life. The Marshall Plan, American democracy, Billy Graham (the preacher, not the prizefighter), and Coca-Cola were conquering much of the civilized world with love and goodness. Dwight D. Eisenhower, that great, smiling symbol of passivity, would soon be running for President, and all the young men who had gone to school on the GI Bill and whose rooms were still filled with bayonets, Lügers, Japanese flags, and photos of Americans standing together in foreign lands would stand up and cheer. And Frank Sinatra, an American Orpheus without wife and pursued by maenads, told a *Time* reporter that life was still good and that suicide was the furthest thing from his mind.

He often thought of this period of his life as a time of slogans and certainty, a dream of peace that rested between the holocaust of the Second World War and that nameless chaos of assassinations and social upheaval that followed the death of John Kennedy.

America looked and sounded different then. The rock-and-roll phenomenon was still over two years away. Young men in rented tuxedos and girls in taffeta and tulle went to formal dances where they did the rhumba, the jitterbug, the samba, and a dippy variation on the old foxtrot. They listened to turgid ballads, drowning in violins, sung by Jo Stafford, Vic Damone, and Perry Como. High school boys took their girls to the movies, and sat in peanut heaven, where they necked a little during long, smoky double features. They hung out in soda shops and drove around in prewar jalopies and envied the rocket fins, the streaks of chrome, and the puffy contours of their parents' automobiles.

Pants were loose and baggy with plenty of room for wallets and handkerchiefs and combs. No one seemed to mind if his pockets bulged. Computers were enormous machines that existed mostly in science-fiction stories. Hamburger was thirty-nine cents a pound. The price of ballpoint pens had dropped from twenty-five dollars (the Reynolds pen, with its own pedestal and its dustproof plastic display case) to a quarter. People ate popcorn and turned off all the lights when they watched television to make dark theaters in their living rooms. Bells rang when merchants punched their cash registers.

The great interstate highway system, with its chain restaurants and gas stations which would do so much to homogenize American culture and destroy village life, had not yet been built. The suburban ranch house was still a daring innovation. The era of supermarkets and franchise food palaces with their high-rise marquees was still years away, and small-town America was made up of caboose-shaped diners, fruit stands, meat markets, dime stores, shoe repair shops, gas stations, cigar stores, and hardwares. It was still an age of shops, and shopkeepers.

More than anything, he thought, it was an age of drugstores. Although he seldom set foot in Heinkel's Drugstore after Norman Pangborn opened his shop across town, it was still the place he remembered best from his grammar school days. He remembered the magazine racks filled with *Thrilling Wonder Stories, Famous Fantastic Mysteries, Mammoth Detective, Amazing Stories,* and *Weird Tales*. He remembered their ragged, powdery pages, their delicious pulpy smell, their bright, slick covers filled with monsters and spaceships and cowboys and beautiful, murdered women in black stockings. It was here amid the overpowering odor of malt and chocolate that he first fell in love with the impossible. He fell in love with ice cream and eternity, with Egypt and Almond Joys, and with the luxury of his own melting sensations in that cool Saturday-morning world hidden behind marble soda fountains and tinted window glass. And Mr. Heinkel, with his screechy voice and his Hitlerian mustache, a child-hater and a penny-pincher from morning until night, was like a monarch ruling in a kingdom he had never traveled.

Dennis Kirk and Frank Aldonotti understood his feelings about such things. The three of them spent nearly all their free time together. They were the Denizens of the Sacred Crypt, and they met every other Wednesday night in his basement to talk about flying saucers and tell horror stories. Harry was not a Denizen, and he did not understand about Egypt or flying saucers or secret societies. Harry was interested in history, and in his strange ability to change it.

Besides Harry Fisher and the Denizens, he had one other friend, a Martian named Ythn. He had met Ythn during the previous winter when he had no friends at all and had spent all the mornings of his Christmas vacation walking in the snow and all the afternoons reading science-fiction novels and pulp magazines and looking out the window. He remembered that it was Thursday night and that he had lain in the dark after finishing Edgar Rice Burroughs's *A Princess of Mars,* unable to sleep. Flakes of snow, glowing in the soft lambency of the streetlight, fell obliquely against his window and then gathered in a powdery drift on the sill. He was thinking about the long descent of the snow through the dark winter night and, a lifetime away, the sands of Mars passing forever through the arid seasons of that bright world. He was thinking of Barsoom, and the beautiful princess. He was thinking of how John Carter had come out of the cave with its strange vapors and raised his arms up to the sky, and he imagined himself walking out into the snow, running down the steep pine bluff and crossing the road into the Watchung Reservation and then standing there with his arms stretched out like wings amid the white branches and the silence. He thought of the ancient Martian canals and the great wall at the edge of the desert that lay so far beyond his outstretched hands. He reached out from under his covers and touched the rough springs of the bunk bed above him, the bed where no one ever slept. The metal frame squeaked.

Suddenly he realized that all along, against the play of his imaginings and longings, he had been listening to something. A tapping at the window. But no, that was not possible. His room was on the second floor. He opened his eyes and turned his head to look at whatever might or might not be there.

A spidery-looking creature with green fur and a large, triangular head crouched against the glass. Tiny suction cups at the ends of its fingers pulsated, and the creature seemed to glow a little, as if it were electrified. The snow falling against its shadowy outline gave it a ghostly and somewhat pathetic appearance.

He got out of bed and went to the window. The creature saw him immediately and came out of its shivering crouch to spread itself against the glass, clinging to the smooth surface with its outstretched toes and fingers.

He tapped on the windowpane with his fist. "Can you hear me? Do you speak English?"

"I speak English very well," said the creature. "Furthermore, I'm very friendly. My name is Ythn and it's very cold out here."

"My name is Roger Cornell."

"I'm very glad to meet you, Roger Cornell. Now could you let me in? I'm freezing."

"You look like an alien."

"Well, for heaven's sake that's obvious enough, isn't it? But don't let it frighten you. Every boy your age needs an alien. Just thank your lucky stars that you've been fortunate enough to get one. Now please open the window?"

He put his hand on the window lock, and then hesitated. "I really don't know you," he said. "My mother told me lots of times not to let anyone in the house I don't know."

"Now you listen to me," said Ythn. "You spend half your life dreaming over all those incredibly lurid magazines and thinking about flying saucers and the like. And here you have a chance to meet a real alien, and you won't even open the window. God, it's cold out here."

"You don't sound like an alien at all. You sound like my Uncle Peter."

"I wonder if you'd be good enough to tell me just what an alien is supposed to sound like," said Ythn. "I thought you'd be pleased to hear me speak the King's English, but I suppose I could make incomprehensible whistling noises, or begin every third word with the letters *fth*, or some such silly thing. Or I could speak Portuguese. Would Portuguese be alien enough for you?"

"I think I'm upsetting you. I'm really sorry. My mother says I have a real talent for saying the wrong thing to strangers."

"Not to worry," said Ythn. "But do try to remember that to me I am a perfectly natural member of my own race."

"Well—could you say something in your own language?"

"Moo goo gai pan."

"That's not your own language. That's something you order in a Chinese restaurant."

"Please," said Ythn. "It's so cold. The snow is getting in my fur. We don't have snow on Mars."

"Mars? Are you a Martian?" He threw open the window. The alien leaped inside, landing on the tips of his toes. Then he squatted on the floor and began to rub himself all over. When he finished, he sat very still for a moment. With his legs bent and his four arms crooked, he looked suddenly inanimate, like a music stand.

"Roger, I can't tell you how much I appreciate this, and I fully intend to pay you back a hundredfold. There's no doubt at all in my mind that you and I are going to become fast friends."

It was clear that the alien—the Martian!—was no threat to him. He had done the right thing, letting him in out of the cold. "Do you live near Barsoom? Have you ever gone sailing on the canals? Are you going back soon? Can you take me with you?"

"I ought to tell you," said Ythn, "that the novels of Edgar Burroughs are riddled with inaccuracies."

Roger began to shiver in his pajamas. He closed the window. "Of course," he said quietly. "They're just novels, aren't they? They're not true at all. I sometimes forget—"

"Now, now," said Ythn. "I wouldn't go so far as to say they're untrue." The Martian's green head tilted a little to one side, and his large gray eyes began to shine softly. The crosshatch of silver cords inside his rigid little mouth blurred when he spoke. Ythn was beautiful, he decided. Like something out of a dream.

"You mustn't be sad," said Ythn. "Mr. Burroughs really did have the right idea about things. You know, we have a Mr. Burroughs on Mars. He writes stories about Unkthanistorn—that's Earth to you. Of course, he was wrong about the details, but with the poet's gift of intuition he did catch the spirit of things very nicely. I daresay your Mr. Burroughs has done as well."

"But how about the flying horses and the great wall and John Carter and the princess?"

Ythn shook his head. "Roger, I know you have a hundred questions, but I have to tell you I'm really very tired. Perhaps we could talk tomorrow—"

"Oh sure!"

"—and in the meantime I have a favor to ask of you. I'm still very cold from my journey and from your nasty weather. Could I crawl in with you? Just for a little while? I don't take up much room."

Roger could see at a glance that his relationship with Ythn would be asexual, and that it would be perfectly safe to invite him to bed. But he hesitated. His perpetually damp sheets, evidence of secret activities he would rather die than reveal, embarrassed him deeply, especially on washdays. He wondered about Ythn's sense of touch and his (God forbid!) sense of smell. Would he notice? Would he be offended?

"Oh, don't worry about all that business," said Ythn. "That's just what people do. We're all human, aren't we?"

* * *

The next morning he asked Ythn if he had come in a flying saucer. He was pleased and mystified to hear that no, he had just come by himself. Could he possibly have used the Burroughs Method? He tried to imagine Ythn with his four green arms raised into the Martian sky, wishing with all his might until finally his soul caught the edge of Earth's atmosphere. *Ythn had come by himself*. Wild.

That winter the airspace over America had been full of flying saucers. The reports in one week over Chicago left him to wonder if there was any blue left in the sky there. Roger loved flying saucers more than almost anything in the world. He was a subscriber to *Fate* magazine, and every month he read the saucer articles, and believed them. Several years earlier, Raymond A. Palmer had led him into the intricacies of the Shaver Mystery when he had edited *Amazing Stories*. Roger still dreamed that Deros and Teros lurked in caves somewhere near Greencastle, but now he had turned his attention to saucers, and the evidence seemed even more persuasive, even more irresistible.

As winter melted into spring, Roger made two other friends, both of them human. Their common love of flying saucers, Raymond A. Palmer, magic tricks, Egypt, pulp fiction, and staying up late made them all the closest of friends in less than a week. Soon, with Norman Pangborn's help, they became the Denizens of the Sacred Crypt. They wrote nearly fifteen pages of club bylaws.

Roger had never had real friends, but he had known for a long time that the only way to have them was to form or join a club. Other people, he believed, made friends because they belonged to the Boy Scouts or the football team or Future Farmers of America or Youth for Christ. He hated those organizations. He hated all organizations he knew anything about, yet he felt the need of one for the sake of these elusive friendships that other people seemed to have. When he was in the sixth grade, he created a secret society called the Invincible Hooded Fangs, which unfortunately had no members and no program except for the vague notion of sneaking around at night when your parents thought you were asleep and doing good in the dark. "The Defenders of Midnight Justice" was its ringing epithet. Later, in the eighth grade, he tried again, this time with the Immortal Cosmic Slashers. And this time the club did attract one other member, a fat boy named Rollo Pflug, who lived on Kent Place Boulevard. Sometimes they would fly model airplanes together at Roosevelt Memorial Field. Rollo would insist on ending with a "club flight," which meant setting a stick model on fire and sending it aloft. "Immortal Cosmic Slashers!" Rollo would scream happily, waving his fat arms and jumping like a june bug while his aircraft burned and fell.

It was the utter failure of the Immortal Cosmic Slashers and the Invincible Hooded Fangs that made the Denizens of the Sacred Crypt seem like such a miracle. Three members, regular meetings, Kool-Aid, and field trips at least twice a week to see Roger Pangborn, who in a sense had invented them and was their spiritual adviser. But most of all, it was being with two boys who would keep his secrets, who were at loose ends without him, who walked with him every day and made jokes and punched him on the shoulder.

Now it was the fourth Saturday in October. The trees along his street turned their leaves away from the sharp, clean wind that marked the cold edge of autumn. But he did not mourn the passing of summer and the beginning of school as he had in previous years. He viewed these things with a kind of poetic melancholy that was new to him. It was as if his new friendships and his books and his magazines had formed a castle from which he saw this great loss with a certain philosophical detachment. And only a season ago, he thought, he had been a mindless ninth-grader.

He ran all the way down the steep hill at the end of Stone Hill Road, feeling warm and easy in his blue canvas jacket, thinking that he had escaped his mother's Saturday-morning job list by less than five minutes. He turned left at the bottom, crossed High Point Avenue, and sprinted down Thistle Street.

He preferred running to any other way of getting around, except on Friday nights when he came home in the dark from Miss Dot's School of Social Dance. Then he liked the speed of his bicycle and the way it lifted him a little above the night. But here in the bright morning, his legs worked like an independent force that let him sail effortlessly through the world. He ran on the balls of his feet, never once coming down on his heels, so that the earth seemed softer when he ran than it did when he walked. Running gave him a clear distance from everything. It put him in another place, and the voices and opinions and threats of other people caught in the wake of his running never touched him. That was important—the feeling that he could leave anything behind that might want to hurt, touch, or change him. Sometimes he imagined that a shadow—not his own, but the shadow of something or someone else—followed him everywhere, and that it was determined to catch him and take something away from him. And he imagined that his legs were growing longer and harder so that he could run faster to escape from the thing that wanted him. Sometimes, especially at night, he half believed that Shadowman had caught up with him and had taken whatever it was without his knowing. *Something is getting lost,* he would think as he lay in bed. *Ythn? What is it that I'm losing all the time?* But Ythn would be asleep underneath the mattress of the bunk above him, his many arms and legs tangled in and out of the springs, like green macramé.

Past the third house on Thistle Street, Roosevelt Memorial Field opened up on his left. He rushed past the deserted baseball diamond with its catcher's screen and water fountain. In a few seconds he came to the second half of the field, marked by the right turn at Recognition Street. At the far point of the angle formed by the two sections of the park, he saw a man in a baggy black suit flying kites. With a large wooden reel strapped to his waist, he stood with his legs apart, smiling at the sky. Three nylon lines stretched upward and then disappeared. High and far away, three kites, orange and blue and green, hung motionless, like bright holes cut in the fragile, paper-thin atmosphere. Roger laughed. Without breaking stride, he turned and ran along the angle of the L-shaped field toward Playground Joe.

"Roger? That you?"

Roger waved, slowed down, came to a stop in front of Joe's pushcart.

"Never saw any kid run the way you do."

"I'm going out for the track team next year maybe," said Roger. "You still got all your stuff? I didn't think you'd be here so late. I mean, it's practically November."

Sometimes Joe brought only his kites to the park. Sometimes he came with everything: kites, carom board, chess, checkers, backgammon, croquet, Monopoly, Rich Uncle. And Roger could remember days when he had everything going all at once. At dusk he would fold things neatly into his push-cart and be off down Recognition Street to God knew where.

"Brought everything," said Joe, "but I don't 'spect much business today. The big kids got football practice down at the high school, and the little 'uns don't spend so much time outside now that it's turned cool."

"I see you got three up already."

"No point coming out here if I can't get least three up." He squinted up into the sunlight where the long droop of the kite strings marked the three bright, tiny shapes.

"Eleven o'clock and not much wind," said Roger. There was something about Joe that made him want to say things like that. Joe was like a ship captain, and Roger wanted to look out into the sea of the world around him and say, *Seven bells and all's well, Joe. Wind southeast. Ceiling twelve hundred.* There was not much wind, but there was some. He stretched his hands and arms up as far as they would go and stood for a moment as motionless as the kites. He wondered how far up they were.

"Wind dies a little this time of day," said Joe. "It'll pick up again after lunch. Always does."

It occurred to him that Joe was one of the most predictable people he had ever met. He said the same things over and over. He brought his pushcart to the park every day in midsummer, then every other day in September and October. Then he disappeared until the following spring. No one knew where he lived, why he didn't seem to work for a living, or what his last name was. Sometimes a new boy would ask him, and he would always say, "You couldn't pernounce it, kid. Just call me Playground Joe."

Joe was a shapeless man with hound-dog eyes, sagging jowls, and a hundred veins branching and popping all over his nose and cheeks. The old black suit he wore every day to the park buttoned tightly over his bulging stomach. A gray scar extended like a streak of lightning from the corner of his left eye to his cheek and down the side of his throat. "Got it in the war," he would say. But Joe never talked about the war. He talked mostly about the strategy of caroms, the ins and outs of kite flying, the best way to hit a croquet ball. Sometimes he talked about what was in the newspaper.

"My job's to keep you kids informed," he would say. "Bet you don't know there's an oil embargo on. Bet you don't even know what an embargo is. Bet you don't know why the Japs came to San Francisco last month."

Then he would smile and read a little out loud from *The New York Times,* something about the new peace treaty with Japan, McCarthy's latest attack on Communism, Eva Perón's visit with the Pope, or the upcoming primary elections. Roger noticed that sometimes the newspaper was a week or two old, and after a whole summer of coming to the park with Dennis and Frank, he began to suspect that Joe didn't really understand much about what he read. His relationship to the contents of newspapers seemed custodial rather than intellectual.

Roger ran his fingers over the surface of Joe's fourth kite, which rested lightly on the green grass, just touching at three points. The paper felt soft and slightly fuzzy, like velvet. But the wonderful thing was that Joe had painted a flying man on the back, a man with long white hair, his arms stretched forward. Blue, with a white star between his shoulders.

"Joe, I didn't know you could draw."

"Used to draw a lot when I was a kid," said Joe. "Thought I'd give it a try."

"A flying man. That's neat."

"That's what I think of sometimes when I fly my kites. A man out in the blue on a string."

Roger smiled. "But what's the man doing way up there? What's he looking for?"

"Don't know. Something you can't see from down here. Something up in the blue."

"But what happens when the flying man goes out too far? What happens when the string breaks?"

"Don't know. Last year I had a string break on me. Never should have used that cheap fuzzy stuff from Woolworth's. Cotton's not worth a damn. Anyway, the string broke and I saw her sail away. Tipping from side to side, looking jaunty as you please. The Good Humor man told me he saw it way over on Warsaw Avenue five miles across town. Probably landed somewhere up in the next county. Or maybe—" Joe looked into the sky again, raised his hand against the sun, and squinted at his three kites.

"Or maybe what, Joe?"

"Don't know. Maybe she went somewhere else. Maybe there are places we don't know about." He shook his head and clicked his tongue. "Lots of nooks and crannies up there."

Roger laughed as he tried to imagine a sky full of nooks and crannies, a sky that looked like his grandmother's living room in Detroit. "Playground Joe loves the sky," he said. "That's what all the little kids say."

"It's true," said Joe. "Had lots of experiences up there. Sky's an amazing place. Love the sky."

Roger had the idea from something Joe had once said that he had been a pilot during the war. There was something sad about that, he thought. He had ridden on the backs of eagles during the biggest and most important war that ever was, and here he was now with his scars and his old scarecrow suit, playing with children and flying kites where he couldn't go anymore. But still, he seemed happy. He seemed to have a point of view about things. Playground Joe loved the sky.

"Joe, do you think there are things up there? I don't mean kites and airplanes. I mean *things*. Aliens. Saucers. Do you believe in any of that stuff?"

"Don't know," said Joe. "Don't believe in anything, really. I just like to watch my kites go up and see what the clouds are doing and sorta keep my eye on things. Always been very curious, you know. That's one thing that—that never got lost."

Joe touched the scar on his neck. He eyes wandered away from his kites and seemed to lose their focus. Roger saw that Joe was thinking about something very far away.

As he watched Joe run his third finger over the silver scar, he wondered who Joe really was. He wondered what had happened to him. "Joe, what's your name? You never told me your real name."

"I forgot."

"Oh, come on, Joe, you can tell me."

"I'm not kidding. I forgot my name."

"That's impossible! You can't forget your own name!"

"I knew it up until about two or three years ago," said Joe. "Then it just sort of slipped away."

Roger was quiet for a moment. He wanted to laugh, and then he didn't. He was sure Joe was kidding him, and then he wasn't. *It just sort of slipped away*. He imagined Joe's name slipping away like a kite with a broken string. He saw it tipping from side to side, drifting high over Warsaw Avenue and then into the next county.

Joe looked down now from his kites and smiled at him. "How about a game of caroms? I still got your favorite shooter."

"No, thanks, Joe. I gotta get going."

"How about some croquet? I could set it all up just for you and me."

"Not just now. I gotta run. Maybe I'll be back after lunch. I got things to do. I'll see you, Joe."

The truth was, he had nothing at all to do, but he was

beginning to feel restless. He had to run. Feel the wind. He got halfway to the street before he remembered to turn back and wave. Playground Joe smiled his crooked smile, showed his yellow teeth.

"See you later!" cried Joe. "Have a good winter! Make some snow forts and drink something hot at Christmas! See you in April!"

Roger stopped running and his hand fell out of the sky. He would have stayed another half hour to play caroms if he had known that this was Joe's last day. Autumn, the four months of winter, all the way to April. That was a long time. Lots of things could happen to a man who didn't even know his own name. He wondered where Joe went in the winter, and how he lived without money. He knew that Joe had been wounded in the war. He knew there were things he never talked about. He hoped he would be okay until spring.

2 | The Hanging Boy

Running down Recognition Street gave him an oceanic feeling. Most of the trees here were saplings, which left a clean, open view of white houses and green lawns. Light was plentiful. The cement island that divided the north and southbound traffic curved at one end and came to a sharp point at the other, and its arrangements of trees, bushes, and stone steps resembled sails, spars, and a poop deck. As he passed Jump Street, he saw the second island, this one long and slender. The streets here seemed unnaturally wide, and the crossings wider still. They made him think of alluvial floodplains, canals, and rivers. Once, he remembered, it had rained for three days in Greencastle, and Recognition Street had flooded. Dozens of children with their sailboats, mechanical submarines, and motorized speedboats had turned Recognition Street, Jump Street, and Thorne Street into a Venusian playground—a vast ocean of the imagination. A hundred ships sprinkled the gray-blue water for six hours until the choked sewers began to run again, carrying many of the precious toys into that blind underworld of rats, decaying leaves, and lost baseballs.

At the corner of Thorne, Recognition Street made a steep

climb back up to High Point Avenue. Here the ocean of grass and cement and white-shingled houses came to an end. Tall elms and oaks flanked the street on both sides. High overhead, their branches intertwined, plunging everything into cool darkness. He crossed the street and stopped at the edge of the shadows near a house that stood on the left-hand corner. There, hanging from one of the side windows, he saw a window box filled with sick roses. A blight of some kind had turned the points of the petals brown and curled the pinkish-brown leaves into grotesque imitations of buds.

He took a few more steps up the hill and saw an old garage in the back, and a stone driveway that opened onto Thorne Street. The grass by the garage and around the side of the house had caught on only in patches over the dusty, gray soil. Too much shade, he thought. Grass can't grow in all that shade. Across from the garage, six steps led up to a back porch where a brown-and-white dog lay curled, his nose buried under his tail. He saw from the way the dog trembled and whimpered that it was dreaming.

He stood on the sidewalk near a large elm tree and stared at the house. There was nothing remarkable about the place. All the shades were drawn on the first two floors, but there was nothing odd about that. His own grandmother always drew her shades during the day for privacy, and to keep the house cool in summer.

Suddenly he saw a boy under the shadow of the elm tree, less than twenty feet away. The boy hung by his hands from a thick branch three feet above his head, and swayed a little from side to side. He wore a polo shirt and wrinkled corduroy pants. The dark silhouette hanging from the tree, seen so suddenly and so close, gave him a chill. He thought for a moment of death. The hanged man in his tarot deck.

"Hi," said Roger.

"Hey," said the boy.

"I—I was looking at your house."

"Not much to look at," said the boy. "Just a house and some sick grass and too many trees. You new around here?"

The boy's voice was so unnaturally loud that it made Roger wince. He could not see his face in the dim light, but he sensed that the boy was grinning at him. "I've lived here since I was ten," said Roger.

"I been here a year," said the boy. "Not much of a town, is it?"

"It's okay," said Roger. "You go down to the park much?"

"I hate the park," said the boy. "Nothing down there but pregnant women and mothers with baby carriages and a bunch of kids screaming and playing baseball and football. I'll be finished with high school in two years and then I'm leaving for parts unknown. You in tenth grade?"

"Yes." He blinked and waited for his eyes to adjust. He felt uneasy. It felt queer talking to someone when you couldn't see his face.

"Tenth grade's got all the bad teachers," said the boy. Still hanging from the tree, he crossed his legs and began swinging in wide circles. "I really hated tenth grade. I had French in tenth grade but I never been to France. You like school? You look like the kind of kid who might like school." The boy laughed. His laughter was hard and sudden, like a mirror breaking.

"It's okay," said Roger. "Not too bad." He stared at the dark outline of the hanging boy.

"So who do you have?"

The boy chinned himself three times effortlessly, then dropped from the tree, landing on his heels. He walked out of the shadows of the elm branches toward the sidewalk. He was tall and muscular, but with an odd, lumbering gait that made him look awkward now that he was on the ground. His black hair curled into a tangle over his forehead. Roger was surprised to see that the boy was handsome in a rough sort of way.

"Who do I have? You mean for classes? I have Figge for World History and for Physics. I have Wakowski for Algebra. I have Simic for Latin and Leibolt for English."

"Leibolt, she's the one to look out for," said the boy. "I got her again this year."

"She was sick with something at the beginning of the semester and we had a substitute who just read us stories," said Roger. "She only came back about two weeks ago."

"Leibolt, she's got an encyclopedia attached onto her," said the boy. "And she never likes anything anybody says or does."

"She seems okay so far."

"Wait till you get to know her."

"It's Miss Simic who really scares me," said Roger. "She screeches at everyone and she's about a million years old. She looks like an orangutan."

"Most ladies over sixty, they look like orangutans," said the boy. "Their faces get flat and they get all this stuff that hangs from their chins and they start to look kind of Chinese. You say you got Figge?"

"For History and Physics."

"Mr. Figge, he's a terrible teacher. Nobody ever learns anything from him. He's got this weak little voice and he's really skinny and he'll do most anything to avoid trouble. He's vice-principal now. Biggest sissy in the world."

"How about Miss Wakowski?"

"She's just a math teacher. What can you say about a math teacher? Jesus, I wish it was still last summer."

"I guess you really hate school," said Roger.

"It's a toilet," said the boy. "They make you do a million things you're not interested in. Me, I could do a lot better on my own. Did I tell you how much I hate the French and the Italians? Listen, maybe sometime I'll show you my attic. I got a lotta great stuff up there."

The boy picked up a stone and threw it at his own garage. "Mrs. Leibolt, she was sick last year too," he said. "She gets these headaches. I think maybe she's got brain cancer."

Roger shuddered, thinking this was a very bad joke. His own childhood had been touched at various times by illness or death whispered in the next room or spoken quietly over his head at the dinner table. His Aunt Clovia, a woman he had never met, had caught something awful in France. His grandfather had rheumatic fever and one day had ceased to exist. Illness, he often thought, was a condition of adulthood, something that was liable to happen when you got older. Like his Uncle John, who went to college, got married, and died of pneumonia. He had always known that apart from his springtime encounters with asthma he would never get sick. Children lived in a glass world of immunities until—well—he did not quite know when childhood ended. Not too soon, he hoped.

But he imagined that the smiling boy who stood in front of him was an exception—he knew something more about illness, and perhaps something about death. And he sensed that the boy's smile was not genuine, not really a smile at all, but a mask that kept his real face hidden.

"You say she gets headaches?" said Roger.

"Yeah, you know. Like women do. Midol and all that stuff. Hey, I got a secret. Bet you can't guess. Ennis tried, but he never even came close."

"A secret about Mrs. Leibolt and her headaches?"

"Forget about Mrs. Leibolt. It's a secret about me."

"Oh."

"You think about it. Hey, did you see my dog? He's up there on the porch. He and Ennis are number one and number two. You could be number three if you want."

"Number three?"

"You know."

"No, I don't get it."

"Hey, you're lucky, you know that? I just decided to show you my stuff."

Roger winced. Two months ago a big skinny kid had said that to him over by the old Catholic high school, and had promptly dropped his pants. But this was the middle of Saturday. Things like that didn't happen on Saturday, at least not in this neighborhood.

"Is that your secret?" said Roger. "That you're going to show me your stuff?"

"Listen, don't always ask me if what I'm talking about now is what I was talking about a minute ago. You done that twice now."

"But you talk about sixteen things at once. I can't figure out what you're talking about."

"Listen, don't think so much. That's Shakespeare. You're not scared of me, are you?" The boy grinned.

"What's to be scared of? I don't see anything to be scared of." Roger felt vaguely angry. "What's your name, anyway?" he demanded.

"Harry Fisher."

"I'm Roger Cornell."

"Hey, I know you. Ennis told me you won the ninth-grade English prize last year."

"You seem to know everything," said Roger.

"Don't worry about it. What did you do to win the English prize?"

"Nothing. I sort of won by default. Mrs. McGilliam hated our whole class, but she hated me least because I was the only one who finished his final project. I built a model of the Parthenon out of Popsicle sticks after we read *Julius Caesar*. Mrs. McGilliam didn't seem to realize that the Parthenon was over in Greece."

"They got more damn awards in this high school," said the boy. "Did you notice that? They got plaques and cups and certificates and trophies and pins and ribbons and letters of merit and scrolls—there's no end to it. They give out awards for just about everything. I bet if you keep your desk clean all year long they'll stick a lollipop up your nose with a pink ribbon on it. C'mon inside. I'm gonna show you all my stuff, remember? I got stuff you wouldn't believe. Don't step on the army."

"The army?"

And then he saw the acorns. Hundreds of them arranged

in rectangles of forty-eight, six files and eight to a rank. Platoon after platoon, all arranged in tight formations in the bare spaces where the grass had died.

"We got two kinds of armies here," said Harry. "The first kind might lose and lose but it can still win the war, 'cause it comes from a big country and has lots of allies and time is on its side. Then we got the Elite Fisherman Army. It has to win every time. If it loses even once, that's it. Most of my good stuff is in the attic. I got this great machine I built with a motor onto it. Listen, did you ever meet Ennis?"

As they came up the steps to the back porch, the dog woke and began barking and beating the back door with his tail. "Atsa good dog, Nunnug," said Harry. "Atsa good Nunny-Nunnug. This here's Roger. He wants to see all my stuff."

The dog leaped on Harry and began pawing at his shirt. Harry laughed and gently pushed him aside. Then the dog noticed Roger. Instantly he stopped barking and sat back on his hindquarters and twisted his head a little to one side.

"Hi," said Roger. "Good dog. What did you say his name was?"

"Nunnug."

"That's a funny name for a dog," said Roger. "That's a funny name for anything."

Harry bent down and hugged the dog and buried his face for a moment in the dog's neck. "He's a good dog," said Harry. "He's a good Nunnug."

No one seemed to be home in Harry Fisher's house. They took two Cokes out of the icebox in the kitchen and then went up a steep flight of stairs to Harry's room on the second floor. The place was filled with stick models hanging on strings taped to the ceiling: Messerschmitts, Focke-Wulf night fighters, Zeros, and one Dornier-219, the "Flying Pencil." On an end table near his bunk bed sat a German submarine, its conning tower, its railings, and its delicate lace of electronic rigging all miraculously carved from a single piece of wood. His desk near the corner was covered with sticks of balsa, tubes of glue, green and blue model paper, and stacks of military decals.

Harry slid the desk drawer open to reveal a tray full of silver dollars, a German Lüger, a box of ammunition, and what looked like the shell of a German "potato masher" hand grenade.

"My God," said Roger. "Does your father know you have all this stuff?"

"My dad, he doesn't come here," said Harry. "He doesn't know too much. He's this guy with a big mouth and no brain. Did you ever see so many silver dollars? Wait till you see what I got upstairs."

A little bewildered, Roger followed him up a narrow stairway to the third floor, which was a single large room with a dormer window and a wonderful pinewood floor.

"This is your room too? This whole place?"

"No one ever comes up here but me," said Harry.

Against the one windowless wall a three-story bookcase ran the length of the room. It held dozens of tiny warships, all carved from balsa with tiny stick guns and little housings and turrets cut and glued together to form the superstructures. They reminded him of the metal ships with the tiny wheels that were sold in dime stores, but these were more delicate, more detailed. Next to the rows of warships sat boxes of games—Monopoly, Rich Uncle, chess, checkers, Camelot and a half dozen others. Next, an army of metal soldiers—little figures cast from lead with shining metal helmets held on by a rivet through the skull. Machine gunners, hand-grenade throwers, sharpshooters standing, sharpshooters on one knee, marchers, mine detectors with gas masks, and finally a row of diers. Roger was fascinated by diers. He remembered checking out all three dime stores in Greencastle when he was in grammar school, looking for different kinds of diers. Some clutched their throats. Some had dropped their rifles on their metal stands and were in the act of pitching forward or backward. Some buckled their knees, lowered their heads, and clutched their stomachs. The diers were by far the most dramatic and the most complete of all toy soldiers. He himself had loved being a dier in sixth grade, and had perfected various falls, grimaces, gasps, and spasms that had amazed all the other children who played war at Roosevelt Memorial Field.

The end of the bookshelf was filled with books. *Jane's Fighting Ships,* an old Encyclopaedia Britannica, a picture history of the Second World War, and finally, at the very end of the shelf, a thin folio entitled *Artists and Models—50 Delicious Poses*.

Other amazing things hung from the bright blue walls: a Catholic Knights of Pythias sword, a real flintlock rifle, two replicas of Spanish pistols, and two Japanese bayonets. In the middle of the room stood a large worktable piled high with white construction paper, sticks of wood, bottles of India ink, and notebooks full of numbers. What an absolutely glorious place, he thought. He had never in his life seen a playroom that was so large, so blue, and so full of riches.

Harry stood in the middle of the floor with his hands on his hips. "You like my hideout? I got a new project in mind. It'll cover the whole table."

"Is that your secret? The thing you're building on the table?"

"Nope. My secret is nothing you can build. You'll never guess it. So I guess you like my dog, even though you're not too crazy about his name, am I right?"

"Harry—I think you're trying to confuse me."

"I got no reason to do that. What do you think of the fleet?"

"You mean all those little boats?"

"Ennis and I have these sea battles sometimes. Each ship has a maximum speed and a maximum range and firepower onto it. We work everything out with rulers and you get to move all your ships in one turn. Ennis, he comes up here and says, 'Hey, Harry, let's play with the fleet.' So we set up a battle and work it out from books. Once we took a whole weekend to do the Battle of Savo Island."

"Who won?"

"We both played the Japs. The Japs won."

Roger was mildly shocked. "Why would you want to do a

thing like that? I mean, play on the Jap side and let them win."

"Because the Japs, they had better ships and better-trained sailors and they had what you call the Bushido spirit. They won every battle at sea until finally at Midway the American fleet, they had this really dumbstupididiot good luck. The Japs, they were much better than the Americans, but the Americans had all these factories. The Japs couldn't make up their losses."

"Oh."

"That's the thing about war. Some countries can make up their losses, and other countries, they can't make up their losses. That's just the way it goes."

Roger had been hearing about the Second World War for years, and he remembered some of the images and sounds of battle from listening to someone named H. V. Kaltenborn on the radio, and from watching the flickering newsreels that came between double features years ago at an old movie theater in Chicago. But he had never heard anyone defend or praise the Germans or the Japanese. He did recall that a man in his father's engineering firm had been accused of being a Nazi sympathizer. The police had talked to him and then one night he was beaten up on the way home from work. His father had been very nervous about it. Was Harry like that? A *sympathizer?* But the war was over, had been for seven years. How could he be a sympathizer when there was really nothing to sympathize with? No Japanese navy, no sons of heaven smashing their fragile suicide planes into American aircraft carriers, no slanty-eyed fanatics bayoneting our boys and burying them alive in prison camps. Was it wrong to sympathize with an enemy who no longer existed? But of course, he thought. That was history. Historians cared a lot about things that didn't exist. Like Mr. Figge, who seemed to care a lot about the fact that Constantinople fell in 1453 and not 1543. Everything was clear now. Harry was nothing more than a harmless Japanese-sympathizing historian, and his attic room was a historian's room. It was a wonderful place. In later years, he would see it over and over again in his dreams.

"Harry, what are you going to be when you grow up? I mean, are you going to build things? Be an engineer?"

"It don't pay to think about all that," said Harry. "That's school counselor psychology stuff."

"I think about it all the time," said Roger. "Problem is, I'm not good at anything. But you could be an engineer. Or maybe a historian. I mean, with all this stuff—"

"An engineer? You mean eight to five and two weeks off in the summer and wearing a white shirt with a tie and the whole works?"

"You have to be something. I might be a psycho-archaeologist."

"What's that?"

"Something I made up. I used to think of it as a person who studies the minds of ancient people by looking at their bones and relics and stuff. Then later I thought maybe it could mean a guy who does part-time archaeology and part-time psychology."

Harry laughed. "You're a little crazy, you know that?"

"That's what my mother thinks."

"Then you must be sane as rain," said Harry. "Mothers, they're never right about anything. We used to live in Minnesota, did I tell you?"

"That's not true. I don't mean about Minnesota—I mean about mothers never being right about anything. But I guess you don't get along with your mom."

"I get along okay," said Harry. "The trick is to stay away from your parents as much as possible and don't ask for too much and don't let them know what you're doing. Did I tell you I was building a whole city out of sticks and paper?"

"That sounds awful," said Roger. "I don't mean about the city—I mean about your mom and dad."

"My dad, he's an assistant section manager up at the electric plant. He's in charge of a bunch of meter readers. He's a jerk."

"That's—that's too bad."

"That's just the way it goes. You can't go around crying because your dad's a jerk. That's Shakespeare. I gotta throw you out now."

"You have to what?"

"My dad's coming home in ten minutes. I got things to do. See you."

"Did I—did I say something wrong?"

"Nope. I just have to get some stuff done. Come back sometime if you got nothing to do. I'm always here in the afternoons. Course, if you got something better, don't bother. I'm not begging you."

"Harry, you're a little strange, you know that?"

Harry laughed. "Don't worry about it," he said. "Don't worry about a thing."

Back out on the dark lawn, Harry again grabbed the limb of the elm tree and began to swing. For an odd moment, Roger half believed that the boy was about to disappear.

"Well, thanks for showing me your stuff," said Roger. "Nice to meet you."

"Anytime."

Roger turned to go, then hesitated. He kicked at the sparse grass. "I wanted to ask you," he said, looking down at his feet. "These two other guys and me have this club that meets on Wednesday nights. We study flying saucers and unexplained phenomena and we trade pulps and read stories out loud. You could come if you like. We need a new member."

"No, thanks," said Harry. "I hate clubs."

"I hate clubs too. That's why I made up this one. It's not like any club you ever saw."

"I hate all clubs. And I hate Buck Rogers and spaceships and ghosts and little green men. All that stuff."

"Give me a call if you change your mind," said Roger.

"I won't," said Harry. "I hate telephones. Another thing I

hate is other people's houses." Harry chinned himself three times and grinned.

The brown-and-white dog whose name Roger had forgotten came down the porch steps and ran in circles around the tree, panting and barking. "Dog's crazy about me," said Harry. "He can't stand it when I go to school."

As Roger walked back out into the light, he saw that Harry was still off the ground. With his careless, easy strength he hung first by one arm, then by the other.

Roger crossed Thorne Street and the park came back into view. Playground Joe was gone, and the two fields looked nearly deserted. It had been an unusual day, he thought. He had talked with a man who had forgotten his own name, and he had met a new boy who laughed too much, who talked funny, and who owned incredible things. All the way home he kept seeing the boy in his mind, appearing and disappearing under the elm tree. Harry was a boy hanging in a dark place.

3 | Sled Dogs, Whiskey, and Frozen Beasts

He did not see much of Harry Fisher in the weeks that followed. Two or three times Roger walked by his house, but there was no one swinging under the elm tree. Once he called to see if Harry had changed his mind about the Wednesday-night meetings. A woman with a dry, distant voice answered. It was a voice that made him think of insects. She told him that Harry was playing with his *things*, that she would give him the message, and that most likely he would not call back, since he hated telephones.

Occasionally he saw Harry in school between classes. When they passed each other in the hall, Harry would smile and jerk his head upward in a quick sign of recognition. "Hey," he would sometimes say. This was the way all the Italian boys who lived on Brick Street said hello to each other, and it surprised him that Harry would ever do anything that looked Italian.

As the weather grew colder and October deepened into November, school got less and less interesting. He remembered having high hopes for tenth grade. He had looked forward especially to World History and English, subjects which he felt would be the ground for everything in life that interested him. But when they studied Egypt and he had tried to tell Mr. Figge about the Cult of Osiris and about the Rosicrucian claim that Amenhotep was the first Grand Master of Occult Knowledge, the man's face went blank, and Larry Norcross and Harriet Emerick began to snicker. When he told Miss Wakowski that Bode's Law was a magic formula that predicted the distances between the planets, she smiled in a distant way and said that was interesting but a little off the subject. He had even approached the terrifying Miss Simic one morning with the confession that he had read some of Tacitus in translation because he heard that his account of Caligula was great fun. But Miss Simic had cried out that she was not even remotely interested in anything in translation and that in any case Tacitus was neither amusing nor truthful on the subject of Caligula.

He wondered why teachers were so difficult, so hard to understand. What made Miss Simic so angry? Was it just that she was upset about being old and ugly? Perhaps the sound of her own voice was as harsh and disturbing to her own ears as it was to others. Why was Miss Wakowski so quiet, so negligent, and so easy? Why did she spend so much time looking out the window, as if she were waiting for someone, or something? Perhaps a man in a shiny blue Packard who would drive her out to Mildred's for steak and champagne? Where was Mr. Figge going from week to week? In Physics he moved from sound to light to gravity to electricity. In World History he talked about the uniting of Upper and Lower Egypt, the rise of the tyrants in pre-classical Greece, Alexander of Macedon, and the Seven Wonders of the Ancient World. His mind was a confusion of precise but unrelated ideas and images. There was something almost astrological about Mr. Figge's lesson plans, as if he saw in the stars that tomorrow would be a good day to show slides of Etruscan kraters. After several weeks Roger began to suspect that Mr. Figge had a great deal in common with Playground Joe: Figge was to history as Joe was to newspapers. They were both merely caretakers of information.

Only Mrs. Leibolt's class gave him any satisfaction. Mrs. Leibolt was demanding, but she used lovely words. She seemed to have ideas about things. Roger noticed too that she looked at her students, something that Mr. Figge and Miss Wakowski almost never did. And he loved the way she sat on the front of her desk and crossed her fascinating, lovely legs and sometimes brushed her hand through her hair when she was thinking. It was an odd thing to watch Mrs. Leibolt. Roger had never before in his life had sexual fantasies about a woman as old as his own mother.

But school was a dream that seemed to recede even as he reached out for it. His many enthusiasms seemed awkward when trapped inside classrooms. He had the general feeling that both his teachers and his classmates thought he read too much and talked too much and looked funny. This stung him more than he could have admitted to anyone. He hated show-offs, and yet he wanted to tell everything he knew—it was all so interesting. He instantly distrusted anyone who was handsome or beautiful, and yet he wanted to be handsome. Even irresistible. He tried to comb a curl into his hair, without much success. He practiced his smile in front of the bathroom mirror, trying to purse his lips a little so his mouth would not look too big. He worried about blackheads on his nose and pimples on his forehead and shoulder blades. Why just on his forehead and shoulder blades? What sense did that make? What was his body trying to tell him? He practiced walking. Some boys, he noticed, walked too much on the balls of their feet and tended to look pretty silly. Others clunked along on their heels, like farmers. The trick was to do neither, to walk with a perfect, natural grace that was neither a clunk nor a pussyfoot. But he saw in the hall mirror that his attempts at this perfection achieved only a fearful, flat-footed stealth that resembled a soldier on the lookout for land mines. Why did social things have to be so difficult? he wondered. Apart from Ythn and the Denizens, he seemed increasingly incapable of making a decent impression on anyone.

Even his parents were more difficult to get along with now

that they were past forty. His mother talked too much, asked too many questions, did too many things for too many people, and got tired too often. His father was nearly always in Hartford. Roger explained to the Denizens that his father was the family ghost—a tall, pale, handsome man with a soft voice and circles under his eyes who came at night and never stayed more than a day or two.

Although Roger was often sad about particular things, he was never unhappy. He was having the best year of his life. The Denizens came to his house every other Wednesday night, and three afternoons a week the three of them would go to Pangborn's to talk and drink orange juice. The double feature changed every three days at the Strand. At night Ythn talked to him about Mars. He could run for nearly three miles without tiring. Flying saucers were everywhere. It was clear that the world was a wonderful place. Ideas and images burst out of him, and there was never enough time to read and think and do everything. Once on a Saturday morning he woke early and lay in bed, thinking about the infinite store of possibilities awaiting him, and he began to laugh. Leaping out of bed, he did a wild dance around his room and crowed like a rooster. Ythn watched from under the covers, leaned back on one green arm, the tentacles of his fingers pressed against his green cheek.

"Adolescence," he said. "I tell you, I am *so glad* to be through all that."

Then he stretched, sat up, crawled up Roger's bookcase, and did a slow Martian pirouette on Roger's stack of *Famous Fantastic Mysteries*.

On the last Thursday in November it snowed for the first time. The snow came down very quietly and evenly on a perfectly windless morning, and lay on the ground like a drift of goose down. It lasted for only a day, but after that things were different. The chill in the air had a different meaning. The water running into the gutters was not rainwater; it was defunct snow, which was a different matter entirely. The great, soundless hinge of the new season was turning. A door was opening somewhere, and soon winter would spill out into Greencastle.

The changing of the seasons was a great event for Roger. He remembered the day his first-grade teacher, Miss White, had set everyone looking for signs of spring. All the seasons had signs, she said. God made it that way. And so Roger had always looked for the waxing and waning of things. He saw the coming of the summer birds, one by one, and their slow departure in October. He brushed away the powdery snow by his front steps in March to see if the grass was still yellow. He felt the nubs of buds on trees as he walked to school, and watched for the cloudy mornings when spring fog drifted along the street, and warm air polished the humps of speckled snow along the edges of Stone Hill Road and Thistle Street. But all that was gone, had been for nine months. Now the signs all pointed to December and the bleak January that would follow.

On the first Saturday in December it snowed again, this time for a whole day in the midst of a high, freezing wind. He said goodbye to autumn.

Plastic Christmas trees, paper snowmen, and cellophane icicles began to appear in store windows in downtown Greencastle. Lines of glass holly and strings of lights made arcs between streetlamps. In another week, merchants would pipe organ music into the streets and people would bustle down sidewalks, bumping into each other and crossing in the middle of the street, and the snow would turn from the lovely adhesive stuff that made such wonderful snowballs to a white powder that would hardly pack at all until it melted a little in your mittens and froze your fingers.

"What do you want for Christmas this year?" his mother said on Monday morning. She stood in her green bathrobe in the kitchen doorway while he sat on the floor in the front hall trying to jerk his galoshes over his shoes without taking off his mittens. It was the second Monday in December. To his right, the large entranceway into the living room glowed with yellow sunlight. In the dining room on the other side of the hallway, two iron radiators sat on their claw feet and hissed.

"Don't know," said Roger. "Haven't the faintest."

"How about a baseball glove? Or a football?"

"I have all that stuff."

"Well, there must be something you want." His mother leaned a little on one hip and smoked her cigarette and looked down at the floor. He knew that men thought his mother was sexy when she stood like that, and he smiled a little. His mother had short hair that curled naturally into a feathery brown tangle that his Uncle Peter loved to run his fingers through.

"I haven't thought about Christmas," he said. "I don't know what I want, and I don't know what to get anyone else. And I haven't got any ideas at all about where I put all the Christmas-tree stuff from last year."

"It's in the basement behind the furnace. Roger, are you okay?"

"Am I okay? Sure, I'm okay."

"Well, I was just wondering. You seem so different."

"Different from what?"

"I don't know. Different from last spring. From last year."

"I'm a year older."

"Your father is worried about you."

"He never said a thing to me."

"You know how he is."

Roger stood up and stamped his boots on the wooden floor. They were at least a half size too small. "No, I don't know how he is. I haven't seen him for three weeks and I don't know how he is and I don't have any idea what he's worried about."

"Your father's job is two hundred miles away. He can't help that."

"What do you mean, he can't help it? That's the job he took, wasn't it? Nobody forced him. Besides, why doesn't he just move us all up to Connecticut?"

"He doesn't think we should go in the middle of the school year."

"So why didn't we go last August?"

"Roger, I can't tell you everything that's in your father's mind. You'll just have to ask him." She turned away from the doorway and disappeared into the kitchen. A moment later he heard her bang pots together in the sink and turn on water. "The job may not be permanent," she called back to him. "That's another thing."

"Is that what he said?"

"No, but that's what I think he thinks. But he did say he thought you were having problems in school, and he's afraid things will get worse if you have to change in the middle of the year."

"I'm not having any problems in school. School is okay."

"Your grades are not as good as they were last year."

"Is that it? He completely ignores me for about a million years, but he spends two minutes looking at my report card and decides I'm having problems. That's terrific."

Suddenly the pots stopped banging and the water went off. "Your father never ignores you," said his mother's voice. "But I suppose—I suppose grades are not really that important. I guess that's not what's really bothering him. Or me."

Roger grunted and pulled, and finally the heel of his left shoe slipped into the bottom of his left galosh. He wrapped his scarf around his neck and buttoned his coat. Just then, one of the hissing radiators in the dining room shrieked, and his mother reappeared in the kitchen doorway.

"I never know," she said, "whether that thing is supposed to do that or whether I'm supposed to call someone and have it fixed." She swore under her breath. "Women never know anything. That's our problem."

She took two steps into the hallway and then yawned and leaned against the banister that led upstairs. "Well," she said, "I thought I knew what I was trying to tell you a moment ago." She looked out the window, and then suddenly she squared her shoulders and tightened the belt on her bathrobe. "You read too much. And you sit in your room and talk to yourself. You never used to do that."

"Mom, I'm going to be late."

"Put up your collar," she said. "The wind out there is awful."

But outside there was no wind at all. The morning was clear and cold. The buckles of his boots snapped and clicked as he ran down the street, sliding here and there, spraying snow into the gutters. A sudden, miniature snowfall glittered through the blue air when he touched the branch of a small maple tree.

At the bottom of Stone Hill Road he turned right onto High Point Avenue. Then, three houses past the top of the rise, he saw a tall boy standing near the curb, his schoolbooks tucked under one arm. When the boy saw Roger, he waved and kicked a spray of snow into the street. It was Dennis Kirk, the second member of the Denizens of the Sacred Crypt.

"Surprise!" shouted Dennis. "It's winter! Time for sled dogs and whiskey!"

"Time to look for frozen beasts in the trackless wastes," said Roger, who had just finished reading H. P. Lovecraft's *At the Mountains of Madness*. He slowed to a walk and punched his friend on the shoulder with his left mitten. "Time to look for Figges and Simics and Wakowskis and other extinct species."

When Dennis Kirk laughed, his round cheeks and his wide mouth overwhelmed the rest of his face. Now, with his large Russian hat and his red scarf wrapped under his chin, he looked clownish and improbable. "A frozen Simic," he said, shaking all over. "How would we drag a thing like that all the way to the Museum of Unnatural History?"

"A real problem," said Roger. "But what else could we do with a frozen Simic?"

"It might make a dandy toboggan," said Dennis.

The third Denizen, a short boy with a round, yellowish face, trudged out of a green house at the corner where Recognition and Iris veered at right angles into High Point Avenue. With the flaps of his leather cap pulled down over his ears and snapped under his neck, his face looked mouselike and vulnerable.

"Hey, Frank! You look like a nun when you wear that hat!"

"Hey, Frank, we're searching for extinct frozen Siberian beasts! Did you know that a Simicus Latinus Obnoxious was found only a few yards from this very spot?"

"Come on, you guys," said Frank. "Do you always hafta act like it's Wednesday night? Do you hafta make up stuff every minute of every day?"

"Dr. Freud told us just yesterday that all this fooling around is a major part of our illness," said Roger.

"If you guys don't hurry up, we're gonna be late for Flag & Bible, and Mrs. Frankenhurst is gonna raise holy heck."

"Frank wants us to deal with reality," said Roger.

"I hate reality," said Dennis. "I remember once in the evening I turned off television for just ten minutes to watch reality. I hated every minute of it. Hi, Frank. Howsa boy?" Dennis punched Frank Aldonotti on the shoulder.

"I'm okay. Come on, we hafta run."

"You got your ghost story ready for Wednesday?" said Roger. "I bet you forgot Wednesday is your story night."

"I never forget whose story night it is," said Frank. "I never forget anything. I have this curse that one of my doctors calls *total recall*. I can remember the darndest things. I can even actually remember things from when I was three."

"I wish I was a genius like Frank," said Roger. "Then I could make all A's in school and my father would be happy."

"I'm not a genius," said Frank. "I just got total recall. There's actually a big difference, believe me."

"A genius is a guy who makes A's in everything forever and ever. That's you, Frank."

Frank shook his head. "To be a genius you have to be smart. You have to actually make things or write stories or do Whiz Kid math problems in your head like Joel Kupperman on the radio. Stuff like that. All I do is remember. It almost sort of gives me the willies sometimes to have all this stuff in my head."

"How many doctors do you have now?" said Dennis.

"I got three. My orthopedic doctor, my allergy doctor, and my regular doctor."

"That proves it," said Dennis. "Only a genius would need three doctors. Roger and I are just not that complicated."

"We don't have as many parts," said Roger.

"But we like it that way," said Dennis. "It's very rococo to have too many parts."

"You guys," said Frank. He was smiling and shaking his head again. "You guys."

They began to run down the middle of High Point Avenue toward the high school, still a half mile distant. They joined hands for a long slide when they came to a patch of ice. They threw snowballs in the air, trying to hit themselves on the head. They shouted things about whiskey and sled dogs and frozen beasts to everyone they passed on the sidewalk. Roger was tall and pale, Dennis still taller but heavier, like a tree trunk, while Frank seemed short and round by comparison, like an eggplant. Linked together and running down the middle of the street, they were brighter and windier than any winter morning.

4 | Hating Great Literature

At eight twenty-eight Roger stuffed his coat and hat and galoshes and mittens into his locker. At eight twenty-nine he burst into his homeroom and sat down in his seat in the second row just as Mrs. Frankenhurst began to take the roll. The excitement of the cold weather, the red pinch in his cheeks, and his bright words with Dennis and Frank all began to dissipate in the dry, warm air. Things began to slip away. He said the Pledge of Allegiance, listened to the sound of someone's voice reading twelve lines from the Bible, and waited for Mrs. Frankenhurst to call his name.

All the hard work came in the morning: Latin, English, World History, and Algebra. In the afternoon after Physics he had two study halls and then the final homeroom period, except on Tuesdays and Thursdays, when gym classes took the place of study halls. "We are bright and quick in the mornings," Miss Simic had once said. "And this is why Latin is always first period! First period, when your young minds move like lightning!" But Roger's mind did not move like lightning in the morning. He was fine until the double doors of Greencastle High School closed behind him, and then he had a tendency to doze, to lose track of things, to fall down.

He was aware now that classes had changed and that Miss Simic—an ancient woman with a gray face and gray-white curls that hung in a little fringe around her head—was questioning someone about the day's translation from their Latin reader. Her sharp, accusatory finger and her loud, thin voice pierced the elaborate indifference of the intelligent students and the simple apathy of the dull ones. One thing was abundantly clear: Miss Simic cared about Latin. Roger did not know why anyone should fall victim to such a strange aberration (though he had done so himself once for a very brief period), but still it was a pleasant change from the confusion of Figge and the quiet indifference of Wakowski.

Today the class worked on a story about a twelve-year-old boy named Marcellus who played the lute with great skill (*cum magna arte*), whose sister was named Livia, and whose father was a grain merchant. On this day they wished their father a safe journey. He, in turn, joked that soon he would be too old for long voyages (*non sum qualis eram*). Their mother, Lavinia, then admonished them to finish their lessons with the learned slave, Aristarchus, before the sun was high. To Roger, Marcellus was an insufferable bore. The boy longed to become a grain merchant like his father, he longed to shake the hand of Julius Caesar as his father had once done, and he just couldn't wait to finish his mathematics so that he could get on to his Greek lessons, which gave great pleasure (*donat magnum gaudium*). *Insufferable*. Like Boy Scouts, Flag Day, assembly programs about hygiene and mental health, football pep rallies, and the utterly antiseptic Hardy Boys with their shortwave radios, their speedboats, and their motorcycles. Insufferable, like all his father's relatives, who lived, thank God, in Cincinnati.

At exactly nine forty-five, Latin ended and English began. But since no one could be in two places at once, this was only theoretical. In practice, teachers granted a five-minute grace period so that English, which began at nine forty-five sharp, did not really begin until nine-fifty. Roger suspected that time in school was different from time anywhere else in the universe. It was always five or six minutes slow, and it never moved continuously, but rather in little jerks and starts. He was fascinated by the way clocks' hands moved only at sudden intervals when they would click, move one minute backward, then three minutes forward. And sometimes, especially in Math class, time stopped.

Roger and twenty-three of his classmates shambled into Mrs. Leibolt's English class, glancing up briefly to make sure she was there. They mumbled to each other, took the long way around to their seats, sharpened pencils, coughed, opened their notebooks. Roger sat down in his chair in the second row. Behind him, a collage of brown leaves and seven perfect papers from the previous week's grammar test were thumbtacked to the corkboard display wall at the back of the room. In front of him, green blackboards silhouetted Mrs. Leibolt's gunmetal-gray desk. To his left, bookcases sat under a row of windows that held back the beautiful, white winter.

Mrs. Leibolt perched on the front of her desk. She was a small woman of about forty with red hair, a narrow waist, and long legs which she had a habit of crossing and uncrossing. Her small, round mouth and her large eyes, which she highlighted with painted lashes and purple eye shadow, gave her a doll-like appearance. This had surprised him, almost shocked him on that first day she had appeared in class two weeks after the beginning of the semester. *Maybe it has something to do with her illness*, he thought. *Maybe she's just trying to look healthy*. Now Mrs. Leibolt looked up and smiled her quick smile. It was her signal that she was ready to begin.

"We have tried," she began in her clear, lyrical voice, "to turn our searchlights into the dark corners of English grammar. I think we've cleared out a few cobwebs and brought in a little fresh air."

Larry Norcross, a tall, handsome boy with black curly hair who was captain of the basketball team, began to groan quietly. He glanced at Curtiss Baylor, a straight-A student and first debater on the school team, who pressed his fingers into a little pyramid and smiled to keep up his mask of attention.

Two seats behind him, Marilyn Sord, the prettiest girl in the tenth grade, stared out the window and combed her hair.

"But perhaps we should take this occasion for a final look at the question of what grammar is, and why it's so important."

Mrs. Leibolt looked down at her copy of the blue-and-red grammar workbook, and her eyes narrowed. "Grammar," she said, "is meaning. It is the structure of ideas. It is our way of knowing that what we say makes perfect sense. First we must have correctness. Then we can have fluency. Finally we can have profundity. Some of you, before you die, may do or say things that are profound—but first you must begin at the beginning. You must have grammar."

Mrs. Leibolt smiled again at her class, evidently pleased with what she had said. Then she placed the grammar workbook on the desk next to her and looked out the window. Roger saw that snow was falling again. It was falling away from the windows, into the streets and against the gables of roofs across Paris Avenue.

"No pianist enjoys five-finger exercises," she continued. "And no pianist will ever play a piano concerto without having played them thousands of times."

The Italian boys who sat in the back of the room stared at her and leaned back in their chairs. Roger could see how they hated English from the way they let their legs fall apart and the way they smirked at each other. Harriet Emerick, an ugly but popular girl, adjusted her glasses and wet her lips and then whispered something to Marilyn Sord. But Marilyn had not yet finished her window reverie. Oblivious to everything, she continued to comb her hair with a large green comb.

"Education is an acquired taste," said Mrs. Leibolt. "There is not much fun in memorizing your list of prepositions, learning to use commas, or expanding your vocabulary. There is nothing amusing about the possessive use of the apostrophe. There is nothing whimsical about learning to use topic sentences and developing them with particulars and details. But gradually"—and here she lifted both arms as if she were outlining the sun—"gradually all this takes on meaning. The outline of your own mental powers becomes clear as you trace it with the tools of language."

Roger did not quite know what it meant to trace the outline of his mental powers with the tools of language, but it had a nice sound. A lot of what Mrs. Leibolt said was like that. Again he looked around the room to see who was listening. Eddie McQueen, a short boy who was uniform and equipment manager for the basketball team and had very bad skin problems, turned his face away and winced. Cynthia Cucinelli, a plump girl with thick eyebrows who never understood anything, smiled beautifully at Mrs. Leibolt. Mary John Grodner, a tall bony creature who found school utterly terrifying, opened and closed her mouth and flared her nostrils as if she were trying to breathe underwater.

"But now we move on," said Mrs. Leibolt, "to the stuff that grammar makes." With this announcement she brought her hands together and looked very pleased. But then, suddenly, something dark seemed to cross her face and she looked out again at the falling snow. "It is sad—sometimes even tragic—to think that people like—well, that ordinary people—have very little imagination."

She was silent for a long moment, and Roger noticed that in her words as well as in her silence there was something odd. *She got off the track*, he thought. *She's lost somewhere*.

Then she looked back at the class and smiled in a distant way, as if the faces of her students were images in old photographs. "But the genius of a great imagination can touch anyone—even ordinary people—and this is the biggest and the most wonderful thing we can ever know. Imagination has wings that go everywhere. Imagination changes the world. And what we are about to begin is a great adventure into the imaginations of some of the greatest writers who ever lived."

A hand jerked into the air. Mrs. Leibolt smiled again, and with a nod of her head she recognized Larry Norcross. "Somebody said that one of the sophomore plays is Shakespeare," he said. "Is that true? Are we gonna have to read Shakespeare again this year?"

"Yes," said Mrs. Leibolt. "We have that good fortune."

The entire class groaned, and Larry, apparently encouraged by all the dismay, went on in a louder voice: "I don't see why we have to read Shakespeare every year. He doesn't even write in regular English. You can't understand a word of it on your own, and then when the teacher explains it all, it's so embarrassing you could just about die."

At this there was a flutter of assent from the class, a little susurrus of whines and groans and titters. *Shakespeare*, he thought. It pained him to admit, even to himself, that he could ever agree with Larry Norcross about anything. *Shakespeare*. All those old words. Nothing but dialogue. An interminable flow of grand feelings and three-hundred-year-old jokes punctuated by *Alarums & Exeunts*. *Shakespeare*. Suddenly he thought of Harry Fisher, and he smiled.

And again Mrs. Leibolt was smiling. "Do you find love embarrassing?" she said to Larry Norcross.

"What?"

"Love between men and women. Does that embarrass you?"

Larry put his hand on his forehead. "Mrs. Leibolt, what kinda question is that? Am I supposed to answer that in front of the whole class? Gimme a break. I'm just a poor basketball player."

There was generous laughter, and Larry flashed his smile at Marilyn Sord and Curtiss Baylor, and at Buck Moore, the strongest and most dangerous boy in the tenth grade.

"Do you think war is embarrassing or corny? Or murder? Or insanity? Or a duel to the death?"

"No. Guess not."

"Well, these are the things that Shakespeare writes about," she said. "Don't be put off by the fact that Shakespeare isn't easy. Nothing worthwhile is easy. Making the first team in basketball isn't easy—it takes talent and practice and perseverance. So does Shakespeare."

Larry Norcross shrugged and sank back a little in his chair. Curtiss Baylor, always cautious, looked thoughtful and nodded at Mrs. Leibolt. Eddie McQueen rubbed his nose and stared at the pencil sharpener.

As Mrs. Leibolt went on to talk about the Four Adventures—Adventures in Fiction, Adventures in Poetry, Adventures in Drama, and Adventures in Nonfiction Prose (also called Adventures of the Mind)—Roger stared at the bright green blackboards that outlined her head. Outside the snow was still falling, and he began to think about the shapes of snowflakes, each one woven with perfect symmetry from strings of ice crystals, each different, like his grandmother's crocheted coasters, each falling through the cold morning from somewhere to somewhere. He wondered who kept track of all the snowflakes and all the butterflies and all the sparrows. Was there a book somewhere, a book of creatures and things, where all was recorded, remembered, held forever? He had read somewhere that in the end the earth itself would be recorded as a round cipher. An *O*.

"—a panorama of new ideas," Mrs. Leibolt was saying. Then she uncrossed her legs and Roger forgot about snowflakes and began to wonder what she took off first when she undressed, what she looked like when she lay down in the dark with Mr. Leibolt. He knew that most of his fantasies about her came out of his feeling that she was mysterious, forbidden. That made her a little more interesting than Cynthia Cucinelli, who was also forbidden but probably available.

Roger had gotten past the bare rudiments of his sexual education the previous summer by talking to Dennis. Until then he had believed that married people *did it* only when they wanted to have children, and that most of marriage consisted of self-denial.

"You think people would get married just to do it three times in forty years?" said Dennis.

"Well, I sort of thought maybe they did it a few extra times just to make sure—you know—it takes."

Dennis laughed. "No, dummy. They do it for fun. My parents are at it all the time. Aren't yours?"

"God, I don't think so. My parents?"

Now Mrs. Leibolt was looking at him and smiling, and for one terrible moment he imagined that she had read all his thoughts.

"Well, Roger?"

"What! What? I didn't say a thing—"

The class laughed. Mrs. Leibolt smiled. "Roger, you don't have to raise your voice. We can all hear you."

"I'm sorry. I was thinking about something—"

"Roger was thinking about Egypt," said Harriet. She grinned and pushed her glasses back up her nose with her forefinger. "Roger never thinks about anything except Egypt."

"Maybe he was thinking deep thoughts," said Buck Moore. Buck was very muscular for a fifteen-year-old, and he wore nothing but T-shirts and dungarees. The previous June he had been named Freshman Athlete of the Year. His straight black hair glistened with Wildroot Cream Oil.

"I think it's a real shame the way school cuts into Roger's brooding time," said Larry.

"Never mind all that," said Mrs. Leibolt. "Roger, I was asking if you'd like to lead the discussion of our first story."

Roger blinked. "The first story," he said.

"I assume you've read the assignment for today," said Mrs. Leibolt. "It is one of the greatest stories in the English language."

Roger could not remember whether or not he had read the assignment, and since he had not been listening, he had no idea which story she was referring to. He decided, as his Uncle Peter would have said, to tack away from the wind.

"I never read Great Literature," he said. "I hate Great Literature. Or at least I hate the stuff people call Great Literature."

Mrs. Leibolt raised her eyebrows and then pursed her lips into something that was not quite a smile. "Roger, I'm a little surprised to hear that from you, of all people. What with all you read and all you have to say—"

"Tell us all about it, Roger," said Larry.

"We all just love to hear you talk about your feelings," said Harriet.

"Now that's quite enough," said Mrs. Leibolt. "Roger has a right to be listened to without all this ridicule. Marilyn, stop combing your hair. Eddie, take that comic book out of your literature book and put it on my desk. All right now, Roger. What were you saying?"

Mrs. Leibolt looked down at him with an expression that seemed to show a kind of calm liberality and measured interest. She was not unfriendly. In a way he trusted her, wanted to tell her about his club, his friends, the things he had been reading. But how much could you tell an English teacher? Someone who divided the year into Four Adventures and talked about the Panorama of Ideas and Voyages into the Imagination. Someone who read Shakespeare for breakfast and thought you couldn't get into heaven without good grammar. Then too, there was something humiliating about the way she took his side against the rest of the class. He saw that without meaning to she was isolating him, showing everyone by her attention and her concern that he was different. Now she was looking at him again, hoping that he would go on and say things.

"Well, that's about all I wanted to say," he said. "There's a lot of stuff I'm supposed to be crazy about that I just can't stand. I got this aunt who reads all this Great Literature because she thinks it's good for her, sort of like mineral oil. She's always sending me these books."

"Could you give an example?"

"Please be very specific," said Larry. "Give us lots of particulars and details. Maybe you could write a poem about it."

A dangerous halcyon calm settled into Mrs. Leibolt's face. "Larry, I am going to ask you just this one more time to be quiet. Roger?"

He took a breath. He saw that Larry was smirking at him. Curtiss Baylor made a guarded, superior smile behind his hand, and Buck Moore rolled his eyes. Roger knew it was about to happen again. It had happened so many times now, and he had never known how to stop it.

"Well, I fell asleep about six times over the first three chapters of *Silas Marner* and twice over the first fifty pages of *Lady Chatterley's Lover*, which is supposed to be real spicy but is really a dud—"

He was pleased by the laughter at the end of "dud." As always, he had them at the beginning, everyone except Larry and Curtiss and Buck and Eddie and Marilyn and Harriet. *Quit*, he thought. *Just shut your mouth*.

"—and I also read this Great Play called *The Three Sisters*, which is a thrilling story about three girls who decide not to go to Moscow. And I read this Great Novel about a guy who deserts the army during the First World War to run off with this girl who gets pregnant. About a million times the author says that they're having a fine time of it, and then the girl dies. Not too much happens in a lot of Great Literature, that's the problem."

At the word, Mary John Grodner gasped and then began to flair her nostrils again. Roger was certain that she was the only girl in the tenth grade who was not sure about the facts of life, and who really believed the joke about *Vagina* being a small town in southern Italy.

"Well then," said Mrs. Leibolt, "what *do* you read?"

"I like Sax Rohmer and Richard Shaver and A. Merritt and H. P. Lovecraft and Edmund Hamilton and Rider Haggard—"

"I don't believe I've heard of any of those writers," she said.

Harriet Emerick adjusted her glasses again and smiled viciously. "Roger has his own private writers," she said. "And he also has his own private little club where he and his friends sit around on Wednesday nights holding hands and trying to scare each other with spooky stories—"

It was happening again, and there was no way to stop it. He felt himself redden. Hatred for Harriet Emerick welled up inside him.

"We don't hold hands!"

He knew instantly, amid all the cruel laughter, that he had said exactly the wrong thing. He remembered that he had once overheard Buck Moore say on the playground that when somebody gets nasty you don't just stand there and say no, I don't *do it* with my mother. You punch somebody in the face.

"Jeff Weems went to one of the meetings," said Harriet. "He said it's all very chummy."

"I bet they put all the chairs real close together for body warmth," said Larry.

The roar of laughter died quickly against the quiet countenance of Mrs. Leibolt.

"Larry."

"Yes, Mrs. Leibolt."

"Harriet."

"Yes, ma'am."

"I'm giving you both blue slips to the principal's office, and I want the rest of you to show a little respect and a little restraint for the rest of the period. And I want you all to remember that there is nothing wrong with people who read. There is nothing wrong with forming a club for people who read. There is nothing wrong with meeting on Wednesday nights. Am I making myself clear? You are not to make fun of people because they are a little different. This country was founded on the principle that people should be allowed the freedom to be different, and it was founded by people who were in fact agitators, original thinkers—"

The bell rang. Mrs. Leibolt held out the two blue slips between her fingers. She had not signed them, and Roger was afraid now that she would relent. But as the students began to murmur to each other and collect their books, she did sign them and hand them to Larry and Harriet, who whispered to each other and stared at Roger.

"Roger and his queer friends are developing their minds," whispered Larry. "Isn't that wonderful."

"They're blooming," said Curtiss Baylor. "Like roses."

Roger made his way toward the door of the classroom, trying to whistle, trying to pretend that no one was talking about him.

"Hey, Roger!" shouted Larry. "Why don't you just go home and listen to your Yma Sumac records!"

"The Lure of the Unknown Love," said Buck Moore. "That's Roger and his buddies on Wednesday night."

"There is no Yma Sumac—did you know that?" said Curtiss. "Her real name is Amy Camus, and she's from Brooklyn—"

Roger took a drink of water out in the hallway and then sank into the blissful anonymity of the stream of students changing classes. But as he found his way into Mr. Figge's room for World History, a girl stopped him. A girl in a green jumper, a white blouse, and white stockings. It was the quiet girl who sat two seats to the right of him in English. He knew that her name was Ruth Jahntoff, but he had never spoken to her. Ruth Jahntoff was not pretty. This was a tragic flaw that many girls had. Not Being Pretty was something like being sentenced to prison for the rest of your life. But as he looked at her, he could not quite see why she was not pretty. It was perfectly clear from the way all the boys ignored her that she wasn't, and yet he saw now that she did *appear* to be pretty. Looks, he decided, were sometimes deceiving.

"I want to tell you something," she said. She was looking at him without smiling or frowning. She looked—but he could not think of the word for the way she looked.

"You do?"

"Yes. I want to tell you not to let things get you down."

"What things?"

"You know. English class and all that."

"Oh, that stuff doesn't bother me at all," he said.

"You're better than they are," she said quietly.

Roger looked at her very carefully. He saw that she was serious. He couldn't think how to answer her.

"Oh, I don't know," he said.

He wanted to put his hand on her shoulder and smile at her. He wanted to say, *Thanks, I needed someone to say something nice to me*. Instead, he turned away. People were watching.

5 | The Forest of Symbols

Instead of going home that afternoon, the Denizens turned north on Paris Avenue, crossed Greencastle, and then made a right on Avondale. The cold air and the white snow brought them to life again. They ran the last two blocks, their book bags dangling and bumping behind them like broken kites.

The single-story brick building at the corner of Avondale and Phoenix had once, twenty-five years earlier, been a beauty parlor run by a Miss Lily-Anne. Fifteen years later someone else bought it, painted it blue, and changed the name to Edwards Auto Parts. But in five years the business failed, and a Jewish man from New York named Norman Pangborn bought the place outright and spent his last twenty-five dollars on a ten-foot sign which he nailed above the window.

The Denizens opened the front door, and bells rang. They stamped their boots on a rubber mat inside and hung their hats and scarfs on the wooden garment tree that stood by the cash register. Coming out of the bright snow made the store seem beautifully dark. Roger took a deep breath and felt the damp warmth all around him and listened to the steam escaping from the valves of the iron radiators.

The three facets of the front window defined a walk-in display area on a raised platform. A fine silver mist covered the glass. On the wood platform he saw pots of spider plants and winter ivy thrive and overflow. The faint green odor of summer drifted in the humid air.

The proprietor appeared from somewhere near the back, smiling and waving. It was always like that. As if he were a magician who poofed into existence when he heard bells ring. He was a slender man, and in this one way he reminded Roger of his father, though Pangborn was neither as tall nor as handsome. He combed his thin, stiff hair straight back over the top of his head. His long nose and his narrow face gave him a birdlike appearance that suggested attentiveness, or quickness. His gray eyes were cloudy and soft, like the mist in the front window. Gray hollows scooped out his cheeks, as if he had spent most of his life hunched forward poring over books with the heels of his hands against his face. He was surely as old as his own father, he thought. But he walked lightly on the balls of his feet like a boy in tennis shoes.

"Well, goddamn it, how are you? I thought you were all dead."

"You're close," said Dennis. "School is killing us. Slowly."

"As long as you have money," said Pangborn. "And as long as you all live until March. I have to pay the rent next week and then the property tax in February."

Roger smiled. He had never been fooled by this kind of talk. This was the man who watched them wander up and down his aisles last summer with empty pockets, the man who said with a perfectly serious face that it was a damn lucky thing they had come in on Thursday since there was a one hundred percent discount on anything up to four dollars.

"Things are tough all over," said Roger.

"You don't know what tough is." Pangborn dropped the load of books he was carrying on the floor and made a gesture of despair with his open hands. "Do you know who my last customer was? A nun. Can you believe it?" He rolled his eyes to the ceiling.

"What did she buy?" said Frank.

"Nothing. She just came in to make sure I didn't have any books that might injure the young. I told her I thought that was a really fascinating possibility but that I didn't quite understand. Did she mean books with razor blades sticking out of the binding? Books with sharp edges? Books with pages laced with belladonna? Or maybe two-hundred-pound books that could break your foot? No, she said, nothing like that."

"Pangborn, you're making this all up," said Frank. He looked up at Pangborn and smiled hesitantly and crossed his hands over his round stomach. "I can always usually tell when you're making things up."

"I swear to God she was here just an hour ago," said Pangborn. "I could smell convent dust all over her. Anyway, here she was telling me how worried she was about books that might injure the young, but she was so cute about it. She blushed every time I asked her a question."

"I bet she did," said Roger. He thought for a moment about books that hurt. *The Necronomicon* and *The King in Yellow*. Books that sickened. Books that killed. Books that opened up like jaws, and inside their serrated pages everything went red. He had the impression that most of the English teachers and all the librarians at Greencastle High School would understand this, and had in fact divided the universe of literature into two categories: books that injured the young and books that did not injure the young.

"I asked her to come by again," said Pangborn. "I told her I would take her out to Mildred's and buy her a roast beef dinner and tell her everything I knew about the injuries done to youth."

"You didn't!" said Frank. "You never said that! Not to a nun! You just couldn't! Did you really?"

"Swear to God. You have to understand that when you sit here all day stacking books and waiting for someone to come in, you get a little funny in the head."

"I read a book that almost sort of injured me once," said Frank.

"Oh, come on," said Dennis. "Sticks and stones can break your bones, but books can never hurt you."

"I'm not so sure about that," said Pangborn. "There's this ancient Welsh saying—books and poems can break your bones but stones can never hurt you. God, wasn't that good? I just made it up. What was the book, Frank?"

"*Ethan Frome*. It gave me the willies. I never even actually finished it. But I sorta glanced real quick at the last chapter."

"*Ythn Froam*? Did you say *Ythn*? I didn't think that was a real name. I mean, not around here—"

Pangborn was standing behind his cash register now, an ancient thing that looked for all the world like a bronze cathedral. He punched it once. Bells rang and the money tray flew open, but Pangborn seemed not to notice. He stared off into the far corner of the store.

"*Ethan Frome*," he said. "Christ, yes. That's a book that could injure you. All that bitterness and bad luck in just a few pages. Yes, that could do it." He looked down at Frank and smiled at him with his gray eyes.

Roger saw in those eyes that he had missed the important thing. "I guess I've read books like that," he said. "Like at the end of *Green Mansions* when Rima gets burned up in the tree and Abel remembers the *Hata* flower. And like in *Panther Magic* when the boy loves the panther who gets taken away by the circus people."

"Sometimes it's good the way books hurt you," said Pangborn. "It sort of prepares you for the big calamities that come up later. A little poison every day helps you to build up your immunity."

"Hey, I like that," said Roger. "That's terrific. A little poison every day."

"I stole the idea from an English poet," said Pangborn.

Frank raised his arms a little as if he were about to make a grand gesture, and then seemed to think better of it. He slapped his sides and smiled his yellow smile. "Sometimes," he said. "Sometimes I think this is the only place where anybody really even sort of understands me."

"This is the House of Understanding," said Dennis. "That's why we come here. Hey, Pangborn, tell us more about the nun. What did she say when you invited her out to dinner?"

Pangborn shrugged and sat down on the stool behind the counter. "She told me she had a previous engagement. Then she ran out. Have you ever heard the sound of a nun running? It's quite an experience. They sort of rustle and jingle. I guess they got all this mysterious paraphernalia they have to wear underneath their habits. Nun stuff. Chastity belts, and all that."

As Roger listened to Pangborn and watched the Denizens, he was aware, all at once, that there were different kinds of laughter. In school people snuffled or gargled or snickered. Here laughter was like bells ringing. *Different kinds of laughter*. That seemed to be the name of something, like a poem or book he would someday write.

"Gosh," said Frank, "if our parents actually knew what we talked about here they'd never let us out of the house, that's for sure."

"Oh, come on, Frank," said Dennis. "All we've been talking about is nuns. Nuns is a very clean subject."

"Listen," said Pangborn, "I got about a zillion things to sort out this afternoon. Tell you what. You guys go through the aisles for a while. I'll meet you at the back for orange juice in about a half hour. Okay?"

"Okay, Pangborn."

"Roger. Wilco."

"Dig you later."

Roger looked up and down the three long rows of metal shelves. The black pole lamps that Pangborn had stationed like sentries here and there made pools of light on the green rug. At the other end of the store sat the long workbench with a pitcher of orange juice and a row of paper cups. Beyond that, three large windows looked out onto a ragged garden of thistles and sunflowers, stiff and broken now, and the brown stems and leaves of a ruined grape arbor all covered with snow. Everything looked beautiful. The smell of the place—

the musty, acid odor of old books and magazines—sometimes haunted him at night just before he went to sleep. Pangborn's Used Book and Magazine Store.

The Denizens fanned out. Roger left his sack of schoolbooks in the middle of the green rug and began to pick his way down the center aisle. He stopped at the old novels—mostly love stories and tales of adventure from the 1920s and earlier. He loved the elaborate cover designs, the baroque curlicues, the oval portraits of bland but secretive-looking women with hairdos that made him think of bird's nests, and bursting floral designs tooled into leather covers. He took down something called *Cowardice Court* by someone named George Barr McCutcheon. As he turned the thick, ragged pages, he saw that each was bordered with a line drawing of vines, flowers, leaves, and hearts which isolated the little island of print on all four sides. He turned to Chapter One: *He's just an infernal dude, your lordship, and I'll throw him in the river if he says a word too much*, said someone named Tompkins. The book was sprinkled with pictures of a woman with the bird's nests coiffure, one of them upside down, as if some bookish gremlin had wanted to see her riding skirt and all her lovely Victorian underthings fall down over her waist.

He had several notions about the lost world that had produced these old books. An age of cut-velvet sofas with velvet tassels and claw feet. A time when rich people had plays in their living rooms and invited chamber orchestras into their salons to play *In a Persian Market*. He had seen the milky ghosts of these men and women floating through old movies at the Strand, and he had listened to his Uncle Peter talk about the old days. *Tapestry time*, he once called it. *People burned incense, women were literary, girls had names like Eleonora and Vilma, and everybody was just crazy about Egypt*.

He reached the back of the store carrying an old astronomy book that contained full-page reproductions of Lowell's maps of the Martian canals, and Richard Halliburton's *Book of Mar-*

vels. He sat quietly for a moment with his new treasures, waiting for the other Denizens.

It was strange now to look back through the aisle to the light from the front window. The books seemed surprisingly quiet, as if they were simply objects, things like lamps and footstools. Only a few moments ago he had opened them, and their images and feelings had leaped out at him. The world, the room, his own hands and feet, even the books themselves had faded, grown light, disappeared in the sudden flow of life that transported him to Baghdad and San Francisco and Mars. Roger knew that books were real. You opened them, and then they opened you. And even the feelings and ideas of people who had been dead a thousand years would leap out of the letters and come alive again in your own brain. To sit on the edge of your awareness and listen to someone else's thoughts speaking inside you—how could such a thing happen? How could you be two people, lost somewhere between the maker, the word, and the listener?

How innocent all the books looked now, sitting in their neat little rows. So quiet and secure and self-satisfied with the edges of their spines rubbing up against each other. Where, he wondered, did thoughts go when you stopped reading? Did they slip back into the books or back into your head or did they hover somewhere out in space, waiting for you and book to come back together? The thought of all these odd choices made him laugh out loud, and the sound startled him. His mother was right. He was different this year. He never used to do all this thinking. He never used to think about his thinking, or think about the fact that he was thinking about his thinking. It was like standing between the opposing mirrors in his bathroom. If you tilted one just slightly and stood a little to one side, you would see images of images of yourself receding into infinity.

Frank turned the corner of his aisle, smiling and clutching a dozen pulp magazines against his stomach. Dennis, who was capable of carrying twice as much as either of his friends, came lurching out of the west aisle and dumped his books on the table. The avalanche sent all the paper cups bouncing across the floor and nearly spilled the pitcher of orange juice. Roger smiled. He had told Dennis many times that he would never be a ballerina.

Norman Pangborn appeared in the middle of the center aisle. "Juice time," he said.

"We're waiting," said Roger.

"Books will make you actually more thirsty than anything," said Frank.

"Very true," said Pangborn. He smiled and rubbed the hollow of his cheek with the fingers of his right hand, a thing Roger had seen him do a hundred times. "I wonder if you boys know the scientific explanation for that?"

"Get ready for another fairy tale," said Dennis.

"The truth is," said Pangborn, "that books stimulate your thinking, and all your thoughts run around in your brain pathways causing friction, and pretty soon your brain heats up and then dries out. This makes you thirsty. That's why old people have wrinkles. They read too much and so their brains dry up and suck all the moisture out of their faces."

"That's terrible," said Roger. "I mean, that's the worst story you ever told."

"I think it's kind of cute," said Dennis.

"Even I know you're kidding," said Frank.

Dennis retrieved the paper cups and set them in a row. Pangborn smiled and poured. The bright orange juice fairly spurted out of the pitcher and filled each cup to the brim. Summer in December, he thought.

"So how are the Denizens of the Sacred Crypt?" said Pangborn. "How are all your projects? And most important, how are you going to pay for all these books?"

"We're keeping a saucer chart," said Roger. "Frank goes to the library and reads all the saucer reports every week from area newspapers and he also gets a bimonthly bulletin from *The Saucerians*. Then he comes over once in a while and puts

X's on this big map of New Jersey we got at the drugstore, and we date all the X's."

"Our sincere hope is that a pattern will emerge," said Dennis.

"Patterns always emerge," said Pangborn. "The problem is not finding patterns. The problem is deciding whether or not you want to believe them. Believing is getting to be more and more of a problem with me."

"We believe in Percival Lowell," said Frank. "We got *Mars and Its Canals* and *Mars as the Abode of Life* in the Denizen library."

"We're building a telescope," said Dennis. "Percival has inspired us to look for canals, rococo as that may sound."

"Actually," said Frank, "we're almost sort of building it. We're sort of actually planning to build it."

"It might be more accurate to say that we're thinking about planning to build it," said Roger. "We have fifty bucks saved in the Denizen treasury. We can buy this kit for two hundred and we can grind our own lenses in about six months and then set the whole thing up in my attic with a sliding panel in the roof."

"You want to see the canals," said Pangborn.

Dennis leaned back in his chair and stared out the window at the broken weeds covered with snow. "It's really just a dream," he said. "The telescope is too small."

Pangborn poured himself another glass of orange juice. "I read somewhere that Lowell had more clear sightings when he turned the power down."

"I don't get it," said Dennis. "That doesn't make any sense at all."

"Maybe when you get too close you can't see the canals. Lots of things are like that. Maybe the canals only appear when you get a little past your eyeballs."

"You mean they're just imaginary," said Dennis.

"No, that's not what he means," said Roger. "I don't know what he means, but he doesn't mean that. Pangborn would never mean that."

"I'm really talking about a book I once wanted to write," said Pangborn. "I dreamed up this story about a blind man. I was going to call it *Visions*. It was about how sometimes you see the best when you can't see anything."

"You mean seeing things that aren't really there," said Dennis. "Like canals on Mars."

"That's not what he means at all," said Roger. "He means seeing like Homer and Milton."

He watched the books sitting on their shelves and the idea was almost clear to him. A book was not just ink on paper. That was not what was real or true about a book. The real thing was inside you. Or perhaps when you raised your arms into the night and saw the real thing, why then you met the truth in a middle place that was neither star nor soul.

He looked across the table at the man who had stimulated all this thinking. Pangborn leaned back in his chair, looking gaunt and quick and thoughtful, his hands stuffed in his dungarees, his long legs stretched out so that only the points of his heels touched the floor. Pangborn was a thinker; that much had always been clear. Roger reminded himself that thinking was generally a bad business, that there was hardly anything in the whole world you couldn't ruin by thinking about it—and yet when Pangborn talked and thought, he saw that thinking gave you a handle on things.

"Anyway, we'd have a lot more money for the telescope and a lot of other things if we had more members," said Frank.

"I got a terrific new prospect," said Roger. "Name's Harry Fisher."

"I know him," said Dennis.

"You do? Hey, that's terrific. I didn't think anyone knew him. What do you think? I mean—"

"He's a little different. Maybe from another planet."

"What's he like?" said Frank. "Do you think he would like us?"

"I met him just once," said Dennis. "Never forgot it. He came out to the playground once last summer."

"I never saw him at the playground. He told me he hated the playground."

"He was up at the corner of the field where Playground Joe sets up his stuff. He just stood around and smirked at everybody. Curtiss Baylor was there, and somehow they started playing chess. Curtiss is of course always happy to play chess with anybody because he destroys all opposition, being the smartest kid who ever lived. But anyway, I watched the moves for a while and then Curtiss began to look real concerned and then finally his face turned red. He and Harry played three games, and I think Harry won every game in about fifteen moves. Old Curtiss couldn't even speak when it was all over. He just turned around and walked away, and Harry laughed at him. God, it was wonderful. You say he's coming to the meeting?"

"Not exactly. He hates clubs. He hates other people's houses. He's pretty weird, but he does all these great things. He builds all these terrific models and then makes up games to go with them. I never saw anything like it. He never uses a kit. He can just look at something and build a model of it."

"Why don't you bring him around sometime?" said Pangborn. "Tell him we have free orange juice."

"The problem is, I never see him."

"Call him on the telephone," said Dennis. "God, I'd love to see him at a meeting. The kid who creamed Curtiss Baylor."

"He won't talk on the telephone. He hates telephones."

"I know who he is now," said Frank. "He's that kid who smiles funny and hangs from that tree. It gives me the willies every time I go past his house."

Pangborn stacked the cups and cleaned the table with a wet rag. "Like I said, tell him to come around sometime. Tell him I got a dozen books on model building and military history. Tell him I'm a good listener."

They were standing now at the front of the store counting up their books and magazines and spreading their dollar bills and quarters across Pangborn's counter. The time had passed so quickly. One brief walk down one aisle, a sip of orange juice, and two hours had vanished.

"We hafta go," said Frank. "It's getting dark soon. I gotta be home before dark."

"You should all come in tomorrow," said Pangborn. "I got four A. Merritt novels coming in. All in multiple copies."

"Are you getting *Seven Footprints to Satan?*" said Roger. "I love *Seven Footprints to Satan*."

"Merritt is an awful writer," said Dennis. "His characters are all like wooden Indians and his plots jump around too much."

"There's something about Merritt that shines through all his deficiencies," said Pangborn. "I used to dream about his stuff at night. I used to dream I was being kidnapped by three strangers on a streetcar who had all these papers proving I was an escaped mental patient. I used to dream I was sailing on this ancient ship with a beautiful woman and that I was on horseback in Mongolia with these Tartar warriors. I remember walking to school in the morning with all this stuff in my head and winding up at the post office."

"Merritt is illogical," said Dennis.

"His books are like dreams," said Pangborn. "Everything seems to mean something even though you don't kow what it is. Reading Merritt is like stumbling through this huge forest of symbols."

"A forest of symbols," said Roger. "Hey, I like that."

"I stole it from a French poet," said Pangborn.

"I used to think that the picture of Shakespeare on Avon pocketbooks was actually a picture of A. Merritt," said Frank.

"A forest of symbols," said Roger. "What poet said that?"

"A stands for Abraham," said Frank. "Did you guys know that? I saw once where a librarian actually wrote *braham* in pencil after the *A* on the title page. That was three years ago when we lived in Peoria—"

Roger looked back at the three long aisles of books. The pools of light from the pole lamps shone brighter now, and the patches of shadow looked darker. Books lay against each other in long rows waiting to leap out at him, or anyone. Suddenly it occurred to him that Pangborn's store was a forest of symbols. You wandered through it, never knowing what you were going to find, always getting lost, never quite knowing where you were. And everything you touched came alive. You resonated to the meaning of things even if you didn't quite know what the meaning was. A forest of symbols. He did not want to come out of it even though he knew it was five-thirty. There were voices outside the forest, and he did not want to know what they were saying.

"See you tomorrow," said Pangborn. "Don't take any wooden nickels. And don't get caught with *Weird Tales* in your social studies notebook."

As Roger turned to go, he looked up past the potted plants into the steamy display window and saw, through the film of water condensing and running down the pane, the shimmering outline of a girl in a green coat. She was standing close enough so that her breath blew silver against the glass. It was Ruth Jahntoff. He did not know how long she had been standing there, watching them. She looked ghostly and beautiful. She waved to him and then walked away.

6 | Shadowman

When he got home that afternoon, his mother informed him that Harry Fisher had called.

"You mean on the telephone? Harry doesn't use the telephone."

"He did this afternoon. He said he built a time machine in his attic and he wants you to see it. Harry must be a very strange boy." She was standing in front of the stove spreading a lemon glaze on three pork chops.

"He's a little crazy," said Roger. "We were just talking about him down at Pangborn's."

"What do you suppose he meant, a time machine?"

"Some kind of joke. Harry loves military history and he has this thing about the Second World War. I guess—well, like I said, it's some kind of joke."

"Nobody from this world could build a real time machine," she said.

It seemed odd to him that his mother would make such a categorical statement about time machines, as if she had seen this to be an important subject and had given it some serious thought. But it was clear that she saw nothing unusual in what she had said. She did not even look up from the noodles into which she was now stirring a pat of melting butter.

"You better wash your hands for dinner," she said.

Roger spent a large part of the evening in his room talking with Ythn and worrying about his health. He knew it wasn't normal to be so tired all the time. He was tired the moment he entered school. He was tired before dinner, after dinner, and into the evening until eleven, when he invariably woke up. He was often dizzy. Why had he fainted three times last month just from bending over to look at books on the bottom shelf at Pangborn's? And why did he pass out cold one Saturday at breakfast when his mother was talking about how she gave blood at the Red Cross during the war? (Her veins, she said, were rubbery, and the needle wouldn't penetrate.) And why did his head roar in the evening before he went to sleep, as if a locomotive were passing through his skull? None of this, he knew, was normal.

He knew that masturbation was ruining his health. Perhaps it accounted for his large Adam's apple (a thing he could hide only by tensing his throat), his small waist, and the fact that his arms and neck were too spindly for his strong legs. Everything about him seemed out of proportion. Closer scrutiny revealed that there was a slight bow to his legs. Worse yet, his calves curved backward from his knees, as if somehow they had been screwed on wrong. Fully dressed, he could eliminate most of these problems through a careful monitoring of his posture, but even this had its disadvantages. People noticed the difference between his usual gawky appearance and his sudden military stance—his shoulders square, his Adam's apple gone, his fists clenched, his head lifted. He knew that people laughed at him.

He reached to the first shelf of the bookcase behind his bed and clicked on the radio. It was pleasant to lie alone, his reading lamp clipped to his bedpost, his books and magazines all within reach, his homework done. And there was a certain luxury in all this secret worrying.

Ythn lay on the rug in the middle of the room. He reached out with one idle green arm to touch the schoolbooks that sat on the card-table desk where Roger did his homework. Above the desk he could see the dim contours of an imitation oil painting, a green-and-blue seascape that his father had given him three years ago for his birthday.

It was eleven o'clock and the news, as usual, was incomprehensible. The baffling truce talks continued in Panmunjom, the French waged war in Indochina, Mohammed Mossadegh sacked two Tudeh newspapers as the Iranian people, destitute now after five months without oil revenues, were beginning to revolt against revolution. Helen Traubel reported in an interview that she was no longer giving voice lessons to Margaret Truman because the girl had refused to cancel plans for a concert tour. Her father, the President, snapped at reporters and fired another dozen government officials amid rumors of corruption, while the smiling wife of a Michigan senator refused to wear her imitation mink in public without the sales slip pinned to the collar. A congressman from New York opined that you couldn't travel in the Midwest without running into cows, dirt roads, and broken signs. Someone located the source of the Orinoco. And finally, Pope Pius XII announced that for Catholics the rhythm method was unacceptable if it was used only to satisfy sensuality and thus avoid the fecundity of union. He added that if pregnancy is dangerous, abstention is heroic. Now what was all that supposed to mean?

He glanced down at Ythn, who was still toying with his schoolbooks, trying to lift his Latin text with just one suction cup.

"Ythn," he said, "I'm worried about my body."

"There's nothing wrong with your body. You are engaged in the great war between adolescence and maturity, and I am here to tell you there is nothing to fear but fear itself."

"Another thing. All the good radio programs are off the air now. *The Clock, The Mysterious Traveler, Broadway, My Beat, Quiet Please, Tales of Willie Piper*—all the good stuff."

"That's progress," said Ythn. "All the money is in television now. But what has that to do with your body?"

"And the news doesn't make any sense. And television is really awful. Did you ever watch television?"

"Television will mature. It's still in its infancy, as you Earth people like to say. Perhaps you and television will mature together."

"I don't want to mature. I hate maturity."

"Hush. Your mother will hear you talking to a Martian."

"I don't care what she hears, and I don't want to mature. I hate adults. I hate them almost as much as they hate being adults."

"But you love Norman Pangborn and you love your mother and your father. And you rather like Emma Leibolt."

"Mrs. Leibolt embarrasses me to death. I never know what to say to her."

"I must say, Roger, that your list of problems doesn't add up to much. You don't like television and you miss your old radio programs and you dislike some adults, and your body—I should point out to you that everybody has one—disturbs you. It's perfectly adequate and it works fine but it disturbs you."

"Well, it's more than that. I'm depressed. I hate everything. Everything hates me. I'm not good for anything. I'm ruining my health with certain habits I've fallen into. I have this feeling I'll be dead before I'm twenty."

"Your childhood will be dead before you're twenty," said Ythn. "*You* will be just fine."

"Something is all wrong," said Roger. "I just can't say it right."

Ythn turned his head to look at him with his large gray eyes. "Try again," he said gently. "Try to say it right."

"I can't. I don't know. Everything is slipping away. It's getting harder to believe in stuff, just like Pangborn says. Half the time I think Yma Sumac is really just Amy Camus from Brooklyn, just like Curtiss Baylor says. Everything is changing. My pants are always too short. Pretty soon I'll be in college and then I'll grow old and that'll be the end of it."

"You don't believe in anything beyond death?"

"You mean God? I don't know. Maybe it's all imaginary."

Ythn sat up on the rug, crossed his legs, and began to glitter. Then he crooked his four arms and put his hands on his hips so that he looked vaguely like an amethyst—all bright facets and sharp angles. "And what about me?" he demanded. "Am I imaginary too?"

Roger looked up from the bed, surprised that Ythn would ask such a question. "Well—I mean—you seem awful real to me," he said after a long silence.

A low oscillating whistle escaped from Ythn's small, immobile mouth that Roger took to be a sigh of relief. "I'm pleased to hear that," said Ythn. "You're only fifteen, and it's a little early for you to lose faith in everything. But then, it's always a little early for that, no matter how old you are."

"I just have this feeling that the end is coming," said Roger. "Maybe that's why Harry built a time machine."

"Harry did what?"

"Harry Fisher built a time machine. He called this afternoon and told my mom. Maybe he feels the same way I do and decided to go backward or forward, like in H. G. Wells. But that's impossible, isn't it? You can't really build a time machine."

"Everyone builds his own time machine," said Ythn. "You build it inside yourself. It takes you anywhere you want to go."

"I don't mean that. I mean it can't be *really* real. Not like rain and lightning."

"Rain and lightning are much more real for some people than they are for others," said Ythn. "Things are unfortunately never simple. Now, the real and the unreal—upon that subtle and shifting distinction a great tale could be told—"

"Oh, come off that stuff. That's—"

"What?"

"That's Shakespeare!"

"I beg your pardon?"

"Ythn, I'm trying to tell you something. I'm trying to tell you that everything is all messed up. I used to love to run more than anything in the world. I never thought a thing about it—it was just fun. Now when I run I wonder why I'm running and I sometimes get this idea that something is following me."

"What thing?"

"I don't know. Shadowman. The thing that makes everything go so fast. Did you know I never shed one single tear when I found out there was no Santa Claus and I never believed in the Easter Bunny at all but that I really fell apart over Jack Frost?"

"I'm afraid I don't follow. Who's Jack Frost, and what has he to do with Shadowman?"

"There's this children's story about Jack Frost. He's this little guy with a pointed hat and a paintbrush who silvers all the windowpanes and paints all the leaves in autumn. I used to think it was so terrific the way he got around. All those millions and trillions of leaves and all those zillions of windowpanes. I used to imagine him leaping from one place to another on those little pointy toes so fast you couldn't even see him. When I was six I wanted to be Jack Frost—can you imagine that?"

"So when you run, you flee from the dark something that steals away all your beliefs. All your hopes. Is that it?"

"I guess. I don't know. It's too many things all at once. It's no wonder Harry built a time machine."

"So you believe in Harry's time machine after all?"

"Harry is awful smart. He can do things no one else can do. And he has this secret—at least he says he does. Maybe that's it. I mean, maybe he really does have a time machine."

"Why don't you ask him?"

"I can never find him. He sort of disappears most of the time. He's like Jack Frost."

Roger loved it when Ythn laughed. His laughter was like chamber music. It chimed and reverberated quietly in six different voices. And now that he was so happy perhaps he would finally tell Roger about the things that really mattered.

"Ythn, tell me about Mars. Tell me about the canals and cities."

Downstairs the telephone rang three times. Then he heard his mother's footsteps coming from the kitchen.

"Mars is mostly desert," said Ythn. "Orange oceans of sand with mountains here and there and huge sand beasts that live beneath the surface. And there are the ruins of ancient cities here and there. No one knows who built them."

"Have you seen them? Have you been all through them?"

Ythn nodded and then raised his four arms and spread out his twenty fingers in a gesture that made him look like a green fan, or a waterfall, or a tree. *If I were a Martian*, Roger thought, *I would do that in church. If I went to church.*

"The green cities," said Ythn. "Their ruins are the most beautiful things I have ever seen. Four hundred thousand years ago there was an elder race we know nothing about. They built all the canals and they raised all the towers and domes out of Martian onyx and marble."

Roger saw that the snow was falling behind Ythn in the dark outside his window. "Who is this?" his mother was saying. "Who is this—" Her voice seemed far away, submerged. A voice not from Mars but from Atlantis.

"—all we know of the elder race is the writing on the walls of the temples of Yoh-Vombis, and an old legend that goes back many thousands of years about—"

He heard his mother calling him from the bottom of the stairs, and then her quick footsteps on the upstairs hall. The door to his room opened.

"Roger?"

Standing in the doorway in her blue bathrobe she made him think of a Sunday-school Madonna, except for the wrinkles around her eyes that came in the evening when she was tired. And the blue vein, just barely visible at her temple, that sometimes pulsated when she was angry or frightened.

He went to the window without answering her. Across the

street he saw the gray shapes of tree branches crossing in the dark, and the vague outlines of snowdrifts.

"Roger, you were talking to yourself again. Did you know that?"

"I was talking to a Martian."

"Roger, I want you to be serious for a minute."

"I am serious. I'm always serious. Even when I'm kidding I'm serious. I guess that's one of my problems."

She came into his room and sat on the bed. Ythn lay on the top bunk, one ear curled and listening. Roger hated it when she caught him talking to Ythn, who never showed himself, who always left him holding the bag. *You might as well be imaginary*, he thought.

"Roger, are you all right?"

"I told you this morning, I'm fine. I always talk to myself. I have—an active imagination."

"Someone just called."

"I know that. I heard the phone ring." He looked at his mother. "What do you mean, someone? Was it Harry?"

"I don't know who it was."

"You mean—you mean he wouldn't tell you who he was? You mean like a dirty phone call?"

"No, not that. Not exactly. It was from a Concerned Mother. That's what she called herself. She said things about you."

Something fell in the pit of his stomach. He was running, but Shadowman was closing in. Someone or something wanted him. Someone or something was pushing too fast, making things happen, taking advantage of the fact that he was only fifteen. Something. A Concerned Mother. A voice without a body.

"What did she say?" he managed to ask.

"I'm trying to remember. The trouble is, it didn't make much sense."

"She talked about me? She said bad things about me?"

"She asked me if I knew what went on at Pangborn's Used Book and Magazine Store. Isn't that the place you and Dennis and Frank go after school?"

"Yes, but—"

"And she asked if I knew anything about anti-Christian book clubs. Isn't that crazy?"

"I can't believe it. They think I'm going to injure the young. All the nuns and all the Concerned Mothers have been deputized and they're going to hunt me down like a dog. Oh God—"

"Roger, what are you talking about?"

"Today at Pangborn's a nun came in and asked him if he sold books that might injure the young. Something like that."

"Maybe there is a connection. But this lady didn't sound like a nun."

"What does a nun sound like?"

"Oh, I don't know. She just didn't. Besides, she said she was a Concerned Mother.

"Maybe she's a Concerned Mother Superior. Oh God, she's gonna call the school—"

"Roger, you mustn't get upset. The world is full of crazy people." She took his hand and he sat down next to her on the bed. She put her arm around his shoulder and gave him a squeeze.

"I know you would never hurt anyone or do anything bad," she said. "But I'm worried about you. I'm worried about the way every little thing gets to you. You get too excited about little things. You probably say things to people that get taken the wrong way."

"Can't keep my mouth shut, is that it?"

"Roger, please. I'm on your side. She also mentioned something about a boy in your class. Larry somebody?"

"Larry Norcross. Oh God, was it his mother, do you think?"

"She said that Larry—what was his name?—he knows what you're up to."

"Larry Norcross doesn't know what anyone is up to. All he knows is basketball and dancing the rhumba with Marilyn Sord and looking pretty and making nasty remarks. I really hate him. He's just awful."

"Well, perhaps you'd better steer clear of him from now on."

"That's awful hard to do. He's in all my classes, just about. He makes fun of everything I say. He has this smirk that all the girls love, and they all titter every time he opens his mouth. I really hate him."

"Then just be quiet when you're around him. Don't argue. Show a little common—"

She stopped in the middle of her sentence and pressed the tips of her fingers over her forehead and then took a deep breath. Then, suddenly, she laughed. "Oh, for God's sake," she said, "don't listen to me. I keep telling you to be weak when I want you to be strong. I keep telling you to make all the female mistakes I made for so many years. But still, I—I don't want people to think badly of you. You're such a good boy. You're playful and imaginative. You're sensitive and kind. I want everyone to know that."

It had never occurred to Roger that he was either sensitive or kind, and he did not want to be thought of as playful. Dogs were playful. He was about to ask his mother just what she meant by calling him that, but then he looked into her face—her sad, beautiful face—and thought better of it. Yes, she was on his side. It was difficult, so difficult, having a parent on your side. The nice things they said about you were always the things you hoped no one would find out, or the things you knew you could never live up to.

She got up and looked around the room as if she had misplaced something. Her cigarettes or an ashtray. "You get to bed now," she said. "It's late. Is all your homework done?"

"Yes."

She went to the door, then hesitated. "Your father is coming home this weekend. I think we ought to do something together as a family. Something really special. Perhaps we could see a play together. They have a special winter series at the Papermill Playhouse."

"You know, we could do a lot of things together if he lived at home. I don't suppose that ever occurred to him."

"Roger, we've been through this so many times."

"Why doesn't he come home on weekends? He doesn't have to work on weekends."

"He has a new job. He has lots of new things to learn. He'll be home on weekends after Christmas. He promised us that, remember?"

"I'll believe it when I see it."

"Your father loves us in his own way. You can't—you can't always have someone love you in your way. Sometimes you have to let people love you the way they know how. You have to recognize the fact that it's still love, and you have to be satisfied."

He understood that, or thought he did. He understood a great deal about his mother and father, about the distance between them. But again he was angry. Too many people wanted him to accept too many things. His father wanted him to accept his absence. Miss Simic wanted him to accept Latin. Mrs. Leibolt wanted him to accept Great Literature. Ythn wanted him to accept the fact that he was growing up. Larry Norcross wanted him to accept humiliation. Norman Pangborn was the only person he could think of who had never asked anything of him. When he grew up, he thought, he would have a bookstore too, but in another city. He would spend the whole day reading and talking to kids and drinking orange juice.

"Well, *would* you like to go to the Playhouse? We haven't been for a year. You could invite a friend."

"Sure, Mom. That sounds great."

Outside, the snow was still falling. Strange how so much snow fell without making any noise. But of course that was because it fell in such tiny pieces. Little flakes, each one drifting in its own space. What would it be like, he wondered, if God let the snow come down all at once?

7 | Dinosaur Football

On the way to school the next morning he told the Denizens all about the telephone calls. Dennis and Frank were both curious about Harry Fisher's time machine, but they had little to say about Concerned Mothers. Finally Frank ventured that this was a terrible thing for a grown-up to do to a nice person like Roger. Then Dennis put in that this was just the rococo kind of behavior that young men must learn to expect from adults.

"Anytime we have a little fun they get suspicious," he said. "They have this everybody-out-of-the-pool philosophy of life. You just have to get used to it. They don't mean any harm."

"I would hate to think that people are getting organized against me," said Roger. "All the teachers and Concerned Mothers."

"And the telephone company and the post office and the city government," said Frank. "What a horrible thing to even imagine. It gives me the willies."

"The march of the malicious mailmen," said Roger.

"Terror on the telephone," said Dennis.

That morning Miss Simic screamed for five minutes at Cynthia Cucinelli for not having her verbs finished. Cynthia smiled and said she was sorry. Tears streamed down her face. She was the ugliest girl in class, and she was the only one about whom Roger had daily fantasies. There was something wonderful about her round figure and her kinky black hair. Her thick, black eyebrows bushed over her bulging eyes, beneath which deep creases ran like pencil marks. How exciting it would be, he thought, to *do it* with such an ugly, friendly, and, he imagined, utterly willing creature. He had never thought that stupidity could be so sexy. It took all his breath away to think about her fat thighs, her round stomach, and her pointed breasts. He suspected that he was the only person in the world who had ever found Cynthia Cucinelli to be an object of lust. Still, when he saw the tears in her eyes he felt ashamed. She was a person, like anyone else. And it wasn't her fault that she was Italian.

When class ended, he found that he could not stand up without embarrassing himself. He piled and unpiled his books, ruffled through his notebook until everyone else was gone. How quick to come, he thought, and how slow to go.

"Roger!" said Miss Simic. "You're going to be late for Mrs. Leibolt's class."

"I was just thinking about what you said, Miss Simic."

"You were doing nothing of the kind."

"Please?"

"No one meditates upon the glories of the pluperfect subjunctive. It's just something you learn."

"Yes, Miss Simic."

"There is no way to get on my good side. You understand that?"

"Yes, Miss Simic."

Miss Simic stood up at her desk and shook her fringe of powdery gray curls. When he looked at her, he decided she had no good side; therefore, no one could ever get on it. There was only one side to Miss Simic, and that was Latin.

In English class Mrs. Leibolt picked her way through several short stories. She asked which of the main characters had tragic flaws. She had questions about rising and falling action. She asked which stories had resolutions and which did not. She wanted to know about point of view. Then she crossed her legs and smiled, and all the Great Literature, whose presence had become dry and feathery under the light of her questions, flew out the window.

After a noisy lunch in the cafeteria, he spent a half hour on the playground playing Smear the Queer with the other tenth-graders. Smear the Queer, a primitive and incoherent form of football, consisted of chasing and tackling whoever had the ball. When the horde of boys converged on the ball carrier and successfully buried him, someone else would take it and become the Queer. The Queer usually had a friend or two to whom he could hand off or pass. When Larry Norcross or Curtiss Baylor or Buck Moore had it, they could depend on six or eight loyal supporters. Roger had no one, since neither of the other Denizens was in any of his classes or even shared the same lunch or recess hour. Dennis, who hated violence, had always referred to this lumbering, disorganized activity as Dinosaur Football.

Roger leaped into the air to intercept a pass from someone he could not see that was intended for someone behind him. For an instant he stood out above everyone, the ball caught in his cold hands. When he came down, he began to run. He turned sharply to the left by twisting his right heel into the snow. Then he stopped, reversed his field, and four of his pursuers ran into each other.

"Smear the Queer!" shouted Larry Norcross. "We really got a queer this time! Smear the Queer!"

Roger did a quick stutter step to avoid Curtiss Baylor's rush, then hurdled over two boys who had been knocked over in the confusion. At the instant he came down, his body still stretched out, he felt a tremendous blow to his left side. He turned in time to see that Larry Norcross had thrown a body block that had caught him just under the ribs. The blow lifted him off his feet and knocked him sideways through the air.

A bright, sudden pain spread through his left side, reaching in all directions, and as he fell he thought of a hammer hitting a glass windshield.

The air went black. Then he felt snow melting against his right ear underneath his cap, saw a flash of blue sky, and heard Larry Norcross laughing.

"You all right?" said Buck Moore.

"Jesus, he looks blue," said Eddie McQueen.

"Can't—can't breathe."

"The little baby can't breathe," said Larry. "Maybe he needs a nice smack on his bare bottom from the doctor."

"Bastard."

"Ooooh," said Larry. "Such a nasty word from such a little baby. Maybe the little baby is upset by telephone calls?"

Roger sat up and blinked. Things came back into focus. He shook his head. "Did you all see—what—Larry did? Did you—all see—that?"

"It's a tough game," said Buck Moore. "If you can't chew, then spit it out."

"If you can't screw the dude, then don't be nude," said Eddie McQueen.

"If you can't shit, get off the pot," said Larry Norcross.

Roger was on his feet now. He was trying hard not to cry. His breath came in gasps. "So it *was* your mother," he said. "You can't—you can't do it yourself, so you get your mommy to fight your battles for you with dirty phone calls!"

"You don't know who it was, you little bastard queer! But I know who it was, and I know about you! Everybody knows about you and your homo friends and your dirty books and your little meetings in the basement! You're gonna get tarred and feathered before this school year is over, you know that?"

The bell rang and people began to drift off. The antagonism between Roger and the handsome captain of the basketball team was familiar to everyone, and of no particular interest.

"One more thing," said Larry. He took a step forward and pushed at Roger with his left hand, and Roger saw too late that Eddie McQueen was crouched behind him. For the second time he went sprawling into the snow.

"Come on, Larry," said Buck Moore. "Playtime is over." He clapped his mitten on his friend's shoulder.

But Larry Norcross continued to stand over him, his fists clenched, his legs spread like a young colossus, his face a mask of hatred. "This is my time," he said through his teeth. "You understand that? You get my meaning?"

Buck frowned. "Larry, you don't have to get into all that. Not in front of this sissy. Your father never meant to—"

"I'm not getting into anything!" shouted Larry. "I'm making a simple statement. This has got nothing to do with my father and his college fraternity and his country club and my big-shot brother with his engineering degree—" His face flushed, and he shook his fists at Roger. Then he turned and walked away.

The second bell rang and Roger was alone in the snow, his side aching, his breath still coming unevenly. He hated Larry, his tormentor, the boy who had everything, including the prettiest girl in the tenth grade, but it had never occurred to him that Larry really hated him back. What was there to hate? Or to be jealous of? And what did he mean, *it's my time?*

He stood up and brushed himself off. It was cold. He lifted his arms above his head. He prayed that Larry Norcross, Curtiss Baylor, Eddie McQueen, Buck Moore, Marilyn Sord, Harriet Emerick, all nuns and Concerned Mothers, and most of the people in the town of Greencastle would fall into a burning pit, and that Ythn would take him to Mars in a real flying saucer. Mars, where there was no winter.

And he prayed that Harry Fisher really did have a time machine in his attic. One that worked.

8 | The Words of the Donkey Spoken to the Cat

In the corner of his basement, Roger had pinned two old sheets to a clothesline and fixed a third one at a right angle to make a small white room that glowed in the candlelight. A door and a set of sawhorses formed the table where the Denizens sat with their two guests for the evening. Roger had painted the table white, and then covered it with Egyptian hieroglyphs laboriously copied from *The Book of the Dead.* He had pieced together several vaguely related sections from Plate XXXII:

I have made offerings to the gods, and sacrificed meals to the shining ones. I have given bread to the hungry, water to the thirsty, clothes to the naked, and a boat to the shipwrecked. May those who see me say, come in peace, come in peace. For I have heard words spoken by the Donkey to the Cat in the house of Hept-Re. Deliver me from Baabi, who liveth upon the intestines of princes.

He hardly knew what any of this meant, but the words pleased him. Once, as he read them over to himself on a rainy night when his parents had gone out to a party, they had made him cry. It was strange, he thought, to let the night affect you that way, and to cry over something you didn't understand. Nothing like that had ever happened to him before.

His first interest in ancient languages came when he discovered one day on the playground that his most secret sexual fantasies had been blessed and dignified by Latin names. But after a brief and unhappy romance with the Roman tongue, he realized that this dull, plodding language did not begin to satisfy his hunger for the strange and the wonderful. Then, one day in the middle of the summer of his fourteenth year, he discovered, misplaced in the history section of the Greencastle Public Library, a translation of the *Papyrus of Ani* together with the original hieroglyphs and an approximate rendering of the sounds of that ancient language. It was love at first sight. He spent the whole summer trying to learn hieroglyphics. He taught himself all twenty-five of the alphabetic characters, most of the prepositional forms, and nearly a hundred ideograms. Writing in Egyptian gave him a special pleasure, though it took him weeks to learn how to make the different kinds of birds and owls. He especially loved the names of gods and pharaohs and famous places. Baabi, the devouring god, was a leg and a foot, two falcons, a leg and a foot, and two quills. *Ba-ahbi*, he thought. Yes, that was how it had been spoken three thousand years ago. He would have to tell Pangborn about that.

The five boys sat on card-table chairs as the diaphanous sheets undulated in the drafty cellar air. A plaster of paris skull sat in the center of the table with a candle burning in its center so that the yellowish light shone out from the mouth and eyes. Other candles hung from a chandelier Roger had made from a barrel hoop and string. Wax dripped on the table. Beads of moisture formed on the cement walls.

The guests who had come to the seventeenth meeting of the Denizens of the Sacred Crypt were Phil Hedley and Randy Hormann. Phil slicked his hair back and had a little rosebud mouth that smirked at everything. He was tracked high in math and science, and his father was a senior engineer at CIBA. Randy Hormann was fat and secretive. It was rumored he had a collection of books that could send him to prison.

"We begin!" said Roger. "Place your hands on the skull!"

Phil Hedley smirked. Randy Hormann looked uneasily to his left and right and then put his hand on the skull with the others. Together the five boys made a star in the semi-darkness.

"For the next two hours," said Roger, "we, the Denizens of the Sacred Crypt, again dedicate ourselves to the terrifying, the ghostly, the mysterious, and the unexplained. Are there any announcements?"

Phil Hedley shook his head and chuckled, as if he had seen an easy card trick.

"If not, we move on to Denizen projects. The chair recognizes Frank Aldonotti."

"We have fifty-two dollars and sixty-seven cents in the Denizen treasury for the building of the Denizen Mars Telescope," said Frank. "But we sort of need some ideas about raising the other hundred and fifty. Maybe we could make things and sell them. Or something."

"What things?" said Dennis.

"I don't know," said Frank.

"We need Harry Fisher for that," said Roger. "God, I wish we could get him to come to just one meeting. He can make anything."

"If we can't get the money by next September it's almost sort of pointless," said Frank. "We'll all be off to college in a couple years."

"I'm going to MIT," said Phil Hedley. "My dad says I can go right into his fraternity."

"That's terrific," said Roger. "But does anybody have any more ideas about raising money? Dennis, why don't you work on that? Consider yourself a committee. Okay, we got one more thing before Frank's story."

"Project Saucerwatch!" said Dennis.

"Right. Frank, you got another report on that?"

After nearly a minute of fumbling with his notebook and stumbling into chairs, Frank managed to Scotch-tape a large area map of central New Jersey, upon which he had drawn dozens of small circles with a ballpoint pen, to the cellar wall. "I can't go through all this stuff," he said. "I got sixty-seven sightings going back three years. But here's a few samples—"

"I don't get it," said Phil. "What's saucerwatch?"

"It's a new German lunch meat," said Dennis.

Frank pointed to the circles on the map and began reading from his notes, giving times, places, and descriptions. He went on for ten minutes.

"This is boring," said Phil. "There's no such thing as flying saucers. It's all marsh gas."

"But we have all this evidence," said Frank. "All these sightings."

Randy Hormann hunched forward and squinted at the map. "But they're just little green circles," he said.

"Maybe we ought to draw pictures to go with them so even dummies can understand," said Roger.

"Maybe we should get on with the meeting," said Phil. "I can only stay till eight-thirty."

Frank stared at Phil's rosebud smirk. "You haven't actually even read any of the evidence," he said. "There's lots and lots of evidence. Did you see the big article in *Life*? One scientist said there was so much evidence that he just had to believe it—"

"Could we get back to the meeting?" said Dennis. "Could you guys fight it out later?"

Roger raised his hands. "If there is no further business," he said, "then we turn once again to Frankus Aldonottus, the mad monk of the catacombs, who has a story for us from the dark crypt of his memory—"

When the laughter ended, Frank moved one of the candles closer to the book that lay on the table in front of him. The flame tipped, wavered, sent shadows of light across his face. He opened the book and held the pages down flat with his open hand. Then he looked up.

"I am going to read 'Cool Air,' by Howard Phillips Lovecraft," he said in a high, ceremonial voice that cracked on the word *cool*. Again everyone laughed. Frank gritted his teeth and closed his eyes. He made a fist and pounded the table very softly. Then he opened his eyes and tried to begin his story.

"*You ask me to explain why I am afraid of a draught of cool air; why I shiver more than others upon entering a cold room, and seem nauseated and repelled when the chill of evening creeps through the heat of a mild autumn day. There are those who say I respond to cold as others do to a bad odour—*"

Roger watched the faces of the other boys in the candlelight, saw their expressions change from politeness, smirking disbelief, and schoolroom vacuity to slow interest. He had noticed that Lovecraft always did that to people. He knew Frank believed with all his heart that HPL was the greatest writer who ever lived; Roger was not willing to go that far, but surely he was *one* of the greatest. And then, thinking of Mrs. Leibolt, he decided there was a difference between things that were great because adults said so and things that were great because somehow they just were. Dickens, Shakespeare, grammar, Sunday school, Swiss chard, and going to bed early on weeknights were all Great Things for Kids, according to, he imagined, millions of schoolteachers, Concerned Mothers, and nuns. But H. P. Lovecraft, Edgar Rice Burroughs, cheeseburgers, walking in the woods, Denizen meetings, early summer mornings at Lake Michigan, and Egypt were all great things according to his way of looking at life. It occurred to him that as he grew older he was slowly dividing the world into two camps: one was official, well organized, dull, and powerful. The other was fascinating and wonderful, but impotent.

As Frank read, his voice became steadier, more natural. After a while he looked up from his book and seemed to stare at some point far outside the room. Randy Hormann, his pudgy fingers folded in front of him like sponges, looked up at Frank with sudden interest.

"He memorized the whole thing," he whispered to Phil Hedley. "He learned it all just for tonight."

Phil shrugged his shoulders. "So?"

"—the whole house, as I have said, had a musty odour; but the smell in his room was worse, and in spite of all the spices and incense, and the pungent chemicals of the now incessant baths which he insisted on taking unaided, I perceived that it must be connected with his ailment, and shuddered when I reflected on what that ailment might be—"

Now there was nothing but silence, candlelight, and the sound of Frank's voice spinning out his terrible story. But Roger knew the story well, and again his mind began to drift. He thought again of the great split he had created in the world, and he decided that Phil Hedley and Randy Hormann belonged on the side with Concerned Mothers, Larry Norcross, and Dinosaur Football. It worried him, however, that as the school year passed, he seemed to have less and less patience with things he hated. And it worried him that the list was getting so long—longer every day—while the list of things he loved did not begin to keep pace.

He knew, of course, that many of his complaints against life were trivial. He hated the jelly slime that spilled out when you turned the key on a can of Spam. He hated television, especially Arthur Godfrey (and all the little Godfreys). He hated gummed reinforcements, used textbooks, kids who said *motherfucker* and *shitass* and wore ducktail hairdos and plastered their hair down with Wildroot Cream Oil so that it looked like road tar. "You have no sense of proportion," Ythn often told him. "You make moon craters out of mud puddles."

Of course he knew Ythn was right. But he also knew there was something lurking behind all these minor and major annoyances, some principle or force that was responsible. It was the thing that followed him everywhere, the Shadowman that haunted and hated him.

"—then, in the middle of October, the horror of horrors came with stupefying suddenness. One night about eleven, the pump of the refrigeration machine broke down—"

The Lovecraft story moved in a prolix and laborious way toward its climax. Roger thought it was a splendid tale and could not understand why it repulsed Ythn. Ythn had told him once that most of Lovecraft's work was unhealthy, the product of a terrible prude who had sublimated all of his perfectly normal human emotions into titillations of forbidden horror. "When your poetic discrimination develops a little further, you will begin to see that HPL has served his purpose and you will go on to higher things," Ythn said one morning. Roger opined that he did not want to develop his poetic discrimination because he hated poetry, though he sometimes admitted to himself that *poetry* was perhaps a feeling about things that went beyond the trivial, sentimental, and stilted confines of *poems*.

Frank's voice began to rise as he came to the chilling conclusion of "Cool Air." Phil Hedley raised his eyebrows. Randy Hormann's jaw fell open, and his gold fillings gleamed in the candlelight.

"*—and the organs never would work again,*" cried Frank. "*It had to be done my way—artificial preservation—for, you see, I died that time eighteen years ago!*"

After a lengthy silence, Randy took off his glasses and began to rub his forehead. "Is that it? You mean he was dead all the time and the cool air kept him from—jeez, I can't talk about it. It's too awful."

Roger felt a thrill of pleasure. Lovecraft triumphs, he thought. Here in his basement, Halloween was still the master, and the little earthlight of dull reason was lost in the larger darkness.

"But it's impossible," said Phil. "You could never keep a dead man going like that on drugs and cold air."

"But it makes a good story," said Dennis.

"How can it be a good story if it's impossible?"

"It's not supposed to be true," said Roger. "It's not something you read in a newspaper. It's a story. It's fiction."

"But it never *could* happen," said Phil. "A good story is something that at least could happen."

"I don't care," said Frank, who now looked a bit disappointed. "I liked it."

"A lot of people think the stuff in the Bible is impossible," said Dennis. "But a lot of people still read it and believe it even though it goes against science."

"That's different," said Randy. "That's religion."

"But Lovecraft is sort of a religion," said Dennis. "He's got Yog-Sothoth and all his friends."

"Cthulhu, who sleeps beneath the ocean!" said Roger.

"Nyarlathotep, the crawling chaos!" said Frank.

"You guys are something," said Phil. "You guys are really something."

"We are the Denizens of the Sacred Crypt," said Roger. "We are the Inhabitants of the Night. The Defenders of Midnight Justice."

"Midnight justice. Jesus. Well, at least I give old Aldonotti a little credit for memorizing the story. That must have taken weeks."

"Frank never memorizes anything," said Dennis. "He doesn't have to. He just knows everything without even trying."

"You're kidding."

"Not a bit. That's why he's taking junior and senior courses in History and English. He reads something once and remembers every word. He can even tell you where all the words are on the page."

"It's really a pain in the neck," said Frank. "I get all cluttered up with all kinds of stuff."

"Like a garbage pail," said Phil. He smiled his tight little smile and his eyes narrowed.

"No," said Roger. "Frank's brain is more like an ocean. It goes down for miles and miles. Millions of things live there."

"Phil wouldn't understand that," said Dennis. "He's never seen an ocean. He has a sort of bathtub way of looking at things."

Phil Hedley chuckled and made a vicious scratch on the white table with his fingernail.

By eight-thirty Phil and Randy had left the meeting, and the Denizens sat together around the table and stared at Frank's map.

"Frank, you did a terrific job tonight," said Roger.

"You really think so?"

"No doubt about it," said Dennis. "Even your map gets an A."

"Gosh," said Frank. "Thanks."

"Of course, I could never understand why you love the most horrible and terrifying stuff as long as it's in a book when you get scared by even the littlest things in real life," said Dennis.

"Everything in a book has to stay in there," said Frank. "But outside of books the whole world is full of scary little things. I just hate all the scary little things. Like when you go down into the laundry room and everything is damp and steamy, and shirts without people in them are hanging on lines and then suddenly the washer turns on all by itself."

"Never mind that," said Roger. "It was a terrific meeting."

"But I almost sort of got the idea that Phil and Randy were laughing at everything," said Frank. "Maybe they can't wait to get to school tomorrow and tell on us."

"I don't know why we invited them," said Roger.

"They were the only ones who would come this week," said Dennis. "We seem to have this reputation."

Frank picked up the plaster skull and held it near the wall so that the candlelight flickered across the map. "I dream about this stupid map at night," he said. "And I think about the sightings. All sixty-seven. I try not to, but it just sort of happens. I can tell you the exact location and the date of the sightings and the names of all the witnesses and what they saw. And I keep seeing circles."

"Circles? You mean the green circles you made?"

"No," said Roger. "He means big circles to connect the lines. To make a pattern."

Frank stood up, found a ballpoint pen in his pocket, and then held it poised for a moment above the map. "Circles," he said. "Like this. Like when you drop a stone in a pond." His pen touched the map, moved from one sighting to another. When he finished, Roger saw that he had drawn three concentric rings over central New Jersey. A spider's web.

Frank put his finger in the middle of the smallest circle. "Look where the middle is!" he said. "Just look!"

"Where? I can't see."

Roger got up from the table and lifted Frank's finger. It was the Watchung Reservation, a forest preserve a mile east of Greencastle. A place full of pine trees and steep hills and rivers and swamps. He had been there a dozen times, or more.

"Could this really be it?" said Frank. "Could this be where it all comes from? It gives me the willies to think about it."

"The Alien Enclave," said Dennis.

"Saucer Central," said Roger.

They all laughed, but when the laughter died away they stood there together in the candlelight, their hands on each other's shoulders, gazing at the web of saucer sightings.

"It's a mystery," said Frank. "It's the voice of the Donkey speaking to the Cat."

"We must make sacrifice to the Shining Ones," said Roger.

"And flee from Baabi, who lives on the intestines of princes," said Dennis.

9 | Time Changes

A week later he made up his mind to stop at Harry Fisher's house after school to have a look at the time machine. He left the Denizens at the four corners and took the plunge down Recognition Street that led to Roosevelt Memorial Field. He remembered how shadows had covered this section of the street all through autumn. Now, with the trees bare, the hill was open to the cold sunlight. He took a long run down the sidewalk and slid the last twenty feet on a patch of ice.

A dozen sparrows, puffed out from the cold, pecked at a spray of bread crumbs that someone had thrown out onto the snow. The stark branches of a black elm cut the sun into seven pieces. A white cat picked its way up the gutter, sniffing at an orange rind, a stiff sheet of newspaper caught in the snow, and a green mitten. It was five o'clock. The brown-and-white dog whose queer name he had forgotten was howling in the yard where Harry Fisher kept his acorn army.

He ran up onto the front porch, hesitated, then pushed the doorbell. Nothing seemed to stir in the old house. He looked up to the third floor, where Harry had his books and ships and antique weapons, but the curtains were drawn shut. He knocked on the door five times.

A bolt snapped back and the door opened. A woman in a brown house dress with yellow flowers stood in the doorway. White streaks ran through her black hair, which had been clipped short. Her mottled, grayish-white skin made him think of the carbonate deposits that surfaced at the edge of the highway along the Watchung Reservation in the wintertime. Fine silver hair grew thinly over her throat and under her chin. She is a gray lady, he thought. He did not know what a gray lady was—the words had just come into his head—but somehow they fit her. Mrs. Fisher, the Gray Lady.

"Is Harry here? He called me a few days ago and wanted to show me something."

"Harry's here okay," she answered in a thin voice. It was the voice he had heard on the telephone, the voice that told him that Harry hated telephones. "He's here but he's busy. He gets mad if anyone comes up when he's working on his things. Are you Ennis?"

"No, ma'am. I'm Roger Cornell."

"Well, you come back later. Tomorrow maybe. He won't see anybody just now."

"He wanted to show me his time machine."

"I'm sure. You just come back tomorrow."

"Does Harry really have a time machine or was that just a joke?"

The woman's face went blank. "Harry has lots of things," she said. "He makes things up in the attic. I don't keep track. You come back tomorrow."

The Gray Lady closed the door. There was something about her that stunned him, left him staring at the doorknob. Her terrible, thin voice, her ravaged skin, her age—how could he and Harry be only a year apart in school when she looked twenty years older than his own mother? And there was an abruptness about her that reminded him of Harry. He had not talked to Harry for weeks, but he remembered how he always seemed to have two or three things in his mind at once, and jumped from one to the other.

He walked back to the corner of Recognition and Thorne.

As he stood there waiting for a car to pass, he heard a sound behind him. He turned and looked back at the tall house with its gray shutters and empty flower boxes. At first he saw nothing, no sign of life at all. But then, just for an instant, one of the curtains moved, and he knew that what he had heard a moment earlier was the sound of a window closing on the third floor.

"Roger? Is that you?"

He burst into the kitchen, his coat already unbuttoned, his red scarf hanging loose about his throat. He leaned against the sink and rubbed his hands and tried to catch his breath. When he looked up he saw that his mother was wearing her long blue dress and had her hair done up in the French roll she liked when she was going to spend a lot of time with other women.

"Aren't you a sight. I was just about to eat without you."

"Sorry."

"Just put your things on the chair. Where have you been?"

"I went to see Harry's time machine, but his mother wouldn't let me in, so I jogged down to the edge of the Watchung to look for flying saucers. The Denizens have decided that the Watchung is Saucer Central for this part of New Jersey."

"I had to ask, didn't I? Listen, I have a League meeting tonight, but I have to talk to you seriously for a minute if you can stand it. Sit down and eat before everything gets cold."

Roger sat down in front of a plate of ham and beans and broccoli. He heard his mother's words, but he was still thinking about Mrs. Fisher, the Gray Lady, and it occurred to him that perhaps the reason she didn't want anyone to visit the house was that Harry was crazy. Yes, that could be it. She didn't want anyone to find out that her son was a candidate for the loony bin.

"Your father's coming home late Friday night," his mother was saying. "He'll be here for dinner, and he told me that he wants us all to do something nice together. Remember I said we might want to go to the Playhouse?"

"Yes."

"Well, I just happened to see Nancy Sharpe today at the meat market, and she has four tickets to *The Student Prince* for Saturday afternoon that she absolutely can't use."

"What's *The Student Prince*?"

"It's an operetta. Your father's seen it. He told me once that it was very good."

"But he doesn't really want to go. He hates to go out."

"That's not true. I called him this morning and told him all about it. He sounded very happy."

"Okay, but what about the other ticket?"

"I thought you might ask someone."

"If I ask Dennis, then Frank will feel funny, and if I ask Frank—"

"I don't mean that. I was thinking you might ask a girl."

He stared at her. "You're kidding."

"Roger, you might as well get started on this sort of thing. Here's the perfect chance. You get free taxi service, and you get to take someone to a real stage show, not just a movie."

"A girl? You *must* be kidding. I can't ask a girl to go to an operetta with my parents. It's ridiculous. People would laugh at me."

"I don't see why anyone would laugh at you."

"I just can't. It's too—"

"Too what?"

"It's too rococo, that's what it is. It's just too rococo."

His mother laughed. "Well, you think about it. Dancing school is tomorrow night, isn't it? You could ask someone then."

"Friday is too late," he said. "You can't ask a girl out on Friday for something that's happening on Saturday."

"I don't know what makes you such an expert. You've never dated anyone in your whole life."

"There are certain things you just know."

"Suit yourself."

After dinner he went into the living room and lay on the rug for a half hour staring into the black fireplace and thinking about his father. He was pleased that he was coming home, pleased that they would all be doing something together as a family. But he had wanted for over a year to spend an evening with his father and tell him about all the changes, all the fears and hopes and confusions. Going to Millburn with two women to see an operetta was not his idea of how to do this. Talking with his father under any circumstances was getting harder and harder. Their brief exchanges always evaporated into clichés and pleasantries and awkward silences. Roger remembered a time when this had not been so.

The Germans had mounted a counteroffensive in a place called the Ardennes, and every day the newspapers showed large maps with black arrows tracing the attack routes. Some American commander said "Nuts" to some German commander, and was instantly famous. And Roger's father, who had avoided the draft for four years because he was in some vital defense industry, had taken him to New York City twice that winter. They visited the Museum of Natural History, the Metropolitan Museum of Art, and the Automat. He remembered that they talked constantly, though he could not recall what they talked about—only the inflection of his father's quiet voice, the way it went flat just before he laughed, and the way it narrowed into a whisper when they walked together through the dark rooms of museums.

They went for long walks. They found leaves in the snow, and his father told their names and then later he traced them on pieces of paper and explained about chlorophyll and photosynthesis. And he drew pictures of all manner of things with his engineering pencils and his soft pastels: ships and buildings and elephants and helicopters and bridges and schooners and ancient catapults and soldiers with spears and maces and shields. And, just once that he could remember, a pterodactyl. He worked quickly and then handed the sketch to Roger, and smiled as if he had made a little joke. His father's smile was never a grin. It was a pursing of the lips and a turning up just at the corners of the mouth. There was something shy in that smile, as if he did not wish to insist that what was amusing to him should necessarily be amusing to others. The memories were all very clear. His quiet, attentive, gentle father who took him everywhere and who came into his room every night with a cup of hot chocolate to ask how his homework was going.

When the war ended, something changed. Roger had often tried to remember just when this happened. There must have been a day, an hour, when he did something or said something that made his father turn cold. Or perhaps it was something at work, something that had nothing to do with him, some terrible truth found in a blueprint or an inter-office memo.

He remembered V-J Day in New York City. Shredded paper falling all over everybody, and soldiers kissing girls right out on the sidewalk, and the streets and buildings crisscrossed with long streamers when people threw rolls of colored toilet paper out of twelve-story windows. That summer his father received a war commendation from someone for designing something, and then they had all gone to Lake Michigan for two weeks, and then he was in the fourth grade at Washington School in Greencastle. Everything was wonderful, except that his father began to get up at night to make tea, and his mother complained of stomach pains. And sometimes he heard muffled voices behind the bedroom door at night and in the afternoon when he came home from school. "Why?" his mother would say. "Can't you just tell me why? Don't you think you owe me that much—" And then one day his father bought a table saw and a lathe and a bench grinder, and set up shop in the garage. He had always been clever with his hands, and now he spent hours and hours making bookends and trivets and small cabinets and lamps and then redwood benches for the backyard. Roger saw little of him in the evening after that.

And then, the summer before he went into ninth grade, they had all gone to the ocean for three days with his Uncle Peter, his Aunt Hattie, and their two beautiful daughters, one of whom he had been in love with since he was four years old. They rented a house on Jones Beach, a three-story mansion surrounded by yellow sand. He remembered that it tilted slightly to the south. They had a wonderful time of it, three glorious days in the middle of the summer. None of the five toilets worked and there was no electricity, but none of that seemed to matter. They had fourteen rooms, the sand went on for miles, and the ocean went on forever.

Each morning when he got up he would look out his ocean-front window on the second floor and see his father swimming alone past the breakers out into the sunrise. That was his father. Swimming alone in a wide place. He knew that swimming was the only sport his father had ever been able to master.

On the morning of the third day he went up to the third floor, searching for a toilet no one had used. He found one in a strange white room with bolts of faded fabric stacked in one corner and two dressmaker's dummies and a blank-faced mannikin standing in the center of the linoleum floor as if spellbound by the dust and the close, stale air. The toilet sat in the other corner of the room next to a small sink, and it was the most unusual toilet Roger had ever seen. It was perfectly circular with no seat, a thin porcelain rim, and a little spout in the middle. He had never seen such a thing. It gave him a queer feeling to use it, as if he had committed some sin whose name he had never heard, or gone somewhere that was forbidden. When he finished, he went back downstairs, undressed in his own room, and looked around for his bathing suit. Suddenly his father appeared in the doorway.

"Oh. Sorry." His father looked up and down his nakedness, winced, and then turned away.

"It's okay," said Roger. "I'm just changing."

But he felt a pang of embarrassment. He had never felt that before with his father. Only a year or two earlier they had taken showers together, and only two or three years before that his father had bathed him, lathered him all over with a soft washcloth. He remembered the look on his father's face when he poured clear water over his head and shoulders, a smile that said how clean and beautiful he was. It pleased him to please his father by the simple act of cleanliness as he looked up from the swirling, soapy cradle of warm water. And now, such a different look. He wanted to cover himself, like a girl. *I'm changed somehow*, he thought. *And it's not okay.*

But later he came down to the beach with his father and Tracy, his secret love, and Barbara, her older sister. They ran together across the wet sand, and after a while he saw his father had fallen behind. This was a terrible and wonderful thing. He was faster than his own father. Not wiser or stronger or braver, but faster. He glanced back. His father looked quiet and frail in his orange bathing suit. He waved, and after a moment his father raised his arm a little and waved back.

He thought about his nakedness and realized he was growing into a man. *My thing is growing longer*, he thought. *And I dangle. I never used to dangle.* Then he thought about his bush of curly hair, and the muscles in his legs, and the little tufts under his arms. Everything was changing. When he ran hard or played Dinosaur Football he smelled sour and milky, like one of his uncle's goats. He wondered if his changing body had offended his father as much as it had offended him. Perhaps, he thought, his growing up was not really forgivable, not really something his father could ever feel good about.

He sat up. At first he thought he was in bed, then realized he had nearly fallen asleep in the living room. It was snowing again outside. He remembered that the newspaper had predicted snow all through the evening. Perhaps there would be no school in the morning.

He went upstairs and dressed for bed. It was not even Christmas, and already he was tired of winter. He wished the thaw would come, and with it the hard green buds and the smell of earth and flowers. Then he could explore the Watchung Reservation with Dennis and Frank and discover a whole fleet of flying saucers and get his name in the *Greencastle Herald* and prove something once and for all to Larry Norcross and Curtiss Baylor.

"I feel like Ponce de León," he said to Ythn as he stared up into the dark. "He spent practically his whole life looking for stuff that wasn't there."

"A sad case," said Ythn. "But perhaps only to others. Perhaps not to Ponce de León."

Friday was interminable. Miss Simic gave an intensive review of fifth-declension case endings. Mrs. Leibolt sat on the front of her desk and smiled, swung her restless legs, reeked mildly of perfume, and talked. She incited lust, resentment, boredom, and occasionally interest as she sketched in the historical background for the age of Keats, Byron, and Shelley, the first subject in Adventures in Poetry. It was odd the way she had suddenly, two days earlier, grown impatient with short stories. She had pressed her hand to her mouth, as if to keep herself from telling secrets, and then, put away her careful lesson plans on O. Henry and turned to poetry. The Romantic poets, she said, wrote some of the greatest poetry ever penned. Their greatness, she went on to say, lay in their ability to express a great and tragic longing for things they could never have, their ability to transfer despair into beauty with the alchemy of their verse, and their sensitivity to the images of nature. Furthermore, they were original. They broke the old idols, melted the metal, and molded anew.

"To do this," she intoned, "to break the old traditions and moralities, that requires genius. And genius is the rarest and most dangerous of all human possibilities—"

Mrs. Leibolt looked out the window at the snow drifted on the far side of Paris Avenue, her lips parted slightly. Roger imagined that she was thinking about faraway geniuses, people she had met long ago in Hartford or Newark.

"You and I," she went on, "may never know in all our lives a man who is a genius. And yet we open our literature books to page ninety-seven and we are in his presence—"

As the students opened their books, a quiet sigh of weariness filled the air, and Mrs. Leibolt concluded that Romantic poetry would live as long as men remembered, that "The Eve of St. Agnes" should be read by Monday, and that failure to do so would mean staying after school and memorizing a sonnet.

History was a blur. Today's discussion had something to do

with the Renaissance, which, he gathered, was the place where Shakespeare lived. In Math class Miss Wakowski stared out the window while one student after another went to the board to solve quadratic equations. At lunch he sat next to Rolfe Gerhardt, the human blitzkrieg, who was probably the only person in the history of the world to think of the peanut butter sandwich as a deadly weapon, and Virgi Prewitt, an awkward, rawboned recluse with long pigtails who spent all her free time drawing pictures of bugs and germs.

After lunch he went to Physics class, where Mr. Figge talked about Einstein. He read something out of a book and then he pulled note cards from a wooden file with the tips of his fingers. Gradually Roger straightened up in his chair and began to listen. Mr. Figge was saying something now about time getting shorter or longer depending on how fast you were going.

"Are there any questions?" said Mr. Figge. He stood at the front of the room looking very narrow and very swaybacked. He ran his fingers through his thin yellow hair, adjusted his glasses, and looked relieved when it was clear that no one wanted to ask anything. The bell rang. Roger went up to the teacher's desk and waited for Mr. Figge to look up from the papers and books he was carefully placing in his briefcase.

"Mr. Figge? I do have a question."

"A question? Oh. That's fine. What is it? Always glad to answer questions."

"You were talking about time. I was wondering if you knew anything about time travel. I mean, do scientists think this will ever really be possible? I read a lot of science fiction, and it happens there all the time. Course, that's just imaginary."

"Yes," said Mr. Figge. "Just fiction, to be sure. Well. Time travel. I'm not too familiar with all that. H. G. Wells, and all. Just an idea, isn't it? A theory."

"I guess it sort of depends on whether or not time is real," said Roger.

"Real?" Mr. Figge scratched his cheek.

"You know. Like a tunnel or something. If time is just on

clocks, then it's just a way of showing how fast things are happening, right? But if it's something—I mean, like stuff you have to move through—well, then maybe someday someone might find a way to move back and forth in it."

Mr. Figge gave him a sudden, pinched smile that reduced his eyes to slits. "Very interesting," he said. "Roger, your ideas are always very interesting. We will have to talk about all this sometime. Very necessary stuff, time. It's what keeps everything from happening all at once, isn't it? Right now it's making me late for study hall."

Another quick smile, and time carried Mr. Figge out of Physics class and into the hallway.

10 | Ruth Refuses to Be Misty

That evening after dinner Roger took a long bath, polished his shoes, and carefully donned his one white shirt, his black bow tie, and finally his black suit. Then, for fifteen minutes, he combed his hair. He gave his tie a final twist, rubbed a spot of Vaseline into his lips, and stared at himself in the mirror. He wanted very much to be handsome, but it was just impossible to tell. He had seen himself too often, and whatever perfections or imperfections might be obvious to others were, for him, lost in the blur of familiarity. Curtiss Baylor and Buck Moore were both good-looking. Larry Norcross was almost beautiful, and girls stared at him openly in the hallways. Frank Aldonotti was a little on the short side and his teeth were not good and he ate too much spaghetti and lasagna. Dennis was tall and sort of shapeless, and his cheeks were too fat, especially when he smiled. But no matter how often Roger looked, his own appearance was still a mystery to him.

By seven-fifteen he was out the door and on his way to Miss Dot's School of Social Dance. He joined Frank and Dennis at the corner, and the three of them made their way down Maple Street and across the railroad tracks to the center of town, where they turned left on Springfield Avenue. They saw dozens of boys like themselves, all dressed in black or navy blue, slightly subdued and expectant, not quite themselves. At first they appeared in twos and threes, then in packs of seven or eight, and finally in a huge flock, like penguins rushing toward the ocean.

Just past the Strand Theater they came to the corner of Springfield and Holpen, which was the edge of the decent part of town. Past this were bars, warehouses, and three-story tenements where the poor blacks and the dangerous Italians lived. But here at this corner, Miss Dot's School of Social Dance held the eastern flank of town against the surging lower classes for six days every week. The school was on the top floor of an old department store that had gone out of business ten years earlier. The Denizens ascended the two flights of steps, hung their coats on the fifty-foot iron bar that served as a coatrack, and walked into the central ballroom. A single chandelier with twelve lights illuminated the entire room, which was lined on the two long sides with folding chairs. In one corner Mr. Waring, Miss Dot's second-in-command, arranged circles of red paper cups around the green Christmas wreaths that decorated three card tables. In another corner, a gray-haired pianist sat at a baby grand piano next to a bald man setting up drums. Miss Dot, a handsome lady with white hair and a white off-the-shoulder gown, talked to the drummer. The drummer, looking very tired, was nodding his head and trying to smile.

The pianist opened with a sprightly rendition of "Ricochet Romance" and then went into "Hard to Get" and "I'll Walk Alone," all fox-trots. The fifty or sixty boys who sat on one side of the room got up and walked over to the fifty or sixty girls sitting on the other side. *Would you like to dance? Why, yes, thank you.* Nervous smiles and bows. Limp hands helping girls to their feet. Much gazing at the floor.

Dennis, who looked huge in his black suit, danced with Amy Gillig, the ugliest girl in the tenth grade next to Cynthia Cucinelli. Roger caught his eye for a moment and Dennis flashed him a quick smile and then rolled his eyes to the ceiling. He could almost hear Dennis thinking: *Isn't this heaven? We ugly boys just love to dance with ugly girls.* He waved to Frank several times, but Frank never looked at anyone when he danced; he stared at his partner's left ear and sweated. In spite of his shyness at social events, Roger always had a good time at dancing school. Almost everyone from the tenth grade was there except the Negroes and the Jews and two Indian girls, daughters of a man named Kashfi, who owned a leather-goods store on Springfield Avenue.

Next to the waltz, the fox-trot was in Roger's opinion the dullest of all possible dances. No one except Larry Norcross and Marilyn Sord did anything but the basic step for the first hour. Everyone moved stiffly and in the same direction—as if someone were herding all the dancers in a great circle around the ballroom. The girls looked pacific, like waterlilies; the boys looked slightly uncomfortable, occasionally grinning at friends, jerking their heads in signs of manly recognition, or leaning away from their partners to whisper something to a member of their own sex. The girls withstood all this abuse with equanimity. "You have to put up with all that," he heard one of them say. "Men are just naturally rude and boring until they get to be eighteen."

Soon the boys began to "cut in." Miss Dot had taught them how to do this, warning that it must be done sparingly and with discretion: *You tap another gentleman on the shoulder and you say, "May I cut in?" And the gentleman must smile, take two steps away from his partner, and say, "Of course." Then partners are exchanged and the dance resumes. Is that clear to everyone?* The boys had also been taught to applaud at the end of each set of three numbers, to sit down on the boys' side, and to stand up and *casually* walk to the other side to find another partner when the music resumed.

During intermission Mr. Waring poured punch and made conversation with the girls. The boys laughed and punched each other. The girls stood in circles, talking about school and admiring each other's dresses.

"Hello."

He looked up from his punch and saw Ruth Jahntoff standing in front of him. She wore a green dress that was the same color as her winter coat, and he saw that she had taken the combs out of her hair and let it fall straight over her shoulders. It was much longer than he had ever imagined it could be.

"Hello," he said. "Another wonderful evening with Miss Dot."

She smiled at him, then said something that was blown away by a burst of laughter from the boys at the punch tables.

After intermission everyone formed a circle and Miss Dot gave her lesson for the evening: the outside turn in the rhumba. "The secret of grace while dancing is always to look *casual*," she said after she had illustrated the basic step with several variations. "Not bored, but *casual*. So many of you boys look as if you are walking across a narrow bridge in a high wind when you rhumba. Always remember that the Latin dances are languid and beautiful, never tense or grim."

He knew that many of the boys had begun to realize that one of the three secrets of social success in high school was the ability to dance, and thus they were all beginning to take their lessons very seriously. All the parties were dance parties. Proms came twice a year. The country club dances for young people came six times a year, and everyone who was anyone at all got invited. It made him laugh to think about all this, and to see that indeed many of the young men around him were at this very moment trying to look very casual.

After the lesson, the boys loosened up a little and began to try hesitations, dips, and conversation steps that broke up the wheel of black suits that revolved around the chandelier. Larry and Marilyn did an exaggerated tango dip that brought a frown and a tap on the shoulder from Miss Dot. Roger sat one dance out and then, looking up, he saw Ruth coming out from behind the screen that led back to the girls' powder room.

"Ruth? Dance with me?"

"Okay."

Even in simple things there was something different about Ruth. Perhaps it was the way she refused to make a fuss about anything. He could not imagine her saying, *Who me? Why, yes, I'd just love to!* He noticed too that she did not smile easily and that she never giggled. But still she looked up at him in her quiet, pleasant way as if his face—the same one he had stared at in the mirror for fifteen minutes nearly two hours ago—somehow gave her pleasure.

He also noticed that her palm was moist. Some girls, he knew, were like that. They came off on you. He remembered a very pretty substitute teacher he had in sixth grade who was like that. He knew the word for this was *clammy*, and he knew it was supposed to be disgusting. None of the popular girls had clammy hands. But still he found it pleasant, almost thrilling. He wondered if he would be able to smell Ruth on his hand and wrist all night long. He wondered if she knew that some secret commerce had taken place, an exchange that no one else could see or know. He wanted to find a way of telling her that it was all right, that clammy was beautiful.

"I saw you outside Pangborn's a couple of days ago," he said as they began to dance.

"I saw you too. Just thought I'd stop and wave hello."

"You looked all misty through the glass."

She smiled a little. "I wasn't misty on my side."

"Beg pardon?"

"I could never be misty," said Ruth.

"I don't get it."

"I mean like Marilyn Sord and Melissa Van Ghent. They're very misty. That's fine for them, I guess."

Again she had surprised him, this time with something he would never have suspected from a girl: a play on words. "I get it. You mean they sort of melt and glow and run all over the place. So sweet to everyone. Sort of like a watercolor painting that got left out in the rain."

She laughed quietly and then squeezed his hand. "No one talks the way you do," she said.

"Everybody says I talk too much. Everybody says I don't know when to shut up. Even my mother says that."

"You try to talk about things that are really important to you. People usually take that the wrong way. People get embarrassed when you try to be sincere."

"That's—that's true." It seemed so true to him at that moment that he couldn't think what more there was to say to her. "Ruth, did you know that you don't talk like a girl at all? Don't get me wrong. I don't mean you talk like a boy. I don't mean you say things that go against being a girl. I don't know what I mean."

"I understand," said Ruth. "You mean I'm not misty."

Again he was quiet for a moment. "I guess that's it," he said finally. "I guess that's exactly what I mean."

"Sometimes I try to explain to my mother that I'm not very pretty and I don't have much personality, but you know how mothers are. They think you're wonderful. But I know I'm just Ruth, and I know my last name sounds funny to most people."

"But you're very sincere," said Roger. "I can tell that just by talking to you."

"Maybe so. Are you sincere?"

"Yeah, I guess I'm pretty sincere."

"I'm more sincere with some people than I am with others," said Ruth.

"Just now you're being extremely sincere, in my opinion," said Roger. It was strange the way she had not taken her eyes off him since they had begun dancing. Most girls, he noticed, looked at the wall when they danced. Or at your Adam's apple.

"Ruth, how would you like to see *The Student Prince* tomorrow? It's an operetta. It's at the Papermill Playhouse. My parents can drive us."

"You're kidding."

"Nope. We have an extra ticket. I can't ask Frank without asking Dennis, and vice versa. So I thought I'd ask you."

"Well, sure. But I'll have to ask my mother. Can you call me tomorrow?"

"Okay."

"It's awful nice of you to ask," said Ruth.

"Not at all—I mean—you know this is the first time I ever asked a girl to go anyplace. It's a lot easier than I thought."

"I don't have too much experience either," said Ruth. "I'm not too popular. I only had two dates in my whole life, and they were both with Eddie McQueen, and he isn't—well, we didn't have much fun. Don't tell anyone I said that."

He thought for a moment and then decided to say something that seemed to fit the occasion: "Gee, Ruth, I thought you had lots of dates."

She pursed her lips as if she were about to smile. "Roger, that was not a sincere thing for you to say. But the truth is, I did get asked out one other time. I didn't go. It was a boy named Harry Fisher."

He stared at her. "Harry? You mean Harry Fisher actually asked you to go out?"

"You know him?"

"Well, not really. I mean, I don't know too much about him. He's sort of a man of mystery. Frank and Dennis and I are trying to get him to come to our club, but he's sort of invisible most of the time. Stays in his room. He builds all these fantastic things."

"I didn't go out with him because he's a year ahead of me," said Ruth. "And—I don't know—something about him was scary. He has this funny way of talking. And when I said no he made this funny laugh and said that was too bad because he wanted to show me a machine he built that could travel through time, and I wouldn't get another chance because something big was about to happen that would change everything."

"That's Harry. He tries to act mysterious. He laughs, but you never know what he's laughing about. Did you know he beat Curtiss Baylor three games of chess in a row last summer at Playground Joe's?"

"I didn't think anybody could beat Curtiss at anything."

"Harry's probably a genius."

"You mean like Frank Aldonotti? Everybody says he's a genius."

"Frank says he's not a genius," said Roger. "Frank says he just has total recall."

The music ended and suddenly Roger realized where he was. He was at Miss Dot's dancing school and he was lost in conversation with a girl, something that had never happened to him before, not ever in his whole life.

Miss Dot raised her arms and smiled. "Mr. Waring and I trust you have had a pleasant evening. We look forward to seeing you in three weeks. In the meantime we bid you good night, and we trust you will conduct yourselves like the ladies and gentlemen you are on the way home."

This was the signal for everyone to form two lines, one for the girls and one for the boys.

"Good night, Ruth," said Roger.

"Good night, Roger. Call me tomorrow?"

11 | Spiritual Exercises

When he awoke Saturday morning he heard water dripping. He put his feet on the cold floor, went to the window, and threw back the curtains. The street was shining wet, and a dark column of slush had formed in the snow under the roof's overhang. What a beautiful morning, he thought. He had not expected a thaw before Christmas.

In fifteen minutes he made his bed and cleaned his room. He looked about with satisfaction. Things in their place had always given him pleasure. One of his earliest memories was putting different buttons in different compartments in his mother's button box. He loved boxes and shelves and dividers. Things that fitted snugly against each other. He loved to unscrew the case of his alarm clock and watch the wheels and springs inside all working together. And he loved the nylon threads tied to his bedpost which led through a system of eyelets and hooks to the pull strings of every light in the room so he could turn them on or off without even opening his eyes. Roger didn't mind dust or dirt, but he hated disorder. "You would have made a perfect little British gentleman," his Aunt Hattie told him one day. "Very neat and very dirty."

He heard voices downstairs, and then he heard his mother

moving about, fixing breakfast. All at once he realized that his father was home and that in the afternoon they would see an operetta and that Ruth Jahntoff was coming with them. All that and the bright sunlight flooding the room and a January thaw in mid-December and Christmas vacation coming in just three days—it was too much to think about. He went into the bathroom and turned the hot and cold knobs for his Saturday-morning shower. Just before he stepped into the steaming water he remembered to smell his left hand. *Ruth,* he thought, *is that you? Are you still there?*

By the time he had showered and dressed, he began to smell bacon and coffee. He ran downstairs, thinking about his father, wondering if he was wearing his blue terry-cloth robe, imagining the expression on his face when he looked up from the table to say hello.

His mother was frying eggs and bacon and buttering toast. His father sat at the breakfast table in his orange pajamas looking out the window at melting icicles. Roger stood there framed in the doorway until his father saw him.

"Well! There's the boy. Long time no see."

"Hi, Dad."

"Sit down," said his mother brightly. "Everything's ready. We're going to have a long, slow breakfast with lots of coffee and eggs and bacon and toast and fruit compote."

"Sounds wonderful," said his father. "I haven't had a good breakfast in weeks."

"You should take time," she said. "It's the most important meal of the day."

The presence of his father in the kitchen seemed sudden, even though he had known for two days that he was coming. He was surprised by all the familiar things he had forgotten, things that seemed strange because, as the weeks passed, they had grown cold in his mind. His father's long white fingers. The way his blond hair curled a little at the edges. His pale skin, and the dark places under his eyes that nearly went away in the afternoon. His thin lips, his muted, shadowy voice, and the way he leaned over tables with his shoulders hunched forward, without looking at anyone. There was an intensity about his father's appearance that seemed almost theatrical. It would have been fitting, he thought, for his father to smoke Du Maurier cigarettes and talk like Brian Aherne. But he was not really like that at all. He was a quiet man, easy to get along with, and down-to-earth. He worked for an engineering firm in Hartford.

His father picked up his coffee cup, closed his eyes, and inhaled the aroma. "How's school?"

"Okay."

"Mom tells me you don't like school as well this year."

"It's okay. It's not terrific."

"Too bad you're not taking math or mechanical drawing this year. Or something I could help you with."

"I'm doing okay. I just get sick of all the busywork."

"Vacation's coming in a week," said his mother. "I can't believe it. Only eleven days until Christmas."

"That's not much time," said his father with a weary smile. "Not much time at all."

"Well," said his mother. "What are you two going to do this morning?"

His father looked up from his coffee. He had not yet touched the rest of his breakfast. "Do?"

"We don't have to leave for nearly five hours," she said. "You two have the whole morning to spend together. I have to clean house. Why don't you go Christmas shopping? All the stores are open. The weather is wonderful. So crisp and clear. Roger, have you been outside yet? No, of course not. You just got up—"

He sensed that his mother was talking too fast, bustling too much. He saw his father respond to this by hunching a little further over the table and closing both hands around the warm cup of coffee.

"Dad doesn't want to do anything," said Roger. "He's had a long trip. He's tired."

"I am a bit bushed," said his father. "Thought I'd sit for a while and read the paper. But what was that about this afternoon? I seem to have forgotten—"

"I told you yesterday. About the operetta."

"I was so tired when you called."

She sat down at the breakfast table and looked steadily at her husband. "The operetta at the Playhouse," she said. "We're all going to see *The Student Prince*, and Roger is bringing a lovely girl named Ruth. It's his first date."

"But couldn't we—oh. I see. Roger is having his first date. Well, that's fine. Well, congratulations. You've become quite the young man, haven't you?"

"It's not a big deal," said Roger. "It's just Ruth. Ruth is this girl I know."

"I see."

"We'll have a wonderful time," said his mother. "And tonight your father can build a fire and we can sit and have popcorn after supper and watch television."

His father set his coffee on the table and rubbed the corners of his eyes. "Well," he said, "I suppose we could do that. That would be very nice, wouldn't it, Roger?"

"But you forget," said Roger. "You can't stand watching television."

"Oh, I don't mind."

"We wouldn't have to watch television," said his mother. "We could just sit and talk. Or play records."

He remembered that the last time his father came home they had tried to sit together on Sunday evening and watch *I Remember Mama*. Roger hated *I Remember Mama*. He had a general hatred for television which he had never been able to explain very well either to himself or to others. For one thing, it occurred to him that there were too many *Theatres*. There was the *Kraft Television Theatre*, the *Cosmopolitan Theatre*, the *Fireside Theatre*, the *Armstrong Circle Theatre*, the *Starlight Theatre*, the *Celanese Theatre*, and the *Lux Video Theatre*, to name a few. And all the stories were about people who fell in and out of love, or people who had amnesia, or people coming back from the war, or people hoping for the big break that would make them successful reporters or lawyers or actors. It was awfully boring. His mother watched television for at least a half hour every morning and at least an hour in the evening, and when Roger passed through the living room he would glance at the milky screen for a few moments to see what was going on. Like the evening news, it was always incomprehensible. Once he saw four men in service-station uniforms singing about Texaco products, and then a man dressed in a rabbit suit came out of the audience. Another time someone named Dave was standing on a bare stage holding the works of a Second World War bombsight. He was saying things about the bombsight, and Roger could not tell if Dave was serious or trying to be funny.

It pleased him that his father also disliked television. He once tried to speak to him about this, tried to say they were alike, had this much at least in common. But he knew this was only a place where two infinite lines intersected on their way to different universes. "We don't have time for that, do we, son?" his father had said. "There's better things to do than sit around and watch commercials. And all those stories. Gosh, we have problems enough without worrying about imaginary ones, right?"

But that was not it. Not what he meant at all. He loved imaginary problems. They were always so much clearer and so much more interesting than his own muddy dilemmas. Nothing could be more exciting, more clear-cut, more utterly refreshing than an intergalactic war, a midnight visit from a vampire, or the discovery of an underground empire.

After breakfast his mother shooed them out of the house. "Go for a walk!" she said. "Do something! Get your blood moving!"

They put on their coats and went outside.

"Sorry you got dragged into this operetta business," said Roger. "I know you want to go to an operetta about as much as you want eczema."

"I don't mind," said his father.

"You know Mom—she thinks it's important we do things together." He was careful to look straight ahead.

"I know I don't get home often enough," his father said. "But that should change. Right after Christmas."

They walked for two blocks before Roger thought of something else to say: "What's an operetta?" he asked.

"Oh, it's one of those things. You know. Like a stage play, only with music and singing. Like an opera, only different."

"How is it different from an opera?" Roger was not at all interested in the difference between an opera and an operetta, but he wanted to hear his father's voice. He wanted to hear him make distinctions, explain things, as he had done so often when Roger was in grammar school.

"Well, an operetta has a different kind of music and I guess it usually has a happy ending. The music is lighter. It's like listening to popular songs instead of arias."

They walked on for a while in silence, listening to the water running in the gutters, watching the silver ice melting from twigs and branches, squinting against the glare of sunlight that glanced off the snow-covered lawns.

"I saw *The Student Prince* once," said his father. "It was in Chicago in 1938. That was fourteen years ago. I was in school then. I went with Jack West and Dizzy McLaughlin."

"Jack West and Dizzy McLaughlin?"

"School chums from the old days," said his father. "Boys I went to college with."

"Did you like it much?"

"What? You mean school?"

"No, the operetta."

"Oh. I don't remember. It was so long ago. It was—I think it took place in a foreign country in a café—something like that."

"That's all you remember?"

"It was so long ago. Your mother and I—we had only been married a year or two."

His father slapped his hands against his leather coat and looked up into the cold blue sky. Watching him, Roger remembered another day, years earlier. Another crisp December morning of sunlight and icemelt. He and his father sat on a white blanket in some backyard having a winter picnic of apple cider and cheese and crackers. His father smiled and pointed up at the sky with one finger as though it were in a special place instead of all over everywhere. *A sky like this is the most perfect thing you'll ever see*, he said. *It's got no sharp corners. It's all the same color and it goes on forever. It doesn't remind you of anything*. It was different with Playground Joe, he thought. Playground Joe thought the sky had nooks and crannies.

When they returned from their walk, Roger went to his room and listened to *The Land of the Lost* and *Let's Pretend.* He had outgrown both of these programs, but he listened to them every Saturday out of loyalty, sometimes wishing that he were still in sixth grade. Then he went through his stack of *Famous Fantastic Mysteries* and began to read the first chapter of an old H. Rider Haggard novel while Ythn stood in the corner doing spiritual exercises. Roger was not quite sure what spiritual exercises were, but Ythn had told him that they were necessary when one wished to commune with the Great Beyond.

Roger suspected that spiritual exercises gave him some kind of energy. Ythn did not seem to eat anything—how could he with that strange immobile little mouth of his? So perfectly round and full of silver filaments. Roger looked up occasionally from his magazine and suppressed a laugh. Ythn looked ridiculous with his legs so stiff, his arms crooked at right angles, and his head drawn back into his thoracic cavity.

"Ythn, can you tell me exactly what you're doing? You look so silly standing like that. You look like a green telephone pole."

"Don't disturb me," said Ythn in a muffled voice. "I'm almost finished."

"Finished with what, exactly?"

Ythn's head screwed out in slow circles. Finally he was himself again. "I believe that should do it," he said.

"You sort of recharge your batteries. Is that the idea?"

"In a manner of speaking. My spiritual exercises bring me into Oneness with the Infinite I Am, as one of your poets puts it. And yes, my connection with the All is the source of my energy, wisdom, and patience."

"You're kidding."

"I never kid. Occasionally I am satirical or whimsical, but I never kid."

"Ythn, are you a Rosicrucian? It really would explain a lot of things if you were a Rosicrucian."

"I don't know. What is a Rosicrucian?"

"A Rosicrucian is a guy who belongs to this club that advertises on the back of *Amazing Stories* and *Fantastic Adventures*."

"And do they also claim their energy comes from the Center of the All-Knowing?"

"Sort of. Here, wait a minute." He turned to the back of a copy of *Amazing Stories*. "Here it is. Listen. They say there is this Secret Knowledge that helped build the pyramids and that this helps you to develop the Inner Power of the Mind. It says here that this is a Rational Method of applying Nature's Laws for turning dreams into reality. They say you can send for this booklet that Explains All."

"A booklet?"

"Sometimes they call it *The Sealed Book*. Sometimes they call it *The Mastery of Life*. It depends on what ad you read."

Ythn sniffed. "Mail-order mysticism," he said. "I'm not sure I approve."

"I guess it doesn't make much sense," said Roger. "All this stuff about the Great Mind and Cosmic Awareness."

"I have no quarrel with that," said Ythn. "The truth is, you people here on Earth could do with a little more faith and a little less reason. In this country you all think you can create paradise with democracy, machines, and a shorter workweek. You do not realize that reason, technology, and leisure time are an absolutely deadly combination."

"Mr. Figge says we should always be logical."

"On Mars we have an ancient saying: 'The man who is completely reasonable is the most unreasonable of men.' Do you understand that?"

"No."

"Well, consider yourself. It would be a grave error for you to abandon many of the unreasonable but wonderful sides to your personality."

"Like what? Name one thing."

"Harry Fisher."

"What about Harry Fisher?"

"You talk about him and dream about him and draw all sorts of conclusions about him, and yet you hardly know him. You have the same relationship to Harry Fisher that the average Christian has to God. You are more affected by his absence than by his presence."

"But that's not wonderfully unreasonable. It's just dumb."

"You do the thing we all must do," said Ythn. "You see that things are more than the sum of their parts. You create feeling and myth where there was only fact. It's like magic. Alchemy. What could be more wonderful than that?"

"I don't get it," said Roger. "Here we're having this nice conversation and all of a sudden you get deep."

"I am saying a very simple thing. I am saying that boy does not live by cereal alone. He needs dreams. He needs to fly on the wings of his imagination—"

"That's just what the Rosicrucians say," said Roger. "Look here, right on the back of *Amazing Stories*. It says, *Thoughts have wings*."

"Someday," said Ythn with a sigh, "I hope you will aspire to something beyond the wisdom of pulp magazines." His mouth filaments began to vibrate again. "I must be patient. And I must remember that you are in for a terrible and somewhat frightening winter."

Roger sat up and put down his magazine. "Am I going to die? I sometimes get this feeling I'm going to die soon."

"No. Nothing like that."

"Well, what then?"

"It's Harry Fisher. He's going to happen to you. Harry Fisher and other things."

"Ythn, you're scaring me. What's Harry going to do? Is Harry dangerous?"

"I can't tell you any more. The truth is, I don't know any more. And I can't tell you how I know what I know, and I can't tell you why I don't know what I don't know. So don't ask."

"But is Harry a regular person? You know what I mean. Is he from Earth, or is he like you? From someplace else?"

Ythn turned his head slowly from side to side and made the beautiful symphonic tintinnabulation that he knew was Martian laughter. "Roger, you have such an imagination. No, Harry is from Earth. Harry is too much from Earth. You'll discover that soon enough."

12 | Heidelberg and Violins

Houses rushed by, and the swift shadows of telephone poles and trees passed over him. His father sat stiffly at the wheel, guiding his old Packard through the noonday traffic. His mother had turned sideways in her seat and tucked her legs under her knees. She seemed on the verge of going to sleep. Roger and Ruth sat behind them, Ruth in a white blouse and a beautiful powder-gray jumper. He watched her leaning back in her seat, her hands open in her lap, her face tilted slightly away from him, her lips parted. She seemed a hundred miles away. He could think of nothing to say to her, and he began to suspect that the whole afternoon was a terrible mistake. Saturday was completely shot—he could not visit Norman Pangborn, he could not play Monopoly or Rich Uncle with the Denizens, he could not read H. Rider Haggard's "Alan and the Ice Gods" in his newly acquired issue of *Famous Fantastic Mysteries*, and he could not talk with Ythn or listen to the radio. And now that he had asked Ruth for a real date he knew he would be somehow committed to her, and this could be enough to ruin his whole school year, or even the rest of his life if he were not careful. What would everyone think when they found out that he had taken Ruth Jahntoff to the Playhouse to see an operetta, and that they went with his parents? Ruth was not the ideal date to begin with. She was a nobody. She was, in some way that Roger did not quite understand, the victim of her own naturalness, her common sense, her inability to put on airs, and her democratic "hello" which she gave to anyone who was nice enough to smile at her. And her name was Jahntoff, which was just awful. When spoken out loud, it suggested a whole series of mild obscenities. An acceptable name for a pretty girl was Morrison or Lewis or Miller—something on that order. Well, he thought, at least Jahntoff was not Italian.

But then she shifted in her seat and brushed her right hand through her hair. Looking at her hands and her long hair, he remembered the dance. He remembered their hands together and the sound of her voice when she told him that she could never be misty. He remembered that she had not asked anything of him. He was not sure what she could have asked, or could have wanted, but he had the clear impression that she had not pushed him into something. It had been enough just to dance and talk. And now, here in his father's automobile, he sensed that the silence between them was not at all awkward on her part. She was perfectly happy to sit and watch the December thaw and listen to the slush whisper under the tires.

From the outside, he could not tell if the Papermill Playhouse was an old papermill that someone had converted into a theater or a new building made to look like something it never was. Inside, a crowd of people pushed through the lobby. Ticket takers and usherettes dressed in red leather, brass buttons, and black boots manned the doorways into the main theater. Toy soldiers, he thought. Officers in the Army of Never-Never Land.

His parents took their seats near the back of the parterre underneath the first balcony, while an usherette led Roger and Ruth down into the orchestra circle. The theater was at half-light, and an orange glow from the stage cast the audience into a jumble of silhouettes. A baroque scroll in red and gold made a border design for the blue velvet curtains. A gold chandelier glittered above them. Roger took a deep breath and shivered. He turned and saw Ruth smiling at him.

"This is really something," she said. "Have you ever been to a place like this?"

"No. Never."

"I think they call this the *legitimate* theater," she whispered.

"It does seem like the real thing," he ventured.

The orchestra pit ascended very slowly out of the dark, and the faces of the musicians glowed like planets as they bent forward into the light of tiny lamps fixed on their music stands, and began to tune their instruments. Roger listened to the weird, oriental cacophony of scales and fragments of melody. Now the conductor in white tie and tails walked onto the podium, and the audience favored him with a brief burst of applause. The orange sunset of footlights faded to a dim glow. The conductor raised his arms, then brought them down suddenly to a flourish of horns and a soaring of violins. The velvet curtains opened soundlessly behind the music, and Roger saw the rooms of a palace aglow with candles and tapestries.

13 | The Paper City, the Wooden Fleet, and the Cardboard Time Machine

Bright images appeared, turned, and vanished like figures on a painted carousel. He ate breakfast, read the Sunday paper, then wandered about the house until noon in his pajamas.

"Roger? Are you dressed yet?" His mother's voice drifted upstairs over the sound of the vacuum cleaner.

"Almost."

"You're wasting the whole day."

"Okay."

White as blossoms on the bow, he thought. Prince Karl Franz at Heidelberg in the spring. Gardens full of flowers and the white outdoor tables and chairs of the Golden Apple Inn and crowds of students all in blue-and-gray uniforms and café waitresses in red and white. A deluge of voices and violins. *White as blossoms on the bough.*

"Roger, do you realize it's twelve o'clock? Don't you have anything to do today? How about homework? How about cleaning your room?"

She was in her bedroom now, and he could tell by the snap of the mattress springs that she was making the bed. But he was thinking now about other beds, and other bedsprings. He was thinking about *doing it* with a soprano. He was sure that if he had been the prince, he never would have left Heidelberg just to take his father's place as King of Karlsberg—boy, was that a stupid idea—and he never would have let the spring and summer slip away into autumn.

He finished dressing and came down into the living room, where his father sat on the sofa in his green smoking jacket reading *Scientific American*.

"Well. How's the boy this morning?"

His father leaned back a little so he could rest his head, but he sat with his elbows in and his legs together, like a man on a streetcar. He had never seen his father *lounge* or *sprawl*. His father *sat*. The magazine rested flat between his legs.

"Just wandering around," he answered. "Maybe I should help Mom with something."

"I think she's about finished. Did you have breakfast?"

"I had some muffins. How'd you like the operetta?"

His father turned a page. "It was about what you'd expect, I guess."

"I didn't know what to expect. I never saw an operetta."

"Oh. Well, that's true."

"Did you like it? I mean, this thing that you expected, was it something that you liked?"

"It was fine. Very colorful."

"Well, that's terrific," said Roger. "You mean you liked all the blues and golds and reds? Or did you mean the pinks and purples?"

His father looked up from his magazine and pinched his mouth into a smile. "Roger, are you upset about something?"

"Who me? What's to be upset about? I'm not upset. I was just asking you what you thought of the operetta."

"I told you what I thought of the operetta."

His father picked up the magazine with two fingers and slid it onto the sofa cushion next to him. Then he looked up again at Roger. It was a look that showed neither anger nor amusement nor bafflement. *I am a goldfish*, thought Roger. *I am swimming in a goldfish bowl and my father is looking at me. He thinks I'm colorful.*

"Roger, why don't you go outside and play? I'm tired this morning, and I'd like to read in peace."

"Sure, Dad. I'll go out and play with the snowman next door. But if you have any other really fascinating insights about the operetta that you just can't keep to yourself, you let me know, okay?"

"Roger, what do you want me to say? I told you—"

Roger went to the hall closet and threw on his coat and pulled furiously on his boots. He did not know why he was angry. So his father had nothing to say about *The Student Prince*. There was nothing unusual in that. His father had nothing to say about his childhood in Cincinnati with his mother and his three anemic sisters. His father had nothing to say about the men who stared at his mother at cocktail parties, about how he felt when he left, early in the morning, to go back to Connecticut for God knew how long, about his three years in the army as a medical technician just before the Second World War, about his own dead father, or about why he had not sold the house and moved his family to Hartford so they could all be together. Why should he have anything to say about operettas?

As he stuffed his scarf into his coat, his mother came downstairs. She had wrapped a white towel around her head, and she wore her white bathrobe.

"You look like an Arab," said Roger.

She smiled. "You going out?"

"No, I'm going to take a bath. I always get my winter coat on when I take a bath."

"I see. You mad about something?"

"Not a chance. I'm cool as a cucumber."

"Your friend called this morning," she said. "I almost forgot."

"What friend?"

"The crazy boy. What's-his-name. Harry."

"Harry called? On the telephone?"

"He gave me another strange message. He said for you to come over if you were bored, but not to call back. He said he would be home if you came over, but out of town if you called on the telephone."

"That sounds like Harry."

"Why don't you go? I need to have a long talk with your father this morning and it would be easier if we were alone."

"I understand completely," said Roger. "Your words shall be the words of the Donkey spoken to the Cat. May your spirit rest in the field north of the grasshoppers—"

"Fine," she said. "See you later."

"Until I return, be purified in the Southern Pool where the Divine Sailors bathe."

She pushed him toward the door. "Out," she said. "And don't come back until dinnertime."

The December thaw continued on into the afternoon. Water ran in the streets, and the shrinking snow held on only in icy, gray patches across the yellow lawns on Stone Hill Road. His anger evaporated in the clear, balmy air, and it occurred to him that things were nearly okay, if not terrific. The nuns and the Concerned Mothers, the teachers at Greencastle High, and Larry Norcross & Company had not coalesced into some midnight conspiracy, as he had half feared. Only one concerned mother had even called. No one had heard from Pangborn's nun. His teachers did not really have it in for him—he was not even sure that Mr. Figge and Miss Wakowski knew his name—and it seemed clear now that their distaste for their profession and their own students was careless and impersonal.

When he got to the corner of Recognition and Thorne, he saw Harry Fisher out on his lawn working on snow projects. Here at the foot of the hill going up to High Point Avenue the snow was whiter and more plentiful, and near the sidewalk stood a tall snowman in a brown shirt with a coal-chip mouth and mustache. A British army helmet obscured the top half of its frozen face. Near the house loomed a jagged, seven-foot ice palace built from hard chips of surface snow that had melted and then refrozen during the night.

It seemed odd to come upon Harry standing there in his own front yard. He had not seen him for such a long time. He was taller than Roger remembered, and more dangerous-looking. His dark image in the middle of the winter was like something cut out of black paper and pasted in a white notebook. With his left arm extended and his mitten flat against the cold wall, Harry leaned carelessly against his ice palace and smiled his crooked smile. A strange and useless thought came to Roger as he stood there watching him: The first time he had seen Harry he had been *hanging*. Now he was *leaning*.

Bits of ice clung to his baggy cord pants and his black leather jacket. He wore a black aviator's cap with flaps that stuck out like mouse ears. Strings dangled from the ends of the flaps.

"Hey," said Harry.

"Hey yourself. I haven't seen you for a long time."

"I been busy."

"I tried to call you a couple times about Denizen meetings."

"Not interested."

"Dennis Kirk says he saw you down at the park last summer. He says you beat Curtiss Baylor at chess. He wants to meet you."

"Not interested. Hey, you want to see some of my new stuff?"

"I want to see your time machine."

Harry laughed. "You think I really got a time machine?"

"That's what you told my mom."

Harry laughed again and Roger shivered a little, remembering how Harry's laughter unnerved him because it always came when nothing seemed to be funny. He led Roger up the back steps and through the door into the kitchen, where his mother, the Gray Lady, was putting stew in the oven. As Harry and Roger passed on their way to the living room, Harry lifted four doughnuts and a bottle of milk from the refrigerator.

"You leave them be," said his mother without turning from the oven. As she peered through the smoky glass window, her kinky black-and-silver hair lifted stiffly from the back of her neck. "Your dad, he needs them doughnuts in the morning. He won't eat nothin' but doughnuts and coffee, you know that. There'll be hell to pay tomorrow if he don't get his doughnuts. He—"

"Ma, will you shut up? Here, I put your crappy doughnuts back, okay? Not even a finger mark. You happy now?"

The Gray Lady turned around, smiled thinly, and rubbed her hands on her apron. "Ain't it terrible the way he talks?" she said to Roger. "Bet you don't talk to your moms that way, do you? No, you're a good boy. I can see that just lookin' at you. Harry, you should be more like your little friend here. You do chores for your moms, I bet. Don't tell your moms to shut up, do you?"

He could not take his eyes off the veins in her face. "No, ma'am," he managed to say.

"Ma, we're going upstairs. Roger, he didn't come in here to listen to all your garbage."

"Used to live on a farm," said Mrs. Fisher. "That was when Horace and I was first married. Now there was a different life, let me tell you. No one ever talked to his moms the way Harry talks to me. No siree. Everythin' changes real quick when you come to the city."

"Ma, for Crissake—"

"But Harry, he don't sass his father, that's one thing. You're a public school boy?"

"Yes, ma'am."

"Well, that's fine," said Mrs. Fisher. She poured herself a cup of coffee from the stove and then spilled a little into the saucer. "I don't take to all the kids around here going to private schools, I can tell you that. Wearing those little blue jackets and learnin' foreign languages. All that foolishness. All those snooty little misters and misses from Kent Place Boulevard—"

Harry's large hand closed over Roger's shoulder and pulled him into a living room full of doilies, end tables, figurines of birds and kittens, colonial chairs, and the smell of wax and lemon oil. The brown-and-white dog lay in the middle of the open hallway adjacent to the living room. His long tail fanned the polished wood, and he raised his eyes mournfully and made a soft whistle through his nose when Harry bent down to pet him.

"Good dog," said Harry. "That's a good Nunnug. No, you can't come up to the attic. You'll mess up the fleet."

Halfway up the stairs Roger saw that the Gray Lady had followed them as far as the hallway. She looked up at them now with what appeared to be a sort of wistful longing. "Nice to meet you, Mrs. Fisher," he said.

"Nice to meet you, Mrs. Fisher," said Harry when they reached the second floor. "Your house was just dreamy, Mrs. Fisher." He laughed in a way that made Roger think of windows shattering. "I *bet* it was nice. I bet it was an absolutely sensational experience meeting my old ma."

"Well, what was I supposed to say?" said Roger. "Was I supposed to say it was just awful meeting you, Mrs. Fisher? Was I supposed to say you're a snerd, Mrs. Fisher? Would that make you happy?"

"Don't worry about it, buddy. That's your problem, you know. You worry about things that don't matter. Did you know Christmas is coming in ten days? Isn't that a laugh. Good old Nunnug. He and me, we take everything the way it comes, no matter what's attached onto it."

Roger shook his head. "Oh. Okay."

"What I'm trying to say is, don't worry about my old ma. She's got this little gray hearing aid. It looks like a piece of snot stuck in her left ear. If she hears you from the wrong side, she gets everything wrong and that's why what she mostly says don't make any sense."

When they came up the narrow attic stairs and through the open hatch into the attic, he saw the large, open room that he had thought and dreamed about so many times. The three high windows that looked down on half of Greencastle. The glorious blue walls with their antique swords and guns. The long bookcase filled with treasures. The enormous wood floor. It was curious now to see what he had dreamed about, to have one impression of things lie upon the other, as if what was real were only a copy or an illumination of what was imagined. Like the image of Harry leaning against the ice palace.

The room was different in many ways. In one corner stood something that looked like a cardboard phone booth. The thing glistened with black enamel paint, and across one side Harry had painted the letters SS in silver. Now what in the world was that? Across the floor, long columns and V's of balsa-wood ships steamed toward a white concrete island covered with dozens of plastic aircraft and bristling with cannons and pom-pom guns. A great battle was clearly in progress. And near the dormer window on the large worktable that before had been filled with sticks and paper and bottles of ink, he now saw the outline of a paper city with houses, streets, telephone lines, parks, and miniature automobiles. To Roger it looked intricate and perfect and beautiful, like something from a museum.

Harry straddled the trapdoor and brushed the ice off his pants. Then he threw his leather jacket down the narrow stairway and came back to the center of the room. He stood there for a moment with his hands in his pockets, smiling at the floor.

"Harry, how did you do all this? I don't understand it."

"Comes natural. I used to live in Millburn."

"Nobody can do all the stuff you do. God, I wish you'd come to a Denizen meeting. Did you really beat Curtiss Baylor at chess last summer? Nobody ever beat Curtiss Baylor at chess."

"Curtiss is a baby," said Harry. "He cries when he loses. Jesus, I'd rather shoot myself than cry. And he really stinks at chess. He's got these two or three snappy openings and then he just plays by the seat of his pants. A wood pusher. He's like the Chinese navy, for God's sake."

"The Chinese navy," said Roger. "That's terrific. I got to remember to tell Curtiss you said he played chess like the Chinese navy."

"Forget all that," said Harry. "Look—here's Greencastle."

Harry snapped on an overhead spotlight and the paper city came to life. And it was Greencastle. There was Stone Hill Road. And Thistle Street and Roosevelt Memorial Field. And across town the high school, the railroad tracks, and then the downtown business area. Everything. Dozens of tiny brown and gray and yellow houses, each no more than a half inch tall, each with windows and shutters and doorways drawn in India ink. Automobiles of silver foil parked in driveways and on the curbs of white streets edged with bushes made from bits of green sponge.

On the south side of town a sharp descent led to a forested area—that would be the Watchung Reservation, where the Denizens had planned their spring expedition to find Saucer Central. Colored sawdust powdered the undulating papier-mâché surface, and together with hundreds of tiny twigs it formed an autumnal forest with hills and valleys and misty swamps of glass and cotton and cellophane.

"I never saw anything like this in my life," said Roger. "Look, there's my house."

"Painted it pink so it don't get lost," said Harry. "Just a little joke."

"And there's Enrico's Leather Goods. And there's Pangborn's bookstore. And there's the Unitarian church, for God's sake."

"Is that what that is? Look around the back—I got this little porch attached onto it." Harry laughed.

"You ought to bring this to school. This is terrific."

"That's the last thing I'd do."

"You ought to. You'd impress the hell out of everybody. Harry, nobody around here can do this kind of stuff."

"Mrs. Leibolt would probably give me extra credit. Jesus, I'd hate that. It would be like I did homework without even knowing it. I never do homework."

"How can you not do homework? You'd flunk everything."

"I do good on tests. That gives me C's in just about everything. What they call a 'gentleman's grade' in college. But I'm not no gentleman and I sure as hell won't go to college.

Ennis told me all about that stuff from what his cousin said. All kinds of Shakespeare courses and lectures and people trying to find out what you want to do for the next sixty million years, if you can imagine that."

"It's what you have to do," said Roger. "I mean, if you want to be somebody. If you want to get a good job you have to plan ahead and go to college and all that stuff."

Harry stood with his hands on his hips, looking down at his paper city. "Never plan ahead," he said. "Never try to be anybody. Never show what you can really do. Never bring any of your good stuff to school."

"Harry, are you kidding? You must be kidding."

"Guess so. I am a big kidder, right? Harry Fisher is always good for a million laughs."

"Harry, I don't get you. You're smiling, but I know you're mad about something."

No, not mad, he thought. *Bitter*. That was his mother's word for it. Harry was *bitter*. Like cold coffee that sits overnight and then your father tries to boil it in a pan in the morning and drink it black when your mother has gone to New York for a League of Women Voters' convention. *Bitter*.

"Harry, you're *bitter*. That's what you are."

"Then you better not take a bite outa me. You could get real sick."

"I don't get you, Harry. I mean, I don't get you at all."

"Then listen, buddy, 'cause I'm only gonna tell you this once. I gotta IQ higher than this house, and I'm here to tell you the war is over. We're all civilians. That's just the way it is. So I just sit up here in the attic and keep comfy. Did I tell you my dad moved us all over from Millburn a few years back? C'mon, let's play with the fleet."

"I'm going to college," said Roger. "I'll never get to be a psycho-archaeologist if I don't go to college."

"There's no such thing," said Harry. "And even if there was, nobody would let you do it except in your own attic. People just laugh. People knock you down unless you knock them down first."

"That's not true."

"Sure it is. Take you. You stick your neck out all the time and people always chop it off. Am I right? You're always in trouble."

"What trouble? I'm not in any trouble."

"The kids at school, they all think your club's for homos. And all the PBS parents, they hear about it and talk to the teachers and then the teachers get scared and think you're working against the school or something. I know how that goes. Just stay in your own territory. Don't tell anybody what you're doing. Learn jiujitsu. Don't join anything."

"You sound like all this happened to you once."

"I used to live in Millburn, like I just said. Did you know Mrs. Leibolt doesn't like you too much?"

"Harry, will you stick to one thing? Honest to God, it's hard to talk to you. And for your info, Mrs. Leibolt thinks I'm okay. She told me just last week that I was a very promising person."

"That's what she tells you when she begins to hate you. She told me that once."

"Mrs. Leibolt always asks me questions. She likes it when I talk in class."

"No, she doesn't. She hates it. I can tell."

"How can you? You're an eleventh-grader. You're not even in any of my classes."

"Do you watch Mrs. Leibolt's legs? Does she sit up on the desk and sort of swing one leg up and down? Ever see up her skirt?"

Roger could feel himself turning red. "What's that got to do with anything? What's that got to do with whether or not she likes me?"

"Don't you think Mrs. Leibolt is sexy?"

Roger could feel a lie taking shape on his tongue. "She's too old to be sexy," he said.

"People are talking about you," said Harry. "People are going to run you up a pole if you're not careful. Let's play with the fleet."

"Harry—"

Harry pointed his finger at him. "Now don't tell me to stick to one thing. You told me that already. I jump around—that's the only way to keep light, you get it? Nothing goes together. That's what all you sissies think—you think things go together. That's why you want to go to college. Things get attached onto other things, but that's about it. Let's play with the fleet."

Harry gestured with a spasmodic jerk of his head toward the dozens of balsa-wood ships arranged in formations all over the floor. The pale gray forces divided into two fleets, while the bright blue had three. Between them lay a white plaster island with antiaircraft guns, mountains, and an airfield. As Roger stared at the patterns the ships made across the floor, he felt vaguely uneasy. A chill ran over the surface of his arms and fingers, like winter frost. He wanted to tell Harry that nothing he said really made sense, that he didn't feel like playing war, that it was time to go home. Instead he stood there amid the intricacies of Harry Fisher's attic and thought about his feet. It occurred to him that it would be really terrible if he stepped on something.

"It looks real," said Roger. "You get the feeling that the ships are really moving."

"It is real," said Harry. "It's the realest game you'll ever play."

"What's it called?"

"Midway."

"Oh, I know that. I heard Colonel Robert R. McCormick talk about that in the middle of the *Chicago Theater of the Air.*"

"Never mind that old fart," said Harry. "He's Shakespeare. He really is Shakespeare."

"We won that one, didn't we? That was the first big victory for the Americans, wasn't it?"

Harry sat down very carefully in the middle of his ships and closed his eyes. "We never should have won the Battle of Midway," he said. "That was the dumbest luck in the world."

"How come you always stick up for the enemy? That's not very patriotic."

Harry hit the floor with his fist, and a boom sounded through the attic. The balsa ships shuddered. One tipped over, resting lightly on its radio mast. Harry leaned over, and with infinite gentleness he picked it up with his thumb and forefinger and brought it up close to his eye. "What I was saying," he said quietly, "is that it was just stupid luck. You see, there was this Jap ship, a straggler. The American planes saw it and guessed from that where the whole fleet was. It was the last chance the Americans had. They—they never should have found the carriers. So by the end of the day the Japs had this big surface fleet and all these transport ships to attack Midway, but Yamamoto, he said *Sashi sugi*."

"What's that?"

"The carriers were all sunk. They got caught with their planes down. You can't win without air cover. *Sashi sugi*—enough is enough. That's what he said. Yamamoto, he was a genius, just like Erwin Rommel. One was in the desert and the other was in the ocean. It's the same thing."

"So what's the point in having a game about Midway when everybody knows how it's going to turn out?"

"That's just it," said Harry. "We don't pay no attention to history. We change history. We give everybody another chance. Just like in my time machine, you go back and you get a chance to do things right. The way they were supposed to be."

The time machine! He had almost forgotten about it. He turned around and stared at the black cardboard booth. "Is that it?" he said. "Is that the time machine?"

"We get to that when the battle's over," said Harry. "First we have to play with the fleet. That's the first part of it."

"I'd rather play with the time machine."

"No, you wouldn't. Now quit standing around in your big clodhoppers and get down over there on your side. Careful where you put your feet. This is the most important battle in the whole war. It's 26 May 1942. I'm the Japanese fleet and you're the Americans."

"How come you have twice as much as I do?"

" 'Cause that's the way it was. I have more ships, but you have extra planes at Midway and you also have better surveillance—that means you find me first and get to make the first attack. It all works out even."

"How do we play?"

"I hafta show you as we go along. Every ship gets to move up to three inches every turn and then I got these charts that tell your range and we use this little shooter that shoots these tiny cotton balls. With the air attacks you drop the cotton balls from your bombers. The trick is to knock out all the enemy carriers and then move in for a surface battle with air cover."

Harry opened a blue folder which he brought down from his bookcase. Inside were hit-probability charts, gun-range charts, maximum-speed lists for different kinds of ships, and a ruler marked in knots and another marked in thousands of yards. He spread these things out on a clear place in the pinewood ocean. As he did so, he began to whistle out of the side of his mouth—a jaunty, tuneless hiss that reminded Roger of air escaping from a radiator.

It was already late afternoon and Roger had homework to do and he did not want to play war. But as he listened to Harry's whistle and saw him move his blue ships toward Midway, he felt weak. Harry was a genius and he had built a time machine—who knows, maybe even one that really worked. He could not imagine what would happen to someone who said no to Harry Fisher.

They crouched on opposite sides of Midway Island, moved their ships according to the speed charts, and checked the ranges of their guns. "—there was a diversionary attack up near Alaska," Harry was saying. "But the main force is right here. Nagumo's carrier force to the north, Yamamoto's main force in the center, and then Kondo's occupation force to the south. That's what they call a three-pronged attack. You know, like on a fork."

"How come you know all this, Harry?"

"I read it in a book. Now the Americans, they knew all about the three-pronged attack 'cause they busted the Jap code and they had all these scout planes all over the place. So on 28 May Admiral Spruance, he left Hawaii with Task Force 17, and on 30 May Admiral Fletcher, he followed, only a little further up north."

There, far out in the wooden ocean, Roger saw the three spearheads of the Japanese attack, and the useless fourth fleet, so far away, already drawing near its attack points at Kiska and Attu. The walls of the room began to fall away.

As the three arms of the Japanese attack force moved closer to the plaster of paris Midway, Roger began to feel the immensity of what was taking place. The Japanese navy was exotic and beautiful, and its ships were not christened for mundane places, but for sensations, images, and dreams—*Red Castle, Flying Dragon, Increased Joy, Peach Blossom*—and the sounds of their singsong names jangled when Harry said them, like wind chimes: *Hiryu, Soryu, Akagi, Kirishima.* He could feel the poetry of war in the high voices of his dangerous adversaries, for this was the Year of the Dragon, and the Japanese, whose engines of destruction were also flowers and myths and fabulous beasts, meant to keep their appointment with destiny.

A distant roar washed across the room behind Harry's voice, and Roger saw that his hand was a thousand feet from his face, and his ships were four hundred miles across the varnished ocean from the Japanese airmen and sailors, whose homeland songs trembled in their throats, and whose spirits were haunted by visions of death and flowers. How, he wondered, could the *Portland, Pensacola, Enterprise*, and *Yorktown* prevail against such powers as these?

Harry talked constantly, easily, and in different voices. Sometimes he was a combat pilot shouting curses in Japanese. Sometimes he was Admiral Yamamoto issuing orders. Sometimes he was Harry Fisher explaining fine points of the game with diffident ease, or commenting on the game's historical accuracy.

Things happened quickly. Roger's tentative strike against Admiral Nagumo's carriers failed, and the Japanese retaliation came within the hour. Harry smiled and pulled up the corners of his eyes with his middle fingers. "When the infidel strikes the tail of the dragon," he said, "the dragon bites off his head."

And indeed it was happening. The Japanese planes came in alternating waves at ninety-degree angles that divided the defensive firepower and made it difficult, according to the probability charts, to turn away from a torpedo attack. In ten minutes the *Yorktown* was torn apart by internal explosions after two hits amidships, and lay dead in the water. Three bombs sank the *Portland*, and four more blew the *Astoria* out of the water.

As the Japanese in the flush of their early victory made full steam for Midway, Roger saw, just for a moment, an opening in the heavy storm clouds offshore, and he realized that he was in Harry's attic and that it was getting late. Soon his mother would have dinner ready. But then the sense of the present fell off the edge of his consciousness, like a ship falling off the edge of the world. He was here at Midway in the spring of 1942, and his mother would not have dinner ready for nine years.

Something had to be done quickly. He decided to combine what was left of his broken fleet and make a surface attack at dusk on the northern arm of the Japanese forces. This was the advance strike force—a ring of destroyers and a wedge of battleships and cruisers protecting the four great aircraft carriers. If he could concentrate the attack of all his land-based aircraft on Admiral Yamamoto's main force and thus prevent it from reaching the carrier fleet until dusk, then perhaps he could break through Nagumo's ring with his heavy cruisers and dive-bombers, sink the carriers, and then escape in the darkness. "A bold plan born out of desperation," he said to himself. He had read that somewhere.

"I know what you're doing," said Harry. His voice seemed to come from the ocean, from nowhere at all. He was invisible, like the black-robed figures who made things work in Japanese puppet dramas.

But for a while things seemed to go according to plan. The land-based planes from Midway harassed Yamamoto's fleet, keeping it out of formation, damaging the *Yamato*, the pride of the Japanese navy, and sinking the ancient battle cruiser *Hiei*. Meanwhile, the combined American forces closed with Nagumo's fleet two hundred miles off Midway. In less than thirty minutes the *Agaki* and the *Hiryu* sank, and the *Haruna* and *Chikuma* took heavy damage and steamed out of the battle area. More important, Japanese plane losses were heavy, much heavier than Roger had hoped for.

"You're going real good," said Harry. "But real good, that's not good enough."

The circle of Japanese destroyers opened into a long line of ships that flanked the American forces, released their oxygen torpedoes, and turned away. In five minutes all the American cruisers were sinking. Harry Fisher turned out the lights on the Pacific Ocean, one by one. Night had fallen.

Roger stood up for the first time in two hours. His back ached from squatting and bending over. His eyes hurt. He rubbed them and then looked out the window and saw that it was dark. God, he thought, what time was it? Had he missed dinner?

"It's only seven o'clock," said Harry, who seemed to have read his thoughts.

"Oh."

"You give up?"

"What else can I do?"

"Nothing. You got practically no fleet."

"Then it's over."

"Right."

"You win, Harry."

"Right."

He rubbed his eyes again. The streetlights outside made a

blur of yellow through the window glass. He knew he had missed dinner, and he knew his mother would be worried. No one in the whole world knew where he was, except Harry. He stared at the scattering of balsa-wood ships, the tiny plastic airplanes, the rulers and graphs and dice. He felt himself growing and pulling away from everything. He felt large again, and the toys looked small.

Harry stood in the middle of the room smiling and looking strange. The one remaining light shone directly above him, so that his face appeared shadowy and melodramatic. There was something about his image—the way he stood there in the middle of the room with his hands on his hips—that made Roger want to push him down the steps.

"Harry, did you ever lose at anything? I mean, like a game of checkers or Rich Uncle or a fistfight or anything at all?"

Harry closed his eyes and shook his head. "Lotsa things I don't do," said Harry. "I never do homework. I never join clubs or go to church. And I especially never *try out* for anything. That's a toilet. But when I do play something, I always win. That's the way it is."

"But what would happen if you did lose?" said Roger. "I mean, just one teeny little loss to somebody not too important."

"End of the world," said Harry. "One loss, that's it. But don't you worry about it. Harry Fisher, he can't lose. Harry Fisher, he's too strong and too smart. Hey, you know how many days it is to Christmas vacation? Wait till you see what I got up here next time you come. I got ideas for an Egypt game that's right up your alley and also I'm gonna put in a whole sky. You won't even notice this place has a roof. You won't even notice you're in a house at all with what I got attached onto it—"

He raised his eyes to the single light, and all the shadows fell out of his face. Harry laughed and shook his fists.

"Harry? Harry, I don't think I should be up here."

"Don't say that, buddy. I'm not the enemy."

"I don't know what you are, Harry. But I have to admit

you scare me. You scare me worse than anyone I ever knew."

"Listen, you don't have to be scared. We just had a little game, right? Just a little game."

"Why did you turn the lights off?"

"That's the way it ends. It gets dark on the ocean. Here, I'll turn another light on. Cheer up, okay? Listen, you thirsty?"

"Yes."

"Knew it. War makes everybody thirsty. I'll go get us some Orange Crush. You just stay here a sec."

Harry disappeared down the trapdoor, and now there was nothing but silence in the attic room, and Roger was still afraid. Something buzzed in the back of his head. He was alone with a paper city, a wooden fleet, and a cardboard time machine. The time machine! He looked up and stared at the black thing that Harry had pushed into the far corner of the attic. He had a queer feeling that it had moved sometime during the Battle of Midway. But of course that was impossible.

He walked across the room, stepping carefully around the fleets of ships. He stood now in front of the time machine. He touched the smooth enamel paint with the tips of his fingers. Then he traced over the silver place that spelled SS. Looking more closely, he saw six small openings under the letters, like breathing holes for an animal. When he put his hand over them he felt tiny gusts of air. Something inside the box was making wind. How could that be? He put his ear to the surface and touched it very lightly with his fingertips. After a moment he felt and heard a faint hum, a vibration. *The time machine is turned on*, he thought. *All the time Harry and I were playing, he had the time machine turned on.*

"What the hell you think you're doing?" Harry's voice behind him was sharp and hostile. Roger turned to see him standing over the trapdoor, two bottles of Orange Crush clenched in his hands.

"I asked you a question, buddy."

"I was looking at your time machine."

"Did you go in?"

"No. Is there a door?"

"Around on the other side," said Harry. "But that's none of your business. Nobody touches my stuff unless I say so. Nobody comes up here unless he obeys all the rules, understand?"

"Sure. You don't have to get mad. I didn't do anything, for God's sake."

"You sure you didn't go inside?"

"I didn't even know you could. But what's in there? Something's humming and making a little wind where those holes are."

"You seen enough for one day. I'll show you the time machine the next time you come over."

"Does it really work? What does it look like inside?"

"The inside is like nothing you ever saw," said Harry. He handed Roger the bottle of Orange Crush. "And course it works. But not the way you think. Not like the time machines in all those magazines you read."

"Is this your big secret, Harry? The fact that you built a time machine?"

"You mean my really big secret? The one I told you about last time?" He shook his head. "You'll never guess that. Not till it's too late."

Harry turned on another light and they sat for a few minutes in the dim attic room drinking soda pop. Something was keeping him here in Harry's attic, but he couldn't for the life of him think what it was. He was hungry and he wanted to go home. The soda seemed to fizz uneasily in his empty stomach, and Harry talked on and on about his projects, about how no one would ever guess his secret, and about how school always went from bad to worse as the year wore on.

After a while he lost track of what Harry was saying. He stared at the blue walls, thinking now of the blue uniforms of the students at Heidelberg. Then he heard the soaring music of the operetta, and he remembered the lovers who parted, saying they would live on memories and might-have-beens. He saw the dark stage, and heard the soft, choral strains of

Gaudeamus Igitur. And then afterward in the parking lot he took Ruth's hand and she smiled up at him, and for a moment he saw the whole operetta in her face.

"Nothing means anything without violins. Did you know that, Harry?"

"What?"

"Never mind. I have to go. I already missed dinner. My mother is going to kill me."

"You just got here, buddy."

"I got here six hours ago. I have to go home."

In the downstairs hallway, Nunnug waved his tail and whined and clicked his claws against the floor. He barked three times. The smell of pot roast and the sound of John Cameron Swayze intoning the news with his Scandinavian twang drifted in from the kitchen. Roger felt the world slowly coming back. John Cameron Swayze, he thought. Good old John Cameron Swayze.

"Did you miss me, Nunnug?" said Harry. He clenched his teeth together as if he were about to bite the dog's nose. "Did you miss Harry? Did you? Are you a good dog?"

Outside the front door now, Roger looked back and saw Harry's figure silhouetted there in the yellow light. "Come back again sometime," said Harry.

"Show me the time machine?"

"Sure thing. We'll take a ride and see the sights."

"That'll be something. See you later, Harry."

"See you later, buddy."

Roger ran down the front steps and out into the darkness. The stars had come out and the air was cold. The water from the melting snow had begun to freeze in the gutters and in thin, brittle sheets over the sidewalks. He took deep breaths of cold air, and his head began to clear. He wanted something to eat. He wanted to see his mother and father, and he wanted to see Dennis and Frank. He wanted to hold their hands and slide on the ice going down High Point Avenue and make a flying wedge into a snowbank. He wanted it to be morning.

14 | Winter Light

Mr. Figge had mentioned a week earlier that the last six days before Christmas vacation perfectly illustrated the principle of entropy. Roger did not know then what entropy meant, but for years afterward the word was bound up in his mind with teachers disappearing before pageant rehearsals and classes dissolving into study halls. For days in history class he had seen the same movies on Egypt and Benjamin Franklin, and each time the film broke down in the same places. He listened to Miss Wakowski read Christmas stories out of *Senior Scholastic. That* was entropy.

"*Senior Scholastic*, now there's a real magazine," said Dennis.

"Their movie reviews are awful," said Frank. "To get a good review in *Senior Scholastic* a movie has to have Orson Welles or Ingrid Bergman in it, or at least it has to be made in England."

"I always read the articles on getting along in school and making friends," said Roger. "They say things like, you have to be sensitive to other people's needs. And here I always thought we were supposed to be insensitive to other people's needs. You know, like Larry Norcross. Look how popular he is."

"The health column is my favorite," said Dennis. "I just love it when they tell me how two of my very best friends are Sally Soap and Wally Washcloth."

"Worse yet, they got pictures," said Frank.

On Tuesday of the previous week, Roger had heard that Virgi Prewitt, the girl who loved bugs and germs, had taken over the art class when Mr. Donato had been commandeered to design costumes for the pageant. He told Virgi to keep the other students going on something appropriate to the season, and so she began on Monday by drawing cold germs all over the blackboard. Apparently the class had not shown much interest until she gave them names and branched out into serious diseases. By Wednesday afternoon she had everyone drawing germ houses, then parks and municipal buildings. By Thursday the class had taped together sixteen sheets of poster paper which portrayed in vivid colors an entire city. On Friday morning the whole school was talking about Virginia Virus, Barnaby Bacillus, Sylvia Streptococcus, Tommy Typhus, Annabelle Antibody, Curt Common Cold, Lawrence Leukemia, and Carolyn Cancer. That same day, William R. Mace, the principal, delivered a short talk over the public-address system about "obscene murals" and threatened "certain individuals" with suspension, but no one took that very seriously. After all, it was nearly Christmas. By Monday morning, the last day before vacation, Virgi's "Christmas Germs" had disappeared. No one knew whether the artist had hidden it away or whether William R. Mace had consigned it to Mr. Klempke's furnaces.

Meanwhile, Rolfe Gerhardt, the human blitzkrieg, had written FUCK in peanut butter across the principal's office window and had later attacked Harriet Emerick with an open-face peanut butter and jelly sandwich. Roger often wondered where his arsenal came from. Did Mrs. Gerhardt buy fifty jars of peanut butter every month and never wonder where it all went?

In spite of everything, the pageant came off well on Monday afternoon. The senior chorus, dressed in white robes, sang nine carols as the auditorium curtain clanked and rumbled up and down on six Christmas vignettes. Marilyn Sord played the Virgin Mary, a role usually reserved for a senior girl. Larry Norcross played a reluctant shepherd while one of the senior boys he hated played Joseph. Curtiss Baylor, who had always been first in everything, was the Angel of the Lord.

At the end of the school day Mrs. Leibolt solemnly passed out report cards for the first term. Roger made all B's except for an A in Latin. "In her class you get scared into excellence," Dennis told him as they walked home through the snow.

On Christmas he gave his mother a gray morning dress which he bought at Schaeffer's Emporium after three agonized hours of window-shopping. He bought his father an electric drill for his garage workshop to replace the one that had shorted out the previous summer. From them he received *The Stars for Sam* (a book on astronomy for young people), *The Dwellers on the Nile* (a book on ancient Egypt which his mother had finally found in a New York bookstore), the game of Camelot, a white turtleneck sweater, and a leather dopp kit full of shaving equipment for the two Saturday mornings each month when Roger shaved the fuzz from his cheeks and chin. From his Aunt Hattie, two novels by Thomas Hardy with a note to his parents saying she had heard that Thomas Hardy was good reading for boys. From his Uncle Peter, a hunting knife, an Arkansas stone, and honing oil.

That evening his father took them out to Mildred's for Christmas dinner, and then to the movies. "Four days at home," said his father over dinner. "I didn't think they would give me four days."

"And you'll be home every weekend from now on," said his mother.

"Just about."

His father tapped a drumroll on the table with the tips of his fingers. "Hope you can put up with me that often," he said.

"We'll do our best." She took his hand across the table and smiled at him. He did not look up, but instead watched the way his wife's hand covered his own on the white linen. Suddenly he pressed his lips together. Roger, watching him, was mystified by his father's face and had no idea what he was thinking.

The week of vacation that followed Christmas was the happiest of the whole winter. A blue silence came to the white, snow-blind mornings. The ice and sun brought all the children of Greencastle out into the streets of the city even as it exiled the shivering adults to their automobiles and kitchens and living rooms. Igloo castles and lawn angels that looked like Christmas cookies cut out of the snow appeared everywhere. Fragile columns of smoke rose in the windless air from chimney after chimney all through the afternoons and evenings. The snow was deep and mysterious. Walking through it, you kept stumbling across things that were invisible, things without names or shapes left over from autumn and summer. A story went around the school playground that Larry Norcross, Eddie McQueen, and Buck Moore had dug a whole labyrinth of tunnels under the snow at Roosevelt Memorial Field and that fifteen second- and third-graders who got lost in the passageways were now frozen solid and would not be found until spring.

"That's an awful story," said Frank. "I just hate stories like that. They give me the willies."

"What good is a frozen second-grader, anyway?" said Roger.

"They don't have much commercial value," said Dennis. "But you can use them for fence posts until they get soft around April or May."

"You guys," said Frank. "I wish you'd quit on that stuff."

Every morning at nine o'clock the Denizens met in Dennis Kirk's bedroom to make plans for the day. The plans were always the same. First, a game of snow football with whomever they found down at Roosevelt Memorial Field. At noon they ate together—the three mothers had reluctantly agreed to rotate lunch duties for the week. In the afternoon they ran downtown to check the movie marquees and make the rounds of all the interesting places, buying pulp magazines and ice-cream sodas and looking over the skeletal remains of the toy and game displays in department stores. At three o'clock they came to Pangborn's to see the new books and talk and watch the white afternoon slip away into dusk.

All through Christmas vacation Norman Pangborn wore a blue turtleneck sweater that made him look cool and princely. He seemed to love the winter, the way it closed them all in together. The cold weather awakened him. He seemed less gaunt, more at peace with himself. The blue sweater, he thought, was Pangborn in winter. It was the color of sky and the color of shadows on the snow. It was also the color of thought. Thought was blue, like infinity. And so, one afternoon, the Denizens came in with a box wrapped in Christmas paper which they put on his back table without a word.

"What's this?" said Pangborn. He picked up the box with one hand and then he looked quickly from one boy to the next. He sat down. "This isn't necessary," he said.

"We wouldn't do it if it was necessary," said Dennis.

"It's Christmas," said Frank.

"Christmas was over five days ago," said Pangborn. "Besides, I'm Jewish."

"So we're a little late," said Dennis. "But don't give us that Jewish stuff. We all saw the holly in your window."

"It's just to pay you back a little for all the orange juice and all the sausages," said Roger.

"And—and other things," said Frank.

Pangborn looked down at the package. His fingers trembled when he opened it.

"It's beautiful," he said.

"We thought you looked so terrific in your blue one," said Roger. "So we got you this one for spring and maybe for summer nights when it's cool," said Roger.

"Blue for winter, green for spring and summer," said Dennis.

"We sort of wanted you to be ready for anything," said Frank.

Pangborn could not seem to look up from the sweater, neatly folded in its bed of tissue paper. He held the box in both hands and shook it once or twice, as if he were panning for gold. "Today is a special day," he said at last. "What should we talk about? We've talked about almost every damn thing there is, I guess. We've talked about geography and geology and the occult and space travel and nuns."

"And we talked about the Arctic Circle and menstruation," said Dennis.

"And we talked about Sigmund Freud and volcanoes and Ingrid Bergman and chastity belts," said Roger.

"And we talked about the Middle Ages and Miss Dot's dancing class and vampires," said Frank.

Pangborn looked up from the table to the grape arbor outside all covered with snow, and the dark silhouettes of houses on the next street, and the light behind them that was already turning red and dying in the western sky. "Then let's begin again," he said. Tears streamed down his cheeks. "Yes. Since we've talked about everything, let's start all over again."

The snow falling every other day was like a veil of dreams. Nothing was more beautiful or more strange to him than the snow which had come so far and changed so much. How could it turn every angular outline into a soft white curve, and yet give every memory, every feeling and sensation, such a clear, sharp edge?

One evening he took Ruth Jahntoff to the Bogart double feature at the Strand. Afterward they met the other Denizens at the Sugar Shoppe, where Ruth told them about B. Traven, the mysterious author of *The Treasure of the Sierra Madre*. According to an article she had read somewhere, no one had ever seen B. Traven, and his publisher sent his money to some address in Mexico that no longer existed. Dennis, who never stared at girls, stared at Ruth. "A very unusual female," he told Roger the next day. "Not your ordinary bobby-soxer."

Roger stopped three times that week at Harry Fisher's house, but the place was always dark. Finally the next-door neighbor, a very pretty but hard-looking woman with two children whose husband had been killed in the Battle of the Bulge, told him that the Fishers had gone off to Minnesota for the week to have Christmas with relatives. It made Roger shiver to think of spending a week in Minnesota at the beginning of January. But it seemed so typical, so much like Harry, not to have mentioned that he would be gone, to say that he would be around when in fact he would not be. Like Playground Joe's sky, Harry had nooks and crannies that no one had ever seen.

15 | What John Keats Meant to Say

Another snowstorm struck the last day of Christmas vacation. Roger got up at five-thirty the next morning to listen to the school-closing bulletins, but no luck. The wind whistled in his ears, the snow sifted down in the cracks between his boots and his trousers, his nose ran, and school began on time.

That morning the teachers smiled at everyone. They seemed flushed, effusive, overly courteous, as if they had forgotten everyone's name and the thirteen days away from school had made them all strangers again. Even the terrifying Miss Simic cracked a nervous smile when they all filed in for first-period Latin.

The weather turned from cold to colder. The snow changed from an adhesive fluff to a dry powder that blew in everyone's face and rested uneasily in rivers and drifts along the edges of streets and across sidewalks. The romance of winter was beginning to wear thin. Even the snowball fights on the back playground during lunch recess had changed into a grim and habitual warfare with hard-crusted embankments and pyramids of iceballs. He remembered how Dennis had come out with them just once and stared at the playground and shook his head. "In December," he said, "we had Winter Wonderland. Now look at it. It's like the Russian Front."

Mrs. Leibolt seemed unhappy about the class discussions she had tried so hard to stimulate earlier in the year. Miss Wakowski wrote quadratic equations on the board and then looked out the window for fifteen or twenty minutes while the class copied and solved them, her pretty face dissolving into gray vacuity, as if the snow had gotten inside her. Mr. Figge did not know what to do with the Renaissance. Only Miss Simic remained the same as the weather grew colder: Latin, after all, was Latin. There was nothing you could do to make Latin more or less than what it was.

As the weeks passed, he found he had less energy for schoolwork and more time on his hands. In the afternoons he listened to the radio and talked with Ythn. Instead of studying in the evenings, he built fires in the fireplace and sat for hours watching the flames and thinking of nothing. Soon he even began to watch television and read the daily newspaper. He took a certain pleasure in these activities because they seemed so meaningless.

The newspaper, especially, was a jumble of things that had nothing to do with each other, and the stories were peopled by beings without histories or personalities, beings who lived in the shadow world outside Greencastle. While the revolution in Iran had cut off oil to America and Great Britain, someone named Macfadden made a parachute jump at the age of eighty-four. Sugar Ray Robinson threatened to withdraw his support from Walter Winchell's Damon Runyon Memorial Fund because Winchell looked on while Sherman Billingsley refused to seat Josephine Baker at the Stork Club. Now what in the world was that all about? The peace talks at Kaesong were going nowhere. Senator McCarthy intimated that Communist sympathizers had infiltrated the highest levels of American government. Joan Crawford tried the thirty-day mildness test and concluded that Camels were good for her T-Zone. An aging concert pianist, dubbed "The Pink Raven" by the French police, wrote poison-pen letters on colored paper, and the husband of Maria Jeritza gave away thousands of umbrellas to her admirers during her comeback tour of the United States. Why, he wondered, would a famous opera singer marry an umbrella manufacturer? *Sashi sugi,* he said to himself. Enough is enough.

"The news doesn't make any sense," he told his mother one afternoon after his father had left for Connecticut.

"It doesn't make any sense to you because you live in a dream world," said his mother.

"Books make sense," said Roger. "One chapter follows another. It's all the same story, and you get to know all the characters."

"The world is not like a novel," said his mother. "You can't expect that. The world is not about anything in particular, and it doesn't have any last chapter and all the ends don't get neatly tied together. You just can't expect everything to be exciting and meaningful. When you grow up you'll have to fix the furnace and make out your income tax and work hard at things that bore you and be nice to people you hate. None of that is much fun, but it's damned necessary."

He knew, of course, that his mother was perfectly right. The world of adults was a collection of necessary but uninteresting news items. He also knew that she was dead wrong, but just how that was so he could not put into words. Miss Wakowski did all the necessary things. She probably did her own income tax, she always started class on time, and she never made a mistake when she wrote an equation on the board, but inside she had turned to snow. That didn't make her wrong about anything, but he knew that being dead was worse than being wrong. If Percival Lowell's canals were more than what was really there, then Miss Wakowski's perfectly correct equations were somehow less than what was really there. Whatever that was.

By the end of February he had given up on ever getting Harry Fisher to a Denizen meeting. He called three times but never got him on the phone. He stopped by the house but was turned away by the Gray Lady. Once, however, he did see Harry after school hurrying toward town in his leather jacket and his leather aviator's cap. He watched him swing from side to side, lumbering through the snow toward downtown Greencastle, his earflaps pointing upward, the loose strings dangling over his shoulders.

The Denizens had met faithfully every other Wednesday evening all through January and February. They collected another seventeen dollars toward the building of their telescope, and Frank found an ad in *Popular Science* for a cheaper but larger lens that would take less than six months to grind. Suddenly the canals of Mars seemed closer. They made definite plans to explore the Watchung Reservation in April when the weather got warmer and flying saucers would be more plentiful. Roger expanded the Denizens' opening invocation from *The Book of the Dead*, and under his tutelage Frank and Dennis learned over fifty Egyptian ideograms, which they used to write notes in study hall that confounded everyone who saw them, even Mrs. Leibolt. It was clear that the Denizens had already learned a great deal that year in spite of the fact that they spent most of their time in school. Things were not going to be as bad as he had feared. Ythn, he suspected, had said a lot of silly things that day they had talked about the Rosicrucians.

During the last week in February, Mrs. Leibolt got halfway through her Adventures in Poetry. Poetry, Roger learned, could be rhymed with a regular meter, unrhymed with a regular meter, rhymed without a regular meter, and unrhymed without a regular meter. The last, she announced, was called free verse. To Roger, it made about as much sense to call a poem "free" because it had no rhyme or rhythm as it did to call a man "open-minded" because he had no education, but he did not argue the point. By Wednesday he had seventeen pages of notes covering these and other distinctions, each with an example copied from the textbook. He had known from the outset that poetry was boring, but he had never imagined that it would be, like the evening news, totally devoid of anything that was either clear or interesting.

At the beginning of Thursday's class, Mrs. Leibolt passed out the midterm examinations on fiction which they had all taken the previous week. At the top of Roger's paper he saw a B-plus in large red letters along with the comment that he seemed to understand the material but tended to wander. Now everyone stood against the wall, and Mrs. Leibolt called off their names, seating them according to their test scores. Roger got the seat at the high end of the fourth row, just missing the "magic six," as Dennis called it. "It's the seating that gives you your standing," he had said merrily.

"I hate this," he whispered to Ruth as he took his seat just behind her.

She turned around and looked at him in her clear, expectant way. "Hate what?"

"This seating business. Knowing who's ahead of you and who's behind. It reminds you that you're always supposed to struggle to get ahead of the next guy and not let the guy behind you catch up."

"Girls don't worry so much about all that," said Ruth.

"Girls are lucky. But I sometimes wonder what Mrs. Leibolt thinks about all this. I mean, she can't root for everybody. She knows that no matter how hard we all try, half of us are going to be in the lower half."

"Maybe she doesn't think about it," said Ruth. "Maybe she just thinks that competition is good for everybody."

"Competition is only good for you if you win," said Roger in a loud whisper. "And if you do, then there's the next guy who's just a little smarter than the guy you beat. And then when you get to the top of the class, there's all the other classes. It's just like the math tests they give every year. You might get to the regionals or you might go to state or you might even get to the nationals, but somewhere along the line you lose. So life is sort of a war against every other person in the whole world, and everyone loses somewhere along the line. Isn't that terrific?"

"That's a terrible way to think," said Ruth.

"It's the way Harry Fisher thinks," said Roger. "I mean, for him everything is military. I'm surprised that he and Mrs. Leibolt don't understand each other a whole lot better."

When everyone was finally seated, Mrs. Leibolt passed around the new seating chart for everyone to sign and then spent the rest of the period talking about Keats's "Ode on a Grecian Urn." For the first time, Roger felt a flicker of interest in Mrs. Leibolt's Adventures in Poetry. He could see that she was an intelligent woman and that "Urn" was a luminous poem. For a moment, the two came together.

"We've talked about the vocabulary and the figures of speech," she was saying. "We've gone over everything line by line. But there's something else, isn't there? There's what the poem means—what Keats was thinking and feeling. Can anyone talk about that?"

"It's about old stuff," said Eddie McQueen. "Statues and flowers and shepherds and stuff like that." He leaned sideways against his forearm, one bony shoulder high above the other, looking like a sparrow with a broken wing.

"The background is classical," said Mrs. Leibolt. "I believe that's what you mean. Many of the things in the poem suggest a pastoral setting that assents to classicism. But what's the occasion? What's happening in the poem? Eddie, will you please sit up?"

"Keats is talking about all the things he sees on the different sides of the pot," said Harriet Emerick.

"That's why it's so boring," said Buck Moore. "Nothing happens. This guy just sits and stares at the pot and gets sensitive about everything."

Mrs. Leibolt took two steps away from her desk and pressed her hands together. "Ah, you say the poet is thinking?"

Buck looked from side to side and smiled uneasily. Then he put his hand over his forehead as if he were shading his eyes from the noon sun. "Yeah. He has all these thoughts."

"What thoughts?"

The boy's face went blank. "Pretty thoughts," he said after a moment. "Poetry thoughts."

The class laughed, and Buck leaned back in his chair and smiled again. Mrs. Leibolt took a deep breath, and her small, round breasts rose a little under her tight dress. Roger stared at her. Looking at her hips, her breasts, her bright red rosebud mouth, and her long painted lashes, he believed there was little more to know about her body that could be known without undressing her. He knew that when she was angry, as she was now, she did not turn red like Miss Simic. Instead she smiled and looked very stiff and pressed her fingers together. He knew that she had a new brassiere that separated and lifted. He knew that if he had been a middle-aged man married to a beautiful middle-aged woman like Mrs. Leibolt, he would have called her China Doll. There was something about her, especially now when she was holding everything back, that seemed not only painted and stiff, but breakable. He imagined that she was ceramic, like Keats's urn, and that hundreds of tiny cracks ran the length and breadth of her. She was brittle. If you touched her, parts would fall off.

"Marilyn," she said in a very clear voice, "what do you think this poem means? Do the last few lines give you any clues?"

Marilyn Sord moved her head back and forth in an elaborate pretense of reading through the poem. Then she gave her teacher a bright smile and opened her hands in a gesture of feminine futility. "I don't have the faintest idea, Mrs. Leibolt," she said musically. "Honestly, everyone is just so smart but me. People have all these wonderful ideas, and I just—"

"That's fine, Marilyn. Anyone else? Roger?"

She called on him without quite looking in his direction, as if she half hoped he would have nothing to say. He knew that if he spoke it would begin again, the thing he hated before Christmas, and so he decided on silence. But there were things he wanted so much to tell her. He wanted to tell her about Playground Joe and his kites. He wanted to tell her that Joe had a hundred scars and wounds and that every year he forgot something he had known the year before. He wanted to tell her about the Flying Man, and about the kites that were always new and rising. The Flying Man would never find the nooks and crannies, but he would never get wrinkles and he would never have to drop bombs on Stuttgart and get shot up by Messerschmitts and watch his mother get hardening of the arteries, to say nothing of himself. All of this he wanted to say because it was like what Keats was saying about the Grecian urn. But he said nothing. And when he kept his silence, Mrs. Leibolt finally did look at him. He shook his head, knowing it would start all over again if he spoke a single word.

"You can't tell a thing from reading the poem," said Larry Norcross. "Look at all the questions about *what* this and *whither* that. Keats doesn't know what's going on any more than we do."

"Those are rhetorical questions, Larry. Do you know what a rhetorical question is?"

Curtiss Baylor smiled and lifted one eyebrow. "A rhetorical question is a question that doesn't call for an answer," he said. "Like in debate. You ask questions sometimes that you know the audience already knows the answers to."

"That's exactly right," said Mrs. Leibolt. "And this poem asks a whole series of rhetorical questions. As the poet turns the urn and new images come into view, he expresses his sense of wonder with questions rather than statements. Do you understand that?"

A low murmur of assent from the class. Marilyn Sord fluffed up the right shoulder of her blue sweater. Mary John Grodner twitched. Buck Moore leaned back in his chair and stared at the empty blackboard. Occasionally words would form on his lips, and his muscles would flex. Outside the bleak windows of the classroom, the crunch of boots had broken up the thick crusts of snow into a patchwork of gray and white. Beyond the school grounds, parked cars lined the gray, frozen curbs of Paris Avenue.

16 | Everything Turns Red on the Russian Front

Lunch in the school cafeteria—an ancient gymnasium across from the main building converted to a kitchen and lunchroom with seventy-five long folding tables, the kind that he remembered seeing once at a pancake supper at the Presbyterian church. The smell of peanut butter, overcooked vegetables, and grease, together with the shouts and murmurs of hundreds of high school students, all coalesced into a kind of sickness, a feeling that human beings were shouting, sweating creatures who put things in one end that came out the other. Roger let himself be pushed through the serving line while overweight grandmothers, their hair done up in netted buns that looked like dead cats, dumped sweet potatoes, white bread, hamburgers, and quivering lumps of green Jell-O into the square indentations stamped into his steel tray. Chow time in block thirteen, he thought. God.

The tray-lunchers sat in one section, the brown-baggers in another. No one knew why. "It works out better that way," he had overheard Mr. Figge say one day at the office. Keep the red rovers in one box and the pearlies in another, he thought. That way things stay organized. He was pleased, however, that nearly all of the Italian boys were brown-baggers and could thus be avoided if you bought your lunch. He tried never to look at them while he ate; he hated their greasy hair combed into ducktails, their pimples, their heavy eyebrows, their leather jackets and secret handshakes and obscene gestures. God, how he hated anything that was Italian. His mother would sometimes play Italian opera on the radio Sunday afternoons, and he would always go to his room or play outside until it was over. The Metropolitan Opera. Fat sopranos and greasy tenors all screaming about their sex life at the top of their lungs. Then, with a twinge of shame, he thought of Frank. Well, it wasn't Frank's fault. Besides, he was not really an Italian Italian. He was more what you would call a person who just happened to have Italian parents.

After lunch he went to his locker and put on his boots and coat. He had no desire to go out on the Russian Front, but there was nothing else to do. It was expected. Besides, there was always an outside chance of hitting Larry Norcross in the face with an iceball.

The winter playground, like the cafeteria, divided into two camps. At the south end near the cyclone fence stood a small, circular embankment made of soft snow. To its enemies the place was known as the White Doughnut; to its friends it was the Eagle's Nest. Seven members of the varsity basketball team and a few of their admirers, including Phil Hedley and Randy Hormann, had made it their own. Two hundred feet away, near the south wall of the main building, stood Fort Texarkana. No one quite knew what "Texarkana" meant, but the fort was a splendid affair, probably because its inhabitants were defense-oriented. Its seven-foot-square sides supported lookout towers at each corner. Two ornamental domes of snow flanked the entranceway where a ragtag army now defended against the attack of the athletes. Roger saw a few seventh-graders, two skinny boys from his Latin class, Frank, a new boy who had just moved from Alabama, and a soft, colorful sprinkle of nameless girls, their long green and red scarfs, powdered with snow, falling behind them over their shoulders.

The attackers loped easily through the snow. Their arms were like slingshots, each of their snowballs hitting someone in the face. The defenders trudged and stumbled through the drifts outside Fort Texarkana. They threw with their wrists and forearms. Even the shapes of their snowballs looked different. The attackers made hard, gray little spheres that looked and felt like cannon shot. The defenders' snowballs were elliptical puffs of cream, innocent things that blooped through the air and made a white mark on your shoulder. Still, the defenders outnumbered their smiling attackers and grimly held their position.

"Roger! We need you bad! Come on!"

As he ran to join Frank, a hard snowball exploded on the side of his head.

"You okay?"

"Who threw that? God, it just about tore my ear off. Was that Larry Norcross?"

"Who knows."

Frank leaned a little from side to side and flapped his hands against his coat, looking vaguely like a penguin. He had pulled his aviator's hat down over his brows and wrapped his purple scarf around his neck. Nothing showed but his eyes and mouth and his pink cheeks.

"Gosh, I hate this," he said. "I don't know why I come out here every day. Dennis never comes."

"Dennis is smart."

Frank looked down into the snow. "I think if just once we could get on the offensive and kick in the White Doughnut, I would quit this forever and just go to the library after lunch."

"Look out!"

A wedge of athletes ran screaming through no-man's-land, throwing iceballs and brandishing small wooden shields. The defenders made a grim semicircle and retreated slowly toward the entrance of Fort Texarkana. For a while the line held; then the aggressors divided into two forces, one attacking straight on and the other circling around to one side. Suddenly Buck Moore and Larry Norcross appeared at the top of the wall and threw one of the lookouts, a seventh-grader, down into the slush behind the fort. Now the air was thick with snow and shouting voices. Someone began to cry.

"Look out behind you! They got us surrounded!"

"My eye hurts!"

"Don't leave any survivors!"

"So how do you like it in your face, you motherf—"

"Kick everything down—"

Now the athletes were all around them and a white mist filled the air. There was no time to make snowballs. Roger grabbed handfuls of snow and simply threw them at anything that moved. All at once something hit him on the side and he fell against the ruined south wall of Fort Texarkana. When he got up, gasping, he saw that the war was over. The defenders stood in a circle surrounded by the smiles and the white teeth of the victors.

"You are our prisoners!" shouted Buck Moore.

Curtiss Baylor laughed. In his gray coat and his black boots he made Roger think of a panzer general. Something out of Harry Fisher's mythology of terror. "Let the girls go," he said. "The rest must be punished."

"Let's just punish one or two," said Larry Norcross. He looked at Roger and smiled.

Roger looked around at his fellow prisoners with their soggy mittens and red faces. Their mouths hung open. Several were on the verge of tears. Frank sat on the ground. He took off his boots and tried to shake the snow out of them. He stared mournfully at his yellow socks, curled his toes, and shivered.

Roger stepped out of the prisoners' huddle and pointed his finger at the smiling basketball players. "This is supposed to be a game," he shouted, "but you dirty bastards have turned it into a war. Every day it gets worse. You feel good when you make a seventh-grader cry, Larry? Does that make you feel like a big man? Does it give you a good feeling when you hit somebody in the face with an iceball? God, you make me sick. You all make me sick."

There was a moment of shocked silence among the athletes. Then they looked at each other and mumbled.

"Who is that guy?"

"Where does he get off?"

"Whatsa matter, buddy. Can't you take it?"

"I know this guy," said Larry. "And I know just where he gets off. It's a station called Homosville, and it's right in the middle of Fairyland." He took a step forward and gave Roger a push.

A sudden rage boiled up inside Roger as he looked into the handsome boy's face, saw the easy confidence in his white, wintery smile. He took a wild roundhouse swing at Larry Norcross and hit him hard on the left shoulder.

The smile faded from Larry's face. "Now you're really in trouble," he said. "Hey, guys, did you see that? The homo wants to fight. The mayor of Queersville wants to mix it up a little."

Now the distinction between the victors and the vanquished was forgotten. All the boys, still breathing hard, linked arms and waited. A fight was about to begin. Eddie McQueen ran all over the playground announcing it, and in less than a minute dozens of others came to press against the weave of arms that gave the two fighters their space.

Roger, feeling a little silly now, began to circle around his tall opponent and flick out his left jab as he had seen boxers do on Friday-night television. But he could not reach Larry Norcross. He could not *tag* him with his left, as Don Dunphy would have said. As they moved around each other, their taunts and their feints and the shouts of encouragement from the ring of boys seemed more and more unreal. He let his guard down a little and smiled at Frank, who was looking very anxious. At that moment Larry clipped him hard on the left ear.

"Good shot, Larry!"

"Hit him in the face, Larry!"

"C'mon, Roger. Don't let your guard down—"

Out of the corner of his eye he saw Frank jumping up and

down in the snow, yelling something. Two people held him back. Then another sharp blow bounced off his temple. His anger was muffled now by fatigue, and by the cold. It was hard to hold his arms up with his heavy coat on. He jabbed again and again at the tall boy's face, but still could not reach him.

Then, as Roger lunged forward, Larry slipped a jab and countered with a short right that had all his shoulder behind it. Roger had never really been hit in the face before, and the force of the blow frightened him. He staggered backward, then caught himself. He tasted blood in his mouth, and for a moment he heard a buzzing inside his skull.

"You got him now, Larry! Wow!"

"Give it to him! Knock his block off!"

Roger rushed back into the center of the snowy ring, swinging wildly. Larry blocked the blows easily with his hands and forearms and then countered again with a left and a right to the face. Then, suddenly, a hard blow to the stomach. Roger sank to his knees. The shock had paralyzed him, and for a moment he could not breathe.

"You had enough yet, you little shitface?"

Roger finally took three deep breaths, got up, and threw himself at Larry Norcross. But after five more minutes of fighting he found that he could no longer hold his left hand in front of his face.

The more often he got hit, the less the individual blows seemed to matter. He felt pain, and yet he did not feel it. It was as if he had retreated to a black space inside him, a cave where he looked out and saw the face of Larry Norcross in front of him. Everything else was a blur. The shouts of the other boys receded to a vague murmur. Something smashed his eye, then a terrible crunch against his nose, and then a blow to his mouth that set him back on his heels. He went down again. Pieces of crusted snow cut into his face. The world turned red. He got up again and moved toward the face of the person he hated more than anyone in the world. But he saw now that the face had changed. The narrow eyes had widened. The sneer had disappeared. The mouth hung open. Now Larry tucked his chin under his right fist and moved away a little, as if something had frightened him.

"Jesus Christ, doesn't he know when he's had enough?" said someone.

"Larry, you better quit. You're gonna kill him."

"He's right, Larry. You better quit."

"I'll quit when he quits," said Larry between his teeth. "I'll quit when he quits, the son of a bitch."

"This isn't a fair fight!" cried Frank. "This is against all the rules—"

"What rules? We don't got any rules."

"The rules," said Frank. "You know, the rules—"

Roger jabbed again with his left and saw the right-hand counterpunch sail over his head. At that moment he saw his chance—his one lightning, lucky chance. He fell forward and threw his right hand, trying to keep his body behind it as he had seen Larry do. The blow caught the tall boy on the mouth, and Roger felt the delicious and wonderful pain of teeth cutting into his knuckles. He saw the boy's head snap back, and he heard him give a little cry, as if he had lost something.

"That's it," said Larry. "I'm gonna punch your lights out—"

"Larry, you better not get too mad. You're a lot stronger—"

"Larry, the principal is gonna be out here in about two seconds—"

"Roger!" He could hear the sound of his friend's voice above all the others. "Roger! Roger! Roger!"

He was strangely aware of where his feet were. They seemed so far away. He saw that he was supporting himself by leaning against the remains of the snow embankments of Fort Texarkana. Everything looked red now on the Russian Front, and time seemed to be moving very slowly. Someone was hitting him in the face again and again, but for a moment he forgot who it was. The force of the blows snapped his head back, sent him drifting. For a while he imagined that his skull had cracked open and that things were oozing out of it. Then he found himself lying in the snow. People were looking down at him.

"God! You killed him!"

"Jesus, Larry, I told you you shouldn't have—"

"Hey! He's looking up at us! Maybe he's okay—"

"Look out! Here comes Mr. Figge!"

"Oh God, are we in trouble—"

He remembered that three girls screamed when they saw him coming down the main hallway, supported by Mr. Figge. He did not remember going into the nurse's office or taking off his shirt, but suddenly there he was. A big blond woman was bending over him. Her face was all pinched up. She was doing something to his cheeks and nose with Q-Tips.

"Don't look in the mirror," she said quietly. Her voice was like cold water. "Do you have a family doctor? Someone I could call?"

" 'Octor 'Utell."

"What? Dr. Buetell?"

" 'Es."

"Fine. Don't try to talk anymore. I'll call your mother first, and then we'll—"

He heard the door open and saw the nurse turn away. Whispers, footsteps, and then Frank looking down at him, his face white with fear.

"Young man, you're not needed here," said the nurse. "No one is allowed—"

"Fr'en'," said Roger. " 'E's good fr'en'."

Frank did not seem to have noticed the nurse. "C'mon," he said. "The ambulance is here. Let me help you get up." Tears ran down his cheeks. He trembled as he put his arm around Roger's waist. "Larry Norcross is getting thrown out of school," he whispered.

Then Mr. Figge came back with someone else and he heard more voices, and then he saw that he was lying on a stretcher looking up at the ceiling of an ambulance. He was rocking from side to side and Frank was sitting next to him. He wanted very much to hear the siren, but for some reason no one had turned it on. He tried several times to speak, to tell Frank to tell the driver that it would be nice to have a siren, but he found that his mouth would not work, and that he could not concentrate on words. Finally Frank, bending over him, put a pencil and a pad of paper in his hands.

Roger looked at the blank paper and forgot what he wanted. Then, without knowing why, he drew a foot, then two small eagles looking left, then another foot, two quills, the sign of the ankh, the water sign . . .

"What's he writing?" said the nurse. Roger was surprised to hear the nurse's voice. He could not see her anywhere in the ambulance.

Frank laughed and brushed the tears out of his eyes. "We're the Denizens," he said hoarsely. "We got to stick together—"

"But what's he writing?"

"He's telling us he was attacked by Baabi, a monster who lives on the intestines of princes."

"What?"

"The word for intestines is *beseku*. Look—see that? No one else knows about that! Only the Denizens!"

Frank burst into tears and held the hand of his friend as the ambulance took a left turn off Paris Avenue and the siren finally began to scream.

17 | Face Music

Halfway to the hospital he sat up and bumped his head gently but painfully on the top of the ambulance. Houses and drifts of gray snow moved past him. Nothing looked familiar. It occurred to him that he had never been to the hospital in Greencastle, although he remembered his mother had gone several times for something called "female problems." He had no idea what female problems were. It did seem odd to think that different illnesses would have genders, like Latin nouns. Would getting your head smashed in by the captain of the basketball team be a male problem? Male problems, he thought. That's why his mother never understood him. He had male problems. Something about that seemed very funny, and a sudden pain shot through his face. Smiling, he thought, was almost as painful as bumping your head.

He saw that Frank was watching him very closely. "You better lie down," he was saying. "You better take it easy."

It was then he realized that something was wrong inside his head. He had known just a second ago where he was going; now he was not sure. And then he saw himself lying in the snow with Larry's face floating above him. *God,* he thought, *I wanted to tear his head off. I wanted to kick him in the crotch. I wanted to give him a male problem he would never forget.*

He caught sight of himself when the cold afternoon sunlight hit the glass doors of the emergency entrance. He nearly fainted. His right eye had pinched shut and turned gray, the color of dirty snow. Something slick and oily oozed out of the cuts beneath it, and ran down his swollen, purple cheek. And in the brief, terrible flash of that image it seemed as if his mouth were split open and teeth were missing, as if someone had hit him in the face with an ax. He thought of war photos of Americans killed on the beaches at Normandy and in the forests of the Ardennes, and German corpses frozen in the snow in Russia. Suddenly he knew that he was not immortal. He was dying. He lived inside a body that would someday be photographed lying in a field somewhere, or in a casket, or in an overturned automobile.

"I can't walk," he said. "I'm sick."

"Just sit down and wait for the doctor," said the voice of the school nurse.

"Where am I? I can't see."

He wanted, as he had so many times before, to go backward. He wanted Harry's time machine. Just this morning, he thought, he was just another maladjusted teenager, and now he was dying. A casualty on the winter front somewhere between Greencastle and Stalingrad.

A doctor whose face was a blight of acne scars smiled at him and told him he was going to be all right but that he would need some cold compresses, about four stitches above his right eye, and a new tooth. The stitches would have to be done after they got hold of his mother, he said. Did he have a family doctor? When would his mother be home? He turned a little to the left and saw Frank's face, and felt a hand on his shoulder. He saw that he was lying in a room with several other people and that the room had yellow walls.

As Roger drifted in and out of time, he heard Frank say goodbye, and he felt someone put pillows under his feet, and he saw a bottle of colorless liquid dangling above his right shoulder. Then the angry whisper of the doctor's voice—something about not letting him go to sleep.

An hour later, as he walked up the front steps of his own house, the cold air made his right cheek throb. The nurse, a hazy, invisible presence at his elbow, helped him along and pressed the doorbell. When he looked inside he saw his mother standing in the dark hallway. He saw her face turn white.

"Mrs. Cornell, we tried to call you—"

"My God."

"It's just bruises, mostly. Nothing serious. But I thought it best to bring him down to the hospital. The doctor just cleaned him up a little and gave him some fluid when he began to go into shock. He has a very mild concussion, and he will need a few stitches—"

"Who did this?"

"He got into a fight—"

"Thank you. Thanks for bringing him home."

He heard his mother close the door behind him. She helped him to the living-room sofa and put a pillow under his head.

"You just stay there," she said. "Just rest."

She went back into the hallway, and he heard her pick up the telephone and begin to dial.

The next morning his mother took him back to the hospital. The doctor smiled at him, asked him how he felt, and put in six stitches above his right eye and another on his lip. That afternoon he spent at the dentist's office. On Sunday evening he heard his mother call the high school principal and explain in quiet tones that she was suing the parents of Larry Norcross and that she might very well sue the school for gross negligence. She added, again very quietly, that she did not think that a man who allowed psychopaths to wander about the playground beating up other children should be allowed to continue as principal.

"You're going to a private school," she announced during dinner. "You can't go to a school that has a mongolian idiot for a principal. God, I wish your father was here. He's supposed to be the man of the family. He's supposed to be handling all this—"

"You don't have to worry, Mom. I'm okay now."

"You're more than okay," she said. "You're too good for that damned school. By the way, Frank and Dennis called this afternoon."

"What did they want?"

"They wanted to know how you were. They are nice boys. I just wish they were interested in something besides vampires and spaceships."

On Monday the principal's secretary announced during homeroom that Roger Cornell and Larry Norcross were to report to the office for a few minutes during first period. A hush fell over the room when the announcement came, and everyone stared at Roger. My face, he thought. My beautiful face. He realized that his beautiful face, along with the rest of him, would appear every day that week in the hallways, in classes, in the cafeteria, and even, if he could brazen it out, at dancing class that Friday.

At the office they met with Mr. Figge, the acting vice-principal, who sat with them for five minutes in the outer office and explained that fighting was not permitted on the playground, that this particular fight had given the school a lot of bad publicity, and that any further hostilities of any kind would lead to an immediate suspension for both of them. Roger stared hard at Larry while Mr. Figge talked; Larry pursed his lips and looked out the window.

That afternoon on the way home from school, the Denizens were quiet. The snow had melted on the streets, and their black galoshes scraped and clicked on the wet asphalt. It was then that Roger felt the sudden and terrible possibility that his fight with Larry Norcross had made cracks in the smooth abode of the Denizens' friendship. *It's going to cost them,* he thought, feeling a vague sickness in his stomach. *It's going to cost them now to be my friend.*

At school he began to stare at people. He noticed after a day or two that conversations died or melted into whispers when he came near. By Wednesday he began to think that people just out of sight and earshot were talking about him, that when he entered rooms he interrupted their gossip and their cruel jokes, things they could not say in the presence of his purple, swollen face. He knew that the opinion put forth in the boys' locker room was that he had been a brave fool to press the issue with Larry Norcross, to accuse him of bad things, and then to fight on after he was beaten. "Typical," said Harriet Emerick one morning just as he walked into Latin class. He knew she was talking about him.

In the cafeteria on Wednesday he was pleased to see Larry hunched over a plate of pork chops and spinach, looking very sour. He was surrounded on all sides by concerned friends.

"Nobody said it was your fault," said Curtiss Baylor. "Nobody even thinks that."

"Well, what was I supposed to do?" said Larry. "Was I supposed to stand there and let him hit me? Was I supposed to apologize for not being a Mortimer Snerd? Was I supposed to cut off my left leg to make it an even fight?"

Curtiss opened his hands in a gesture of futility. "You're not listening," he said.

"Everybody knows it's Roger's fault," said Buck Moore.

"Everybody saw him hit you first," said Eddie McQueen.

But as the days passed, a strange bond seemed to form between Roger and Larry, a thing neither of them could have anticipated. They saw each other everywhere. When they met in the hallways, they stared at each other. No one mentioned one without mentioning the other. It was as if they had written a book that everyone in the school had read. Yes, he thought, that was it. They were co-authors of The Big Fight. Once when he turned to look at him in Mrs. Leibolt's class he caught him looking back—not with rage or contempt, but with something else. He had seen that expression many times before, but never on the face of Larry Norcross. It was, or would have been on someone else, a look of quiet envy.

He knew that in weak moments he had looked at Larry in such a way. Larry, after all, was prominent and popular. He was tall, athletic, handsome, and very sure of himself. He went steady with the most beautiful girl in the tenth grade. His mother was chairman of nearly everything in Greencastle and practically owned the country club. His father managed a business consultant firm and owned two large department stores in Newark. His big brother had just graduated *magna cum laude* from some big university. And finally, he was the only kid in dancing class who could do all the outside turns in both the rhumba and the samba. The more Roger watched him, the more he saw that Larry Norcross was everything he wanted to be, and not to be. Perhaps—perhaps Larry felt the same way about him? After the first flash of wonder, the chances of such a thing being true seemed very dim. There was really nothing that Roger could do well, at least nothing that anyone else could possibly care about.

Still, the suspicion lingered that in some dim way the boy envied him. Larry never seemed happy, or at ease. He was restless, angry, sarcastic. He had a narrow range of interests and tended to talk about the same things over and over. Except for sports and pretty girls, school bored him. Except for his elite circle of athletes and country-clubbers, people bored him. And except for Curtiss Baylor, whom he treated with a kind of circumspect courtesy, he hated anyone possessed of intelligence or talent. In a way, Larry reminded him a little of Harry Fisher. They were both selective, intense, and intolerant.

By Thursday afternoon the school was filled with rumors. One he overheard in the main hallway was that the Denizens, Rolfe Gerhardt, and Virgi Prewitt were all members of a conspiracy to discredit American athletics by damaging the reputation of the captain of the basketball team at Greencastle High School. Mrs. Norcross, the story went on, had invited the leaders from church and social groups around town into her parlor to discuss the problem.

"Is that what people really think?" said Frank.

"It's what everybody is saying," said Roger.

"Nobody could believe something like that," said Dennis. "It's just too dumb."

"The coefficient of dumbosity that a particular statement has doesn't have much to do with how many people believe it," said Roger. "Like all those people who believe in Joe McCarthy and watch *I Led Three Lives* like it's a religion. They think the Communists are putting saltpeter in our hamburger and poisoning our water supply and destroying our monetary system." Roger grinned at his own hyperbole. He was not quite sure what the monetary system was, but neither, he suspected, did anyone else.

"That's politics," said Dennis. "I never think about politics. Politics is really boring."

"But it's a perfect example," said Roger. "Joe McCarthy is this man who has a voice sort of like a buzz saw, and he thinks you're a Communist if you don't keep your grass cut, or if your sister once gave a glass of water to someone who lived in a city where they once had a Communist rally in 1918. You know, that sort of stuff. And look how Hitler got everybody in Germany to believe that it was okay to make war on anyone who wasn't a member of the Master Race, and that was just a couple years ago."

"So you think—you think people could really believe all those things about us?" Frank winced.

Suddenly the implications seemed too dangerous, too close to being possible. "I guess not really," said Roger. "Not here in Greencastle. I mean, people just like to talk."

Frank smiled and looked down at his shoes. "The war's over," he said. "Maybe people are different now. Maybe people learned something."

But when Roger went to his locker the next morning he saw that someone had written HOMO HORROR across the metal door in purple chalk, and underlined it three times. *God,* he thought. *This is it.*

Hardly an hour passed that he did not think of the moment when he saw himself in the glass doors of the hospital emergency entrance, the moment when everything in his life changed. The whole week proceeded from that moment. Everything looked and felt different. "But that's perfectly normal," his mother told him. "I remember once your Uncle Peter got hit on the head with a barn door when he was sixteen. He told me that he couldn't stand to touch anything made of rubber for a week and that everything he ate tasted like cod-liver oil." Roger took some consolation in this, but he did not tell his mother that he felt dizzy when he got up in the morning, that he could not bring himself to answer the telephone, that he had a terrible fear of doorways, and that he could not read anything for ten minutes without getting a headache. Everything was changing. That was what Shadowman wanted.

When he got home from school on Friday afternoon he found that he was alone. He saw from her note that his mother was doing the week's shopping. He wandered from room to room for a few minutes, feeling the house slowly getting dark. It occurred to him that he had not changed his clothes for three days. He undressed, went into the bathroom, then stopped to stare at himself in the mirror. The swollen eye and swollen cheek, the splotches of purple, the six stitches just below his right eyebrow, and the one on his lower lip all made him think of some creature newly put together by a mad doctor. But the rest of him, he noticed for the hundredth time, was almost equally ugly. He wondered how long his clothespin waist would continue to support life, and how long his upper half would at least continue to maintain effective commerce and communication with his lower half. His long neck, bent in the middle by a prominent Adam's apple, sank between his broad, bony shoulders. His arms dwindled to almost nothing just above the elbows, then flared out into muscular forearms. Like Popeye, he thought. Bright clusters of acne spread over both his shoulders and down his pectoral muscles like a swarm of red hornets. No one in the world had ever seen all this except his mother and father. He never took showers in gym class, since it was not mandatory, and he never went swimming in the summer without his T-shirt. He remembered, staring at himself, that he had never really thought about his body until he was thirteen. He never felt greasy, or wondered what he smelled like. He never watched his blackheads turn day by day into whiteheads, or tried to square his shoulders when girls passed by, or worried about his voice cracking or whether his walk was masculine or feminine. His body was like an incarnation of his thought, a thing that responded instantly to his will. Now it had grown ugly and smelly. And he knew now that it could be hurt, and that someday it would grow old. Shadowman again. Stealing something from him every day. Part of the problem, he knew, was that he thought too much, spent too much time alone. And thinking about how he thought too much, and noticing that he was thinking about how he thought too much—that was no help at all.

When the kitchen clock showed six and his mother was still not home, he decided to fix himself some Cheerios, a banana, and a little side dish of baked beans. That would keep him going until he got home from dancing class. Ythn sat across from him at the kitchen table while he ate. The Martian leaned forward, rested his small chin on the points of his wrists, and let his twenty fingers play over his face. This sign of Martian reverie was something Roger had seen before. It was as if Ythn was playing himself, making music that no one else could hear, something that turned him inward, like rain.

"Roger, you look terrible," he said after a long silence.

"How clever of you to notice."

"And you feel terrible."

"Wait till I get to the dance tonight," said Roger. "I'm going to scare the hell out of everybody with my face."

"I see. You are going to dilute your misery by giving it to others." Ythn closed his eyes and seemed to listen to his fingers.

"Something like that." He imagined smiling at all the girls until his scabs cracked open. Thinking about it almost made him regret his return trip to the dentist that week and his perfect new tooth. "I have to get back at Larry and all his buddies. I have to get back at the school."

"You hate school?"

"I hate school. I hate Greencastle. I hate everything."

"That's very democratic," said Ythn. He spoke very quietly now, and his mind seemed to be elsewhere. Roger watched the Martian's fingers rise and fall on his cheeks and eyes and mouth. His face was changing, very gradually, from green to blue. This was something different, he thought, even for Ythn.

"It's just that everything gets so complicated." He didn't know what the change in color meant, but somehow it made him want to explain things to Ythn as clearly as possible. "All I want to do is read and talk to my friends and listen to the radio and run around the park in my sneakers and maybe take Ruth to the movies once in a while. But no matter what you do, it has sixty hundred other parts that you don't even know about. Everything has parts, and those parts have other parts."

"Parts," said Ythn.

"Right. You know, like when you're little and you think everything is solid but then later you discover that everything is atoms and molecules and mostly empty space. Ythn, will you stop doing that with your fingers?"

"In the beginning," said Ythn, "everything was one. A great white light that lit up the edges of eternity. Then everything broke apart. Exploded. And now for billions of years everything in the universe has been getting further away from everything else. Each year that passes drives our solar system further away from every other solar system. The dark spaces between the stars grow larger, and every year we are more alone than we used to be. It is hard—very hard—not to live your life that way. Not to let all things get further away from all other things as you grow older."

"Ythn, you keep forgetting I'm only fifteen. Honest to God, if I had a nickel for every time you went over my head in the last four months I'd have about fourteen dollars."

"I am sorry. Are you enjoying your cereal that's shot from guns?"

"That's the other kind."

"Oh, yes. Quaker Puffed Wheat Sparkies."

"They changed the name," said Roger. "It's just Puffed Wheat now. And I don't think it's really shot from anything."

"There are many things like that on Earth," said Ythn. "Humans say one thing and mean another, or they say something that has no meaning at all. Did you know there is no nourishment in cigarettes? And yet humans are always writing about how good they are for you."

"That's advertising," said Roger. "Adults advertise everything. *When coughs and wheezes fill your chest, refreshing Kools still taste the best.* After you listen to all that stuff for a while, you don't know what to believe."

"That's what I was talking about," said Ythn. "Ideas drifting away from experience, words getting further away from truth, and people living more and more by themselves. They watch machines instead of each other."

Ythn removed his fingers from his own face and spread them apart in the air, like fans. Then he reached across the table with his longer-than-human arms and placed sixteen of his fingers on Roger's nose and ears and cheeks and eyelids. "But you and I," said Ythn, "we must never let anything come between us."

He began to detach first one finger, then another. The tiny suction cups pulled at his skin a little, then let go. Strangely, there was no pain, although the whole right side of Roger's face was very tender. Then he felt other fingers coming down, and then others lifting. It made him think at first of summer rain, cut grass, flowers, all the odors of the green earth. And then he noticed that the fingers alternated between his ears and eyes, and his cheeks and forehead. At the end of each phrase, one finger brushed across his eyelids. He knew that Ythn was making music. No, not music. Something else. A different kind of harmony.

"This is what we do on Mars to express the idea of unity," said Ythn. "The fingers are all part of the hand which is a part of the arm which is a part of the body which is an aspect of consciousness which is a part of everything."

"You make face music," said Roger.

"Yes," said Ythn. "We make face music."

Roger saw in his mind the universe of stars all speeding away from each other, and he imagined the great white light which had once been all of them together. "You believe in everything coming together instead of getting further apart," said Roger.

"Yes," said Ythn. "And I believe in you."

Roger closed his eyes. The harmony Ythn made on his face was more intense now. He could feel the buzz of the frail wrists and arms behind the fingers. He had always known that Ythn was electrical. "Ythn, you're the only person in the whole world who can say that kind of stuff without embarrassing the crap out of me."

"I know. Isn't it wonderful?"

Roger smiled. "I guess that's why you're here."

"It's one reason," said Ythn. "There are others."

Roger took a bath, shaved some of the pale hairs on his chin, and then began to polish his black shoes. He did not yet have a tuxedo, something that many of the tenth-grade boys had for country club dances and school proms, but he did have a black suit, black shoes, black socks, and a black bow tie.

"You look so adult when you dress for dancing," said Ythn. "You look like a man with a profession."

"I'll never have a profession," said Roger. "I'm too screwy and disorganized to have a profession."

"Maybe you'll be a poet or an artist," said Ythn.

"No talent," said Roger. "Being impractical doesn't necessarily mean you're brilliant or artistic. That's a mistake my mother makes all the time. When I'm confused she thinks I'm being *sensitive*. And when I don't get a thing done for a whole weekend, she thinks I'm being *thoughtful.* Honest to God, I look like a penguin in this outfit."

"On Riga 17," said Ythn, "there are laws against practicality. People buy dreams from each other and only the poets and musicians are allowed to run for public office. Anyone who is caught doing anything useful for more than forty-five minutes is put in the desert of Yoh-Vombis for six days with nothing to eat but hook roots and fizz water."

"I wish I could see Riga 17," said Roger. "Just for a second."

"That's not difficult to arrange," said Ythn.

As Roger struggled with his bow tie, Ythn began to buzz. Two pairs of arms appeared behind his back in the mirror image. They encircled him, and once again Ythn's fingers began their walk across his cheeks and forehead. "A little more face music," he said, "and Riga 17 will appear before your eyes. So to speak."

Soft bursts of color exploded in his brain. Then, as Ythn slipped two fingers over Roger's closed eyes, he saw the Rigans, silvery creatures who looked very much like human beings except for their hands and feet. They balanced on huge silver medallions, beautiful things made in openwork patterns that reminded him of Celtic symbols. The medallions floated a few hundred feet over an ocher desert. Near the horizon, red spires and arches broke through the surface of an inland sea. The images flickered for a moment, then disappeared.

"I don't want to go to dancing class," said Roger. He spoke in a reverent whisper. "I want to go to Riga 17. I want it to be like in Edmund Hamilton. I want an atom bomb to explode in my face and send lucky me a thousand years into the future. I want to travel through hyperspace and fight intergalactic evil and have a whole planet for my castle. I want to be a Star King."

Ythn released all his fingers from his friend's bruised face. His mouth filaments vibrated. He made a sudden sound like organ music, and touched the tip of Roger's nose with a single finger.

"You are a Star King," he said.

18 | Miss Dot Defends Her Reputation

That evening he took an intense satisfaction out of terrifying all the girls at dancing class. It pleased him that conversations died wherever he went. Faces withered when he approached. He felt like a flamethrower moving through a field of weeds. In the third set, he cut in on Marilyn Sord, something he had never done before. As he danced with the most beautiful girl in the tenth grade, he smiled maliciously and played a tune very lightly on the small of her back with his right hand.

"Nice evening," he said.

"Yes," she said in a faint voice.

"You dance divinely."

"Thank you." She gave him a quick, terrified look.

"I must tell you about face music," said Roger. "Face music is when you run all twenty of your fingers over someone's face. It makes these colored lights shoot off inside your brain, and then you start to dream about creatures from other planets."

Her face flushed. Her white hand trembled. She gave meaningful glances to other boys gliding by with other girls, but no one cut in.

"It helps if you have suction cups on the ends of your fingers," said Roger.

Marilyn Sord stared at him. "God help me," she said.

During intermission he stood with Dennis and Frank for ginger ale and cupcakes. For the first time in his memory he did not know what to say to them.

"You're laying it on a little thick," said Dennis at last. "You got to take it easy. People will think you're a disease."

"I can't help it," said Roger. "I just hate everybody."

Larry Norcross, Buck Moore, and Curtiss Baylor glanced at him as they passed by, glasses in hand, walking back to the boys' side of the dance hall.

"Our three club members don't seem to be getting along tonight," said Curtiss.

"Trouble in homo heaven," said Buck. "How sad."

But Larry, after his first quick glance, looked straight ahead, said nothing. He wore a small Band-Aid at the corner of his mouth.

At the end of intermission Miss Dot formed all her tenth-graders into the familiar double circle, and she and Mr. Waring demonstrated the basic steps to the tango. "Blue Tango" was still near the top of the Hit Parade, and many of the tenth-graders, including Roger, were curious about its intricate stops and starts. Dancing the tango was a mark of sophistication, a coming of age. It was something the seniors did at the country club dances.

"The tango," Miss Dot was saying, "is unlike any other ballroom dance because of its very high style. Its most distinct feature is its use of *attitudes*. I should explain to you that an *attitude* is a place in the dance when the dancers pause, holding a certain position—"

The two-man orchestra played "Flamingo" while Miss Dot and Mr. Waring demonstrated. Her sunlamp tan looked beautiful, he thought, against her gray hair and her white gown. The demonstration ended as Mr. Waring brought her into a low dip and then turned her suddenly so that her gray hair brushed the floor. The boys whistled and hooted. The girls looked utterly astonished. "I wouldn't do that with a girl in a million years," whispered someone. "Miss Dot is going to get her hair dirty," whispered someone else.

Each boy in the outer circle tried one step three times with the adjacent girl in the inner circle, then moved on to the next girl. Roger always watched how the boys moved. Ships passing in the night, he thought. You touch someone, then you move on.

He wondered what Miss Dot must have looked like when she was twenty. He saw the bright look she gave Mr. Waring when she came out of the tango dip, as if something had quickened her, taken her breath away. He wondered if Miss Dot had ever *done it* with anybody. It occurred to him that a pretty girl his own age would look something like Miss Dot in about thirty-five years. It occurred to him that Miss Dot was a real person. There was something going on inside her, just as there was something going on inside him. Once he had been quite sure that there was nothing inside teachers, except lesson plans.

When it came time for girl's choice, Ruth walked over to him. He stood up without a word. The music started. She rested her head against his shoulder. "This is the first time you've danced with me tonight," she said.

"I'm too ugly to dance with," he said. "Don't look at me."

"But you danced with everyone else. You danced with Marilyn Sord and you asked her about the weather."

Roger laughed. "Tonight I'm only asking the girls I really hate."

She gave him one of her rare smiles. She was coming off on him again. He could imagine the moisture from her hand running into the lifelines of his palm, the ones that told everything. It was like a blood transfusion. Perhaps, he thought, she was trying to save his life.

"Ruth, did I ever tell you about face music? Face music is

when you run all twenty of your fingers over someone's face. It makes these colored lights shoot off inside your brain, and then you start to dream about creatures from other planets."

Ruth smiled again. "That must be one of those Egypt things you and Frank and Dennis are always talking about." She looked up at his bruised face. "How does it go? Like this?" She lifted her left hand off his shoulder and touched his purple cheek very carefully with her fingers.

"Yes," he said. "Just like that. That's face music. I have a friend who does it with more fingers, but not nearly as well."

Ruth closed her eyes. "I'm playing 'Orchids in the Moonlight,'" she said.

At the end of the class the tenth-graders made their double line and each shook hands with Miss Dot and Mr. Waring and bid them a pleasant good evening. Miss Dot and Mr. Waring smiled and said it was good of them to come. But as Roger turned into the hallway, Miss Dot called out to him in her soft, mellifluous voice.

"Mr. Cornell? That's right, isn't it? I wonder if I could have a brief word with you?"

"Certainly, Miss Dot."

"Could you wait in the hallway? Just for a few moments?"

"Certainly, Miss Dot."

He went out into the hallway and pretended to check through his wallet and look for his hat until nearly everyone was gone.

Frank waited for him on the stairway. "Roger? You coming?"

"Just a sec. I have to go to the men's room. You go on down."

In another two minutes the old building was quiet. He heard the wind blowing outside, and the voices of all the tenth-graders drifted up the two flights of stairs from the dark street below. He stood alone in the long, shadowy hallway looking in at the bright ballroom with its glass chandelier, its rows of empty chairs, its random collage of paper cups and napkins.

He heard something rustle behind him. He turned, startled, and saw that it was Miss Dot. Standing there in the dim light she looked ghostly with her white dress and her soft gray hair.

"Oh," she said. "Did I startle you? I am sorry."

"It's okay."

"I won't keep you long. I wanted to tell you about a little problem I'm having."

"A problem."

"Yes. Mr. Cornell, you dance very well. Did you know that? I was watching you this evening."

"No, ma'am. I didn't know that."

"You are a little too fast. Especially in the fox-trot when you turn into the conversation step. Your girl gets behind sometimes." She gave him a quick smile and cocked her head a little, as if she had said something whimsical. "But essentially you do very well. You have grace. And grace means intelligence. Did you know that, Mr. Cornell?"

"That grace means intelligence? No, ma'am. I didn't know that."

"Stupid people are never graceful. I daresay ordinary people are never graceful. But you—" She squared her shoulders and pulled at the points of her off-the-shoulder evening gown. Tenth-grade girls did that constantly, but he had never seen Miss Dot do it. Again he wondered what she must have looked like when she was twenty.

"But of course you must have guessed that I have not detained you just to compliment you on your dancing."

"Yes, ma'am. You said you had a problem."

"Yes. Quite. I do have a problem. Mr. Waring and I have been getting telephone calls."

"Telephone calls," said Roger.

"From mothers mostly." For a moment she did not seem to know how to go on. "These mothers—they seem to be worried about certain things that are going on in Greencastle, especially in the high school."

"It would be natural for them to call you, ma'am." He said

this without a trace of sarcasm. "I mean, you have good taste and good judgment about things." He was not going to make it any easier for her.

Miss Dot looked at him very carefully. Her eyes narrowed. "It's very nice of you to say so," she said. "But I'm afraid the things *they* are saying are not so nice."

"What are they saying, ma'am?"

"They are saying that you are responsible for getting the captain of the basketball team in trouble, that you consort with undesirables, that you belong to a club that is involved in—well—illicit practices, that you frequent a certain bookstore in Greencastle that is known to be a bad influence on young people. They say you have caused a great deal of trouble in school."

"None of those things are true, Miss Dot."

"That may be so. You seem like a very nice young man to me. You seem very polite. Very conservative. But if I were you I would not dance with young ladies who put their fingers all over my face."

"It's true that I sometimes dance with young ladies who put their fingers all over my face, but all those other things are lies."

"I'm sorry," she said. "But I'll have to ask you not to come back to class for the rest of the year. It will take that long for—well, you know—for your face to heal. You are a sight. I'll admit you don't seem to be—well—that's enough said. I am sorry."

She turned away from him and walked into the brightly lit ballroom. He knew that she wanted him to go, and so he stood there looking at her. Finally she turned around, and he was surprised to see that her face was flushed.

"Try to understand," she said. "I have my own reputation to maintain. Everything depends on one's reputation in this business. I may look like a woman of society—"

She closed her eyes for a moment and rubbed a spot on her forehead with the tips of her fingers. "But I am not that at all," she continued in a quieter voice. "I am an unsuccessful actress from New York trying to make a go of it here with Mr. Waring in this godforsaken town—"

"I can't come for the whole rest of the year?"

"The school year is over in less than three months. It's not that long. You won't be missing that much—"

He could feel tears of anger and humiliation forming in his eyes. He had been trying to make things difficult for her by being polite and sincere and innocent, but now he had lost control of everything. It seemed so unjust. He had never wanted to hurt anybody, but so many people seemed bent on hurting him. He did not want Miss Dot to see his tears, and so he turned away from her and ran down the two flights of stairs. He flew past Frank and Dennis and leaped onto his bicycle.

"So long," he said in a frail voice. "See you tomorrow."

He pedaled like mad through the dark, gliding silently down Springfield Avenue, and then up Maple Street. Water trickled in the gutters, and moonlight gave a soft lambency to the lawns and roofs that were still covered with snow. It was almost like running in the summertime; nothing could touch him but the wind. For a few minutes he forgot about his face and Miss Dot and the high school and the vague conspiracy of mothers. He raised both his arms in the dark and felt the danger of it as he pedaled, the wind running like cool silk between his fingers.

19 | Memorizing the Names of All the Streets in Berlin

Again he remembered how his first grade teacher had explained that the passing of the seasons was a profound and mysterious process full of interesting signs and portents. March, he remembered, was supposed to come in like a lion and go out like a lamb. And now it was happening. During the last two weeks of the month the temperature rose into the forties, and the snow hung on only here and there—under a bush, in the crotch of a tree, in the angle of a gabled roof. From every corner came the bright sound of water washing into sewers. The weather alternated between rainy mornings full of wind and darkness, and mild, silent afternoons during which fog would drift up High Point Avenue and gather in a pool at the bottom of Stone Hill Road. Sometimes it separated into long columns that moved between houses and then settled, like a great silver-white sheet of gauze, over Roosevelt Memorial Field. Winter was giving up the ghost.

Roger's face healed quickly, leaving only a slight dent in his lower lip that he hoped women would find attractive, and a splotch of bluish yellow under his right cheek that would fade to nothing by the end of the month. The strange taste in his mouth went away. He began to answer the telephone again, holding the receiver an inch or two away from his ear until he was sure who was speaking. And even his strange fear of doors had somewhat lessened, though he still had the sharp and unequivocal impression that doors were the interface between the known and the unexpected. They were dimensional. Spooky. If you walked through one, you left something behind. You were not the same person in one room that you were in another, and there was that quick, painful moment under the arch when the person you were got replaced by the person you had just become. He had no explanation for this, except the vaguely comfortable feeling that he was going crazy.

Still, he had hopes that everything was returning to normal. The Denizens continued to meet every other Wednesday evening at Roger's house, and they still waited for each other at the four corners for their walk to school in the morning. But as they turned onto Paris Avenue and the high school came into view, Roger ran on ahead so that by the time Frank and Dennis entered the schoolyard he was nowhere to be seen. He knew they both understood the necessity for this. He was both pleased and dismayed that they never mentioned it. Pleased because his act of consideration and the need for it were humiliating and unspeakable. Dismayed because the silence was a distance between them, something cold and uncomfortable.

In school Roger continued to be a curiosity. Everyone knew that his mother had sued Mr. and Mrs. Norcross. Everyone knew that he had been thrown out of dancing class. He was sure that people were making up stories about him just as they made up stories about Rolfe Gerhardt and Virgi Prewitt. When people spoke to him in the hallways, he simply glared at them. When teachers called on him, he was careful never to give the expected answer and never to say anything very pleasant. Mrs. Leibolt smiled at him sadly and shook her head. Mr. Figge ignored him. Miss Wakowski looked through him as she seemed to look through everyone. But the terrifying and utterly unchangeable Miss Simic shot questions at him every first period, which he answered instantly. She struck her Latin book with the flat of her hand when she spoke, and her voice, coming so early in the day, was like a glass of ice water in his face.

"Roger!" she cried out one morning. "Do you remember asking me about Tacitus and Caligula?"

He watched the veins in her pink face, and the tight, thin lips that quivered when she was angry. She must be a hundred years old, he thought. That was one reason why she was so scary. He swore to himself that when he grew up he would try to get a law passed that would make all teachers retire at thirty-eight.

"Well?"

"Yes, Miss Simic. I remember."

"And what did I say? Does anyone in this class remember what I said?"

"You said that Tacitus exaggerated. You said we shouldn't trust anything he said about Caligula."

"Caligula was a bad boy," said Miss Simic. "He made mistakes. But Tacitus, with his nasty desire to sensationalize, made him into a monster. And just what do you think of that, Eddie?"

Eddie McQueen dropped his pencil. "What? Oh. Um, people shouldn't do that."

"Tacitus was a historian," said Miss Simic. "He spoke Greek and he knew mathematics and philosophy. But he did not stick to business. He was a gossip. A gossip is one of the very worst things any human being can be."

Roger looked behind him. He saw that all twenty-six of Miss Simic's students were sitting very straight and wide-eyed with their Latin books open to the correct page. They were looking at her, waiting for the lesson to begin.

Gradually Roger gave up on homework except for the twenty minutes after Flag & Bible during homeroom period when he rushed through his daily Latin assignment. He had always known there were boys who did no homework. The Italian kids from Brick Street on the north side of town. The ones who wandered through school with thick eyebrows and black combs in their back pockets. They wrote words on the stalls in the boys' bathroom. They never read anything aloud in class. They never turned in themes in English class or took foreign languages. They walked around school with their eyebrows arched and their mouths slightly open in what Roger took to be an expression of vague anticipation. With this fixed on their faces, they nodded to one another. Now, he thought, he was one of them.

In the afternoons and evenings he did very little. He was always tired. He took a nap when he came home from school, and after dinner he lay on his bed and listened to the radio until he again fell asleep. Sometimes he would stare at the bedsprings seventeen inches above his nose while someone named Galen Drake talked about the ancient Greeks, French wine, the World Series, Indian herbal remedies, the life of Teddy Roosevelt, the history of the city of Berlin, and the importance of brushing with Craig-Martin toothpaste.

"Why do you find all this aimless talk so congenial?" asked Ythn one evening just before midnight. "Isn't miscellany just what you claim to hate about the evening news?"

"Galen Drake is friendly," said Roger. "The news is never friendly. The news never tells you about how gay Paris was in 1930 and how Hitler loved Wagner and how he changed the names of all those streets in Berlin before the war."

When he was less exhausted he sat in the dining room in front of the beautiful Zenith console which his father had bought his mother for Christmas one year. He loved the way the cobra tone arm barely touched the records, bobbing a little, like a reptilian angel floating lightly on water. He would listen for an hour or so to *Nights in the Gardens of Spain*, the Grieg piano concerto, and his Jo Stafford recording of "Early Autumn." Sometimes he was aware that he was listening to music. At other times he followed corridors of sound that turned, branched, and opened into enormous rooms.

"I sometimes get lost in music," said Roger.

"A Martian philosopher once told me that all the things we love are like labyrinths," said Ythn.

"Interesting but unclear," said Roger.

"Think about it," said Ythn.

But instead he looked at his fragile albums of records, remembering that most people were now buying the long-playing kind because they didn't break and took up less space. He knew that this was a neater and more efficient way to listen to music, but Roger hated neatness and efficiency. He wondered if it were even barely possible that by the time he grew up men and women would find something neater and more efficient than *doing it.* Something with machines, or pills, or mirrors. It would be just his luck, he thought, the way things were going.

During this month of the Lion and the Lamb, he thought a lot about Harry Fisher. Harry, as far as he could see, was alone in the world, isolated from everything except Nunnug and his attic world of models and games. It was perfectly obvious that Harry needed a friend, and he tried twice that month to call on him. But Harry was neither at home nor away. He was in the attic.

On the last Saturday evening of the month his mother went out with her League friends to a movie, and he sat alone in the dining room listening to music. It was near midnight when the telephone rang. He pressed reject, and the cobra tone arm lifted off the record, clicked three times, and snapped into its off position. The telephone rang again in the foyer.

"Hello?"

Something cackled and whirred at the other end of the line.

"Harry? Is that you?"

Sudden laughter. "You bet."

"I can't believe it! You're on the telephone! What's that funny sound?"

"Some of my new stuff."

"Harry, I can never get ahold of you. You never seem to be home and you never answer the telephone."

Harry laughed again. "Call me Lamont Cranston."
"What's going on, Harry?"
A long silence. "Someday, buddy, I may tell you what's going on. But it's more likely that you'll just find out. Read it in the newspapers, maybe. You should see all my new stuff."
"How's the time machine?"
"Ennis, he came up and saw it yesterday. We thought we might take this little trip back to Berlin in 1941."
"Berlin in '41. That's nice. Just like Galen Drake."
"I got this map from a cousin in Minnesota once. Did you ever see a German map? Nothing like ours. German maps, they got these different colors and little pictures of buildings right onto them. I got it all in my head now."
"In your head?"
"I memorized the name of every street in Berlin. I can take you anywhere you want to go."
"Harry, why would you want to do a thing like that? It must have taken you weeks."
"I can memorize anything in three days," said Harry. "I got this new system I worked out. I hear you been having problems."
"What? Oh, you mean school. Don't worry about it."
"I hear you got beat up."
"I'm okay. I hit him back a couple times."
"I hear a lotta stories about you."
"I bet you do."
"I told you never to bring your best stuff to school," said Harry. "I did tell you that. You didn't listen, did you?"
"I didn't bring anything to school."
"You know what I mean. I mean, don't bring *any* of your good stuff. In school everything is Shakespeare and basketball. Real hotsy-totsy. Listen, I'll see you."
"Harry, don't hang up. I wanted to ask you—"
But Harry, who was the most abrupt person Roger had ever met, had already hung up. The dial tone hummed in his ear. A chill ran through him. If the dead could speak, he thought, they would sound like dial tones.

20 | Creatures from Another Galaxy Take Over Greencastle

On Sunday morning it snowed for two hours. The snow fell through an intermittent slant of sunlight, making a layer of white fuzz that rested lightly on the sidewalks and streets. Roger knew in his bones that this was the last snow of the season. By late afternoon it was gone.

At five o'clock his mother drove up in her four-year-old Studebaker and spun the wheels on the gravel as she turned into the driveway. He had been dozing in a chair in the sun room, and it startled him to see her leap out of the car and rap on the window.

"Come out," she said. "We're going for a ride."

"I don't want to go for a ride. I'm tired."

"You've been tired for weeks. You spend too much time in the house."

"I need to rest."

"You get too much rest. You need fresh air. I want you out of the house. Come on. I mean it."

He groaned and stood up and made a point of staggering out of the sun room, nearly falling into the bookcase. He hated it when his mother got all excited about something, because he knew she expected her excitement to be contagious. He opened and slammed the front door and took a deep breath. The air was cool and humid, but not unpleasant.

His mother stood in the driveway waiting for him. She wore a very official-looking blue suit and she had her hair pulled back into a tight bun so that she looked a little like Eva Perón. This was her League of Women Voters outfit, and he hated it.

"Get in quick," she said. "We'll go for a ride down by the reservation, and then we'll stop for some hamburgers and fries down at the diner so we won't have to fix dinner or do dishes. We'll have the evening free."

"Take it easy, Mom. I just woke up."

She bounced the car back down the driveway and then took a right at the bottom of the hill, off toward the state highway that ran along the edge of the Watchung Reservation. Two years earlier, he and his mother and father had gone for a ride every Saturday and Sunday out into the country. They never had any destination, which seemed peculiar until he realized that almost all the families on Stone Hill Road packed everyone into their cars on Sunday and drove nowhere. This was called the Sunday Drive, or going for a spin.

"I am so glad to be a League member," his mother was saying. "It's about the only time I get to be in the company of women who have any brains."

"I guess most women are kind of dumb," said Roger. "I mean, except for schoolteachers."

"Most women around here read Jack Woodford novels and listen to soap operas and clean house and worry about their hair. But at the League it's different. We have all decided to support Adlai Stevenson for President and conduct an open forum next month on the ethics of Senator McCarthy. I don't suppose you even know who those people are."

"McCarthy fights Communism and Stevenson probably fights something else."

"You hate politics, don't you? Never mind. I have some other news."

"What?"

"Your father is taking a week off beginning next Friday. We're going to have a party his first night home."

"You're kidding."

"Some people from your father's company are driving down to Newark for a convention and then they're coming here for the evening. It's kind of important that we do this every once in a while."

"You mean this is not a party where you relax and have a good time. It's more like one of those parties where you have to make the right impression on the right people so you get a raise instead of getting fired."

His mother smiled. "Well, I wouldn't put it quite that way. But that's the general idea."

"I'll just stay in my room."

"You'll sit in the living room and say hello to people for at least fifteen minutes."

"With my face?"

"Your face is fine now. Just a few shadowy places. Even that should be gone in a week."

"Going to adult parties is sort of like turning on the evening news," said Roger. "It's not terrific."

"Fifteen minutes," she said. "That's not much to ask."

"Is this what you're all excited about? Is this why you're jerking the car all over the road and talking so loud and everything?"

His mother made a fast right off Thistle Street onto the highway. Now the world was filled with sunlight and air, as the residential district gave way to trees on the left and a high cliff on the right. He opened his window.

"Well, I did meet with three lawyers today. They all wanted to have an informal hearing on Sunday, can you imagine? Mrs. Norcross was there. She agreed to settle out of court for six hundred dollars. I got a lot of satisfaction out of that."

He stared at her. "Six hundred dollars," he repeated.

"It's not the money," she said, smiling at the road. "It's the way she gave in. I kept saying I wanted to go to court and that parents of psychopathic children are responsible for their behavior. She flinched a little every time I opened my mouth. God, it was wonderful."

"What's *psychopathic*?"

"A psychopath is a person who doesn't care about other human beings and who doesn't know good from evil. I told them that boys like Larry should be put away until they learn they can't go around beating on people."

"Did you really say all that? I wish I'd been there."

"Those country club pretty boys and their rich parents," she said with something close to a sneer. "They think they run this town. They think they can get away with anything. God, I was so mad. I went into detail about your gashes and your tooth and your stitches and your concussion. Mrs. Norcross didn't say a thing. Not until the end."

"And then she finally said something?"

"Her lawyers were shushing her the whole time—I think they were afraid she would say something that would really get me furious and then everybody really would have to go to court and everyone's name would get dragged through the papers—but on the way out she whispered something. She said that sooner or later the truth would come out. I asked her what she meant, and she got this prim little smile on her face and said something about bad influences and how it probably wasn't *entirely* our fault that you turned out the way you did. I told her that if she spread malicious lies around town about you or us she would wind up in court for sure, and that this time there would be a few malicious truths from our side of the fence. All that business about Mr. Norcross and his women and all his connections with labor unions and gangsters. She didn't say a word after that."

"Mrs. Norcross has a lot of connections," said Roger. He did not quite know what that meant, but he had heard his mother say it about various people, especially women.

"She's president of Christian Alliance and she's best friends with the lady who's president of Parents for Better Schools this year. And she has all these connections through the Episcopal Church and the country club. The Episcopal Church and the country club are practically the same thing, by the way. Anyway, you can't get much more important than that here in Greencastle."

"Do you think—do you think she'll try to make more trouble?"

"I don't know." His mother glanced at him and then looked back at the road. A shadow of pain seemed to cross her face. "You have to realize—that is, people are always going to make trouble for you. That's the kind of person you are. You will have bad enemies and very good friends."

"Deliver me from those who feed upon the intestines of princes," he said.

"You're talking Egyptian," she said. "God, how I hate it when you talk Egyptian."

"Well, join the bandwagon," said Roger. "Just about everyone I know hates just about everything I do."

"That's not true. You have friends."

"You don't know anything about my friends." He was thinking now that for the first time there were things that the Denizens didn't feel they could talk about. He was thinking about how he had to run ahead just as they turned onto Paris Avenue.

"I didn't say I knew anything about them. I just said they were good friends. Frank is a good friend. He sticks up for you."

"I know that!"

His mother winced. "Why should it make you angry when I say Frank is a good friend? That's nothing to get angry about."

"My friends are my own business. I just don't like it when you—I don't know. There are certain things I don't like to talk about."

His mother stared ahead at the road. She looked very grim now. "All I said was that Frank is your friend. That's *all* I said."

"Okay, so I got mad at nothing. So shoot me."

He listened to the ragged sound of the wind. On his right,

chalky sedimentary cliffs rushed past him, their jagged outcroppings and sudden indentations forming a kind of rhythm. On his left, a rocky field and then a dense rise of pine trees. This was the Watchung Reservation. His mother drove on for six or seven miles and then turned left at a sign that said HORSESHOE VALLEY—SCENIC VIEW. This was where he and his father and mother had driven every Sunday until his father's job in Connecticut had taken him away from the family nine months earlier.

"You're very much like your father in one way," she said quietly. "He is so easily offended. I am always offending him, but I never know why. With him, it's a very quiet thing. With you, it's noisy."

"Mom, I don't want to talk about this."

"Fine. What do you want to talk about?"

"When did you say Dad is coming home?"

"Next Friday. The same night we're having the party. I'm hoping you two will do something nice together over the weekend."

"Like what?"

"Oh, I don't know. The things men do. Go to a ball game or go out to a movie or do a woodworking project. Something."

"Dad won't want to do anything. Not unless you plan it. Not unless we have tickets for something and he has to go or waste the money."

His mother was quiet for a long time. They reached the midpoint of the horseshoe curve, and Roger looked down into the valley described by the road, a valley that was already deep in the shadows of the afternoon. He knew that the cliffs left the valley dark in the morning and at dusk. Only for an hour or two at noon would it take the full light of the sun. He wondered what kinds of animals lived in such a place. How pleasant it must be, he thought, to live in a twilight land. A cool place with steep cliffs where nothing came or went, and where no one would ever think to look for you. As his mother drove on, the valley rotated on its midpoint like a dark green spool. Then he saw a small flight of birds rise out of the shadows of high branches, circle for a few moments, then disappear back down into the trees.

"Your father—he's having a very difficult time. He loves you very much. I hope you realize that."

He looked away from the valley and then took a deep breath and exhaled. He closed his eyes and tried to imagine himself floating down into it, touching the floor of the forest. "He has a funny way of showing it," he heard himself say.

"He works very hard. He's not ambitious for himself—he just wants us to have the things we need. He wants to give you a good college education."

"All the things you say he feels and wants are things he never tells me anything about. I just have to take your word for it, don't I?"

"Different people express love in different ways."

"Mom, I don't want to hear about all this."

"Well, you're going to hear about it. There are certain things you have to understand. Things about your father and me."

"But all that—that's none of my business."

"Then what is your business? Egyptian hieroglyphics? Is Egyptian hieroglyphics your business?"

"Mom—"

"This family is your business. You're old enough now to take a little responsibility for the way we feel. Do you understand what I'm saying?"

"I guess."

"Well then—" She brushed her hair out of her eyes and then began to tap on the steering wheel. For a moment she did not seem to know how to go on. Roger pressed his nose into the wind and looked down into the valley.

"Roger, will you please close the window? I have to shout to make you hear me. I was trying to say that your father has given us everything. Everything except—"

"Except his time."

"That's not fair, and that's not what I was going to say. Your father's time is not his own."

"He didn't have to take the job in Connecticut. He knew he would be away most of the time."

"He did what he had to do."

"He did what he wanted to do. And what he wanted to do was get away from us. We—we make him uncomfortable. That's why he won't sell the house and move us to Connecticut."

"Roger, you're making this very difficult for me."

"Every time I say what I think or feel people tell me I'm making things very difficult for them. I don't understand that. I mean, I really don't understand that at all."

"That's because you won't shut up. Now listen to me. When I married your father, I was the happiest person in the world. Your father was a handsome and sensitive and gifted man. I just assumed that we would have a perfect marriage."

"Mom, are you sure you want to tell me about all this—"

"Yes! Now listen to me! I'm trying to help you. There are some things you need to know about your father. I was about to say that after your father and I had been married for a few weeks, I began to realize that he's not like other men. I naturally thought that we would confide in each other, share all our secret feelings. That never happened. He has always been very kind and considerate. I don't think he's raised his voice to me once in all these years. But he's always been terrified by anything personal. He is embarrassed by his own emotions, and by other people's. He can't help it. It's just the way he is."

Roger had the feeling that his mother was not just talking about social intercourse, and this embarrassed him. But he knew that what she was saying was true. "He was different once," he said. "I mean, when I was little."

"That was the happiest time of his life. All of your feelings and discoveries—he felt differently about that. You were a little person. You were all beauty and innocence. There was nothing about you that threatened him. He would play with you for hours on the floor in the evening. Everything was good then."

"I remember that," he said. "Sometimes he would turn all the lights off and lie on the floor and shine a flashlight in his face and tell me he was the man in the moon. He said nothing could ever hurt me if I stayed in the dark with the man in the moon. Then he would set me on top of his stomach and talk about craters and volcanoes and moon men."

He saw tears in his mother's eyes. "I didn't think you could possibly remember all that," she said. "You were only three. God, that was so long ago."

"But something happened," said Roger. "I don't know what it was, but something did happen. I always sort of thought that I disappointed him somehow. Or did something awful. Like that summer we went up to Lake Michigan."

"Your father was brought up by four old ladies—his mother and his three older sisters. He never really had a childhood, and when you came along he tried to live it through you. And then you started to grow up. It never occurred to him that that would happen."

"He saw me this one time in my bathing suit. He made me feel awful. I didn't do anything wrong, but he made me feel awful."

"He saw you growing up. He just hated that."

They came to the end of Horseshoe Valley Road and turned right onto the highway. In a moment the valley disappeared behind them around a bend in the road. It was almost dark.

"You are very precious to me," said his mother. "It's really—well—a miracle that you ever came into this world. And every time I see you two together I realize how terribly different you are, and that breaks my heart a little. But then I think how much the same you are, and that breaks my heart even more. You mustn't be isolated the way he is. You mustn't be afraid of the world. You mustn't just drift off in your own direction, away from everyone."

"That's what the whole universe is doing," said Roger.

"You spend too much time alone and you read these perfectly awful magazines and you don't seem to have any sense of direction. Of course, I'm a fine one to talk. I haven't done anything positive about my own life in years. Your Uncle Peter told me once that I should have had three children or gone to law school. Or both."

She laughed a little and wiped tears away from her eyes with the flat of her hand. "That was good advice. Your Uncle Peter has given a lot of good advice that no one ever seems to pay any attention to."

It was strange to hear his mother talk about his father and about her own life. He knew that it had some connection with driving around a forest at sunset. It was getting dark and her hands were occupied, and she could not look at him. "Don't you dare tell your father about any of this," she said. "He would just die if he found out. He would never forgive me."

That evening after dinner Roger sat in the living room looking at the newspaper headlines without quite seeing them. It had been an exhausting afternoon. He wanted to bicycle down to Katz's Drugstore for the April copy of *Amazing Stories*, but the thought of it made his leg muscles ache. *Frantic Calls from Chicken and Pig Farmers*. The smart thing to do, he thought, would be to go to bed and wait for Galen Drake. He did not want to think about all the things his mother had told him. *Lighted Objects Crash in Swamp*. What was all this? He looked again at the headline:

SAUCERS REPORTED OVER GREENCASTLE
FARMERS REPORT CREATURES IN WATCHUNG WOODS

It seemed deeply significant that he had just been there, just driven past the woods without even knowing. A meaningful coincidence, he thought. Like something out of a book. But of course the Denizens had known it all along. The Watchung was Saucer Central. He folded the newspaper around the article and began to read:

Frantic calls from chicken and pig farmers in and around the city limits suggest that strange lights have been seen in the sky above the Watchung Reservation. Reports also suggest that one of the lighted objects crashed into the swamp. Late this morning, Harry Suggs, a hired hand, reported seeing "men with green torches" walking through the reservation at three in the morning. The police have not yet ascertained what Mr. Suggs was doing at the reservation at that time, or who he works for.

Manley R. Seldon, an egg farmer, whose property lies just north of the woods in question, reported this morning that his chickens would not lay because of "them blasted green things." Upton Whywood, a Millburn grammar school teacher, who was driving through the area late last night on Highway 17, reported seeing "something funny in the sky above the woods" and that his car engine "nearly konked out a couple of times" until he got north of the reservation.

Greencastle police chief John Hasmer was reached by phone late this morning and told *The Herald* that there have been saucer reports from in and around the reservation area ever since the saucer craze began three years ago. "It's just one of those things," he told our reporter. "Sometimes it's pyramid clubs, sometimes it's Communists, sometimes it's Cary Grant, and sometimes it's flying saucers."

Police skepticism is not shared by the Newark branch of the Saucerian Society, which sent a mimeographed report to *The Herald* this afternoon containing a list of seventy-five saucer sightings in New Jersey since 1949. The report indicates that we are being visited by beings "much wiser than we are. Beings who will ultimately be the saviors of mankind."

Chief Hasmer concluded his phone call by warning Greencastle residents that events such as these always "bring out the lunatic fringe." He added that he had received a phone call from a hysterical woman who told him that "Communists, Martians, certain racial and non-Christian religious groups,

> and a small band of emotionally disturbed high school students are hell-bent on taking over the town and handing it to the Devil." Hasmer added that Governor Driscoll has issued an official statement to the effect that all reports of strange phenomena in the skies of New Jersey must be viewed with "calm skepticism."

Roger read the article three times, very slowly. Then he unfolded the paper, put it under his arm, and walked into the kitchen. "Mom," he said, "I want you to read this."

"I can't just now," she said. "We got to talking so long out on the reservation that I stupidly forgot to take us out to dinner and now I'm stuck with the dishes."

"I'll do the dishes."

"Wash or dry?"

"Both. You just sit down here and read the paper."

"I don't get it. What's in the paper?"

"Creatures from another galaxy are taking over Greencastle."

"That's nice," said his mother. "Maybe they'll make some changes. Maybe they'll do a better job down at the high school of monitoring the playground. Maybe they'll tell all those church clubs and parents' organizations to keep their noses out of education and politics."

Roger smiled at his mother and snatched the yellow scrub brush out of her hand. He had never felt so calm, so excited, so clear, so absolutely in charge of his own self. He would call the Denizens before they went to bed this evening. They would meet at Pangborn's tomorrow after school. That weekend they would make a secret expedition to the Watchung Reservation. On the following Monday they would present their findings to the world.

21 | Pangborn's Passivity

On Monday morning the saucer craze hit Greencastle High School. Virgi Prewitt made a six-foot effigy out of balsa wood and toilet paper and hung it on a tree above Paris Avenue. No one seemed to know where she got the balsa wood. No one knew how she managed to hang it from a limb fifty feet above the ground. For two hours it stopped cars in the street. It was a feat worthy of Harry Fisher, he thought. When the firemen cut it down just before lunch period, everyone in Mrs. Leibolt's tenth-grade English class watched through the window.

It floated, slipped sideways in the wind, and for a moment it seemed clear that the thing was gathering power and heading for the window. Harriet Emerick shrieked. Curtiss Baylor raised *both* his eyebrows. But when the saucer hit the ground and broke open, everyone saw that it was nothing but sticks and paper.

The morning light cast Mrs. Leibolt into shadow as she stood by the window, looking out. He could see the silhouette of her long lashes, a wisp of hair out of place, and the perfect curve of her left hip. She was like a black paper doll. If she turned sideways, she would disappear.

"Half of you believed that something was inside," she said in a quiet voice. "But you can see now—it's nothing. Just one of Virgi's pranks. Now can we get back to 'The Lady of Shalott'? We have to finish this today. Tomorrow we begin Adventures in Drama—"

At three forty-five that afternoon the Denizens met at Pangborn's Used Book and Magazine Store to plan their secret expedition to the Watchung Reservation. They found the front door open and heard the whine of a vacuum cleaner. Inside, stacked furniture and bags of refuse. The smell of iron radiators and rust and mold giving way to soap and water and fresh air blowing in through open windows.

Pangborn smiled and turned off the vacuum cleaner. "Well, for Crissake, I haven't seen you guys in weeks," he said.

"We've been very confused," said Dennis. "The flying saucer attack on Greencastle has destroyed our neighborhood and left us homeless orphans."

"I can see that things are crashing down on all sides as usual," said Pangborn. "That means it's time for orange juice and doughnuts."

"Orange juice and doughnuts," said Frank in a religious whisper.

"Let's clean up this place a little before we eat," said Roger. "I mean, this is really a mess."

"Before we eat?" said Frank. "You mean before we even actually have one doughnut?"

"I hate it when people help me," said Pangborn. "That's not my idea of a party at all."

"I'll finish vacuuming," said Roger.

"I'll mop the front," said Dennis.

"I guess maybe I could dust or something," said Frank.

"Goddamnit," said Pangborn. "Can't we just sit and talk? I'm not going to pay you a cent for all this, I hope you know. I never hire anybody for anything."

"We don't expect you to be grateful," said Roger. "All we ask is that you stay out of the way."

In less than thirty minutes the rugs were clean, the tables and bookcases were dusted, the trash was taken out back, and the windows were shining. The whole place smelled and felt different. The four of them wiped their hands on their shirts and sat down together at the back table, where the orange juice and doughnuts waited. Outside the back window a cardinal and two wrens pecked at a feeder which Pangborn had set out for the returning birds.

"It would have taken me a week to get all this work done," said Pangborn. "A whole week."

"The things we do here we'd never do at home," said Dennis.

Roger took a sip of cold orange juice and watched the cardinal flutter his feathers as he perched on the edge of the feeder and cocked his head first one way, then another. Behind his bright plumage, the trees were full of buds. As time passed in that silence of sitting together around Pangborn's table, it seemed also to go backwards. Was that possible?

Once time had been simple. It was only what clocks measured. Now the time outside of him seemed to move at various speeds, but always in the same direction, while the time inside moved backwards or forwards, depending on what he saw and felt. Just now the taste of the orange juice and the smell of books and the bright bird outside and the precious, fragile symmetry of the four of them around the table together had pulled him back into last summer, even as the time in that other world outside him moved into spring. He looked at the others, hardly daring to speak. What if something in his voice or in the words he chose betrayed his happiness, his desperation, or his love? Would his friends all retreat in embarrassment and fear? Pull him instantly back into winter?

"Looks like we came on a good day," he said cautiously.

Pangborn poured juice for everybody, opened the box of doughnuts, and smiled at the assortment of chocolate-covered, cream-filled, and sugar-dusted delights. "If you mean," he said, "that it's a good day because we have all this lovely time without any interruptions, then every day is a good day. Business is really lousy. And to top it all off I get this call yesterday from somebody named Mrs. Daniel S. Treet."

"Heard the name," said Dennis.

"You see her in the paper sometimes," said Roger.

"She's the president of Parents for Better Schools," said Frank. "She's real sincere but she talks kind of funny."

"Really? Well anyway, she's got this voice that sort of melts all over the receiver, like warm Velveeta. She tells me that the education of the young is a great mission in this country and that the future of the world depends on the youth of America. I tell her that the rest of the world may possibly have plans of its own. She says, 'Ha-ha.' Then she says that education doesn't take place exclusively in the classroom, as she's sure I know. I tell her that since she's sure I know this then maybe it wasn't worth the time it took to tell me. More 'ha-ha.' Then she asks me about secret clubs for boys and books sold under the counter and things that have to do with s-e-x. I tell her that I don't know much about secret clubs for boys, that I don't sell anything under the counter, and as for sex, I tell her that I never have anything to do with married women and she better stop calling me."

"You never said that," said Frank. "You didn't. Did you really?"

"Swear to God. After she hung up I called the police and told them I got a crank call from Mrs. Daniel S. Treet and that she wanted to know about sex and secret clubs for boys. The officer I talked to sort of cleared his throat and ahem'd and ahum'd and finally said he would look into it but please not to mention this to anyone, and especially not to say anything that could be misinterpreted. I said what did he have in mind, and he said just to keep my nose clean and my mouth shut and not act smart, and if anyone else called I should be respectful since it just might be an honest citizen making an honest inquiry. Isn't that the stupidest damn thing you ever heard? The police are worse than the nuns."

"People are just nervous," said Dennis. "There have been a lot of crazy things going on."

"People are *very* nervous," said Frank. "It gives me the willies when I think how nervous people are."

"People always think there's a conspiracy," said Pangborn. "If you like lacrosse better than baseball, people look at you funny, and pretty soon someone remembers another guy who liked lacrosse better than baseball who used to sell military secrets to the Russians. And if you vacation in Europe, it means you have a taste for foreign things which means that you think America is not quite good enough for you which means that you're probably an anarchist or a revolutionary which means that you probably have guns and dirty pictures in your basement."

"I'd like to know who *they* are," said Frank. "The people who think all this stuff. That's exactly what I'd really like to know."

"It's all the church and country club people," said Roger. "All those people who think the most important part of education is Flag & Bible."

"And when you do something they don't like they don't tell you about it," said Pangborn. "They tell other people who already agree with them about what you did. They all buzz around on the telephone for a few days and then maybe they have a meeting in some church. And then pretty soon you have this panzer division of housewives and ministers marching down to the library or writing letters in the newspaper or invading the town meeting."

"Like they did two years ago," said Dennis. "When Mrs. Norcross and Mrs. Treet and all those people from Parents for Better Schools got all the stuff about human reproduction cut out of the book after Mary John Grodner fainted that day in science class."

"I remember that," said Frank. "I just hate that kind of stuff."

"It's power," said Pangborn. "Power is something I don't understand. I guess what I understand is non-power."

Roger leaned forward into his chocolate doughnut, and as he ate he thought about non-power. "You mean like reading and talking and sitting around looking at things and generally having a good time," he said.

"That's the idea," said Pangborn. "It's called passivity. Damn, I just love passivity. I'd stand up and fight for passivity just about anytime."

"Is that because you're Jewish?" said Roger.

"No, no," said Frank. "That's *Passover*. *Passivity* is from *passive*. *Passive* means when you don't do anything."

"My father hates all forms of passivity," said Dennis. "He keeps telling me that I read too much and talk too much and that I should work harder and be tough and show people I can take it and dish it out so they'll respect me. He says I should be the best at something or there's no point in being anything. He's a lawyer."

"I have another idea," said Pangborn. "Don't be tough. Don't show people you can dish it out and take it. Just be one of those people upon whom nothing is lost."

"I don't get it."

"I stole that from Henry James."

"Who's Henry James?"

"He's this guy who said to be one of those people upon whom nothing is lost."

"That's a really great definition," said Dennis. "It's like saying that the *Greencastle Herald* is what you wrap up the garbage with on Sundays and Thursdays. But come to think of it, that's a pretty good definition of the *Greencastle Herald*—"

Roger put the last half of his third doughnut down on the table and stared at it. "I think we're all here again," he said in a careful voice. "I mean, like it was last summer. And like Christmas vacation." He never took his eyes off the doughnut.

"We know we're here," said Dennis. "It's perfectly obvious that we're here. Everybody has to be someplace, and this is—"

"I don't think that's what Roger means," said Pangborn. He got up and went to the window. Roger looked up now and saw him standing there, hands on hips, gazing out into the garden, where small wedges of snow were caught here and there, like dragon's teeth, amid the green shoots and the dead weeds. "Last month—last month I thought the winter would never end," said Pangborn. "I thought I'd never get through it. But the days go by, one by one, and pretty soon it's over. Then somehow you feel sorry that another season's gone. You look back and you say to yourself, that wasn't such a bad season, now was it? I had some good times. I got a green sweater for Christmas."

He saw Dennis stare at Pangborn and then turn to him, openmouthed. What was the man talking about? It was perfectly clear. Pangborn was talking about love and loneliness. He tried for a moment to imagine what it was like to live alone, like Norman Pangborn. What would it be like to fix all your own meals? Wash the pee stains out of your own underwear and clean up all your own dishes? What would it be like, he wondered, to live alone in a house without parents, without relatives visiting in the summer? At this question his imagination failed him almost completely. All he could think was that at night all the rooms would be dark except where you remembered to turn on a light. The store, he thought, was all that Pangborn really had. The beautiful, wonderful, endlessly mysterious store. It was his salvation. And his prison.

For a few minutes they all sat without speaking. They watched the birds and listened to the afternoon wind, and drank the last of the orange juice. And then, unaccountably, Roger thought about the man in the moon with his flashlight, and then the dark green valley caught in the dusty twilight where he and his mother had driven, and then, suddenly, he remembered why they had all come that afternoon to Pangborn's Used Book and Magazine Store.

"We have to talk about our expedition," he whispered. "We have to make secret plans while we're all still here and while—you know—while we still have time."

22 | The Palace of the Man of Bad Luck

On the way home that day he saw Harry Fisher moving hundreds of acorns across a bare patch in his backyard. An early-spring campaign, he thought. And this time von Rundstedt would win and Zhukov would lose.

"Harry? I haven't seen you in a month! How's it going?"

Harry looked up from his war. "Hey."

"Listen, I have something terrific to tell you. But you have to promise to keep it a secret."

"I never make promises," said Harry.

"Oh, go stick it, willya? Listen, I'm gonna tell you anyway. The Denizens are going on an expedition next Saturday."

"That's kid stuff."

"No, listen. Frank and Dennis are going to be outside my house at five-thirty in the morning. We're gonna sneak out before our parents are even awake. We're gonna explore the reservation. There's a big stream and some high woods and an old granary, and then further on there's this swamp and an old rowboat stuck off in the weeds that we can use. We got stuff for breakfast and everything."

"And you're gonna look for flying saucers."

"Well, sort of."

Harry's broad smile was one of pure contempt. "And give the two-fingered salute and drink water out of real canteens and be brave and true and everybody helps everybody else. And then it's Junior G-Men looking for evidence of weirdness in the woods. Well, let me tell you, there's lots of weirdness in the woods, but it's not what you think. Mostly it's stuff you step in that you wish you hadn't—"

"Now wait a minute, Harry—"

Harry laughed. "Next time you come around I'll show you the time machine," he said. "I got some new stuff attached onto it that'll knock your socks off."

The following Monday, Mrs. Leibolt began her dreaded Adventures in Drama, which meant Shakespeare, and then, even worse, a Greek named Sophocles. Shakespeare, she told her class, lived in the Renaissance, which Roger now knew was an old time, not an old place. She added that his plays were written in something called Early Modern English, and that originally all the women's parts had been played by young boys. She went on to say that Shakespeare's great talent lay in his ability to deal with Eternal Questions, and that the power and beauty of his language and the depth of his characters had been a joy to intelligent and cultured men and women for hundreds of years. Roger put his head down on his desk and tried not to think about it. Adventures in Drama, as any fool could plainly see, was going to be even worse than Adventures in Poetry.

When he arrived home on Friday afternoon, he saw a man in a gray suit bending over the fireplace in the living room. Then he remembered that tonight—tonight of all nights, when he wanted to get to sleep early—his parents were having a party.

The figure at the fireplace drew small twigs out of a wood box and arranged them one by one on the grate. When he had built them into a mound, he placed a little tent of kindling on top. Presently he stood up and turned to see Roger standing there in the foyer, watching him.

"Dad." He smiled and gave his father a little wave, a flutter of his right hand.

"I'm building a fire for tonight," his father said. "You have to start with these little shavers and then gradually build up. There's a trick to it." He took a match from his pocket, flicked it once with his thumb, and tossed it into the middle of the twigs. A small curl of smoke soon burst into a little cage of fire. His father watched it grow and then carefully placed three split logs on the andirons with his fingertips.

"I'm home for a few days. Took a week off, you know."

"I know. Mom told me."

His father made a little clicking sound with his tongue. "Never did that before. Thought it was about time, though. Thought maybe we could spend some time together."

"Sounds great."

"Fine. I have to change now. Did your mother tell you about tonight?"

His father brushed past him, patting him on the shoulder, and ran upstairs.

For a few minutes after his father's departure he wandered through the house, feeling all the differences. His mother had opened windows, and a clean, cool breeze moved briskly through the rooms, drawing out the stagnant winter air and the stale odor of his father's cigarettes. The dining room smelled like lemon wax, and on the table sat a boat-shaped arrangement of cut flowers that his mother had ordered two days earlier from the florist: daisy-flowering chrysanthemums—brilliant round heads like small suns, interlaced with ferns, with stalks of baby's breath forming a delicate outer atmosphere of white dots.

His mother sailed through the foyer with the vacuum cleaner on her way to the living room. "Isn't that pretty? Purple and yellow and green and white. I just love it."

"It's real nice."

"Parties are usually such a terrible disappointment," she said in a loud, gay voice. By now she had vanished into the living room. "But I love getting ready. I always think, this time everything will be perfect—"

At six o'clock his mother opened a can of ravioli and cut up some cucumbers and green peppers. They ate in the kitchen, his mother full of nervous energy and talk about who was coming, his father smiling, trying to look happy, saying over and over again that he had never before taken days off in April. At seven o'clock Roger stood before the bathroom mirror in his blue suit. He smiled at himself and inspected his new tooth. He combed his hair and rubbed at the fading, shadowy bruise on his right cheek.

When he came downstairs, seven or eight people were standing in the foyer, and he felt a gust of cool air from the open door, heard nervous bursts of conversation, saw faces break into quick smiles. The men stood together in a little circle. The women took off their hats and faced one way and then the other as they took turns examining themselves in the hall mirror.

Soon the early arrivals settled into the living room, and his father made drinks, smiling and nodding at everyone and sipping his ginger ale as he mixed and poured and served. His mother brought cheese and bacon hors d'oeuvres into the living room on a stainless-steel tray. Another breath of cool air, and more people arrived. Roger carried coats up to his parents' bedroom. Time passed. The cigarette smoke thickened. Occasionally his father would rise to open or close a window. The men talked about politics and business, and the women talked about movies, vacations, and interior decorating.

Roger began to see the party as a vague, mindless beast, a cloudy creature drifting from one part of the house to another, sometime detaching parts of itself, sometimes resting quietly after settling itself into a circle, like a cat. Watching the party sing and talk and move about was almost as random and meaningless as watching television. He did not understand why his parents' friends tried so hard to be happy, to laugh at things they obviously did not think were very funny or pretend interest in some pointless story about office secretaries, in some instant movie review, or in someone's excruciating anecdote about buying a dress for her seventeen-year-old daughter. He felt a certain tentative sympathy now with his father, who looked very tired behind his smile. Often, for minutes at a time, he caught him staring at the fire, not listening to anyone. At such times his smile faded to nothing.

Although he understood very little of what adults said to each other at parties, he had a very clear sense of what they felt and what their expressions and gestures signified. It was odd, and after a while even interesting, to know what people intended, without knowing what they meant. As two men talked about closed shops, collective bargaining, and government mediation, he failed utterly to understand their meaning, but he saw clearly that one man showed contempt for the other by the careful way in which he explained everything and by the smile that lifted only the corners of his mouth. But the *contemptee* did not understand this about the *contempter*. He knew only that he was getting a lot of attention by asking what he thought to be sharp and precocious questions. Another man stiffened his face when he talked to women in an attempt to look thoughtful and mature. His mother's friend Alice was the only woman who sat on the floor. She said almost nothing, but she smiled sometimes when the men spoke, and then she leaned back and clasped her hands behind her head and closed her eyes, as if to dismiss all their trivial stupidities, things that were not worth answering or arguing. She was tall with very black hair that parted in the middle. She was the only woman at the party besides his own mother whom he ever would have called beautiful.

At midnight a dozen people retrieved their coats and then lingered for a few more minutes in the foyer. Someone opened the front door, and the rush of air made everyone talk louder and more quickly. A half dozen goodbyes echoed down the front walk as his father and mother stood in the front doorway, waving and shivering.

Now the party was quieter. People brought their empty glasses into the kitchen and then settled themselves in a meandering semi-circle around the living-room fireplace, whose red coals made a pleasant sound, like crinkling tinfoil. Presently his mother came in with a tray of cups and a pot of coffee. She then turned off a light in the corner. Roger knew that she did this for *atmosphere*. He had learned recently that the word *atmosphere* meant two different things, neither of which was visible.

Roger sat just outside the circle of fire watchers, trying to remember names. There was Ed and Betty Nye, Bob and Nancy Sharpe, Lee and Mildred MacWhinney, and a younger man in a powder-blue suit named Peter Lawrence. Mr. Lawrence, he observed, had broad shoulders and a pink face, and he drew faces in the frost on his glass and laughed too much and agreed with everyone. Roger's father sat near him in a chair next to the fire. His pale face and his long white fingers gave him a marbleized, otherworldly look.

The men talked about Panmunjom and Admiral Joy and Heartbreak Ridge and recent rumors that the Yellow Peril was about to invade Taiwan and the monotonal insinuations of Senator Joseph McCarthy that the Secretary of State was soft on Communism. Roger felt these vague and enormous events slip by him, peopled by men and women whose names he could not remember. Only the odd, useless things stuck in his mind. In the midst of a recent economic crisis in Egypt, the editor of an Egyptian newspaper sent reporters to Sakelta to check reports that the entire population turned into cats at sundown. The investigators reported that this was nothing but foolishness and superstition. The adult population was entirely unaffected by the ancient *Pasht* of the pharaohs; it was only the children who turned into cats, and this happened, they added, only occasionally. In Iran there was chaos and revolution, and the oil fields had been shut down. All this was dull, but the man, Mossadegh, was a fascinating creature to watch in newsreels—his narrow shoulders, his incredible nose, his alien robes, and the haunted look in his eyes. Roger knew very little about him, only that his heart was sick and that he conducted his negotiations now from the *Sabeh Gardnieh*—the Palace of the Man of Bad Luck. Who would ever name his house, or any house, the Palace of the Man of Bad Luck? What would such a place look like? he wondered. Perhaps a maze of mirrors that always led back to the beginning? Perhaps an old hotel with wooden ceiling fans turning very slowly, and old men sitting in the lobby with nowhere to go? Mossadegh had driven out his own king, the Shah, and now the British. He was alone with his oil refineries, which did not work without all the people he had driven away.

But the men were no longer talking about Iran. Ed Nye, a heavy man with gray sideburns who spoke in a loud voice, who owned six hunting dogs, and was vice-president of something, complained that the annual inflation rate had reached nearly two percent, that the damn unions were running the country, that the U.S. highway system was a mess and that you couldn't drive anywhere anymore, especially in the Northeast, and that the New Jersey Turnpike would probably take twenty years to complete, the way things were going. Everything, he boomed, was being ruined by gangster unions, Communists, and egghead intellectuals.

Bob Sharpe, another engineer with black-rimmed glasses and a crew cut, who pointed with his pipe and moved his free hand in little circles when he talked, shook his head and blew superior smoke rings. "We ought to hear from the younger generation," he said. "Something to counterbalance all this reactionary nonsense. I wonder what Johnny's boy thinks about all this."

It shocked and offended him when adults referred to his father as *Johnny*. *Johnny* was a little kid who needed a pat on the head and a nose wipe. He did not like the man's wide, boat-shaped grin, his white teeth, or his crew cut. And he did not like the man's pipe pointing at his nose.

"I've heard a lot about you from your father," said Mr. Sharpe.

"Dad talks about me?"

For some reason Roger did not understand, everyone laughed.

"Well, Johnny doesn't talk much, but when he does it's about you. He says you're a real genius."

Roger was dumbfounded. "I'm not a genius."

"He says you spend all your time reading and thinking."

"I do read a lot."

The whole room was silent now. Everyone seemed fascinated by what he was saying. *It's because I'm a kid,* he thought. *They think it's cute when a kid talks up to all the big guys.*

"And what do you read?" said Sharpe.

"Mostly junk." More laughter. Roger blushed.

"I read junk myself," said Sharpe. "Detective novels, mostly."

"I was explaining to my teacher a few months back that I hate Great Literature," said Roger, who was now feeling angry and had decided to give them all a little dose of his own thinking. "I mean, like stories about people who give each other a comb and a watch chain for Christmas, only one cuts her hair to pay for the watch chain and the other sells his watch to pay for the fancy comb. All that stuff with irony. I'm not too crazy about irony."

For the third time there was general laughter. "Your son is quite a talker," said Bob Sharpe.

"And honest to boot," said Lee MacWhinney.

"And he hates Great Literature," said Ed Nye. "By God, he can't be all bad."

"That's for sure!" said Peter Lawrence. He shook his fist once and winked at Roger.

He could not understand why Mr. Sharpe thought he was quite a talker, since this was the first time he had opened his mouth all evening. He did not see why Mr. MacWhinney thought that expressing a preference was an especially honest thing to do. He did not know why not liking the kind of literature the world esteemed to be good was something to be admired.

He was about to speak again, but now the flow of conversation had passed over him and gone somewhere else. The men were talking about a new book by a recent Yale graduate which attacked that university for being liberal, atheistic, and anti-democratic. Mrs. Nye thought it was a shame that Robert Walker died pining away for Jennifer Jones, but she thought it was a good thing that hemlines had finally come down. Mrs. Sharpe indicated a weakness for the poetry of Edna St. Vincent Millay, but did not know what to do about her skin coloring. Roger wondered if he would find all these things interesting when he grew up. He wondered if he would sit with other grown-ups drinking alcohol and being animated. At the moment it did not seem likely.

His father rose from his chair, mumbled something to Ed Nye, and went upstairs. His mother walked out to the kitchen with a tray of dirty coffee cups. Mr. and Mrs. MacWhinney stood up and yawned. Mrs. Nye said something about indirect lighting and how it had been a lovely party.

Roger slipped out of the living room and went upstairs without saying good night to anyone. It occurred to him that he had promised his mother he would stay for fifteen minutes, but instead had sat in his chair near the fire for hours. He could not think what in the world had kept him there all that time. He had listened for a while to the conversations, but mostly he had daydreamed and stared at the fire. Where had all the time gone?

He reached the top of the stairs and turned left past the bathroom, thinking of nothing, when he heard a keening sound, high-pitched and intermittent. He stopped in the middle of the hallway and listened, caught between fear and curiosity. Then he remembered that his father had come upstairs only a few moments before him, and he saw that the door to his parents' bedroom was ajar.

He took three quiet steps down the hallway and then, very gently, pressed his hand on the door, which soundlessly opened a few inches. Inside, the little reading lamp on the wall over the bed cast a weak, yellow glow which left the corners of the room in darkness. The bed was empty. His father crouched in the corner, his face pressed against the wall. His whole body shook. The faint, high sound he made was like a small child crying in his sleep. He smashed his right fist against the wall, and then fell to his knees. It was as if he were trying to get out.

Roger stepped away from the doorway, walked on tiptoe to his own room at the end of the hall, closed the door, and locked it behind him. Think of nothing, he thought. Think of running in the summertime. Think of stars and silence. But then he went to the window and looked out and remembered that somewhere across the world there was a desperate man who had thrown out his own king and would not accept help from foreigners, a man who could not make things work because of all the people he had banished. His father was like that. He didn't know how or why. His father had shut out everyone and closed off all the avenues of commerce. He lived alone with his sick heart, and his house was the Palace of the Man of Bad Luck.

23 | Nothing Happens in Any Particular Way

Something rang in the dark, and he reached out in his blindness to slap at the alarm clock. Consciousness came like a silver knife in his head. No, he thought. A thousand times no.

Ythn lay in bed with him, his four furry arms wrapped around Roger's chest, his head pressed under Roger's armpit. "Get up," whispered the Martian. "You have an appointment with destiny."

"Oh, shut up."

He had been dreaming of sailing on the ocean in a white schooner, and now it was dark and cold, and he was sure that Frank and Dennis had turned off their alarms and gone back to sleep.

"None of that," said Ythn. "It's time to get up and look for spaceships."

"Oh, come on."

"Whose idea was this?" said Ythn. "Did I suggest this little adventure? Did I tell you to get up at five-thirty and wade through the swamp? Come on, get up. The Denizens of the Sacred Crypt are waiting."

Roger rolled onto the floor. When he opened his eyes, he

found himself standing in the middle of his room. In the darkness he saw Ythn dissolve into glittering motes of dust and then reappear in various hues and intensities. Roger groaned, staggered toward the window, caught himself by putting his hands against the glass. He spread his fingers and felt the cold travel down his palms. And then, in the bleary light, he saw them—two figures dressed in army surplus fatigue jackets and knapsacks, standing in the pale starlight and looking up at his window.

Hanging as he was at the brink of consciousness, it seemed like a dream that they had actually come, that the expedition was beginning, that he was about to go outside before daybreak of his own free will. He flashed his ceiling light once and saw them wave up at him. *My God,* he thought, *we're all crazy*.

He brought everything downstairs and dressed in the living room. Finally he donned his own fatigue jacket, his boots, and his knapsack filled with eggs and bread and cooking utensils. As he labored there in the silence, he sniffed the sweet odor of cold embers, and fragments of the evening came back to him. Politics and cigarette smoke. The desperate and helpless feeling that came when he saw his father weeping in the bedroom. As he thought of these things, the morning expedition seemed more and more reasonable and less and less absurd.

Ythn checked to see that his buttons were buttoned and pronounced him ready to go. He stood now by the open front doorway. The pale blue light of pre-dawn flooded across the foyer. Standing there in that strange light, Ythn once again looked strangely unreal.

"How did you do that this morning?" said Roger. "I mean, when you changed into dots and disappeared."

"I change colors. I scintillate. I occasionally glow. It's an emotional thing that's very natural to Martians. But I never discorporate. That was just your imagination. You had just arisen from the arms of Morpheus, remember?"

"The arms of Morpheus?"

"I am trying to learn Earth mythology. I meant to say that you were just waking up. The point, my young friend, is that you must learn to tell the difference between that which is real and that which is illusory. But this is no time for talk. Your friends await. Hurry."

"Why don't you come with us?"

Ythn stood before him now in the doorway, his spidery outline silhouetted against trees and dim sky. He seemed to be looking out across the street toward Frank and Dennis. "You know I can't," he said.

"Why not?"

"You know perfectly well why not. Now hurry." Ythn made a contrapuntal sound with his voice box and then reached out and touched Roger's cheek and ear with one hand. "A little face music for good luck. Now go. For heaven's sake, go."

As he ran down the front steps, the knapsack jiggling on his back, he took a deep breath of cool air and felt his mind clearing. The Denizens slapped each other on the back and laughed quietly in the dark. Then they took off, side by side, up Stone Hill Road toward the row of houses at the end of the curve that led to the bluffs.

"Jesus," said Roger, "we must be nuts."

Dennis laughed again. "No doubt about that."

"I never even actually thought we'd make it," said Frank. "We almost sort of didn't."

"I hope we don't get into trouble," said Dennis.

"The only place the newspaper said was really off limits was Horseshoe Valley Road and what's south of that," said Roger. "We can easily turn back to the highway if we get that far."

"We're going to see a sunrise," said Dennis. "I haven't seen a sunrise for about six years."

"And we're gonna actually have breakfast on a mountain," said Frank.

"God, the air feels good," said Roger.

"I wouldn't do this for anybody but you guys," said Dennis. "I really wouldn't."

They jogged on in silence for a few minutes. Sometimes their elbows brushed against each other. Roger listened to the quick breathing and puffing of his friends and watched the stars grow weaker in the periwinkle ocean above him. He knew now that the morning was a miracle, that their meeting at five forty-five had just barely happened. It was like giving Ruth something for Christmas that he could not afford, something that his mother would never let him buy if she knew, something that would be misinterpreted and make him look ridiculous. Something magnificent.

Overhead the moon is beaming, he thought, remembering the operetta. *White as blossoms on the bough.*

"White as blossoms on the bough," he said, puffing.

"What?"

"Nothing."

"You said 'white as blossoms on the bough,' " said Frank. "That's what you said."

"Then why did you ask?"

Again they all laughed quietly. It was early morning in Greencastle, and the Denizens were hunting for spaceships.

They came to a house with pillars—that was the Butler mansion—and trespassed across the side lawn and into the backyard and the thicket beyond. A path led them down a steep incline. Trees clung to the side of the hill, their roots exposed here and there, forming deltas of twisted sinew under their feet, while their branches hung above them, brushing their faces like nightmare spiders in the dark. Rocks skittered under their feet and things whispered in the underbrush only a lifesbreath away as they passed.

Then once again they came to firm footing. They ran out into a narrow clearing, crossed the gray asphalt highway, and sprinted into the wide field on the other side. Soon they slowed to a walk, and Roger turned and glanced back at the black rise of the bluffs, already a quarter of a mile behind them. Ahead to the east stood an evergreen forest.

They crossed the open field and made their way into the woods. For a while Roger could not see. He lifted his hands in front of his face so as not to smash into things. His boots sank into a dry crunch of needles, and he breathed in the green fragrance of hemlock and spruce and the acid, blackwater smell of winter mulching into spring. And in that blindness, something burst inside him. He knew that morning had come.

They felt a slant now to the land, and as they climbed, a cool wind ruffled their hair. It was not long before they came into a clearing near the top. Birdcalls floated from tree to tree. A pink smudge touched the eastern horizon. Near the center of their clearing they found a drift of leaves caught beneath the branches of a fallen tree.

"Look," said Roger. "The sun's coming up. This is terrific."

"Time for breakfast," said Frank hopefully.

"This is really something," said Dennis. "You can see everything from up here."

The Denizens dropped their knapsacks and for a moment they stretched and blinked and walked in circles.

"And nobody in the whole world knows where we are," said Roger.

They built a fire out in the open and cooked sausages and eggs in a skillet Frank had borrowed from his mother, and then fried slabs of rye bread in the sausage grease. When that was gone they ate oranges and swigged ice water from Frank's canteen. The edge of the sun left the horizon to begin its long arch through a perfect blue sky. The wind subsided. The chatter of insects and birds faded away. The Denizens leaned against the fallen tree and watched the dawn brighten into morning.

"Well," said Roger after a long silence, "we accomplished the first part of our mission. We made it to the top of Machine Gun Mountain. But so far I don't see any signs of saucer landing areas."

"We have two more places to go," said Frank. "Maybe we'll have better luck once we get further away from the highway."

"I think you guys are taking all this a little too seriously," said Dennis.

"We have to go down the other side of the mountain," said Roger. "Then we turn south and follow Moonshine Valley about two miles down to the granary. That's our second observation point. Then we go through another little forest on the south side of the granary and go by this little marsh that leads to the Henrietta Mackelroy Swamp."

"Everything in this reservation has a name," said Dennis, "and none of the names make much sense. Like Machine Gun Mountain. Where do people get that stuff? You don't see any of those names on the map."

"Those names are all from about twenty-five years ago," said Frank. "I read an article about that in the *Herald* by Wilbur J. Hastings three years ago last January. He said there are twenty-seven different place names, but he said none of them are official. He said Watchung Reservation is the only official name."

"What does Watchung mean?" said Roger.

"The article didn't say. I asked my dad and he didn't know either. Nobody seems to know."

Roger rolled his fatigue jacket into a ball and put it behind his head. Strands and feathery tufts of cirrus and altostratus clouds drifted thousands of feet above him. "Frank, will you remember all this tomorrow? I mean, will you remember everything, like when you read a book?"

"Life is different from books. It's harder. When I remember life it's never quite actually like it happened." Frank waved his arms and opened and closed his fingers as if he were trying to gather words out of the sky. "I get hundreds and hundreds of these pictures of things," he said. "It's almost sort of the same as life except that everything is separate."

"I don't get it," said Dennis.

"He means he can't remember everything in life the way it all goes together in time," said Roger. "He means that when he remembers life it's like snapshots instead of movies."

"That's it!" said Frank. "I couldn't say it right, but that's it! Last summer when I was sick in bed with that stomach business and with asthma, I told my nose and throat doctor that I could just lie in the dark for hours and turn over millions of pictures in my head. He thought I was crazy."

"So right now," said Dennis, "right now you're taking all these pictures with your head?"

"Guess so," said Frank.

"I envy you," said Roger. "You never have to work in school. You just know everything. You're just like Curtiss Baylor."

"I don't really *know* anything," said Frank. He looked out into the woods where all the green was shining in the morning light. Above the line of trees they all saw a flight of birds so far off they were little more than motes of dust near the horizon, pen-point scratches in the blue air. The birds moved in a long, slanting line, like geese, but there was no telling what they were at that distance. "I see all the words and all the pictures," said Frank. "But that's it. My brain is like a comic book. You guys, you're the thinkers. You know how to figure things out."

"I hate thinking," said Roger. "Thinking spoils everything."

"I try to avoid anything that's too serious," said Dennis.

"C'mon, you guys. You know what I mean."

"You're too hard on yourself," said Roger. "You have to remember that Dennis and I—well, the truth is, we couldn't do without you.'

"You couldn't? Is that true? It isn't. Is it really?"

Frank looked so pathetically happy that Dennis finally had to turn away. He gathered together all the paper wrappers, the egg carton, and the orange peels and threw them into the fire. Then he stood up and shook out his fatigue jacket. "I'm a little worried about the swamp," he said, changing the subject. "I hate getting my feet wet. Did you say there was a boat down there? The kind that floats?"

"Sure," said Roger. "I used it lots of times. And when we get to the other side, we just go on for another couple miles and we come out on Horseshoe Valley Road."

"Fine," said Dennis. "But listen, you guys don't really expect to find flying saucers in the swamp, do you?"

"It would be a neat place for someone to hide," said Frank. "Nobody hardly ever goes there."

"Well," said Dennis, "maybe this is our lucky day. Maybe we'll find a dozen flying saucers. Maybe we'll string them all together and drag them home like a mess of fish."

"Maybe they're good to eat," said Frank.

The idea of edible spaceships seemed funny to all of them. They poked Frank in his round stomach and called him "yellow fellow." They rolled in the dead leaves and tried to bury each other. They danced all over the crown of Machine Gun Mountain, their shouts and their laughter fading out into the trees and sky.

The rocky descent on the eastern slope was difficult, and many times the Denizens grasped at niches in the rock, or held on to roots or branches of scrub vegetation that clung to the steep hillside. But soon they came out into a soft forest of spruce trees. As the tall trees grew thicker and thicker, the morning turned back into darkness under a canopy of shadows. Roger had the distinct feeling that no one had been here for a long time.

Once he heard something scurry away. Twice something snorted. The forest seemed alive with things he could not see, and he thought now about the aliens who had been reported here by farmers and schoolteachers. He could not escape from the feeling that something wonderful or terrible was about to happen. He waited for it, looked where the light went, breathed deeply and smelled the green darkness all around him.

In a half hour they came out into a two-hundred-foot-wide clearing that extended as far as he could see from east to west. A narrow rise in the land running the way of the clearing showed where the railroad had once gone, but the tracks went their way for only a few yards before disappearing under a bed of thistles and ivy. The granary sat on the north side, a hundred yards to the east.

"Boy," said Frank, "we could die here and no one would ever actually find us for years."

"That's not what I need to hear," said Dennis.

"All we have to do is climb to the top," said Roger, pointing to the granary.

"No, we don't," said Dennis.

"I been there a zillion times," said Roger. "It's perfectly safe if you're careful."

"I want to go someplace that's perfectly safe even when I'm not careful," said Dennis.

"We came all this way," said Frank. "We hafta do what we said."

The granary was a narrow four-sided building that made Roger think of tombstones and monuments. One patch of the rough concrete facing, yellow now in the morning sunlight, had broken off about halfway up to show the brown, skeletal pattern of metal support rods. A narrow window, the glass long since shattered, showed high up on the south side. Lower down, a thick pipe pointed out over the tracks. Under this, a raised, open doorway where the Denizens managed to climb into the building.

The first room was a large open area with doors leading into smaller rooms, one filled with a jumble of torn wire and fuse boxes and circuit breakers, the other empty. At the center of the large room stood the grain elevator. Walking around it, they saw that it was a line of metal scoops attached to a pulley enclosed on three sides by a wooden shaft that went through the ceiling. On one side, a vertical tunnel with an iron catwalk went all the way to the top.

"This isn't the way I remember it," said Roger.

"How's that?"

"I don't know. I just remember it was—it was different." Perhaps, he thought, it was only that the smell of corn and grain had vanished. Now there was only the vague, acrid odor of dry wood and dust.

"There's a storage pit on the other side of the elevator," said Roger. "Over this way."

They walked past the elevator and through a narrow space into another room, where their boots crunched and slid over dry kernels of corn. As Roger's eyes adjusted to the light he saw an iron grate in the wooden floor. It was attached on one side with iron hinges. He bent over, took the grate in both hands, and lifted with all his strength. Slowly it squeaked open. He gave it a push and it crashed onto the wooden floor, bouncing and making a hollow thud. Beneath them now, a black hole.

"Use your flashlights," said Roger. "There's a ladder on this side."

"I'm not going down there," said Frank. "Not for a million bucks."

"It's just a storage room full of old corn," said Roger. "But it's kind of fun because it's underground."

"Fun because it's underground," said Dennis. "I see."

"Oh, come on," said Roger. He took Frank's flashlight and beamed it down into the hole. It revealed nothing but a ladder leading down into a yellow haze. "Just come on down for a sec. I swear there's not a single thing down there that can hurt you."

"I have allergies," said Frank. "I'm not even supposed to think about places like this."

"I get hives," said Dennis. "I think I'm having an attack."

Gradually they began to see the outlines of the underground room as their eyes adjusted to the dim light. And then, when Dennis turned on a second flashlight, they all saw to their horror that small animals had fallen through the grate. Near one corner, a fine layer of dust covered the skeleton of a squirrel, transforming it into a strange, delicate work of art. In a mound of corn lay the remains of a cat, and near it the dusty and half-covered outline of something else, a larger animal whose identity he could not even guess.

"Sorry, guys," said Roger. "I didn't remember all the dust. And all the dead stuff."

"I hate dead stuff," said Frank. "Dead stuff gives me the willies."

"Let's just go up to the observation room," said Roger. "The ladder is right by the grain elevator."

"What's it like up there?" said Dennis.
"It's terrific. Lots of neat things. Come on, I'll show you."
"Is the ladder safe?"
"Sure. It's a terrific ladder."
"I suppose there's more dead animals up there?"
"Nope. Just pigeons. Live ones."
"Oh, that's just great," said Dennis. "We're going to get attacked by herds of pigeons protecting their eggs. This is the season for all that stuff, you know."

But in spite of all their fears and protests they began to climb the dark shaft, Roger leading the way. The narrowness was at once comforting and uncomfortable. Roger did not like the close walls, but he found that when he tired he could lean back and rest against the elevator.

He climbed one iron rung at a time, feeling the cool, hard metal press into his warm palm and into the arches of his feet. A small alcove filled with chains and coils of rope opened up on his left. He thought of the fun house he had gone through once at a carnival. The narrow corridor, the cloth corpses rising out of coffins, and the rubber bats shrieking against his face. But this was a quiet place, something from long ago. Even the odors were distant, hard to identify through the veil of dust and time. Here and there along the shaft, light fixtures hanging in banded metal cages made him think of bumblebees.

The shaft opened, as Roger promised, into a large room at the top of the granary. A mosaic of shattered glass, bird droppings, dry corn, oak leaves, and metal slugs covered the floor. Crossed beams and an overlay of sheet metal formed a ceiling over the wooden walls. Two smashed windows faced north and south. In the center of the room the enclosed grain elevator made an arch, and in the middle of the arch a roundhouse of metal tubes had been bolted to a circular platform. The tubes, moving out in different directions, sank through the floor to hidden rooms below.

"Jesus," said Dennis. "What a place."

Then from the south window came a wild squawking and

scratching and beating of wings. Creatures flew in the window, raising clouds of dust. They settled in one corner and turned their heads sideways to stare at the Denizens.

"Killer pigeons," said Dennis.

"Oh gosh, let's get outa here quick," said Frank.

"Pigeons can't hurt you," said Roger. "Honest to God, you two guys are the biggest sissies I ever saw. Two pigeons fly in a window and you go into a panic."

"We're cautious," said Dennis. "Caution is supposed to be a sign of intelligence."

"What's all this machinery?" said Frank, his eyes still fixed on the pigeons.

"What we got here is a little piece of American history," said Roger. "Fifty years ago all the farmers brought corn to the granary here and sold it to the railroad guys. But then some of the railroad guys sold some of it to these other guys who made secret whiskey in the woods, which was against the law."

"That was when they had prohibition," said Frank. "They passed the Eighteenth Amendment and then they had it from nineteen twenty to nineteen thirty-three. Gosh, I wish I could forget some of this stuff."

"My uncle says the whole place was full of cops and crooks," said Roger. "He says two guys were trapped right here at the granary with this girl, and when they made a break for it the girl got away with a bullet in her chest and finally fell over dead in the swamp and sank."

"There are millions of stories about the reservation," said Dennis. "You never know how things really happened."

"It's like with the saucers," said Roger. "I mean, they could be anything. It depends on who you listen to and what you want to believe."

"But we're investigators," said Frank. "We got to find out the truth. That's why we came here."

"But the more you think and the more you find out, the more sides there are to things. We're just having fun out here, right?"

"That's what drives me nuts," said Roger. "When you really try to think about things, they get muddy. But if you don't think about anything, then everything is perfectly clear."

"Maybe the problem is that nothing ever really happens in any particular way," said Dennis.

"You guys," said Frank. "Do you always hafta talk like that?"

As Roger listened to the squawk and coo of pigeons in the high room of the defunct granary in the middle of a forest with a meaningless name considering the possibility that nothing could be found out because nothing ever happened in any particular way, he told himself that he was nevertheless an investigator. Frank was right about that. He was supposed to keep his eyes open, try to figure things out. There were certain things that Denizens had to do, and this was one of them.

He went to the broken window and looked out. Frank and Dennis stood behind him and peeked over his shoulders. On the south side of the clearing lay another forest, this one nameless so far as they knew, and beyond it, traces of a wide swampland, still milky and indistinct beneath wisps of morning fog which the sun had not yet burned away.

"The light is funny out there," said Roger.

"You're right," said Frank. "It's sort of alien-looking."

"If there is anything interesting out there," said Dennis, "we're not going to find it by getting all moody and pretending to see things."

"But it does look strange and mysterious," said Frank.

"It's just misty. Sort of Walt Disney-looking. And it's probably very mushy, and we're probably all going to get very wet."

Then the fog lifted a little, and Roger saw a flash of water, a log, a stand of flowering weeds and green branches.

"It's all green," said Frank.

"Springtime in the swamp," said Dennis. "We wouldn't want to miss that, now would we?"

As Roger watched the fog dissipate, he thought of his blindness in the woods just before dawn, and the sounds of the animals moving about in the brush. He thought of the birds whose voices had announced their arrival on the mountain. And then, for no sensible reason, he remembered Pangborn talking about Percival Lowell, the astronomer who had seen canals on Mars where no one else had seen them. *Something is going to happen,* thought Roger. *Something is going to happen when the mist is gone and the seeing is good.*

"What's that?" said Dennis.

"I don't see anything," said Frank.

"Follow my finger. Just past the edge of the trees."

"I still don't see anything."

"Somebody's out there. He's walking along the edge of the swamp. Can't you see? Look. Right there. No, there he ducked into the forest—"

"Are you sure it was a person?" said Roger. "Maybe it was an animal of some kind."

Dennis withdrew his arm from the window. "Maybe."

"What did it look like?"

"Just a dark shape. I couldn't really see anything much except that it was moving."

"I never saw a thing," said Frank.

"Wait. There it is again."

And then, just for an instant, Roger saw what his friend had seen. Something shadowy moving along the edge of the swamp. It stood upright and was too large to be anything but a man, and yet it was clearly not a man in the way it loped forward and moved its head from side to side.

"You're right," said Roger. "There is something down there. Right by the water. Now we *have* to investigate."

Frank and Dennis looked at him. Neither spoke.

"Well," said Roger, "this is what we came for, isn't it? To explore the swamp? To explain the unexplained? To look for mysteries to solve?" It seemed the wrong moment to mention aliens and flying saucers.

In five minutes they had climbed down the shaft and walked out of the granary into the sunlight. They walked across the tracks and into the southern forest of the Watchung Reservation. Roger felt the cool air against his face and the soft layer of pine needles under his boots. How pleasant it would be, he thought, to lie down in the shadows for an hour and sleep.

As they climbed over a small rise, he stopped for a moment to look back at the granary. It was brilliant now in the sunlight—high, narrow, and strange, like a monolith left by aliens. He focused on the window near the top and imagined that he saw himself there. *Just a few seconds ago,* he thought, *there I was and here I was not*. He wondered what the difference was. Without time, he thought, everything would happen all at once just like Mr. Figge said. Funny how everything got separated into moments. Funny how time made ghosts of everything that was not today, now, this instant. This was another trick of time, the second he had discovered that week, and it spoke again for the power of abstract thought that he had come to hate, the power that made him a stranger to everything, the power that made all the pictures of the world divide into parts and drift away from each other. As he turned away from the yellow building with its overgrown roads and tracks that crossed and went nowhere, he struggled to put the meaning of what time did into words, but then, mercifully, the green woods touched him, brushed against him, and the words vanished.

Soon the woods grew thicker and the walking became more difficult. In places the ground turned soft, and he would go ankle-deep into a spongy sink of weeds. The air seemed heavier and more aromatic. Swamp wrens chattered and flew in every direction; their tiny, pointed voices scratched the air, like needles. Then the trees ended in a long curve. They had come to the edge of the first marsh.

"I don't see any boat," said Dennis.

"It's further on," said Roger. "We have to walk around this big curve and then cross over to the swamp on the other side."

The marsh was like a beautiful illness. At the shoreline where they walked, leaves of cattails rose out of the mud like clusters of swords, and further out, the heart-shaped leaves of the arrowhead weed speared the clear surface in threes and fours, each group producing one slender column of flowers rising above the water like threads of white smoke. And still further out, clumps of grassy sedge and the flat, overlapping leaves of the lily made passageways opening into a central patch of clear water. Here a white bird skimmed across the silver-dark surface, leaving a scratch that widened, then disappeared. And in the trees above the Denizens and all along the water's edge, red-winged blackbirds flashed from branch to branch and cried out into the heavy air: *kon-ka-ree kon-ka-ree*.

"Willya look at this place," said Frank.

"A perfect place for aliens," said Roger.

"This is like a Frankie Laine record I once heard," said Dennis.

"Keep a lookout for unexplained phenomena," said Frank.

"What does unexplained phenomena look like?" said Roger.

"It's round," said Dennis. "Unexplained phenomena is always round. Sometimes with funny tubes and flashing lights."

They circled around the western side of the open marsh, their boots sinking into the black ooze, then hiked through a stand of poplar and beech to a dark place where the land sank down to another muddy shoreline. Beyond it, tall trees rose out of the water as far as they could see.

"Is this it?" said Dennis.

"This is it."

"This is even creepier than the marsh," said Frank.

"How far does it go?" said Dennis.

"It ends a few miles north of Horseshoe Valley Road," said Roger.

"Maybe the thing we saw in the woods lives out in the swamp," said Frank.

"I hope not," said Dennis. "I really hope not."

Resting against a nearby tree they found the ancient rowboat Roger had promised them. It was silver with age. On either side, oars had been jammed upright into the mud. A rusted tin can for bailing lay in the stern.

"This thing's not swampworthy," said Dennis.

"Sure it is," said Roger. "All you have to do is pack weeds and a little mud up in the bow. That's where it leaks."

"Weeds and mud? Did you say weeds and mud?"

"It holds for a while. You'd be surprised."

"Did Captain Nemo ever put weeds and mud in the bow of the *Nautilus*? Did Admiral Nimitz ever put weeds and mud in the bow of the *Enterprise*? Do you really expect us to go along with this?" Dennis poked at the hull of the rowboat and shook his head.

"The swamp is only about two feet deep in most places," said Roger. "If worse comes to worst, you'll get your legs wet."

"I hate getting wet," said Dennis. "It's undignified."

The three of them turned the boat over. Following Roger's directions, they lined the bow with broadleaf weeds and fresh mud.

"If this works, it'll be a miracle," said Dennis.

"If you two guys sit in the back, the bow will be out of the water most of the time," said Roger. "Trust me, for God's sake."

Frank and Dennis rowed while Roger sat in the bow, on the lookout for shallows and hidden obstacles. The rowboat glided slowly through the water. Above them and all around them trees rose out of the swamp—cottonwood and river birch and black willow. Slender trees that seemed too long and frail, sometimes leaning a little to one side as if they had not found solid footing in the wet, uneasy earth. Where the earth broke the surface, tufts of giant cut-grass shot out every which way, like witches' brooms. Suddenly on their right, a tracery of black branches lifting out of the water. Near it, a brown log covered with green turtles. This was not like the marsh, he thought. It was darker, and full of unexpected mysteries, like Pangborn's bookstore. A forest of symbols.

The water was an intricate counterpoint of impressions, something so beautiful he had no words for it. At the bottom, a pattern of overlapping leaves, all gold and brown. Green streaks of swamp grass grew up through the leaves, all bending away in the same direction. Against this played the blue-green reflections at the surface and the tiny silhouettes of water spiders skittering and zigzagging, barely touching the water with the tips of their feet.

Time moved slowly. Small noises became loud and resonant. He felt a strange happiness knowing that he was lost in this strange place, alone with the only people he had ever loved besides Pangborn and his mother and father. The word *adventure* came to mind. An adventure, he thought, was something you didn't need to explain to anyone, not even yourself. He smiled a little as the rowboat moved through the labyrinth of trees and water.

He noticed that the buttress of mud and leaves was beginning to give way. Pieces of it floated in the inch of water that covered the bottom of the boat. Almost without thinking, Roger began to bail.

"We're sinking!" said Frank.

"Not yet," said Roger. "We have a little time. Keep rowing."

He knew that he ought to be alarmed at the prospect of sinking, but the swamp did not seem quite real. It was more than real. It was an intention, a presence, an arrangement of meanings that came not in words but in colors and shapes and odors. It was odd, he thought, the way the light came and went.

On his right he saw the remains of an old tree trunk sitting upright, submerged a foot or two below the surface. It was turning slowly in the water, the result, apparently, of some pocket of current coming from a deep spring. The broken roots moved in a circle that made him think of a spider, and then an alien creature, and then the arms of a dead man.

"Look at that!" said Dennis. "Isn't that the craziest thing you ever saw?"

"It almost sort of doesn't even look real," said Frank. "I hate things like that. Things like that ought to stay in books where they belong."

"Everything is strange here," said Roger. "This is—this is not the way I remember it."

"That happens to me all the time," said Dennis. "Maybe it's because nothing really does happen in any particular way, like we said."

"You know this is a perfect place for aliens?" said Frank. "I sort of hate to say it, but it is."

"Just keep rowing and I'll keep bailing," said Roger.

"But one thing is definite," said Dennis. "We're sinking. Roger, am I getting through to you? I said *sinking*. You know, like going to the bottom of the swamp—"

The rowboat eased into a wide stretch of water where openings appeared in the high branches and leaves, so that patches of sunlight touched the surface of the water. Here the swamp was suddenly quiet, as if the slant of light from above had driven everything else into hiding.

Roger bailed, thinking of the stump turning in the water. He glanced ahead, and then back at Dennis and Frank. He bailed again. He knew that Dennis was right—they were sinking. But for the moment that seemed strangely unimportant. An uneasy, restless feeling touched him as he listened to the silence, and then it came to him that he had seen something. He looked up quickly, startled by the realization that he had *seen* and yet not *noticed* whatever it was. Now, all around him, trees and water. Stumps. Clusters of water lilies, bright green against the shimmering surface.

There it was. Something standing waist-deep in the water about forty feet away. He had twice mistaken it for a stump. It was dark and shaggy, like the shadow he had seen in the trees an hour earlier. It had a face. It watched him with wild eyes. All at once Dennis snatched the bailing can away from him and began to scoop water out of the hull and throw it into the air. The boat tipped sharply to one side.

"Did you see that?"

"What?"

"Over there."

"I'm trying to bail," said Dennis. "Don't tip the boat over—"

"Something in the water. It had a face. It's the thing we saw before, whatever it was—"

As they all looked to where Roger pointed, the rowboat turned sideways in the slow current and snagged on a confusion of branches where two trees had fallen across each other in the water. The branches reached out, enfolded the boat, brushed against his shoulders.

"Look out!"

"It's okay. We can push off with the oars—"

"There's too much water in the boat—"

"Roger, I can't swim—"

Then, from somewhere, a series of splashes, as if someone were trying to run through shallow water. "There is something out there!" said Frank. "I can hear it now!"

"Never mind that!" said Dennis. "We're sinking and the water's way over our heads!"

Roger took Frank's paddle and plunged it deep into the water. He could not find the bottom. "Grab the branches!" he said.

"Oh gosh, I'm gonna get wet!" said Frank.

"I knew we never should have come out here!" cried Dennis.

"Just grab the branches!" said Roger.

The rowboat slid sideways as they reached out. Water poured over the side. Roger pushed past the outer branches and got both his arms around the trunk. He sank down to his waist in the cold water as the rowboat disappeared beneath him. Then, thrashing and gasping and grunting, all the Denizens pulled themselves up on the trunk, straddling it, so that their feet trailed in the water on either side.

"I thought that thing was coming toward us," said Frank.

"No," said Roger. "We scared it away. It went underwater."

"What a mess," said Dennis. "What a stinking mess."

"How come the boat sank?" said Roger. "Wood is supposed to float."

"Our camping stuff!" said Frank. "My mother is gonna kill me if I lose her only frypan—"

“We should have known better,” said Dennis. “We just should have known better.”

Roger said nothing. By leaning forward on his hands, he lifted himself up and moved in little hops along the log toward the shore.

“This is called crotch-hopping,” muttered Dennis. “You jump up a little and then bang your crotch on the log. Roger gets a real kick out of it. He thinks maybe we can form a team and enter the Olympics—”

“Shut up!” said Roger. “Just shut up!”

When they reached the shore, they took off their soggy fatigue jackets and boots and squeezed out their socks. As they stood there soaking wet and without their jackets, Roger saw how different they were. Dennis was a tree trunk leaning in the wind. Frank was a yellow pear, his T-shirt clinging to him so that the shadows of nipples showed through. Roger was a stick, a mandrake root, a weed. He had to hold on to keep from being washed away. For a moment he had the feeling that the three of them did not go together.

“There was something out there,” he said, thinking of their mission, thinking that they were still investigators.

“You were the only one who saw it,” said Dennis.

“I sort of almost saw it,” said Frank. “It was the same thing we almost saw from the granary.”

“It was just some hobo taking a bath,” said Dennis. “And he didn’t go underwater. He just splashed his way out of the swamp and ran.”

“What did it look like?” said Frank.

“It didn’t look like a person,” said Roger. “It didn’t look like a person at all. It had this face. I only saw it for a second. Maybe less than a second. Then it went under.”

“Look over there,” said Frank.

He pointed out toward the tree where Roger had seen whatever it was that he had seen. Bubbles were rising in the water. Bubbles from out of the muck at the bottom of the swamp.

“What’s making it do that?” said Frank.

Dennis stared out over the water. He shook his head. "It can't be," he said. "We're just kids. Nothing like this could really happen. We're kids and we sometimes imagine things—"

"There *is* something out there," said Roger. "I know there is."

"But we don't know what. We'll never know. It's too deep to go out there without a good boat."

Two minutes later they saw their rowboat with all their gear floating toward shore, just an inch below the surface.

"I suppose someone should go out there and get all our stuff," said Dennis.

"I'll go," said Roger, trying to sound quietly dignified.

Dennis bent over and tried to squeeze water out of the cuffs of his pants. "Look, I know it's not your fault the boat sank. None of this is really your fault. It's just that—"

Roger was already out in the water. Mud and leaves swirled about his ankles as he reached for the ghostly shape of the rowboat drifting underwater. "It's just that what?" he said, without turning back.

"It's just that I hate to get wet," shouted Dennis. "Getting wet is very, very *rococo*."

It took another hour of hiking for their clothes to dry. At eleven-thirty they cut up apples with a paring knife and fried two cans of Spam over a fire. They talked about what they had seen, what they had not seen, what they had almost seen. Early in the afternoon they came out into a field just south of Horseshoe Valley Road. They were surprised to see rows of cars parked along the berm of the main highway and a police cordon across the road.

"I don't think we're supposed to be here," said Roger. "We better duck down in the grass—"

"Too late," said Frank in a quiet, terrified voice. "They see us."

Three troopers in powder-gray uniforms shouted something in their direction. Then they began running across the field toward them. The first trooper had his pistol drawn.

"Oh my golly gosh," said Frank. "We're really in for it now."

"We haven't done anything," said Roger. "Just remember that. We haven't done one single wrong thing."

The state trooper closest to them slowed to a walk when he got to within twenty feet. He put his pistol back in its black holster, leaving the buckle and flap open. He was a tall, heavyset man with blond hair, dark glasses, and a fair complexion that turned pink at the cheeks.

"What you kids doing down here?" he said in a soft voice.

Roger stared at the starched crease in the man's pants. "Exploring."

"Well, that's nice," said the trooper. "Now suppose you tell me just what you were exploring and where you came from."

"We came down from Greencastle," said Roger, trying to sound both cheerful and matter-of-fact. "Of course, we wanted to avoid the restricted area. We haven't stumbled on it by accident, have we?"

"The whole Watchung Reservation is restricted for three days," said the trooper.

"The announcement in the paper didn't make that clear. It said—"

"Never mind what it said. What it said was just words in the paper. What I'm telling you now is that the whole reservation is off limits. What's your name?"

"Roger Cornell."

Frank raised his hand, as if he were in a classroom. "Roger and Dennis and I are members of this club," he offered. "It's our job—that is, we think it's important to investigate any unexplained mysteries in the area. That's what our club's all about."

The man turned his soft smile on Frank. "Son, I want you to shut up until you're spoken to. Is that clear?"

"Yes, sir."

"You've got no call to talk to him like that," said Roger. "He was just trying to help."

The state trooper raised his eyebrows. He looked down at

Roger and smiled again. "Son, I'm the state police, case you haven't noticed, and I'm telling you that you're living dangerously. Now I'll forget you said what you just said if you all give me your names and tell me one at a time just where you been."

Dennis looked at Roger, and then at Frank. "I'm Dennis Kirk. We were just exploring, like Roger said. We climbed up Machine Gun Mountain and then came down Moonshine Valley to the old granary and then explored the Henrietta Mackelroy Swamp."

"I'm Frank Aldonotti, and he's right about where we went, sir. I'm sorry if I spoke out of turn, sir."

"I should run the three of you into the county detention center for the day," said the trooper. "Let your parents come and pick you up. Teach you all a little lesson. You all knew you weren't supposed to be sneakin' around here, now didn't you?"

The Denizens stood in a narrow file, more or less at attention. It occurred to Roger that it had been a very, very long day. Making it even longer was the state trooper looking down at him with his fixed, predatory smile. The black leather chaps on his pants flared smartly to each side, like wings.

"And just what do you have to say about that?"

"I don't think—I don't think—"

"You don't think what, sonny?"

"I don't think you should try to scare us like this when we haven't done anything wrong," Roger heard himself say. "I don't think the police should ever do that."

The trooper stared at him for another moment, and finally the smile faded. "You two boys, you go on home. And don't let me catch you anywhere near here again. You with the smart mouth, you come with me. I heard of you. Cornell. Yessir, I heard of you several times this month. Been gettin' calls from upset mothers about you, Cornell."

He took Roger by the arm and led him past the blockade and past several dozen onlookers to his police cruiser.

"Don't you want to know what we saw?" said Roger. "We saw some things you'd be very interested in. We thought we could write it all up, and—"

"You didn't see anything," hissed the state trooper. "There's no such thing as flyin' sassers."

24 | Romeo and His Problems

"Can you imagine how we felt when the police called? We had no idea where you were. We got up this morning and you were gone. I didn't know what to think—"

"I meant to leave you a note. I forgot."

With one hand his mother opened the front door of her old Studebaker, and with the other she pushed him in. As she came around the other side, she glanced sharply back at the police station. A moment later she slammed her door and twisted the key in the ignition. The engine sputtered and came to life.

"You have to learn to keep your mouth shut," she said, staring into the traffic.

"That's what everyone tells me."

"You talk too much."

"I know."

"You don't care about anyone else's feelings. You argue about everything. You offend people."

"I'm sorry."

"You're not even slightly sorry."

He turned his head just enough to look at his mother without seeming to. "You should have heard those policemen," he said. "They came on like the SS. They enjoyed every minute of it. That one guy was especially awful."

"Someday you're going to get into terrible trouble. You're going to shoot your mouth off to the governor of New Jersey or some Newark gangster or Joe McCarthy. You're going to forget where you are and who you are and you're going to get killed or beaten up or thrown in prison for twenty years. You have to remember this is 1952. People don't say what they think. People who say what they think wind up in front of the Un-American Activities Committee."

"I hope you know we didn't do one damn thing. All we did was come out of the woods and blink. And I didn't say anything until this big guy with the pink face tried to scare Frank."

"I can just imagine."

"All they had to say was, 'Hey, could you kids go somewhere else? We're conducting a search here.' But no, they have to wave their guns around and stick their chests out and act like Junior G-Men. Big stuff."

His mother pulled the car to the side of the road and braked so suddenly that he fell off his seat. She stared at a fire hydrant. "There's just nothing I can say, is there?" she nearly shouted. "There's just absolutely nothing I can say to convince you to show a little respect, to be just a little political once in a while."

"Mom, you'll get a ticket if you stop here."

"Roger, you can't talk to the police the way you did."

"I hate the police. I hate teachers. I hate politicians and ministers and nuns and doctors. I hate J. Edgar Hoover."

"Roger—"

He could see that she was trying hard to stay mad. Without knowing why, he loved her for it. "Don't smile, Mom. Your face will crack open."

"Damn you."

"Mom, I'm really sorry. I know I make a mess of everything."

"You don't make a mess of everything. You're a good boy.

You have good friends and you have wonderful ideas rattling around in that weird head of yours. I wish I had half your brains. I just don't want you to throw it all away—"

"You're right. I'm sorry."

"Don't tell me I'm right and that you're sorry. That does no good at all."

"Okay. I'm not sorry. You're not right."

Now she did smile. "This isn't getting us anywhere, is it?"

"I guess not. But still it's kind of nice—I mean, it's—"

"What?"

"I sort of like it when you worry about me."

"Well, I'm your mommy, aren't I? I'm supposed to do that."

"My mommy," he said, squeezing her arm. "My beautiful mommybuckets."

"Mommybuckets," she said. "You haven't called me that in five years."

"Mommybuckets, mommybuckets, mommybuckets," he said. "Mommybuckets."

She rubbed her hand over her forehead and closed her eyes. "Lord," she said. "Sometimes I think I should have been a nun."

When he came down for breakfast Monday morning, he saw his mother drinking coffee and mashing a cigarette into a saucer. She was also reading the *Greencastle Herald*.

"Where's Dad?" he asked.

"He's sleeping in, thank God. I'm afraid you're going to have to read this. And I'm afraid you're going to have to prepare yourself for whatever happens at school today."

"What is it?"

"Your little escapade with Frank and Dennis got into the paper this morning."

He could feel himself turning red. He sat down. "Anything for breakfast?"

"I haven't even thought about breakfast. I've been sitting here smoking and drinking coffee and worrying."

His mother handed him the paper. "I'm going upstairs to wake your father. It might be a good idea if you were gone by the time he gets down."

Without another word she left the room. He stared after her for a moment. Then he fixed himself a large bowl of Cheerios and began to read:

> Police investigations of the Watchung Reservation east of Greencastle have so far revealed no evidence of any unusual activities or presences. Since the recent local reports of saucers and "green men," the reservation has been the subject of intensive investigations by state as well as local officials. Police chief John Hasmer told our reporter last night that nothing has turned up during the two-day search, although the number of reports about strange phenomena in the area have increased dramatically in the last 48 hours.
>
> He added that three Greencastle High School youths, all members of a club devoted to "Lovecraft" and other occult practices, were picked up in the area early Saturday afternoon. Sergeant Sidney Barris, the state trooper who apprehended them, suggested that they may be behind a series of "practical jokes" in the Watchung area. Two of the club members were released, but the third, Roger Cornell, was taken down to police headquarters and later released into his mother's custody. Barris indicated that he would make a full report to the juvenile authorities and to local police if any solid evidence showed that teenagers were involved in "weird or subversive practices" or "practical jokes at the expense of the populace."

He threw the newspaper across the room and then dumped his breakfast in the sink. He picked up his books, went out into the foyer, and crashed against the new screen door, which flew open and clattered against the wooden siding of the house. He ran all the way to school, feeling the hunger building in his stomach, the ache growing in his calves, the pain spreading through his chest. Twice he looked back and saw Dennis and Frank behind him. They waved and called out to him. *God-*

damnit, he thought, *why weren't their names in the paper too?*

As he entered the school's main hallway, he heard gasps, whispers, quiet bursts of laughter. At the end of the hall he saw Curtiss Baylor and Eddie McQueen smiling at him. *God,* he thought, *this is going to be the worst day of my life.*

In Latin class that morning, Miss Simic's flat, gibbonlike face twice fixed its attention upon him. He felt reduced, somehow inhuman. He had dreamed once that her steady gaze could turn teenagers into anthills.

Mrs. Leibolt sat behind her desk at the beginning of English class, furiously correcting one paper after another. She looked, he thought, a little *too* busy. When the bell rang she glanced up, saw that everyone was seated, lifted her chin a little, and brushed back her hair with her right hand. He saw that she did not look quite right today. One of her long lashes was askew, and there was a gray smudge on her cheek—an imperfection in the thick, creamy blur of makeup she always wore.

She began her lesson by summarizing the third and part of the fourth act of *Romeo and Juliet*. Roger, who had given up on all homework except for the fifteen-minute Latin translations he did in the morning during Flag & Bible, had not read the play. Still, he had a fair idea of what was going on from her daily summaries, from class discussion, and from his quick skimming of the text during class. She was asking now about how Friar Laurence intended to unite the lovers, and what had gone wrong with his plans. The answers from the class were sporadic and uncertain, but she wove them together into a coherent pattern, adding a word or phrase here, coaxing out an additional, reluctant insight there. All year he had admired this quality in Mrs. Leibolt—her ability to tolerate nonsense, her knack for getting people to talk even when they had nothing to say.

Harriet Emerick was saying now that Juliet's family was *just out of the question*. Larry Norcross nodded and said that went for the whole play. Everything was based on coincidence and everybody talked too much. "No one," he said, "ever had that much to say the morning after his wedding night." Five or six members of the class laughed at this in a sort of quiet, strangled way. The others sat in shocked silence. Mrs. Leibolt raised her eyebrows, smiled, and then explained something that Roger did not understand about the conventions of love and rhetoric.

It occurred to him that no one in class was really interested in *Romeo and Juliet*, that the play was just something to jump off from, something that let his classmates express their opinions on related matters. But Roger was not sure now about his own attitude regarding Shakespeare. Officially he was still a hater of Great Literature. The superiority of Henry Kuttner, Edmund Hamilton, Clark Ashton Smith, and H. P. Lovecraft over Shakespeare was abundantly evident. But he was having his doubts about *Romeo and Juliet*. There must be something good, he thought, about a play that the rest of the class thought was silly. He did like certain parts of it. The dueling scene and the graveyard humor of Mercutio were appealing. Something about the idea of a counterfeit death was fascinating. And in some places the language was—what? *Beautiful* was the only word that came to mind. Lovecraft was infinitely more frightening and more powerful, but Shakespeare was sometimes beautiful. He knew that Lovecraft did not express very much that had to do with beauty or love, and that perhaps even the great HPL had his limitations. He thought for a moment about the murder of Paris and the double suicide—it all seemed so desperate and so unnecessary. If only the plague had not come, and if only Friar John had delivered the note. But still, all the bigwigs with all their money and power who thought about nothing except proper marriages, prestige, and hating people who had the wrong name, they all got what they deserved. *See what a scourge is laid upon your hate, that heaven finds means to kill your joys with love*. Damn right.

All at once he realized that he had lost track. He looked up at the teacher and then at his classmates. They were all talking about something. No one seemed to have noticed his absence. Then, from across the room, he saw Ruth looking at him. "Hello, Roger," she said with her lips. It was almost supernatural, he thought, the way she could look so pleased and happy without actually smiling.

As Roger ran his fingernails over seven years of knife and pencil markings on his desk, the discussion again went on without him. Buck Moore opined that too much of the play was based on luck. Marilyn Sord said that she was sure that the play was very *deep*, but that she had never understood *ancient literature* because people talked so differently back then. "It's just me, I guess—the way I feel," she said with a beautiful smile. Mary John Grodner turned the pages of the play and frowned at all the words. Curtiss Baylor listened to everyone else and then finally raised his hand to say that he thought the play could be interpreted as a satire.

Mrs. Leibolt smiled and then tried, toward the end of the period, to explain that the task before them was not to evaluate the play but to understand it.

"For example," she said, "what happens at the end of the play? What about the *import* of the *denouement?*"

A gray silence settled over the classroom. Mrs. Leibolt smiled her quick smile and glanced from one student's face to the next. "More specifically, what about the final exchanges between Montague and Capulet and the Prince? Roger? We haven't heard from you today—"

A chorus of groans and whistles, a titter of laughter. Roger did not look up, but he could feel the class all around him, and out of the corner of his eye he saw the edge of the morning paper pressed under Harriet Emerick's social studies notebook. And he could feel Mrs. Leibolt's eyes. He knew she was hoping now that he would save her from the failure of having to explain what everything meant, and he knew, too, that calling on him was a last resort. He tried to keep his face stiff and noncommittal. Moments passed, and he saw that someone had written the words SNEAKY PETE in the lower left-hand corner of his desk. He smiled.

"Roger?"

"No comment."

"You don't understand what happens at the end of the play?"

"Not too well. It seems awful silly in some places, and I know it's not supposed to be. But I sort of like the way the families get just what they deserve for being so nasty to each other. And I sort of sympathized with Romeo and Juliet. I mean, they didn't want to start wars or punish anyone or collect taxes or win arguments or get famous. They just wanted people to leave them alone. That's really not so unreasonable, is it?"

Now he did look up at the rest of the class. Everyone was listening, and he decided, on an impulse, to go on to another point: "But it's hard to figure out if Shakespeare wants us to think Romeo and Juliet are okay and the rest of the world is crazy, or if he wants us to think that they're crazy and should have stayed home in the first place."

"Shakespeare doesn't want us to think anything," said Buck Moore. "He's dead."

"That's not a serious point," said Mrs. Leibolt. "That's merely an interruption—"

"But Roger is serious, isn't he, Mrs. Leibolt?" said Larry Norcross, who could contain himself no longer. "Roger is always serious. I guess that's because he's in his mommy's custody—"

"You don't understand what it means to be serious," said Roger. "You're not serious about anything except your muscles and your curly hair and all the girls that hang on you all day long—"

Larry flushed. "I don't think you know too much about girls," he said. "You and your little club of fairies. You and that guy from the bookstore and your buddies meet almost every day and you do that Lovecraft stuff, just like it said in the paper. The whole school knows about it—"

"I can't believe my ears," said Mrs. Leibolt in a sudden, quiet voice. "You have both forgotten where you are. This kind of talk is an insult to Shakespeare and an insult to the class. I want you both—"

"Then tell him to shut up!" said Roger. "You tell that—that smirky idiot that he doesn't understand anything. I'm not—I'm not—"

But he could not say it, could not explain to the whole class that he was not a homosexual, had never been a homosexual, did not plan on becoming a homosexual. A murmur rolled through the class and then, suddenly, everyone was talking.

Mrs. Leibolt stood in front of the class with her hands on her hips. "You will all be quiet," she said. She spoke very distinctly, but she did not shout. "You are supposed to be talking about Shakespeare. Instead, you are destroying Shakespeare."

"How can we do anything right with people like that in class?" said Eddie McQueen, pointing to Roger.

"Don't you know about all the trouble he's caused?" said Harriet Emerick. "Didn't you read the paper this morning?"

"Not another word from anyone," said Mrs. Leibolt. "Not one word. I am giving this class an extra assignment. You will all write a five-hundred-word paper entitled 'Romeo and His Problems.' It's due at the beginning of class tomorrow, and pity the student who does not have his or her paper ready. You may begin now. This instant. Roger, I want to see you in the hallway."

Roger left his seat with a display of infinite weariness, and walked out into the hallway. Mrs. Leibolt followed him, closing the door very carefully behind her.

"Now, Roger," she began in a curious rasping voice that Dennis had once called "Leibolt's hallway whisper," "you can see what a negative effect you have on my class. I don't know what you've done or haven't done, but there's just too much talk about you."

"Mrs. Leibolt, it's not my fault when Larry Norcross—"

"Shush. I'm trying to explain something important to you. I'm trying to explain that instead of paying attention to Shakespeare, people are staring at you and whispering. I don't suppose you're aware of that—you spend most of your time looking at your desk—but you are a very disruptive influence. Now don't misunderstand. I'm not blaming you for everything. I know the boys bait you. I know they can be very cruel about little things. But you must understand that there is something about you that inspires disorder and anger in others. I think you have to admit that I've tried my best to be patient and to stand on your side whenever possible. But you are going to have to modify your behavior. You are going to have to stop antagonizing people."

"I haven't done anything," said Roger. "I told the police—"

"I'm not the police, Roger. I'm your teacher, and I'm trying to help you. And I think the most helpful thing I can do for you at this point is to insist that you keep silent in my class for the rest of the school year."

"You called on me. No one else had anything to say, and—"

"That was my mistake. I won't make that mistake again."

She gave him a benevolent smile and leaned forward a little and pressed her forefinger into the V where her bright green dress came together above her breasts. There was something in what she had done that deeply confused him. He looked down at his shoes and tried to think. "You're like all the others," he heard himself say. "I thought—I thought you were different, but you're like all the others."

"Go back to your seat, Roger. And don't forget that Dr. Mace wants to see you sixth period."

"He does? Nobody told me that."

"You didn't get a note?"

"No."

"It probably never got delivered. Things have been a bit confused this morning. I had a long talk about you with Dr. Mace during homeroom, and he said he would send a note. But I understand he's had about six telephone calls and about three visitors since then concerning the article in the paper. He's quite upset."

"Did you know we didn't do one single thing? We just had a breakfast cookout and hiked and rowed across the swamp."

Mrs. Leibolt turned away from him and opened the door to her classroom. "Don't forget," she said. "Sixth period."

25 | Roger's Exeunt and Adieu

Roger floated through the rest of the morning. Mr. Figge talked about the *aftermath* of the First World War. Nothing he said seemed to make much sense, which was not unusual, but Roger was fond of the word *aftermath*. He remembered that in second grade he had assumed that it meant a quiet time after you finished doing your arithmetic.

After Physics he made his way to the principal's office. An older woman with gray hair pulled into a bun, wrinkled cheeks, and a very trim figure stood behind the counter. He had never spoken to her, but he knew her name was Miss Mozart. Briefly he wondered how much of her figure—her flat stomach, her narrow waist, and her pointy breasts—was real.

"Dr. Mace wants to see me, ma'am."

The woman nodded. "What's your name?"

"Roger Cornell."

"Oh yes. He'll be with you in a minute. Just sit down."

The other secretary was much younger, but her hair was also gray. Their faces were blank and impassive as they moved about in the large outer office of desks and filing cabinets. One straightened papers on a desk and then sharpened pencils. The other opened a file and ran her thumb down the row of tabs. They seemed to do these things without thinking, without knowing where they were. As if their thoughts were elsewhere. Librarians were like that, he thought. Librarians were cool and distant, always thinking about something else. He imagined dozens and dozens of librarians and secretaries walking around on a plateau above an endless desert, surveying the sands with a kind of passive immunity as they carried things from one place to another and typed up book lists and attendance sheets. *All the same to them the rising sun and all the same the close of day.* Like nuns. That was a poem he could not remember, written by some man with bad lungs who loved a Polish teenager.

Mrs. Leibolt was also very cool and calm, but it occurred to him that she was not at all like a secretary or a librarian or a nun. Something glittered behind her eyes. Some terrible need, perhaps, that she had never expressed or satisfied. He remembered that he had liked her very much in October even though she used big words and loved poetry. She had taken an interest in him and encouraged him to read and think. But gradually some change had taken place, as it had years earlier with his father. By January she was only tolerating him, doing her duty. He had gone too far. He had talked too much. He tried now to think just when the change began. Was it the time he talked about hating Great Literature? Or was it the time he came to class with his face all purple and lumpy after his epic battle with Larry Norcross? As he thought about it, he began to feel obscurely guilty, as if he had unwittingly destroyed something that Mrs. Leibolt had been trying to build. Something perfect and clear. Something where all the parts fit together. Something with bilateral symmetry. Some shining and impossible thing that was slowly breaking her heart.

"Dr. Mace will see you now, Roger."

Miss Mozart opened the half door at the end of the counter, and then she opened the door to the inner office. Roger was taken aback when he saw Dr. Mace standing there. He had expected him to be sitting at his desk in the far corner, shuffling through reports, not acknowledging his presence for a minute or two, then finally looking up and saying, "Roger Cornell, I presume," or some such thing. But here he was standing in front of him like a tree. He was a tall, hawk-faced man with a narrow chin, a long nose, and a crewcut. He wore a blue suit and a black tie.

"Come in, Roger."

He extended a white hand and Roger took it and felt the sinews and bones close to the surface pressing into his own palm. A firm handshake, but not painful. It was a wiry hand, he thought. *Dr. William R. Mace is very tall and very wiry.*

"Why don't you sit over here in front of the desk," he said.

Roger had never spoken to the principal before, and he was not sure he had ever heard him speak except formally at assembly on Friday. At assembly his voice was piercing over the loudspeaker, like a bird of prey. But here in his office he seemed quiet and relaxed, and his voice was soft and reassuring.

Roger sat down in one chair that formed part of a semicircle of chairs in front of the principal's large, square desk. Gleaming in its polished wooden splendor, the desk was perfectly clear save for a long black pen stuck in a black inkwell, and a single sheet of paper perfectly centered on a green blotter.

"Now then," he said. "We seem to have a little problem here, don't we?"

"Yes, sir."

"Why don't you tell me about it."

Dr. William R. Mace leaned forward and rested very lightly on his elbows. He made a little pyramid in front of his face with his hands, and smiled. For a moment Roger imagined that he had been a basketball player in college. Light on his feet. Lean and fingertip quick. Dangerous, tall, and in control, like a Negro.

"Well, sir, it's all a mistake as far as I can see. You see, we have this club—"

"Let me interrupt you for just a moment if I may," said the principal, smiling. "I should tell you that there's no point in telling me the whole story. I have a number of reports on what's been happening and I daresay I have followed your activities quite closely, as have Mr. Figge and Mrs. Leibolt. What I need from you is any further thoughts you may have. How do you feel about what's happened? What do you think we can do to alleviate the situation? Further thoughts, that's what I had in mind. They tell me you're a very bright boy. I assume you do have some further thoughts?"

"Further thoughts," said Roger.

"Yes."

"Well, I don't know, sir. Right now I can't think how all this got started or just what I can do about it. I don't—"

The triangle that Dr. Mace had made with his hands collapsed. He looked into Roger's eyes and nodded his head. For a moment Roger suspected that perhaps the principal cared about what he was saying, that there was something more to him than quickness.

"I don't want everyone to hate me," said Roger.

The principal raised his eyebrows. "Well, my goodness, of course you don't. You're a good boy and you don't want to cause trouble. You don't want to be hated. You're very sorry all this ever happened."

"Well, yes. But I really—that is, I still don't know what I did that was so awful. What's all the fuss about? My mother says I talk too much, but that can't be everything. I can't figure it out. Mr. Pangborn—he's the man who owns the bookstore down on Avondale—he thinks there's a monster with no head that lives everywhere and causes all these problems. I mean, that's the expression he uses."

"We've heard quite a bit about Mr. Pangborn in recent weeks," said Dr. Mace. "I gather that he has—how shall I put it?—a very active sense of the humorous and the imaginative."

"That's true. He has a way of putting things."

"Well, perhaps these reports from your teachers will be a bit more helpful than Mr. Pangborn's imagination. Of course, they are just routine. When we have problems with students in this school, I ask the teachers to make out these informal reports. Nothing for the permanent record, you understand. Unless, well, unless the problem becomes really serious."

Dr. Mace looked up and down the sheet of paper in front of him and then cleared his throat. Then he placed his hands flat on the desk and looked up. "I'm going to tell you what they all say about you. I'm not going to read you their exact words; I'm going to give you my impression of their impression. You understand?"

"Yes, sir."

"Briefly then. Miss Wakowski seems to have no opinion at all. You seem to have made very little impression on her one way or the other. She says you're rather quiet. Mr. Figge says you smirk at him and that you have a sly way of suggesting that you are superior to everyone, including the teacher. Mrs. Leibolt indicates that you have the ability to do the work, but that you have no discipline, no common sense, and she further states that you are disruptive and a bit egomaniacal. That is, you are concerned only with yourself, not with others. She adds that you have stopped doing your homework and that your grade average is suffering because of this. Miss Simic—and this, I think you will agree, is surprising—Miss Simic says you are an ideal student."

"Miss Simic said that?"

"Yes."

"I wonder, Roger, if you can explain why different people have such different opinions of you."

"No, I don't think I can do that. I—"

"You seem to change into a different person when you move from one classroom to another."

"Teachers are different," he ventured.

"I daresay. And what do you think of Miss Simic's opinion? I don't imagine you were even aware that she held you in such high esteem."

"No, sir, I wasn't."

"Miss Simic is a hard taskmaster, isn't she? No nonsense in her class, is there? Everything kept on the straight and narrow. No sympathy, lots of hard work, no excuses accepted, never a smile, and very little praise for good work. Am I right?"

"Yes, sir. I guess so, sir."

"And yet she says that you are an ideal student. Here in your hour of need she stands up for you. You can't explain that, can you?"

"No, sir."

"Let me offer you a small insight into human nature. People are not what they seem. If you are concerned only with yourself, only with your own accomplishments and needs and problems, you never know that. Miss Simic has worked very hard for you all year long, and you have never given her a thought, have you?"

"No, sir. Not really."

"Well, it's clear that she has given you a thought. More than just a thought. Miss Simic is a Latin teacher. That is her life. And she has given you her life."

The principal's words rang in his head, like cathedral bells. Tears came to his eyes. *Miss Simic had given him her life.*

"I didn't know—"

"Let me go on for just a moment. She has done for you what you so far have been incapable of doing. She gives of herself. She sees herself as part of the community which is this high school. She works for the greater good. Do you understand?"

"Yes, sir."

He could feel the tears running down his cheeks. It seemed to him now that he had brought everything down upon himself. It was all pride, the tragic flaw, just like in Shakespeare. While Miss Simic had been busy giving him her life, he had been busy defending and attacking various things. She was a teacher, and he was a warrior like Harry Fisher, who hated school and had no friends, except for Nunnug and the perhaps imaginary Ennis.

Dr. William R. Mace opened his left-hand desk drawer and pulled out another single sheet of paper, which he placed squarely on top of the first. He leaned forward and raised his eyebrows and nodded his head a little as he read. "I suppose there are some specific questions here," he said after a moment. "There is the question of your relationship to this Pangborn fellow who runs the used book store. There is the question of your club and its activities. There is the question of your fistfighting on school grounds and your disruptive classroom activities. And finally, there is the question of your trouble with the police and their suspicions that you are in some way connected to this flying saucer hoax."

Roger blinked. "The question of all these things? What do you mean, the question of all these things?"

Dr. Mace looked up sharply. "Surely you see that these are all questions. That is, they involve questions about your behavior and your character."

"Dr. Mace, I can see that I haven't been very sensitive to the feelings of other people. I guess I'm not a very sensitive person. I guess I say things I shouldn't. But beg pardon, sir, there are a lot of other questions. It sort of depends on which questions you ask, it seems to me."

"How do you mean?"

"Well, there's the question about the police dragging me into the station when they knew I hadn't done anything. There's the question about Larry Norcross beating my face to a pulp. There's the question of all the ministers and old ladies and nervous nuns in this town who gossip about things they don't understand."

"Roger, you're the one being examined here."

"I understand that. And I really am sorry about not appreciating Miss Simic and about being insensitive. But there are all these other things. Things that people do that I'm just not responsible for."

"Everybody else is to blame. Is that it?"

"Dr. Mace, that's not what I said."

The principal smiled. "Roger, I can tell you're a good person. You were not unmoved by our little discussion about Miss Simic. I could see that. Now listen to me. I'm going to tell you a secret. It is not the really evil people in this world who do the most damage. Hitler, by himself, could have accomplished very little. It's all the rash idealists, the romanticists, the prideful and emotional people, all full of their own dreams—the ones who jump in headfirst before they stop to think where they are going and where they are leading others. Perhaps without realizing it, your immaturity and poor judgment have helped to create the conditions that any public official fears most."

Dr. Mace leaned back in his chair and looked past Roger to the painting on the wall behind him. "Roger, I think it's important for you to know that we are very close to mass hysteria here in Greencastle. The police department and Parents for Better Schools and the Christian Alliance and numerous individuals are beginning to see some sort of conspiracy. Three mothers called me this morning to explain that there was a plot to destroy America working through the high schools. They went on to mention a club of high school students devoted to a form of devil worship called 'Lovecraft.' They said the club is inspired by the owner of a used book store that specializes in alien religions and pornographic magazines sold under the counter. They also talked about outside influences—Communists who come in flying saucers armed with guns and subversive literature who meet the Lovecraft people and other students in a forest outside town. One lady insisted that this is happening all over America and that Senator McCarthy is the only man in the country who understands the grave dangers that threaten us all. Roger, do you see what we're up against?"

"Yes, but it's all so crazy. Everybody's going crazy—"

Dr. Mace smiled.

"Well—what do you think I should do?"

The principal took a deep breath and then exhaled. He pressed his open hands flat against his desk. "I don't know what goes on at your club, but I would disband it. I don't know what goes on, if anything, at Mr. Pangborn's bookstore, but I would stay away. Permanently. I don't know who starts the fights on the playground, but I would stay off the playground for the rest of the year. And I would be very quiet in all my classes. Keep a low profile until all this blows over."

"That's a lot to ask, sir."

"The alternative is suspension. Possibly expulsion."

Roger stared at the principal's hands, which had been in constant motion since the beginning of the interview. Now he interlaced them and wiggled his fingers up and down. *Open the church and there's all the people.* All the dirty, nasty little wigglers who go to church every Sunday and gossip the rest of the week.

He tried to think what his life would be like without talking to anyone, without Pangborn, without his Denizen meetings on Wednesday nights. It was clear to him that too many things had already been lost. Miss Dot, with her sunlamp tan and her beautiful manners and her reputation to maintain, had told him that he could not dance with any girls for the rest of the year. Mrs. Leibolt did not want him to dance with words. And now, because people would not leave him alone, he was supposed to drift away from everybody and everything. Like Romeo, he was supposed to leave Verona and go to God knows where.

"Expulsion," he repeated. He could think of nothing else to say. "Expulsion."

"Now, now," said Dr. Mace. "There is no reason why we need to resort to such an extreme measure. We're on your side, Roger. We'll help you any way we can if you'll just give us a chance."

Dr. Mace stood up and smiled at Roger and rested all ten of his fingertips on the bright surface of his desk. Roger, taking this as a sign, began backing toward the door. He did not want to turn; he did not want to let Dr. Mace out of his sight as he retreated. A strategic retreat, as Harry would have said. Always keep your eyes on the enemy.

"Thank you, Dr. Mace."

"You're welcome, Roger. I'm sure things will work out. I am so glad we had this chance to chat."

"You've made it all so simple. I just need to find some way to kill myself without making too much of a mess."

"How's that?"

"You want me to kill myself. You want me to kill everything that matters. That's it, isn't it? You want death. You want everything to be quiet. You want Romeo and Juliet to take poison. You want to burn down the whole city to make it safe for dead people."

"Roger—"

Roger backed into the door. He reached behind him and turned the brass knob. Like Romeo, he would make his exit. Exeunt? He couldn't think which was correct.

"Goodbye, Dr. Mace. Dr. William R. Mace, I make my exeunt. I bid you adieu."

26 | Wonderful Things

A wake of whispers followed him down the hallways where he walked. People watched him, talked about him with their hands held obliquely in front of their mouths.

Every morning that week, strangers wandered about the hallways of Greencastle High School, or stood in the main office smoking cigarettes and staring at the floor. He recognized Mrs. Daniel S. Treet from her picture in the paper. She was a tall, gaunt woman with a long nose. Dressed in a plumed hat and a brown jacket with padded shoulders, she made him think of an enormous vulture. He recognized Reverend Hairston Wilcox from the Friday assembly program he gave on cigarettes and alcohol when Roger was a freshman. He was a short, rounded man of about fifty with a mound of curly white hair so crisp and brilliant that it looked unreal, like cotton candy. Twice he saw the chief of police out of uniform, talking with students.

In the afternoons there were usually notes Scotch-taped to the door of his locker. On Thursday:

> Please vacate your locker. Only human beings are allowed to have lockers.

On Friday:

Dear Weaselface—please go to the playground immediately. We just finished reloading.

On the following Monday:

Why are the police, the teachers, the churches, the American Legion, and the kids at school all against you? Have you considered the possibility that something might be wrong with you? Please answer in the space provided.

Roger answered in the space provided:

What is wrong with me is that I mind my own business, I read too much, and I try to answer people when they ask stupid questions. For these wrongdoings it has been decided that my throat will be torn out with a red-hot grappling hook next Wednesday at high noon on the playground. Won't you please come and cheer?

Your friend,
Roger

Roger spent nearly a half hour composing his note. He was especially pleased with the image of the grappling hook, but there was no evidence in the days that followed that anyone read what he had written in the space provided.

The Denizens canceled their Wednesday-night meeting. Frank had a cold, and Dennis called at the last minute to say that his parents were taking him out to dinner and would not be back until after ten. Still, he saw his friends every day on the way to school. They talked about the coming of summer, the new digest-sized magazines, and the possible demise of *Amazing Stories*. *Weird Tales*, they knew, had died several years earlier. *Unknown Worlds* and *Stirring Science Stories* were ancient history.

"Maybe in three more years there won't be any pulps," said Frank.

"Maybe all we'll have is *Reader's Digest*," said Roger.

"Maybe we'll spend the rest of our lives reading about little old men who always win at bingo and are kind to baby chickens and are the most unforgettable character someone ever met," said Dennis.

"It's pretty depressing," said Frank.

"It's not terrific, that's for sure," said Roger.

For Roger, everything was depressing, though he tried to keep up a brave front. At home he sat in front of the phonograph every afternoon. He lay in the dark every evening listening to his radio. In the mornings before school he stared at himself in the bathroom mirror, wondering why the person in front of him had no energy for anything except abusing himself and growing pimples. He felt useless, abandoned, and vaguely guilty about a dozen things that did not really seem to be his fault. *When you grow older you will see that everything is your fault*, he told himself. *That's maturity*.

He found that he could not concentrate well enough to read more than three or four minutes at a time. Instead he listened on his radio to the ramblings of Galen Drake and let his mind drift. How quickly he had run through the previous summer in his white socks and tennis shoes. Each day was a green whisper, a fantasy of impressions and possibilities. Then he thought of the sudden freedom of Christmas vacation. His black rubber boots clicking through the snow. Watching the vague white world through Pangborn's steamy window. Most of all, he thought about the expedition. The taste of eggs and sausages on a mountaintop. The secret histories of the granary. Boating through the swamp, and the face of the creature, the alien that he, like Percival Lowell, had either seen or not seen in that flash of an instant. Had any adventure ever been as wonderful? Had anyone ever had better friends? Had anything ever turned out so badly?

The next Monday Ruth was absent from school. On an impulse, he called her that evening and was told by an angry male voice that she could not come to the phone, and he better not call again. In the background he heard someone crying. He told himself that the person who was crying could have been anyone—Ruth's mother, an aunt or grandmother, anyone at all. He had never heard Ruth cry, and had no idea what her crying would be likely to sound like.

If Ruth wanted to cry, he thought, that was her business. He had always tried to be nice to her. He had taken her to the Papermill Playhouse, hadn't he? He always danced with her at dancing class. Was it his fault that she was unhappy? It made him angry to think that the answer to this question was probably yes. *It's not my fault that it's my fault,* he thought.

"I have to be myself," he told Ythn as they lay in bed together that night. "I can't just be some other person that's going to make everyone happy."

"Perhaps you could be yourself without trying quite so hard," said Ythn.

"You have something to say about everything, don't you?"

"Metallurgy, engineering, and popular culture are my weak areas," said Ythn. "Now go to sleep."

"I can't. I slept all afternoon."

"Not to worry. Here, let me touch."

He touched Roger's temples and ears and eyes, and a web of dreams stretched, like spun glass, between Ythn's many fingers.

On Tuesday, Sonny Vacca, Stan (the Man) Pignatari, and Freddy Cucinelli followed him all the way home, and painted a black X on the sidewalk in front of his house. That evening Frank called to tell him in a trembling whisper that someone had smashed in the front window of Pangborn's store and sprayed red paint all over the display area. On Wednesday morning three members of the basketball team whose names he did not know caught him in the hallway to tell him that because of all the trouble he had caused there had been a gym locker inspection that had turned up several embarrassing items that had very nearly resulted in a three-day suspension from team practice.

"You," said the tall blond boy who held him against the

wall, "are now one of the untouchables. We better not see you downtown or at Roosevelt Field or in the locker room. We mean it, snotface. You're a dead man if we see you *anywhere.*"

On his way home from school he saw that the three Italian boys were following him again. They walked slightly hunched over with their hands in their pockets and their black hair combed back on both sides and shining in the sunlight. Sonny Vacca, the largest of the three, waved to him. His malicious smile was marred by a gray tooth and a chocolate drool that had dried in the corner of his mouth.

"Hey, chicky," he cried out. "Chicky-chicky-chicky—"

"Somebody's gonna beat the shit outa you someday."

"And somebody's gonna teach your Jew bastard friend a few lessons. Maybe push out a few more windows and smash his face in a little."

"Hey chicky, you hear us? Chicky is pretending he don't hear us. Chicky is homo. Homos don't hear too good."

Roger turned to confront them. He saw they were still thirty feet away. In his hatred, he decided to risk his life on those thirty feet and his long legs and the fact that these greasers were out of their territory.

"Three guys against one!" he shouted. "That's typical, isn't it? It sure is easy to see why all you Italian bastards fought with Hitler. Hitler and Mussolini, that just about says it for you guys, doesn't it?"

Roger turned and ran. At first it seemed they would reach him, but soon he found his stride, and by the time he passed Recognition Street at the four corners he had left them far behind.

"You better run, you—"

"Get you for this, you motherf—"

"Smash your face—"

As he came to the bottom of Stone Hill Road, he smiled for the first time in three days. How easily the Italians were defeated, he thought, by a little knowledge of history.

That evening there were several telephone calls which his

mother would not tell him about, and further developments reported in the *Greencastle Herald* by someone named Truman Greenwood. He had an instinctive feeling that anyone with a name like that was sure to make a mess of things.

According to Mrs. Daniel S. Treet, president of Parents for Better Schools, there have been some disturbing additions to the Greencastle Public Library in recent months. In her view this is part of a general pattern that has been developing in this area of the country. "The future of our country depends on the kind of structure our children are getting in various educational areas," she told this reporter in a special interview. "And there may also be foreign developments at work in our community that are simply not healthy factors."

When asked to comment on this, Reverend Hairston Wilcox, minister of the United Evangelical Church here in Greencastle, opined that the recent saucer hoax, the influence of unwholesome literature in a local bookstore and in the library, and other recent disturbances and cult activities in the high school all point to "nothing less than an attack on the moral fiber of our children." The symptoms of this danger, he stated, are "a disrespect for teachers, policemen, clergymen, and other legitimate authorities," and the formation of clubs and cults that are "anti-Christian and anti-American."

Both Reverend Wilcox and Mrs. Treet agree that the school authorities are doing everything they can to remedy the situation and are in no way responsible for encouraging ideas which are "foreign to our faith and our way of life." "We are working closely with the high school principal," said Reverend Wilcox.

Also interviewed by your reporter was Miss Teresa Scotti, the head librarian at Greencastle Public Library. In discussing the possibility that certain books were not appropriate for circulation, Miss Scotti replied that there was a long-standing dispute over library acquisitions, and that various "burn lists" have been received in the past two years from several local organizations, including the American Legion, the Women's Christian Alliance, and PBS. The list included *Catcher in the Rye* (a novel), the novels of John O'Hara, certain pagan literatures from pre-Christian times, a number of English plays, the works of Lenin and Freud, and the poetry of Walt Whitman. Miss Scotti, in a strongly worded statement received just this morning at the *Herald* office, stated that "librarians generally pay no attention to the threats of crypto-Nazi elements in the community, though it is disappointing to see that the war we recently fought to free the world from fascism did not free it from some of its American counterparts." (The complete text of her remarks will appear in Saturday's *Herald*.)

Mrs. Treet and Reverend Wilcox told this reporter that civic leaders would be holding informal discussions with Norman Pangborn, owner of Pangborn's Used Book and Magazine Store, at his premises on Thursday afternoon to achieve a frank exchange of views.

Roger read the article three times before he began to picture in his mind what would happen on Thursday afternoon. Mrs. Treet and Reverend Wilcox and a hundred other concerned citizens would all be there, sniffing over Pangborn's treasures. The police would come to ensure order. It would be a regular circus. He wondered what they would all think of Pangborn's stacks of pulp magazines. All the maidens with golden brassieres being attacked by fungoid monsters from another galaxy. He wondered what they would think of the broken window and the red paint. Roger shook his head. Pangborn was in trouble and it was his fault, like everything else.

After school on Thursday the Denizens ran the whole way down Paris Avenue and then turned onto Avondale Boulevard without breaking stride.

"This could be another very bad idea," said Dennis.

"Listen, you guys don't have to come," said Roger. "I mean, it doesn't matter if all of us don't show up—"

Frank stared mournfully at the sidewalk. "We hafta stick together," he said. "What would Pangborn think if we didn't? Something horrible could happen if we don't stick together.

Something that could actually even be too horrible to talk about."

"Frank, I wish you would make sense," said Dennis. "Nothing you say these days makes any sense."

Roger looked down at Frank and saw a face consumed with sadness and chagrin. "Dennis, that wasn't necessary—"

"Maybe I can't figure things out the way you can," said Frank. "But I sure can remember. And if we don't all go to Pangborn's today, then this summer I'm gonna tell you every single day how we used to be something but how it isn't that way anymore because we didn't stick together."

"All I said was, this *could* be a bad idea. I didn't say anything about—"

"And don't tell us how *rococo* it is to stick together," said Frank. "Just don't say that, okay?"

"I wish you guys wouldn't argue," said Roger. "This whole business is more my fault than anyone else's. You don't have to get mad at each other—"

"We all talk too much," said Dennis wearily as they all slowed to a walk. "That's one of our problems. Let's all just shut up. Let's get this over with."

When they reached Pangborn's Used Book and Magazine Store, things did not appear to be nearly as bad as Roger had feared. Some high school students loitered outside, whispering to each other and fingering the long points of broken glass clinging to the edges of the window. Past the streaks of red paint that desecrated the display area inside, he saw a dozen ladies walking up and down the stacks, rubbing their chins, removing books with thumb and forefinger, and gazing thoughtfully at titles. Reverend Wilcox was there, as were Mrs. Daniel S. Treet and three men in gold-braided American Legion caps.

Norman Pangborn sat on the counter next to his ancient cash register, with his arms crossed in front of him. He wore dungarees and a white shirt open at the throat. He also wore glasses. Roger could not recall ever seeing him wear glasses before. He did not like the way he looked in them, and it occurred to him that this was Pangborn's attempt to look more like a schoolteacher or a minister. Roger wished he would take them off. He tried several times to catch Pangborn's eye, but could not.

"We better not go in," said Dennis.

"We could embarrass him," said Roger. "It's better if we stay outside."

"Just so he knows we're here," said Frank.

A small crowd began to gather outside, and then three policemen arrived in a squad car. At four o'clock, Mr. Figge arrived along with three other teachers from the high school. Roger saw Pangborn slide off the counter and shake hands with everyone who came in. He nodded at people and pointed to the stacks and said things in a quiet voice that Roger could not hear from outside. Finally he looked out and saw the Denizens standing by the broken window. He gazed at them for a moment without any show of recognition. Then he pulled his glasses down over his nose and made a crimped little comic smile. The Denizens smiled back.

"He hates those glasses," said Roger.

"He's just wearing them for the occasion," said Dennis.

"I guess they're something to sort of hide behind," said Frank.

Soon a crowd of something close to two hundred people had gathered on the sidewalk and in the street. A nervous-looking young man in a threadbare black suit distributed anti-Communist leaflets. The three Legionnaires tried to get everyone to sing "God Bless America." A Good Humor man, looking like an attendant from the state hospital, parked his square white truck at the curb and was immediately surrounded by high school students, who were soon licking grape Popsicles and eating sundaes-in-a-cup with wooden spoons. Standing in a circle near the store entrance were seven men in green-and-white sweatshirts and knickers with the words BAILEY'S BEVERAGES stitched across the front. Two boys in caps wove in and out of the crowd shouting headlines and waving newspapers in people's faces. And sitting on the curb, a coatless reporter dressed in a white shirt with a red bow tie wrote in a green notebook. He was a young man, pale and chinless, with a little mustache that drooped down just slightly at the corners of his mouth. To Roger he looked very much like someone whose name could be Truman Greenwood.

"This is a circus," said Dennis.

"It's what I was afraid of," said Roger.

"But nobody's doing anything," said Frank. "Nothing's going to happen."

When he looked, he saw that people were leaving the store and that Pangborn had turned the lights out. Roger saw him standing now in the doorway watching Mrs. Treet, Reverend Wilcox, and the Legionnaires, who stood around a wooden box that seemed to have appeared from nowhere. As the three Legionnaires held Mrs. Treet by the elbows and lifted her onto the box, she gave a little cry of delight and fear. She was, he thought, an odd-looking woman. She looked to be about forty-five, very tall with a long, pointed face and a little rosebud mouth. She wore a gray dress and clutched a black briefcase under her shoulder.

"We're not going to make speeches," she entoned in a high, frail voice, "but we thought that at this point in time it would be good to share with you a few concerns about why we're here."

The teenagers at the Good Humor truck looked up at her for a moment when she began speaking, then went back to their whispers and their laughter. Reverend Wilcox and the three men from the American Legion stood almost at attention. Others milled about in a loose semicircle in the street.

"We came to you here this afternoon," she went on, "to offer our sympathies to Mr. Pangborn about the windows and the paint. And in the light of some recent happenings and facts we also wanted to examine his choice of literary offerings in order to see just how these materials might be affecting our young people."

Mrs. Treet stood in front of the broken window. The spears

of glass hanging from the edges formed a large oval hole in which she seemed to stand. She was the unconscious center of a great, accidental design, and after a moment Roger imagined that, like Wonder Woman, she had just smashed her way through the window in her never-ending fight against evil and corruption.

"—we don't pretend to be literature experts," she was saying. "But we who work with Parents for Better Schools like to think that we know right from wrong and good from evil. And we're here to tell each and every one of you that we have some good news and some bad news." Mrs. Treet smiled brightly at everyone and then pulled a note pad from a pocket in her dress.

"We have found—uh—yes, here it is—some good history books and some foreign magazines I'm sure would be beneficial for our Jewish descendants here in Greencastle, and some Italian magazines for the same purpose to the Italians. We also found some good old-fashioned novels of the fictional type we all know. The bad news is that we have found violence and almost nudity and also aliens from other planets on some magazine covers and suspect more of the same inside. We also found a small majority of foreign authors including one Russian and one or two books by perverts like Walt Whitman who was a known homosexual, and another book by Howard Fast who is on our list. As I said, we are not literature experts, but we are not completely ignorant of these matters. We are working in our own way for a better America. Every day I pray to our good Lord that all the scientists with their nuclear experiments about things they have no business in don't get atoms in the American water supply. And every day I pray that PBS can do its bit to push godlessness and trashy books and lust out of the minds of our young teenagers. We do hope and believe that Mr. Pangborn will join with us in this mission—"

At first Roger tried to listen to what Mrs. Treet was saying, but found that impossible. Instead he looked at faces. He wandered to the back of the crowd. He listened to whispers.

"What's she talking about?"

"Dirty books."

"Oh. Who's the guy in the bookstore?"

"He's the Jew from New York. He sells the dirty books."

"So that's what all the fuss is about?"

"He's also soft on Communism, or something. That's what they say."

"Oh."

Roger turned around and saw that he had lost Dennis and Frank. Somehow he had assumed that they would follow him, just as they had followed him down the mountain and into the swamp. But they were hidden somewhere in the restless and vaguely angry crowd of people that had grown larger since the Denizens had arrived.

Norman Pangborn had not moved from the doorway of his bookstore. He looked up into the trees and then down at the box where Mrs. Treet stood. Roger could see that there was nothing in his face. The afternoon sun, shining off his glasses, turned his eyes to silver.

Soon Mrs. Treet, the lady who did not want atoms in her water, stepped down from the box and was replaced by Reverend Wilcox. As he ran his right hand over his perfect white curls, he asked the Lord to give them all the wisdom to know what was true and the compassion to forgive those who did not. The Reverend then went on to thank Norman Pangborn for his tolerance and hospitality, and assured him that the police had several leads concerning the "misguided youths" who had broken his window.

"What we need here," he said, "is a frank exchange of views between the high school teachers, the city librarians, the Christian Alliance, PBS, and Mr. Pangborn about just what children ought and ought not to be reading. What we don't want," he said, turning to Pangborn, "is pornography. What we don't want is Godless Liberalism or Modernism. What we don't want is books that glorify foreign ways, foreign religions, or foreign governments at the expense of our own. Thousands and thousands of our boys gave their lives just seven years ago because Europe and Asia had gone over to paganism and atheism, and we don't want that here." The Reverend raised both his arms, spread his fingers, and looked upward, as if he were holding up a wall. "We all know what happens to a country without God and without respect for authority. History has given us many painful lessons on this point."

Reverend Wilcox lowered his arms and turned to Norman Pangborn. He smiled. "And that's why we take our education very seriously here in Greencastle, Mr. Pangborn. And that's why we're all here today. We're here to begin a new crusade for decency. A new crusade for the Christian vision—the Shining City on the Hill."

Faces brightened. A ripple of applause moved across the surface of the restless crowd. The young man in the black suit waved his leaflets in the air, the high school students whistled and cheered, and the Good Humor man rang his bells and gave out six free vanilla cups. Again Reverend Wilcox smiled and raised his arms in the air, turning first one way and then another, like a prizefighter who had just scored a knockout.

Housewives shouted questions into the air. One woman asked how one contacted book and magazine distributors and whether suits could be brought against them. Another asked if it would be possible to get Miss Teresa Scotti fired from the library. Another described in detail the covers of three pulp magazines and then held them in the air for everyone to see. Another said she had caught her own son with an old copy of *Weird Tales* hidden inside his English grammar workbook. She had further noticed a non-Christian tract entitled *The Mastery of Life* that he had obtained by responding to an advertisement on the back of *Amazing Stories*, and wanted to know if Rosicrucians did the work of the Devil. Another said she had heard that known Communists had infiltrated the magazine industry just as they had infiltrated the movie industry two years earlier, and that *everyone* had better watch what she read and what she allowed her children to read.

The inchoate voice of the crowd murmured its agreement. Then several people asked questions at the same time, and soon everyone was talking. The police, sensing that perhaps something was about to go wrong, moved to the front of the store and called for silence. And then, suddenly, Norman Pangborn, who had stood alone in his own doorway for over a half hour, took three steps down the sidewalk and leaped up onto the wooden box. Just as suddenly, the crowd was silent.

Reverend Wilcox pulled at his sleeve. "Mr. Pangborn, I don't think this is the time for you to respond to our remarks. I think we need to talk privately before—"

Pangborn stood with his hands in his pockets, looking down at the ground. Then he glanced up at the crowd. The longer he stood there saying nothing, the more silence there was. Even from the back of the crowd, Roger could see the deep shadows under his cheekbones and under his eyes. Perhaps he wasn't eating enough. Perhaps there was no money in the big cash register. Perhaps business was bad, and would now get even worse.

Pangborn took off his glasses.

"I don't really have a lot to say," he said in a clear, easy voice. "I hate making speeches and I feel a little insecure standing here in the middle of all you educated schoolteachers and ministers and reporters. I never went to college myself."

Reverend Wilcox gave him a painful smile. "Mr. Pangborn—"

"But I did want to thank Reverend Wilcox for assuring me that something was being done about my smashed window and all the red paint. And I certainly appreciate Mrs. Treet's concern about the same, and I want to thank her too for her invitation to help her fight atheism and trash."

"Mr. Pangborn, we do appreciate—"

"Please let me finish. I want to admit straight out that I am guilty of many things. I sort of gathered from Mrs. Treet and from Reverend Wilcox that you are all here to see just how guilty I am and just what I might be guilty of. Well, let me tell you, it's even worse than you imagined."

"Mr. Pangborn, I really don't think—"

"First of all," said Pangborn, "I'm guilty of disliking almost the entire adult world. Adults seem to know a lot of useful things that make me feel very inferior when I have to spend much time around them. Things like how to make money and how to be respectable and how to wear a gray suit without looking like a jackass. All of my friends are kids from the high school. I've had my fill of the adult world and what it has done to this planet in the last forty years. Another thing I'm guilty of is that I don't seem to know the difference between moral and immoral literature. Mrs. Treet and Reverend Wilcox really have the jump on me there. To me, all books seem moral—isn't that the craziest thing you ever heard? Imagine thinking that anything a kid wants to read is suitable for that particular kid. And finally, I am guilty of the corruption of youth. As you can see, I have saved the worst for last."

Many people laughed at this, and even Reverend Wilcox smiled briefly. But Mrs. Treet raised her eyebrows in surprise and indignation, and then waved her hands, trying to get Pangborn's attention. Now she was talking, but her high, thin voice, unlike Pangborn's, did not carry over the sounds of the crowd.

"To be more specific, there are three boys who come in two or three afternoons a week. I serve them orange juice, which no doubt makes their stomachs too acid and spoils their dinner. I sometimes give them a free book or two, which no doubt encourages financial irresponsibility. And I encourage these young men to engage in all manner of impractical things that will do them no good at all in later life. I encourage them to read and dream and think and talk, all of which will get you a cup of coffee at Maxwell's Diner if you have a dime."

Again there was sporadic laughter, followed by questions that Roger could not hear. Not wanting to miss anything, Roger tried to push his way toward the front of the crowd. Some woman, he thought, was asking something about vampires.

"It's perfectly normal for you to disapprove of what your

children read," Pangborn said in reply. "Parents have been doing that for years. Generally speaking, most adults disapprove of most children because they think children should be nothing more than short adults. This is seldom the case. The truth is, you just shouldn't feel called upon to approve of everything your kids read. From their point of view there is nothing wrong with what you call junk literature. Great men have been nourished on junk literature. Junk literature is very American, just like baseball."

As Roger got closer and closer to the front of the crowd, he heard more and more voices. An undertone, a hubbub of muffled words coming from all directions.

"Slick, isn't he?"

"Too slick if you ask me."

"Seems to know a lot."

"An intellectual."

"Those creeping socialists, they're all intellectuals. Always got their noses in books instead of doing honest work."

Now he was close enough to see the lines of sweat forming on Pangborn's forehead. Close enough to see him staring out over the crowd with his cheeks pinched and his eyes narrowed to a squint, as if something were blinding him, or as if he were staring out into darkness, trying to see the faces of his accusers.

"We don't want you here!" cried the man in the black suit. "We don't need all you foreigners with your books and your ideas and your religions! Go back to where you came from!"

Mrs. Treet and Reverend Wilcox and the three Legionnaires turned toward the sound of the man's voice. Mrs. Treet gave a little gasp, and the Legionnaires mumbled something to each other. Roger saw that they were all embarrassed by the man's outcry.

Pangborn nodded and smiled. "I have seen this happen before," he said.

Reverend Wilcox stared at the man in the black suit, then looked up at Pangborn. His mouth fell open and the muscles in his cheeks knotted. "Mr. Pangborn, I hope you don't think we subscribe to that man's blindness and bigotry. We never intended—that is to say, none of us ever dreamed—"

"Yes," said Pangborn. "I have seen this happen before. I was there. My father and mother were there."

"No one knows what the hell you're talking about," shouted an old man dressed in a red lumberjack's shirt, and the crowd laughed for him just as it had laughed for Pangborn, moments earlier.

"Jew bastard!" shouted someone else. "Two thousand years ago you murdered our Lord, and now you want our kids—" The shrill voice came from a woman far off to the left, a beautiful blond lady in a gray slack suit with a gold butterfly pinned to her lapel.

At this, a dozen mothers gasped, and Mrs. Treet gave a little cry of pain.

"I'm telling you, I was there when they broke the windows of shopkeepers," said Pangborn, his voice rising. "I was there when they burned all the books and then burned all the people. My father and my mother—"

Now the crowd was silent, waiting for him to go on. Roger looked back and saw the Good Humor man with his white jacket and his white pants and his glassy look, and then it seemed to him that they were all Good Humor men and women standing about in their ice-cream suits, not knowing what they had heard, thinking that it must have been something.

"My father and my mother," he repeated. "My father—"

Roger pushed a man and a young girl aside and broke through into the open space around the wooden box, and at that moment Pangborn saw him. Tears filled his eyes. He put his glasses back on, looked up at the sky, and pulled out a handkerchief.

"Hello, Roger." He smiled. The tears ran down his cheeks. "Glad to see you. I'm having sort of a tough time up here, as you can see—"

"Hello, Mr. Pangborn."

"I was wondering—did you find anything in the Watchung? I know you were hoping to find something to—well—verify your theories—"

"Yes, we did," said Roger in a loud clear voice. "We found—" And then, as he tried to think of just what it was they had found, he remembered other expeditions, other hopes and dreams, and other beloved patrons. "We found wonderful things!" he said. "Wonderful things!"

He wanted to say more. It was like running down the dark street after dancing class, wanting to shout into the night that you were in love with music and in love with every girl who ever lived, but not knowing how to say everything all at once. Then, as tears filled his own eyes, he did what seemed to him an absurd thing: he cupped his right hand and saluted Norman Pangborn. As he did this he felt a rush of pride and sympathy, and he thought of Romeo and Juliet, who went mad for each other and died for each other, and he thought of the Denizens coming out of the green dark to the top of Machine Gun Mountain, and he thought of the thing they had seen in the swamp and the Star Kings leaping from one star to another and Playground Joe and the Flying Man, and all these things rubbed off on him, the way Ruth Jahntoff rubbed off on him when they danced, and he knew there was no way to say it all, no way to say what was at the heart of everything he loved, no way to pay Norman Pangborn back for what he had given.

"Thanks, Mr. Pangborn," he said. "Thanks a zillion times. Thanks for all the stuff you did for us that nobody else would ever do."

Pangborn took off his glasses for the second time. He rubbed the lenses with his handkerchief and then squinted up at the trees across the street. "Sometimes," he said. "Sometimes there are no words. But please—all of you—don't think that all my confessed sins are noble or that my intentions are honorable simply because this young man appreciates me. I don't spend time with the young in order to mold them into splendid young men and women, as you do. I do it only because it makes me happy."

He put his glasses back on and got down from the box. He patted Roger on the shoulder, a thing he had done a hundred times if he had done it once, and walked back into the store.

Truman Greenwood, the chinless reporter with the drooping mustache, sat on the curb writing in his green notebook. Mrs. Daniel S. Treet caught her breath several times, started to speak to no one in particular, looking frantically in all directions. Reverend Hairston Wilcox stared wide-eyed at the doorway where Pangborn had disappeared. His face turned white, the color of his miraculous hair, and he clutched himself around the middle. It was as if someone had stabbed him in the stomach.

The mothers and the high school teachers began to wander off. The students chewed gum and waited for something else to happen, and the Good Humor man got in his white truck, started his engine, and smiled at the street in front of him.

"But what about Lovecraft?" said one Legionnaire. "No one asked him about practicing Lovecraft."

27 | The Girl Whose Name Was Not Really Evelyn Casablanca

He dreamed about looking up at the dark ceiling in his bedroom and watching squares of light sweep across the room when cars passed in the street below. He was alone in the house, hoping each time the light moved to hear the crunch of tires on gravel as his father's car turned into the driveway.

He sat up and rubbed his eyes. He was not in bed. He was on the living-room sofa. Outside it was nearly dark and the sky was very cloudy, and for a while he wondered if night were about to fall or if morning had just come. Then he remembered Pangborn standing on the wooden box and the tears streaming down his cheeks and the terrible look on Reverend Wilcox's face and the noisy ignorance of the crowd and the jingling of the bells from the Good Humor truck. What day was it?

He remembered walking home from the bookstore and locking himself in his room. He remembered coming down at midnight when his parents were asleep to fix himself a cold baked bean and pickle sandwich for dinner. And he remembered thinking there would be more trouble in school after what had happened, after what he had said in front of the whole town. All the whispers behind his back. All the quiet laughter and all the ugly jokes.

He spent the next morning in bed with Ythn and a bottle of aspirin, listening to Arthur Godfrey and Phil Cook and soap operas. He was only vaguely aware of the fact that he had skipped school, that three people had stood across the street and stared at his house for nearly a half hour, that others had passed in slow-moving cars and honked their horns and shouted things, that he had forgotten to bring his books home, that the principal had called early in the morning and that his mother had shouted at him and hung up the phone.

He got up and lurched across the living room. Something buzzed inside his head. His stomach felt empty. It was Friday night and his mother, he remembered, had gone to a League meeting. He came into the kitchen and saw his father sitting in the dark, smoking cigarettes. He turned on the light.

"Dad?"

His father gave a little gasp and turned his face away. The sudden light had blinded him. "Roger? That you? I couldn't find you."

"I was on the sofa. I fell asleep."

"Funny. I looked all over. Never saw you there."

"You should turn on a light. You shouldn't sit here in the dark."

"Yes. Well, it gets dark so gradually I hardly notice. But then it always gets dark gradually, doesn't it? Ha-ha. That's silly. Just lost track of time, I guess. Thinking about work. I have to go back tomorrow morning."

"Tomorrow is Saturday."

"Yes. We have a division meeting in the afternoon. No rest for the wicked."

"Did Mom say we should go out to dinner?"

His father nodded. "And I thought afterwards—that is, if you don't have anything on the docket—we could take in a movie. But then you probably have plans, don't you? Wouldn't want to keep you from anything."

"Plans?" He blinked. "That's a funny word. *Planz*. I guess

I have *planz* to stay home and do nothing. Listen to the radio."

"Fine. I didn't think—that is, I knew I should have asked you yesterday."

His father leaned forward, his elbows on the kitchen table, and put his hands over his face. Roger could tell by the smell in the kitchen that he had been sitting and smoking with the windows closed for some time. "It's not that," said Roger. "I just don't want you to have to take me somewhere just because Mom's gone. I know you hate to go out on weekends."

His father put out his cigarette. "Oh!" he said. "Well, no. That is, I wouldn't mind. We could talk. See the sights."

Roger washed his face in the kitchen sink and then went upstairs to put on a clean shirt. Gradually the dull headache that always came when he slept early in the afternoon disappeared, and by the time they arrived at Maxwell's Diner his head was clear. He ordered chicken croquettes, mashed potatoes with gravy, green beans, and apple pie with a slice of cheddar cheese.

Maxwell's Diner, like every diner he had ever seen, was shaped like a railway boxcar. A counter with stools ran the length of it on one side. The other side held a row of booths with red plastic seats and wooden tables. Brass wall lamps with little red shades filled the whole place with light.

As he ate dinner with his father, he watched the two black-haired men turn hamburgers and spoon mashed potatoes and "toss salad" onto thick plates and bowls. There was a beautiful rhythm in the way they did things. The tall, muscular man turned his wrist just so to make a hollow in the mashed potatoes and inundate them with gravy all in one motion. He cracked two eggs at once, one with either hand, over the black griddle already half filled with hamburgers, toast, pan steaks, and pork chops—little islands of food frying in a black ocean. He sharpened knives against each other, flashing silver X's in the air, cut a tomato into thin slices in two seconds flat, crooked his fingers through the handles of three white mugs and filled them with black coffee, never spilling a drop. The tall man turned and smiled at the shorter man and said something that did not carry over the crackle of frying food and the whoosh of the dishwasher.

How clean and useful and self-contained their world was. A land of delicious smells and steamy dishes emerging out of the Conestoga-shaped dishwasher, like white spirits born again from a cloudy underworld. He gazed at the thick white mugs with their broad, curved edges, slightly rough to the touch, each one like the others. They did not break if you dropped them on the table.

"It's safe and warm here," said Roger. "Cozy. Everything works. Everything is clean and simple."

"Clean and simple," said his father. "That's good, isn't it? Yes."

There was a double feature at the Strand: *The Blue Dahlia*, an Alan Ladd adventure thriller from several years earlier, and *The Brasher Doubloon*, another B movie, also from the archives. But the Lyric featured a five-year-old Technicolor musical which Roger decided on since he knew his father had to drive to Connecticut the next morning and would not want to sit through a double feature.

The rain broke just after the movie let out. He hoped it would last. There were few things nicer, he thought, than going to sleep with rain on the roof, and the window open just a crack so you could hear it coming down, falling miles and miles through the night.

When they reached home, the house was dark. "Mother's late," said Roger.

"They have election of officers tonight," said his father. "Mom is always late from her League meeting when they have election of officers."

Roger was tired even though he had rested all morning and slept most of the afternoon. But as he started to go upstairs to bed, he saw his father in the kitchen again. This time he was standing by the sink pouring Scotch into a glass. Roger stopped on the stairs to watch. He thought of all the silence between them, and he thought of that evening after the party when he had found him weeping in the bedroom.

Then his father turned and saw him. Roger expected him to freeze for a moment and then make a little grimace of a smile and raise his glass. *Cheers. Bottoms up. Going to bed so soon? Time to catch forty winks, eh?* But instead he put down his drink and came to the doorway and looked up at his son.

"Roger?"

"That's my name."

"You tired?"

"Sort of. A little maybe."

"Listen. Why don't we—why don't we take two glasses and a bottle of Burgundy and some cheese and apples out to the garage? I have two lights out there now and there's the old sofa. We could sit for a while and listen to the rain."

"Really? You really want to do that?"

"This is—you know—my last night. I thought we could talk."

"Great, but I don't drink. Mom would kill me if she found me out there in the middle of the night guzzling Burgundy."

"Mom doesn't have to know."

"Mom doesn't—are you kidding?"

His father shrugged. "I guess it's not such a good idea. It's late, isn't it? I should get to bed early—"

"It's a great idea," said Roger quickly. "It's an unbelievably terrific idea. I never tasted Burgundy."

Roger bounded down the stairs. His father looked pleased. Together they cut up two apples and some sharp cheddar and put it all on a large plate with a bottle of red wine and two jelly glasses. His father dumped the glass of Scotch down the sink.

The springs twanged and the garage door slid upward and rested on its track against the ceiling. His father lit two kerosene lamps, which cast a diffused yellowish light over his workbench and the sheets of pegboard filled with tools that ran the length of the garage. Above them, pieces of plywood and lengths of two-by-fours hung from a crosshatch of rafters.

Roger and his father sat for a few minutes at the dark end of the garage and listened to the rain. They left the door open since the wind had died and the rain was coming down straight. It was a warm spring shower, the kind Roger remembered running out in when he was small. They sat together on the worn-out sofa his mother had thrown out of the house three years earlier, and spread the food and drink on the cushion between them.

"Always liked this garage," said his father. He poured wine and they clinked their jelly glasses together.

"You made lots of nice things out here," said Roger.

"It's clean and peaceful. Like what you said about Maxwell's. Here it's just you and your tools and the smell of wood. Very simple. Like me." His father forced a little laugh. He looked out at the rain. "Did you like the movie?"

"I liked the ending where Tony Martin gives Peter Lorre this funny look and then gets killed trying to make it to the airplane, sort of like he's saying to hell with everything. And I liked the beginning where all his friends give these signals so the police can't get him out of the Casbah. The rest of it was okay. Tony Martin is too pretty and he sings too much."

His father smiled. He finished his glass of Burgundy and poured himself another. "I don't pay too much attention to the story," he said. "I just watch the Technicolor. How's the wine?"

"Not terrific," said Roger. "Sort of like iodine. But it's not too bad with cheese and apples. Dad, I don't think I ever saw you drink before."

"Sometimes late at night I come downstairs and take a nip when—that is, when I can't sleep. Roger—"

"That's my name."

"I understand—that is, your mother tells me you're having a tough time."

"I can stand it. I'm not getting into any more fistfights."

"Your face—it's, well almost back to normal," said his

father. "Yes. But I heard there was sort of a disturbance yesterday? At your friend's bookstore?"

"That's just part of it."

"Well, if there's anything I can do—you know. Glad to pitch in."

Roger stared at his father. "Pitch in? You can't pitch in, Dad. You're leaving tomorrow morning."

His father nodded and then turned his face away. "What I meant was, if there's anything you need to talk about—" He tapped his fingers on the wooden plate and then suddenly drained his jelly glass and refilled it. "I'd be more than happy to listen."

"There really isn't much to tell. I got in this big fight and got my face smashed up. I antagonized one of my teachers by talking too much. All kinds of people think I'm the leader of some perverts' club. All the athletes and all the Italians hate me and want to beat me up. I'm not allowed to talk in any of my classes and I got thrown out of dancing school for the rest of the year and I guess Mrs. Treet and Reverend Wilcox think I'm part of some anti-Christian conspiracy. I'm flunking all my subjects except Latin and I'm probably going to get suspended from school next week. That's about it in a nutshell."

His father leaned back very gingerly on the sofa so as not to upset the wooden plate between them. He tapped a cigarette out of his pack of Lucky Strikes. His face, still turned away and full of shadows, did not seem to respond in any way to Roger's list of disasters. "Strange," he said. "The way things work out."

Roger laughed. "Strange? You think it's strange? Is that all you can say?"

"What I mean is, all your troubles in school. You're a good boy. You like people. You never—I mean from what I can see—you always liked school and you never looked for trouble."

"I have two terrific friends, but I'm not even too sure about them anymore. Everybody else hates me, and I really hate them back. I just hate their guts."

His father inhaled and then blew vague clouds of smoke into the lantern-lit darkness. Outside, the rain made a hissing sound on the cement driveway. "No one ever hated me," he said.

To Roger, this seemed a very strange remark. Did he mean to say he felt sad or lonely because no one ever hated him? That would be like being sad or lonely because you were the only kid on the block who didn't have acne.

"But of course there's a reason for that. Oh yes. A good reason." His father laughed, finished his glass of wine, and poured another.

"Dad, I think you're drinking too much of that stuff too fast."

"It's just wine. You can't get too high on wine."

"Maybe you should have some cheese and apples."

"Your mother thinks—she seems to feel you should be more political. But I don't think you could do that. You always say what you think. You go right into things. Some people—what I mean is—they can't do what you do. They just fold up their tents and steal away with the Arabs."

"With the Arabs?"

"Right. You know. They stay away from everybody." He gave another short laugh, then sucked on his cigarette.

He thought now of Norman Pangborn, the man who always said what he thought. In his mind he saw him standing in front of the uncertain, muffled hostility of the crowd. He knew that his own father had always suffered by comparison, but now, as he sat listening to the rain, the difference did not seem to matter.

"I don't do very much, though," he said. "You do all the hard work so Mom and I can have it easy."

"But you don't have it easy. Not easy at all. Not simple and clear and bright, like Maxwell's Diner."

"Mom told me once about all the things you do. All about your designs for watches and timing mechanisms and how you worked on radar during the war."

"What I do is very simple," said his father. "But there are

other things I find difficult. You know me. I go with the Arabs." His father took a long sip from his jelly glass and then leaned back. "I want to tell you a story."

"A story? You never tell stories."

"Guess not. But I want to tell you one now. It's about me. Something I did once."

"Great. I love stories."

"It's going to be hard to tell. It's about embarrassing things. Sex. I guess you know about sex?"

"Jesus, Dad. I'm fifteen."

"Oh, that's right. I guess we never did have our little talk about the birds and the bees, did we?"

"No. I learned from the other kids. And Mom got me this book about the sacredness of having babies. It was pretty funny, but I sort of got the idea. Did you say you were going to tell me a story?"

"I did. It happened when I was twenty-four years old. I was in the army in Puerto Rico. I was a medical technician in a hospital and I lived in the army barracks in San Juan."

"You were in the Medical Corps?"

"Yes."

"Oh, that's right—I knew about that. Mom told me."

"It was a long time ago. Way before the war. I couldn't get a job anywhere, so I joined the U.S. Army. I was in the Medical Corps for three years. I hated the Medical Corps." He took another sip of Burgundy and then set the glass very carefully on the wooden plate. Roger saw him smile down at the plate as if he had successfully performed a difficult sleight of hand.

"Puerto Rico," said Roger.

"Puerto Rico," said his father. "The home of the flying cockroach, tropical rain forests, venereal diseases, pretty girls, starving dogs, and the U.S. Army."

"That's funny," said Roger. "Dad, you said something funny."

His father raised his eyebrows and cocked his head a little to one side. "At night we could go to the movies, but they turned the English down so far you could barely hear it, and

I couldn't read the Spanish subtitles. But there were these bars all over downtown San Juan. And in the bars were these—girls."

"Prostitutes," said Roger cheerfully. "Dad, did you ever have anything to do with prostitutes?"

"Roger, let me tell the story."

"Well, that's what you're talking about. I mean, did you?"

"Yes, they were prostitutes, and no, I never had anything to do with them. Not in that way. But I did get to know this one girl. She used to sit down at my table and we used to talk. This was a year before I met your mother."

Roger laughed. "You're telling me you used to sit at this table with a prostitute before you met Mom."

"Yes. I mean, no. That is, I didn't—I sat with her and we talked. She told me all about herself. She liked me, but she sort of knew that I wasn't interested in—well, you know."

"You were short on cash." Roger giggled.

"Well, yes, as a matter of fact. I was saving for a Chevrolet for when I got out of the army. I figured it would be much easier to get a job if I had a Chevrolet."

"Dad, you really are hilarious. I didn't know you could be hilarious."

"I don't mean to be. I'm trying to tell you a story. It has to do with how I am and how you are. But now I've forgotten the point—"

"You were talking about the girl at the bar and what Puerto Rico was like."

"I'll never forget Puerto Rico. Puerto Rico was just awful." His father finished the last of the wine and then ran his fingers over the label of the empty bottle and smiled, as if he were deciphering a message. "In San Juan they had these narrow little streets that were always crowded. Everything smelled like rum and rotting food and sweat and piss. I'll never forget that smell. And there were dogs and cats everywhere. All the females were starving and all the males were sick. And then there were barefoot children wandering all over the streets beating the animals or begging for money, and sometimes families set up their radios and sofas and beds between the buildings. I often wondered what they did when it rained."

"Sounds awful."

"And when you took the 9 Cantera out of the city past Miramar and Santurce you saw the same thing. Prostitutes. Old men selling fried pork skins. Children begging to shine your shoes for a nickel or a dime. Pregnant animals. But the traffic moved a lot faster, so there were a lot more dead animals. They were the lucky ones, I guess."

"But wasn't it nice out in the country?" Roger knew this was a stupid thing to say, but he was trying to get his father to stop talking about human misery. There was enough of that on the news.

"I heard it was beautiful in the country, but I never got out there. They said the Condado Lagoon was beautiful too, but all I saw there were little shacks for changing clothes that the natives used for toilets, and all the pregnant dogs and dog dung. I guess the beach must have been beautiful. I never noticed."

"You were telling me about prostitutes," said Roger.

"I don't think I should say any more about that."

"But that was the whole point," said Roger. "You were going to say something about this prostitute that was the whole point of whatever it was."

"Oh yes. Well. I was saving for a Chevrolet."

"Never mind about the Chevrolet! What happened with this girl you met?"

"I told you—nothing happened. That is to say, something did happen, but not *that*. She told me all about herself. Her mother and father died when she was little, and she got married at fourteen. And then she had a baby who died of pneumonia, and her husband ran off with a male tango dancer, if you can imagine that. She lived with several men, and then she had another child when she was eighteen. I think she said that one lived almost a year. Her milk was no good, and the man she was living with at the time wouldn't let her take the baby to the hospital. When I met her she seemed very happy all the time. She was very pretty and she wore these flouncy dresses with fancy ruffles on the sleeves. But I remember how all her sadness came out in bits and pieces. Why am I telling you all this?"

"Because you've had four jelly glasses of that red stuff. So what happened? You said that something did happen."

"Well, I came to Prado's three times to talk with her. The last time she unbuttoned one of those fancy sleeves and showed me her arms. They were all scarred. I don't mean from needles. She used to—to slash herself with razor blades. Not down by her wrists where it might have killed her, but up in the fleshy part."

His father held up his forearm and made slash marks with his fingers. Then his lips slowly parted and his eyes widened, as if the memory of the strange woman had terrified him.

"She was a Negro, and her name was Evelyn Casablanca. She had this very light sort of chocolate-looking skin. It looked good enough to—well, what I mean is that her skin was perfect except up on her forearms. And the terrible thing was that the cuts never really healed. She used to slash herself in the same places every time, and it got so that after a few months she didn't have to use razor blades anymore. She could just go *swish* like this with her fingernail and suddenly her arm would start to bleed."

"God, that's awful," said Roger. "It makes me sick to my stomach to think about it. Why would anyone ever want to do that? It's like—it's like trying to kill yourself by inches."

"Anytime you go out into the world of people you have these problems," said his father. "All the pain and all the emotion. I can't—I never could—" He shook his head. He fumbled another cigarette out of the pack and finally got it lit.

"She told me that she cut herself when there wasn't enough food and her milk went dry. She said that sometimes the baby would suck the blood when that was all she had to give. And she did it when her grandmother told the priest about her. And she did it when the police closed up the bars one weekend, and she did it at night when she was too tired or too hungry to sell herself and during the afternoons when it was so hot in the summer that you could fry eggs on the sidewalks, and during the late summer when the fever came and all the stomachs of the poor children would swell up like watermelons."

Never in his life had he heard his father, or anyone else for that matter, talk about such things. He had suspected for several years that the real horrors of human life were economic rather than Lovecraftian, but he did not want to think about that. It made him feel queasy, just as the wine had made him feel queasy. He was glad the bottle was empty.

"Your father should not be telling you all this," said his father. "You're only fifteen, and your father is talking too much. Your father is drunk."

"It's okay," said Roger.

"Your mother is going to be very angry. She doesn't—she doesn't quite approve of me."

"She does," said Roger. "She says all sorts of nice things about you."

"Did I tell you that Evelyn Casablanca was not her real name? She had this one little vanity left. Isn't that funny? She didn't care what anybody knew about her and she had no hope for anything in the future, and she knew she would get sick again in July and she knew that in two years her skin would begin to wrinkle a little and her stomach would go bad and no one would want her. But still she wanted to call herself by a pretty name. That little lie was the only pretty thing she thought she had any chance of holding on to."

"But she was pretty, wasn't she? Didn't you say she was pretty?"

"She was pretty, but she was not a pretty person, and she was never pretty to herself. She inspired lust. Men never dreamed about her—they dreamed about that little bird's nest between her legs. She had an animal attractiveness. She smelled good to men. But she never—she never inspired anything, and no one ever cared about her. Do you understand that?"

"No."

His father laughed. "I guess you're too young to know about lust."

"I know all about lust," said Roger. He looked down now into his own empty wineglass. "I mean, I know what it feels like to want somebody."

"You're a smart boy," said his father. "That's what I tell everyone." He reached over and patted his son on the shoulder. Not as Pangborn did, clapping his whole hand on Roger's bony clavicle, but just touching with his fingers, as if he were a prisoner reaching through the bars of his cage to touch some loved one.

"Truth is, I'm dumb," said Roger.

"You're more than smart," said his father. "You have what Evelyn had. You go right into things. You can look at all the feelings and all the blood, and in a year or two you'll see that life is very tragic and you'll go right into that too, and you'll be all right. But you'll cut yourself. Bring all the pain into one place so you can look at it. It's your way of telling God you're sorry for being human. You have to cut yourself—either that or you have to cut other people. That's what it's all about. That's what I'm trying to tell you."

"Dad, I know you don't mean to, but you're really starting to scare me. I don't understand any of this stuff, and I think maybe we should go in now and fix some coffee—"

"I never could face up to it," said his father. "I just ran. I was so jealous of Evelyn because she always went right into things. I wanted her to think I was too good for her, so I never went with her up the elevator with the wire cage into that old building that had all the cardboard rooms. I never—I never—"

"Dad, are you okay? You're really scaring me to death—"

"I never learned to go right into things. Did you know I wanted you to be eight years old forever? I wanted to burn all your books and kill all the librarians and bomb the movie theaters and murder all those boys in leather jackets who taught you all the dirty words you never said around me. I never wanted anything to change."

"Dad—"

"I heard her real name once. It was Chita Rincon, or something like that. But I always thought of her as Evelyn."

"What happened to her?" Roger did not want to know what happened to the girl whose name was not really Evelyn Casablanca, but he felt the need to say something. He did not want his father to drift off alone into his red haze of Burgundy and memories.

"I don't know. I left Puerto Rico, got discharged that same year, moved to Chicago, got a job, and met your mother. I never saw her again. I suppose she's dead now. She said the summer fever would get her in five years."

"That's awful. Puerto Rico must be about the awfullest place in the whole world, next to Armenia."

"I forgot something. I forgot the most important thing. About Evelyn."

"What's that, Dad?"

"She always cut herself the worst when she fell in love. She told me the only way God would ever forgive a prostitute for falling in love would be if she opened all her cuts at once."

That night in bed he thought, just for a moment, that he understood. His father lived in Hartford because he could not stand the thought of people loving him and needing him, and he could not stand the thought of loving and needing others. He lived in Hartford because he was unworthy, and he did not want to open all his cuts at once.

28 | Everything Gets Killed by Imaginary Snow

At eight-fifteen on Saturday morning, Roger, in his blue-and-green-striped pajamas, opened the front door and said hello to Truman Greenwood. The young man clutched his green steno pad against the single-breasted lapel of his sports jacket. He held out his other hand and tried to smile, but the smile faded when Roger came out onto the porch. To Roger he looked vulnerable and absurd with his receding chin and his droopy mustache.

"Are your parents home?"

"They're asleep."

"Oh. Well, it's really you I need to talk to anyway. You're Roger?"

"My name is Roger Cornell. Why did you ask for my parents if you wanted to talk to me?"

"Why did—oh, that's easy. There's a reason for that. You see, I'm supposed to talk to the parents before I interview anyone under eighteen."

Roger stared at the young man in the sports jacket, feeling very angry and very sure of himself. He could see that Truman Greenwood wanted to be invited inside, and that he did not want to stand out on a porch at eight in the morning with a barefoot juvenile delinquent wearing striped pajamas.

"But since your parents are asleep I guess we don't have to bother them. Would you consent to a five-minute interview?"

It occurred to Roger that the man was probably less than ten years older than he was, and that the assumption of youth being interviewed by maturity was a thin one. "Glad to, Truman," he said. "What's on your mind?" He grinned at the reporter, who looked down at his note pad.

"Do you suppose we might step inside?"

"Like I said, my parents are asleep. They don't like strange people in the house when they're asleep."

"Oh. Well, that's okay. Why don't you just tell me about the Lovecraft Conspiracy? You know, in your own words. I have a feeling that this whole thing has been greatly exaggerated, and I thought it would be good to get your point of view on this, so to speak."

"What's the Lovecraft Conspiracy?"

Truman Greenwood chuckled. "Well, as a matter of fact that's my own term for it. I thought it was kind of catchy. It refers to all this business about obscene books and secret meetings and practicing Lovecraft—you know. All this stuff that everyone's been getting so excited about."

"Let's see if I've got this straight. You made up this word and you want me to explain what it means?"

"Well, I thought—"

"I can tell you one thing. You can't practice Lovecraft. H. P. Lovecraft is a writer. You read Lovecraft."

The reporter looked up from his notes and his face turned red. "I'm well aware of the fact that this Lovecraft is also a person," he said. "I've been told, however, that you have talked with Lovecraft and that Lovecraft has been seen with high officials of certain Eastern governments."

"It would be kind of tough for me to talk with Mr. Lovecraft," said Roger. "He died in 1937. Dead people don't talk much. They just don't mix well socially. Sometimes they go for hours without saying a word. I guess you didn't know that."

Truman Greenwood took a deep breath. "Okay, kid. If that's the way you want it—"

"How do I want it?" said Roger. "You come up here without an invitation at eight in the morning and you ask me all these questions about things you got your mind made up about anyway and you write all these lies in your newspaper about stuff you don't know a damn thing about and you think you know how I want it. Well, just how do I want it?"

"I'm gone," said Truman Greenwood. He sneered at Roger and then made an Italian gesture with his right hand. Roger stepped back into his house and slammed the door hard.

When he turned, he saw his father standing in the foyer. He was dressed in his gray traveling suit with his blue tie and black shoes. "Give 'em hell," he said. He spoke so softly that for a moment Roger was not sure whether he had heard or imagined his father's voice.

"I didn't know you were there," he said finally.

His father smiled. "That's my problem," he said. "No one ever knows I'm here. My own fault. Nobody else's."

His father pursed his lips, as if he were trying to keep something from showing on his face. He held out his hand. Roger took two steps that closed the distance between them. Suddenly, inexplicably, he thought about the Puerto Rican girl who slashed her arm every time she fell in love.

"I'll be gone for two weeks this time. I don't want to go, but I have to."

"I wish you could stay for another day," said Roger.

"I wish—what I mean is, I wish I didn't have to go at all," whispered his father. Instead of looking at his son, he watched himself shake hands, as if his hand and his son's hand were independent creatures saying goodbye to each other.

"But you do," said Roger. "I mean, you need to get away. I didn't used to understand that, but I think maybe I do now. It's too much for you here."

"Too much?"

"Mom and I bother you. We talk too much and we want

to go places and do things you don't want to do, and we always crowd you with all our feelings. I know how you hate that kind of stuff."

His father winced. "I can't talk about those things when I'm sober," he said. "But I can tell you that the difficulties of living with people are nothing compared with the difficulties of loneliness."

"Well then, why—"

"There's something else. Something else besides—besides the way I am. My job in Hartford is only temporary."

"You never told me that."

"Well, it's not exactly temporary. It's just—well—I'm always afraid things will turn out to be temporary. It's happened before."

"You mean you think you'll get canned? I don't get it. You're a terrific engineer. Mom says you're real smart."

"It's not how smart you are. You have to be clever. You have to find ways of making yourself look good. You have to say the right thing at the right time. You have to know how to go to lunch with people and how to be informal, but not too informal. You have to spend a lot of time with the right people without seeming to do it on purpose. I'm not very good at all that. Matter of fact, I'm no good at all."

He picked up his briefcase and smiled at the floor. Roger could see that he was trying to extricate himself, and he braced himself for one of his father's formulaic goodbyes. *Well, back to the salt mines. No rest for the wicked. Catch you in two weeks. Take good care of Mom.* But instead he put his briefcase down again, carefully, against the wall. He put his hands in his pockets.

"So you see," he said, "I don't feel permanent. Takes me a long time to feel permanent. It's so easy for people like me to get pushed aside, and I didn't think—well—I know you have good friends here. I know you love Greencastle. You live in a nice house and you go to a nice school. I didn't want to take you away from everything and have you start over just so—you know—just so I wouldn't have to fix my own supper."

Roger stared at his father. He realized suddenly, terribly, and very clearly that his father was trying to protect him from all his failures, real and imagined. *If you are not worthy of the people you love it's better to suffer the agonies of loneliness*. Was that something he had read somewhere?

"You think if we stay in Greencastle we'll be safe, is that it?"

"Hartford is full of strangers," said his father. "I didn't want you to have to go to a place that was full of strangers."

Roger reached up and touched his father's shoulder and then pressed his nose against his gray suit and closed his eyes. His father trembled a little. Roger smelled shaving soap and Aqua Velva, and then a soft white hand fluttered against his cheek.

"Don't ever give up," said his father in a voice that was hoarse with emotion. "Be like Eisenhower. Don't let the bastards grind you down."

He did not know why love was such a fearful act of courage for his father, or why he trembled when he touched people, or why he lived in such a lonely, distant place. His father needed and hated his Palace of Bad Luck, and as Roger leaned against him he knew, as he had never known before, the terror and the strength of his father's love for him.

"Drive real careful," said Roger. "Don't *hurt* yourself."

As April bloomed into May it seemed to him that all the bastards *were* grinding everyone else down. Pangborn's store was closed by the police on the grounds that it had become "a source of public disorder," although the town council reported to Truman Greenwood that this was a temporary closure and that "even now the situation was being evaluated." Another article in the *Herald* reported that Roger Cornell, a local cult leader, had refused to talk to reporters about his club, his cult activities in the Watchung Reservation, or the Lovecraft Conspiracy. Greenwood reported that subsequent talks with school board officials indicated that an organized conspiracy now existed to subvert American youth. The FBI, the board said, had been informed. And then Roger's mother, after a long talk on the telephone with Dennis's mother and Frank's mother, told him that both of his friends had been forbidden to attend Denizens' meetings, and that in effect the club had been disbanded.

During the second week in May, Rolfe Gerhardt and Virgi Prewitt were both suspended from school. Rolfe had terrified three teachers by rushing into the faculty bathroom, driving them out with curses, and clogging all the toilets with peanut butter. Virgi Prewitt was charged with talking back to teachers, punching Eddie McQueen in the stomach, hanging spaceships from trees on school property, eating pumpkin seeds during study hall, and drawing pictures of diseases. And then one morning after Flag & Bible, the principal announced over the school intercom a new policy concerning Conduct and Citizenship. All playground activities would now be monitored by teachers or by volunteers from PBS. There would be no wandering about during study hall periods for any purpose whatsoever. The school library would be closed except during the weekly library periods on Friday. There would be weekly, unannounced locker inspections. Two- and three-week suspensions would be handed out routinely for any behavior which the principal or the vice-principal felt could be described as "Bad Citizenship" or "Blatant Disrespect for Authority."

The first inspection was limited to the athletic lockers, and it turned up a variety of interesting items, according to the school grapevine: a box of shotgun shells, four pink rubbers, two hunting knives, rotting fruit, photos of naked women, wet underwear, bags of used Kleenex, and a collection of "indescribable" twelve-page comic books. The next morning four members of the varsity basketball team were suspended from all practices and also from the final game of the season. "Things are much worse than we imagined," said William R. Mace during the Friday assembly. "Appropriate steps will be taken to sweep our school clean of these sickening influences." That same day after school the four exiled basketball players caught

Dennis Kirk on the playground. After a brief scuffle, Dennis went home with a black eye and a message to the effect that if Roger the Queer was dumb enough to come to school the next day they would all cut swastikas on his ass with an X-acto knife.

In spite of parental decrees, Roger tried to schedule one final meeting of the Denizens for the last Wednesday in May. He called his friends on the telephone. Frank whispered that he had a muscle spasm in his back and neck and that headaches were making him throw up three or four times a day and that all three of his doctors insisted that he stay in bed. Dennis was quiet for a moment and then said he would try to come, but probably couldn't. "It's okay," Roger managed to say. "We can get together this summer. Maybe after the bookstore opens up again." He hung up the phone, ran upstairs, and threw himself on his bed, cursing everyone and everything.

When all the flowers in Greencastle came into bloom, Roger was sick in bed for three days with asthma. He had had asthma attacks every year in the spring since his fourth birthday, but this was the first time one had kept him out of school. During the day he sat up and tried to breathe and listen to the radio. At night he gasped for air and drifted in and out of a weary, twilight sleep. Sometimes, at two or three in the morning, his mother would appear in his doorway and call him to come downstairs. She would put a spoonful of Vicks Vapo-Rub in the teakettle and then make a steam tent over him with a sheet, and he would breathe the vapors until his bronchial tubes began to open. This would give him two hours of quiet sleep before morning.

He thought, from time to time, about Dennis and Frank. The idea of the summer coming and going without them was just unthinkable. Together they were an airtight ship moving through space and time. Together no one could ever hurt them or make them lonely. Together they could never run out of anything. Alone, he was a boy with pimples who read too much. Alone there was practically no reason to go outside the house. Alone he would become something like his father. Or worse, something like Harry Fisher.

He thought as little as possible about Ruth. He did not want to remember the way she looked at him in class. He did not want to remember her quietness, her simplicity, her unfaltering and amazing honesty about everything and everyone. He did not want to hear in the dark the sound of her weeping over the telephone as his own lungs whistled and shrieked against the spring pollens that drifted in the night air. *It's God's judgment*, he could hear Reverend Wilcox say. *It's God's judgment for the sin of pride and the sin of abusing yourself with Vaseline and the sin of not listening to the good advice of your betters*. But the notion, even in the middle of the night, that God came down all the way from heaven just to give him asthma in the springtime struck him as vaguely humorous. Did God also give colds to people who took His name in vain in the autumn? And in the winter did He arrange auto accidents for people who couldn't make it to church, and in the heat of the summer was He responsible for venereal disease as a way of punishing marital infidelity? He had to sit up in bed when he laughed, but even then he felt for a few desperate seconds that he would never again get enough air. A half hour later he realized that it had almost killed him to laugh at God. He looked up into the dark, and wondered.

When he returned to school he did not look at people in the hallways. He did not hear the voices of his teachers or take down their homework assignments. The announcements after Flag & Bible were voices from another planet barking commands in an alien tongue. In the mornings he left fifteen minutes early for school and then sat on a toilet in the boys' room until the first bell rang so that he would not have to see Dennis and Frank. He did not want to see the doubt or fear in their faces, or hear the distance in their voices. He did not want to look at Dennis's black eye. He did not want to test their friendship and find that it was wanting.

* * *

After dinner on Wednesday evening he sat on the radiator by the front living-room window and watched the night come on. It was the evening of the last meeting of the Denizens of the Sacred Crypt, and he was sure that no one was coming. As he watched all the useless spring flowers lose their color in the darkness, it came to him that he had the power to kill the springtime and throw the world back into winter. He waved his hands and saw the snow begin to fall. Soon it covered all the green grass and all the tulips that his mother had planted the previous summer. Soon, he thought joyfully, everything would be dead. Snow would blow through all the classrooms at Greencastle High School and by tomorrow afternoon all the teachers would be found stiff at their desks, or standing at the blackboard, chalk frozen in their fingers, like Pompeiian figures caught in the midst of something trivial.

Then, plowing through the white drifts that covered Stone Hill Road, he saw Dennis Kirk in his old sweater and jeans and green sneakers, looking very tall and square. It was odd that he did not seem at all bothered by the icy sheets of snow blowing across the street or by the sub-zero air or by the death of all life forms in the town of Greencastle. Presently he walked up the front sidewalk and knocked on the door. After the third knock, Roger went to the door and opened it.

"Hi," said Dennis.

"Hi," said Roger. "I was thinking about snow."

29 | Roger and Ythn and Dennis and Fwuppy

Dennis smiled and slapped his gloves on the radiator. "Snow," he said. "Well, that's just fine. I come all the way over here for our Wednesday meeting and you tell me you're thinking about snow."

"Dennis—is it really you?"

Dennis punched him on the shoulder. "I said I'd try to make it, didn't I?"

"You must have had trouble with your mom and dad about this. And God, I'm really sorry about your black eye. It looks awful, but I can tell you from experience that it goes away a lot quicker than you think."

"My dad told me I couldn't come to the meeting and I told him that leaving you here all alone would be kind of a crappy thing to do and I was going no matter what he said and he said we'll see about that and I slammed the door. The last thing I saw was my father with his mouth open. Don't worry about it. We fight all the time. I think he sort of likes it. And don't worry about the black eye. That's just a little present from the basketball team."

"I didn't think you'd come," said Roger. "Frank couldn't make it."

He led Dennis out into the sun room and they sat down together in the two black swivel chairs his father had brought home from the office. Roger felt tears in his eyes and a trembling in his throat. He had never cried in front of Dennis or Frank, and he tried mightily not to now. "I mean, I really didn't think you'd come," he said weakly.

"You said that."

"I didn't want you to see me like this," said Roger. "This is really embarrassing. I know you hate this kind of stuff."

"You're right," said Dennis. "I hate it when people get soggy. But I think I can stand it with you better than with my mother. As long as your face doesn't get all wrinkled and you don't throw your arms around me and call me your *big boy.*"

Roger shook his head. " I made such a mess of everything. And now I just sit here in the dark and think how much I hate myself, and I think about my pimples and my long neck and I don't do anything for hours. People talk to me, but I never hear anything anybody says."

"You stuck up for Pangborn."

"I what?"

"You stuck up for Pangborn. After you wandered off to the other side of the crowd, things got a little tense and then right out in front of God and Greencastle you shot your mouth off, as usual. I never could have done that."

"I don't think it did much good."

"It did me a lot of good," said Dennis. "It made me realize that none of this stuff is your fault. Well, not much of it, anyway. From now on we walk to school together and we go to Pangborn's like always. That's the important thing. That is, as soon as Pangborn's opens up again."

"That's too dangerous for you," said Roger, who was conscious now of a sudden nobility. "All the Italians and the whole basketball team and Larry Norcross—"

"You have to take the long view," said Dennis. "Imagine me about fifty years old sitting in the middle of the winter with my *aged wife* just like in that awful poem by Tennyson that Mrs. Leibolt makes everybody read. And then I remember for the six thousandth time that I didn't stick up for my best buddy after he stuck up for old Pangborn. Now how do you think that would make me feel? Don't you figure that avoiding all that every day when I'm sitting in my rocking chair is pretty important?"

"I guess so," said Roger. "Thanks."

"God," said Dennis. "This is like something out of an old Ingrid Bergman movie. Or maybe a couple of fags on their first date."

"I'm sure glad you came," said Roger. The tears streamed down his cheeks. He punched Dennis on the arm.

"I wouldn't have missed a wonderful party like this for the world," said Dennis. "Me and Percival Lowell just love this kind of stuff."

"Percival Lowell?"

"You remember all that stuff that Pangborn was telling us? About having faith in things? I guess it's just another reason why I had to come. You follow the gleam. You and Percival both stick your foot out in the dark and then you leap. I can't say it. It doesn't make sense. God, I hate this kind of conversation."

"I know I'm always jumping around in the dark," said Roger, seizing the image. "Making a mess of everything. Like when we went to the Watchung. Everything turned out so bad."

"That's about the dumbest thing you ever said," said Dennis. "That was a great day. That was the greatest thing we ever did together."

He dared now to look up at Dennis, who was grinning and rocking back and forth in his father's chair. His round red cheeks, his purple eye, his bulky frame, and his shiny black hair, parted in the middle, all made him look like a comic character from a silent movie. Roger felt a surge of unreasonable happiness. In his mind he canceled the snowstorm.

"Do you really think so?"

"You want me to say it again? God, you are so embarrassing. Haven't you got any Kleenex?"

"We have to make plans," said Roger. "We really have to make plans this time. I mean for the summer. For everything."

Dennis laughed. "Roger, if I had a nickel for every time you said *we have to make plans*, I'd have about seventeen dollars and thirty-five cents. Did you know that?"

"But this time we really do. Life is getting very serious."

"God, I hope not. What kind of plans?"

Roger thought for a moment. "I don't know," he said finally. "Maybe you're right. Maybe that's just something I say. Maybe we can't make plans because nothing is ever what we think it is."

"Maybe we're all crazy," said Dennis.

"I know *I'm* crazy," said Roger. "I have—listen, I never told anyone about this—I have a little friend."

"We both have a little friend. His name is Frank Aldonotti. He's crazy too. He has total recall."

"No, I mean even littler than that. His name is Ythn. He's a Martian."

Dennis smiled. "Oh. That kind of friend. I have one of those too."

"You do?"

"He's a stuffed lion. I've had him since I was seven. He talks to me at night."

"A stuffed lion. You're kidding."

"Not a bit. Roger, how did we get onto this?"

"That's terrific. Ythn talks to me at night too, mostly."

"I guess most kids have imaginary friends," said Dennis. "Ours are just lasting a little longer than most."

"It's not fair to call Ythn imaginary," said Roger. "Ythn is like the Martian canals. Sometimes you have to set your telescope on blur before you can see what's really there. What's really there is not just the facts. Facts are dead, like Miss Wakowski. What's really there—it's what holds all the facts together. Something between real and imaginary. I don't know. That's my problem—I never really know what I'm talking about."

Dennis shrugged. "Maybe it's like that other poem that Mrs. Leibolt makes everyone read. Maybe the most important things are not just the facts on the outside of the Greek pot. Hey, this is deep stuff. I'm going to have to roll my pants up."

Then Roger had an inspiration. "Truth is Ythn, Ythn Truth! That is all ye know and all ye need to know!"

"Unheard lions roar sweeter!" said Dennis. "Pipe to the lion ditties of no tone!" He laughed again. "Maybe that's what the Donkey really said to the Cat in the House of Whatever."

"I ought to read that poem again sometime," said Roger. "But I probably won't. I hate poetry. Poetry is pretty embarrassing."

"The pot poem is okay for a poem," said Dennis. "The problem is that Mrs. Leibolt thinks it's okay for Keats to go around hearing music that isn't there because he's a Great Writer, but she doesn't think we have the right to do anything except appreciate Keats. We're never supposed to hear our own music. You know, I hate it when we talk this way."

"You should hear Ythn sometimes," said Roger. "He really gets deep. I mean, he's way over my head most of the time."

"Fwuppy keeps me informed on current events. He reads the paper, if you can imagine that."

"*Fwuppy?* I don't believe it. Fwuppy and Ythn. Ythn and Fwuppy."

"If you tell anyone about this, I'll kill you," said Dennis.

"Likewise," said Roger.

30 | Traveling Through Time

On Thursday morning the humidity rose. Mrs. Leibolt moved relentlessly through the last two hundred lines of *Oedipus the King,* and then talked about the semester essay due now in less than two weeks. Mr. Figge was frantic because no one had turned in either of the last two experiments in Physics, and also because he was five days behind schedule in World History with only three weeks left in the school year. Miss Wakowski announced that they had come to the end of the year's work in Geometry and that in the days that remained they would have study hall and review exercises. Miss Simic, with half-moons of sweat shadowing her armpits and with her throat and cheeks glistening in the dusty, sunlit classroom, carried on as usual.

"Miss Simic sweats like a pig," said Eddie McQueen.

"Miss Simic has a face like a monkey," said Buck Moore.

"Miss Simic teaches very hard," said Roger.

"We don't talk to homos," said Larry Norcross.

"Yeah," said Eddie McQueen. "We don't talk to homo-commie-lovecrafts."

That afternoon he walked home alone. Instead of going south on Paris Avenue and then cutting southwest on High

Point Avenue, he made the right turn early just to be safe from the athletes, the Italians, and the graduating seniors with their automobiles who knew his route and in recent days had been trying to ambush him. Otero was a very old street full of elm trees and shadows and sudden patches of sunlight. It was strange to see no children anywhere this time of day. Here all the houses were smaller, with grape arbors or narrow paths of flowers and stone walkways separating them. Old women watered their gardens behind wrought-iron fences. Cats lapped at plates of milk left on doorsteps. Grass grew in narrow rectangles between curbs and sidewalks. *Old*, he thought. Everything here was *old*. He wondered if the people who lived here had ever gone to high school, had ever been young, had ever thought they would someday grow old and live on this quiet street where no one ever went because it was not on the way to anything.

He stopped to look in on a small herb garden growing against the side of a narrow two-story house. Bordering the garden was a stone pathway leading to a tiny backyard where flagstones surrounded a goldfish pool. A white-haired woman in a green dress stood above the pool, casting bread into the water and talking quietly to her fish.

Once there had been a time when nothing ever changed or grew old. He had been young forever, secure from mortality in the arms of his father and mother. But now the years were passing, just as they had passed for all the old people who lived on Otero Street. Yesterday he was a little boy only dimly aware of yesterday and barely able to imagine tomorrow, and now he was rushing through high school and would soon be in college, and in no time he would graduate, take a job, and wait for his first gray hairs. God, he thought, what a life.

Even Greencastle was only temporary. Someday it would turn brown and wither away, like the green castle of his childhood. The town was paper-thin and fragile in time, like the beautifully detailed miniature that Harry Fisher had built in his attic. Everything was slipping away. He knew now that there was no point in standing out in the summer night with his arms uplifted, waiting for miracles. But he also knew that he was on the edge of another dream, something else to take up his waiting and wondering. This new conception of life was unclear to him, but he knew that it was centered upon his awareness of the separateness of things. It was centered upon his belief that something was terribly wrong with the world. And it centered upon the fascination and fear that came when he looked in upon his own consciousness, saw his mind moving through time, thought about his own thinking.

When the old woman turned around and smiled at him, he smiled back. The street was so quiet, so beautiful. All the new blooms opening in old places. What had he been thinking of? He shook his head and smiled to himself. Why was he thinking so much now, and why was he remembering so little?

From Iris Street he made a right turn onto Recognition, thinking that he would take a quick run by Roosevelt Memorial Field to see if Playground Joe had set up yet for the summer. But before he had a chance to begin the long descent, he saw a brown-and-white dog barking in the street. It was Nunnug. When he saw Roger, he wagged his tail and ran up to him, his tongue lolling in his mouth, his breath coming in short, joyful pants.

"Hey, boy. Where's Harry?"

He petted the dog and scratched him behind his ears. Then he looked down Recognition Street to the house where Harry lived, but there was no indication of life or movement. During the early spring, the gray shadows of new leaves had mottled the pavement, but now the street had the appearance of midsummer—a dark tunnel with all the high branches arching across.

He ran down the hill with Nunnug at his heels, and in a few seconds he reached Harry's house, the last one before the wide streets with their grass islands opened into sunlight.

"Hi!"

"Harry! God, you scared me!"

Harry leaned against his tree, grinning at him. With his black shirt and pants, he was branches and trunk rather than arms and legs. "I was standing right here. You didn't see me."

"It's dark here at the bottom of the hill," said Roger.

Harry laughed. "It's a little game I play. I stand real still, and people, they come down the hill from High Point, and I say, 'Hi.' Not real loud so they got any reason to get mad, but just sort of sudden. *'Hi!'* Like that. You'd be surprised how many people jump outa their skin."

Harry shifted his weight, chinned himself easily with one arm, then dropped to the ground and came out to the sidewalk. It was odd the way Harry walked. He leaned first one way and then the other as he planted his feet flat on the ground. It was as if his insides were full of machines—gears and pistons and compression chambers that made him lunge and start and stop. Harry was awkward but powerful. It was a safe bet that he could punch out Larry Norcross on the playground about as easily as he had destroyed Curtiss Baylor at the chessboard.

"C'mon in if you got the time. I got something up in the attic I think you said you wanted to see."

"You mean the time machine? Harry, are you finally going to show me the time machine?"

As they moved toward the porch, Roger saw that hundreds and hundreds of acorn army men had been crushed by some invader. Amidst this vast military disaster Nunnug ran in happy, mindless circles, his tongue still rolling in his mouth like a wet noodle.

"Nunnug likes you," said Harry. "You're the only kid in the whole neighborhood he really likes. I got some new stuff, did I tell you?"

"I want to see the time machine," said Roger.

Harry laughed. "I bet you do," he said. "I just bet you'd like to see the old time machine after all the bad times they been giving you up at the old high school. I was wondering yesterday about that. Yessir, I said. Old Roger just may not make it through tenth grade what with all the crap he has to take." Harry looked up in the air and laughed again, as if there were some great thing beyond what was at hand, something beyond them that was too funny for words.

"Most of my stuff is too secret for outsiders," said Harry. "But seeing you're down in the dumps, I'll give you a peek. C'mon, Nunnug."

Roger patted Nunnug and then, with some reluctance, followed along behind the dog and his master. "You and your secrets," he said. "I'm getting to the point where I don't believe you really have all these secrets. Course, I don't believe in much of anything anymore."

Harry grinned. "You should talk to Ennis. He believes everything. Did you see Virgi's saucer? What a laugh. Virgi, she always brought all her best stuff to school every single time."

"And that's another thing," said Roger. "I mean about Ennis. The school secretary told me there is no kid in the senior or junior high whose last name is Ennis. Course, you can't trust anybody in the principal's office—"

"Been checking up on me, eh? I like that. Well, maybe Ennis is his *first* name."

"Maybe Ennis doesn't exist, just like your big secret."

Harry laughed. "Maybe not."

"You know, Harry, I never see you in school anymore. Sometimes I think maybe you don't exist either."

"I'm right here," said Harry. "For the time being."

"I bet you're flunking out same as me," said Roger. "I bet you still don't do any homework."

"All my work is homework," said Harry. "I do all my work at home. But I don't need Mr. Figge to tell me about the Renaissance, and I don't need that hotsy-totsy Mrs. Emma Leibolt to tell me about what Shakespeare said. I just drift. Know what I did last week?"

"No, what?"

"I drifted into the chess club meeting after school just to see what was up. They had membership day, or something. I beat three guys in about fifteen minutes, and Mr. Newhouse, he gets all excited and says wouldn't I like to join. What a laugh. I just whistle a happy tune and stroll out with my hands in my pockets."

"But you should join," said Roger. "You could be a school champion. You could get a free train ticket to Newark for the state tournament."

He said this without much conviction, knowing that Harry had been right all along about high school not making any sense. Roger had tried to bring some of his best things to school, and it had worked out badly, just as Harry had predicted.

"That's Shakespeare," said Harry. "All that mucky-muck. The trick is to do it but stay out of it. Know what I mean? Play a few games to let them know what's what, and then fade out. Can you imagine me in a blue suit crammed on a bus with my elbow in somebody's armpit talking about how much I want the team to win and getting interviewed by the *Newark Evening News* and telling everyone how Johnny Nothing gave me the toughest match of my life and how lucky I was to beat Ricky Nobody because he's a swell guy and how the coach is an inspiration to us all? You got a picture of that? It's a toilet. I'd hafta break my spine to join the chess club."

Harry opened the screen door to the kitchen. When they were both inside, he let it bang behind them. "You want a Coke?"

Roger stared at Harry, trying through his bewilderment to understand the hatred and the fear that burned at the center of what he had said. He knew that it was very close to his own fear and his own hatred. "Harry, I sometimes think you could outtalk the whole world all at once. And you know something, you're probably right about the whole business. I mean, the chess club is not terrific. The whole world is not terrific. There's not too much sense in trying to plan ahead and be somebody 'cause the world is full of fat guys with big cigars and nuns and Concerned Mothers and principals and schoolteachers and dentists. So why think about the future? Why think about anything?"

Harry opened his mouth and closed his eyes and chuckled just once. The Great Cosmic Chuckle, Roger would call it later on when he talked about Harry Fisher. It was as if all the funny and bitter things in the world had come together at the circle of his open mouth into something too strong for laughter. "Sometimes," said Harry, "the future is all I think about. But it's not what you think. It's not what anybody thinks. That's the big secret. The biggest secret of all. What I mean is, I have an appointment."

"An appointment? I don't get it. You mean an appointment with destiny, like in a Bette Davis movie?"

"Something like that." Harry leaned against the white refrigerator in his mother's kitchen and looked out the window.

"Harry, there you go again. Everything with you has to be a big production number. I mean, what's the use? Who cares?"

"You need to try out the time machine," said Harry. "I got her all wound up and ready to go."

"I have to admit I'm curious," said Roger.

"Well, then c'mon upstairs. Watch out for Nunnug."

As they climbed the stairs to the second floor, Nunnug skittering along behind them on the varnished steps, he wondered what changes Harry had made in the attic. He had thought about it and the time machine so often that it was difficult now to remember what the place really looked like. Ythn had once told him that every time you think about something you change it, and that a man named Heisenberg had discovered something called the Principle of Uncertainty, which was a scientific expression of this idea. Roger did not know who Heisenberg was, but he was beginning to understand more and more that thinking had a lot to do with the way things were.

"I'd like to get Mrs. Leibolt up here sometime to play with the fleet," said Harry. "We could let her be a Chinese merchant ship. Send a torpedo right up her crotch. She really asks for it. The way she's always so hotsy-totsy all the time about everything. So smooth. The way she sashays around the room and sits on the edge of the desk and swings her legs. She really asks for it."

Roger winced. Was that the way Harry thought about girls? About doing it? He could not imagine Harry taking a girl to the movies or kissing her on her front doorstep and whispering goodbye. He wondered if he lingered over his early-morning erection or locked himself in the bathroom when he got home from school. *A torpedo in the crotch*. God, that was Harry all over.

"I guess you don't like Mrs. Leibolt very much," he said.

"She talked about me to the principal last week," said Harry. "Curtiss Baylor never forgot how I creamed him at chess last summer. So he told her I had strange things up in my attic and that I was probably practicing Lovecraft and that I was a very close friend of yours. But that don't bother me. I just whistle a happy tune until—well, until."

"Until summer."

"Forget about summer," said Harry. "Summer is just a rumor."

Harry put Nunnug in his second-floor bedroom and then led Roger up the narrow stairway to the attic. Roger held his breath, thinking there might be vast changes, but he was not prepared for what he saw when Harry opened the trapdoor, grabbed his wrist, and pulled him up.

Many things were the same. The dormer window, the swords and guns hanging from the blue walls, the high, vaulted roof. But the changes were incredible. Harry had painted the floor blue and he had made islands out of clay, with tiny sandy beaches and green forests and gray mountains three or four inches tall. In one corner the Japanese fleet steamed toward some invisible enemy. Above his head, a rolling expanse of clouds drifted at different levels all the way to the ceiling. Harry kicked at a switch on the floor and the whole room burst into light. Green and gold and yellow halos outlined the cotton clouds and filled them with a soft lambency. Roger felt himself rising out of his own misery into Harry's dark-bright attic world.

"Harry, you did it again. You're a genius."

"Right."

"This is the most terrific thing I ever saw. And the clouds are moving! How did you do that?"

"The clouds have strings attached onto them and the strings are attached onto a track that's got this quarter-horsepower motor onto it that I geared real low. If you're quiet you can hear the hum."

The clouds moved slowly across the heavens, the high cirrus and stratus going east and the lower cumulus moving north to south. Colored shadows played across the ocean and across the blue walls hung with weapons. And behind everything, the distant and barely audible hum of the power that moved.

But he noticed after a moment that other things stood outside the illusion of ocean, islands, ships, and clouds. The huge model of Greencastle that Harry had once threatened to burn sat on its table against the dormer window. Even across the room he could see the tiny trees, roads, houses, and automobiles. Then, as he turned around, he saw that most of one wall was covered with something that looked like a maze. The painted passageways merged, separated, came to dead ends, opened into pools of green and blue. Halfway up the wall, several of the passageways came out into yellow nothingness, above which floated a large golden disk. At various points in the maze, adhesive corks had been stuck to the wall, and glued to each cork was a tiny wooden carving—a bird, a unicorn, a snake, a lion, a spider, a cat. "It's a game," said Harry. "It's called Amenhotep the Fourth." And in the farthest corner, the time machine rose like a black obelisk halfway to the high ceiling.

It was a little too much to take in all at once. Too many different things, he thought. Oceans and warships and mazes and sun disks and time machines and model cities and colored lights and cotton clouds moving on invisible strings. Too many different things all going in different directions. Just like Harry.

"That's a funny name for a game" was all he could think to say.

"It don't mean anything," said Harry. "The cat and the snake, they're against everything else. They try to travel up through the maze to get to the sun. They win if they get to the sun."

"Sounds very Egyptian," said Roger. "You know the Egyptians worshipped the sun, and Amenhotep was the pharaoh who thought that the sun god was the only god."

"It's a joke," said Harry. "It's nothing. That's why I gave it a silly name. Did I tell you I attached a phonograph onto the time machine?"

They removed their shoes and walked across the ocean in their socks toward the black box that loomed in the corner. "*This* is what you could call my big production number," said Harry. "I got this little room inside with all my time travel equipment. When the machine starts, you can just watch, or you can step outside the window."

"There's a window?"

"Inside there's a window that goes outside. But not to *this* outside. If you cross over you can only stay for a minute. You got to get back before it goes or you're stuck in that time forever. No one will ever find you. Another thing. Sometimes—just sometimes—the time you see outside the window gets inside the time machine, and then you have to get out quick or you'll get stuck in time just like if you stayed outside the window too long."

"It all sounds kind of dangerous."

"Not if you follow orders. Just keep cool. Do like I tell you."

Roger touched the black wall of the time machine and noticed again the narrow vents, the currents of air, and the faint vibration that made the tips of his fingers feel fuzzy.

"Harry, is this your big secret? The thing nobody knows?"

Harry hesitated. "No. Not exactly."

"Harry, is this a joke?"

Harry laughed. "Everything's a joke. This is no different. But still this here is a real time machine. Best anyone ever made."

"And you want me to go inside?"

"That's what *you* wanted," said Harry.

"Harry, you wouldn't do anything crazy, would you? I mean, this thing isn't going to hurt me, is it?"

"It's just this big cardboard box I made from these two big things my dad kept suits in," said Harry. "Just go on in and set the dial and flip the switch and keep your eyes open. Just keep cool and remember that the danger, that's nothing. It's only the danger of getting away from a lot of stuff that don't matter."

Roger stared at the black box, and his fear told him that the things of this earth did matter, that he was not cool like Harry either was or pretended to be. Still, he had waited for months for this moment whose meaning seemed to change before his eyes. He saw that the door was just a large square C cut into the cardboard. He bent it open by pulling a string, and then he stepped inside. Harry grinned and closed the door behind him.

Inside, things were very bright. White lights against white plasterboard, and clocks ticking everywhere. He felt a moment of panic, but as his eyes adjusted he saw there was probably nothing to fear.

On the narrow wall directly in front of him, a great miscellany of devices sat on white shelves, all illuminated by eight white bulbs blinking on and off. On the top shelf, an old radio gang with a knob and a dial marked *Egypt*, *Middle Ages*, *Dunkirk*, *Midway*, and *Far Future* sat next to a mirror aimed at a set of lenses. On the next shelf, coils and magnets, and a serpentine jungle of electrical circuitry with resistors and condensers and radio tubes. On the bottom shelf, an old tape recorder, a large metal fan with a black safety frame and black blades, and a phonograph turntable with no tone arm. On it was a record painted with dozens of angular designs suggesting birds, snakes, lizards, suns, and moons, all in bright shades of red and green and gold. Only Harry would think to paint pictures on a phonograph record! Everything on the three shelves was more or less connected. Wires and tubes ran through holes drilled everywhere in the shelving.

On the right-hand wall adjacent to this tangled fantasy of machines, Roger saw a window cut out of the painted cardboard. Behind it, another white wall, again illuminated with bright lights, apparently from above. He stared at the window, thinking that this was where the past or future would appear. And if he stepped through into the narrow corridor—why was it that there seemed to be so much more space inside than outside?—he could get lost in some other time. But no. This was only a joke. Something out of Rube Goldberg.

"Set the dial and flip the switch," said Harry. His voice, muffled through the cardboard, seemed a hundred miles off, and fading.

He stood for another minute looking at everything. Then he set the radio dial for Egypt and turned the switch to *on*.

Immediately the fan began to oscillate and hum, and he felt a breeze run over his ankles. The blinking lights intensified. Things began to whirr and click. A beam of white light focused through the row of lenses and onto the mirror, and the ticking of the clocks seemed to grow louder. The turntable began to rotate, so that the bright designs blurred into an Archimedean spiral, a whirlpool of colors all sinking into the center. Suddenly, he was afraid.

He could not bring himself to look at the window, but he sensed that something—something was flickering across it. Shadows. Markings. The smell of ozone filled his nostrils. Did this mean that something had gone wrong? Was the time he was afraid to look at coming through the window? As his fear changed to terror he turned around and pushed against the cardboard door and fell out into the room. He heard himself gasp. All around lay the blue ocean, the islands, the blue wall with its maze and sun disk. Above him the clouds moved back and forth and whirred.

He expected a sharp remark and the sound of Harry's laughter. Instead Harry stood over him with his hands on his hips. It seemed to Roger that he was waiting for something.

"I couldn't stay in there," said Roger. "I got scared."

"What did you see?" said Harry. He spoke almost in a whisper.

"I didn't see anything. I was—I was afraid to look." He looked behind him and saw through the open door that everything had stopped and gone dark.

"I got it fixed so that when the door opens it turns off," said Harry.

"That's terrific. Hey look, could I try it again? I just—I didn't know what to expect. I've never been in a time machine before."

"It takes an hour to reset," said Harry.

"Oh."

"Sorry, buddy."

"Listen, you just have to let me try again later. Maybe I could come over tomorrow. Maybe—"

"You shoulda stayed in until you saw something," said Harry. "You shoulda done what I told you." Harry kicked the switch on the floor. The clouds stopped moving and the colored lights went out.

"We have to get outa here. My mother's gone shopping, but my father's gonna be home in about ten minutes."

"Is that a problem? I mean, doesn't he like all the stuff you do up here?"

"He's my father," said Harry. "That tells the story, doesn't it? Are you sure you didn't see anything out the window? Didn't you look even for a second?"

"No."

Harry thought for a moment. "Maybe it's just as good you didn't," he said. "Maybe you're too different from me. Maybe you're not ready for the big jump. Me, I been ready for a long time now."

On the way downstairs he stopped to free Nunnug, whom he had locked in his second-floor room, and to stuff something into his shirt. Nunnug barked and followed him, his tail smacking against walls and railings and chair legs as they made their way out through the kitchen and into the backyard.

Roger took a deep breath. The wind and the shadows and

the green grass dazzled him. It was as if the outside world had vanished from the universe when he stepped inside Harry's house, and now, miraculously, had re-created itself.

He could think of nothing to say. He had seen too many things too quickly. He could not imagine anyone doing all the things that Harry did, reaching out in so many different directions. What, he wondered, would it all come to? Where was Harry trying to go?

"Harry, where did you go when you used the time machine?"

Harry looked around at the shattered army of acorns. Then he found a stick and threw it across the yard and watched Nunnug chase after it. "I never did use it yet," he said. "I wanted you to be the first. You know, sort of like I'm the inventor and you're the test pilot. But I'll give it a whirl tomorrow, maybe."

Nunnug dropped the stick at Harry's feet and then looked up mournfully at his master. Harry picked up the stick and threw it again.

"Nunnug, he doesn't need a time machine," he said. "He just eats and craps and pisses and sleeps and barks and runs around and gets petted. He's a good dog, aren't you, Nunnug? He's a happy dog. Found him half dead in a parking lot downtown. Just a no-name dog. Nonadog. Nunnug. But Roger, he's not like Nunnug. He's all sad 'cause he got chicken and flunked the time machine test. Maybe we oughta give poor Roger a present."

Harry pulled something out of his shirt and handed it to Roger without looking at him. It was a hunting knife in a brown leather sheath.

"Harry, I don't—"

"Open it up."

Roger undid the metal snap and withdrew the knife. It glinted silver. A little scallop near the tip brought the blade to a sharp point, and a thin blood groove ran the length of it. *English Sheffield*, it said in tiny letters where the blade met the horn handle.

"It's beautiful."

"Take it."

"You mean you're giving it to me?"

"How many times do I have to say it? It's a present."

"But it's too much just to give away. I mean—"

"It doesn't go with my stuff at all," said Harry. "My father gave it to me about five years ago when—well, just get rid of it for me, will you? Give it away if you don't want it. It's a garbage knife. You know, Boy Scout stuff. You're kind of a Boy Scout type, so I thought you might be able to use it."

"I should trade you something."

"I gave up trading."

"Harry, I don't know what to say. It's a terrific knife. I never had a good knife—"

"Look," said Harry, "it's a real simple thing, okay? I been trying to get rid of it for weeks. Don't think—don't think for a second that I—"

Harry's face turned red. He clenched his teeth. "Sometimes—sometimes people like you really get under my skin." The words were slurred, barely comprehensible. "You think because I show you all my stuff—you think because I give you a crummy knife—"

He snatched the knife away from Roger, stared at it, then, very gently, put it back in his hands.

"Harry? You okay?" He wondered again if Harry was crazy. He had heard somewhere that being a genius was very close to being crazy.

The two boys walked around the front of the house and stood for a moment just at the edge of the forest of shadows that marked the end of Harry Fisher's domain.

"Thanks, Harry."

"Christmas in springtime," said Harry. "Me, I'm Santa Claus. Just paint my ass red. Listen, I'll see you later."

Before he turned away, Harry made a little sign with his hand, a jerk of his wrist with his fingers held stiffly together. Roger could not remember ever seeing Harry *wave* to anyone. Harry *signaled.*

With the knife in his right hand, he began to run home. He thought again about the time machine. It was more than what he thought it would be. It was not a joke at all. He had the feeling that somehow it had worked, or had almost worked, or would have worked if only he had stayed inside a little longer.

He glanced back just once, and for a moment he saw Harry Fisher standing inside his screened-in front porch. Harry seemed to be looking out at something, but at that distance there was no telling what he saw or what he was thinking. Roger was too far away now to see even the outline of his face, but he noticed, in that brief instant, a bright spot on the screen where Harry pressed his hand.

31 | *Sashi Sugi*

In grammar school Roger had believed that he, like Frank Aldonotti, possessed total recall. But by the time he entered junior high it was clear to him that his eidetic memory, though amazing in some ways, was very selective. He knew the names of sixty different Egyptian gods and could write several informative sentences about each of them in hieroglyphics. He remembered the names and faces of everyone who visited on Christmas day in 1948. He remembered whole paragraphs from novels, even their position on the page. On the other hand, there were whole years that were missing from his life, and when he looked back, trying to recall feelings and images, there would only be the vague memory of being seven and perhaps something very dull and trivial, like having to wear knickers. Today was another day, the seven hundred and eighty-eighth Friday of his life. But in the years to come there would be no other day whose moments and hours he would remember with such coherence, and with such intensity. It was the thirtieth of May, and the year was 1952.

He remembered something in the paper that morning about Reverend Wilcox, something that brought to mind the image of the man sitting before Pangborn's shattered window staring at the square of space where Pangborn had disappeared, looking like a man bleeding to death. The article in the paper reported that he had resigned his post as pastor of the United Brethren Church, saying that he was a dull old man and that "all those who have followed me have been led away from the heart of humanity into dogma and superstition." It was an odd thing, Roger thought, coming from a man who had never been anything but an anthology of slogans.

He remembered that he had paid twenty-two dollars that morning at the principal's office to replace the books he had lost. He remembered that Dennis Kirk's purple eye had begun to turn a sickening yellow. He remembered that there had been a very unhappy hour with Mrs. Leibolt. It was their last class period of Adventures in Drama, and she had ended it by ticking off the elements of tragedy according to Aristotle, and then discussing how tragic heroes have tragic flaws, usually a prideful or blindly passionate nature. And she had talked about how Greek tragedy was, for modern audiences, less spectacular than Shakespeare's for a number of reasons, one of which being that in Greek drama the main action happens offstage and is merely reported by a messenger.

"We do not see how Jocasta hangs herself or how Oedipus tears out his eyes with the clasps from her robe," she said with unnatural calmness. "And thus the dramatic meaning is to some extent lost upon us."

Harriet Emerick clicked her tongue. Buck Moore mumbled something and shook his head. Mary John Grodner made a square of horror with her mouth and clapped her hands over her ears. Then Mrs. Leibolt drifted back to the question of pride and blind passion:

"We see these things in our own lives," she said. "That is why Shakespeare is so powerful, so modern. We see people among us today who become enthusiasts. People who are misled by their beliefs or their feelings. People who make terrible mistakes even though they are not evil people."

She glanced briefly at Roger, and for a moment he feared she was about to say something about him—perhaps that he was the cause of all the strange and awful things that had been said and done in Greencastle for the last three months. He knew in his mind that she would never do such a thing, and yet he expected it. He saw his name on her lips. He wanted to cry out, to shout obscenities and light fires all over the room with his eyes.

"We live in a romantic age," she went on to say. "An age that Shakespeare and Sophocles would hardly have approved of. We live in an age in which the Romeos and the Macbeths and the Othellos and the Hamlets seem to be threatening everything. They are no longer beautiful but tragic figures who must, ultimately, surrender to the larger system of order. You all know what is happening now in American movies and in American literature and in politics. There are enemies everywhere. Even here—yes, right here—in Greencastle. Standards are shaken. Decency is ridiculed and God is mocked. You know, of course, that Dr. Mace and all the teachers have been made deeply aware of this and that we now have new policies concerning absences, tardiness, disrespect toward teachers—"

Everyone had heard all this before from all of the other teachers except Miss Simic, who never bothered with anything but Latin. But there was a quietness now in Mrs. Leibolt's manner, a quietness that everyone feared. It meant extra homework, a trip to the principal's office, or a surprise quiz.

"There was a boy just this morning," she said. "A junior. He has been disrespectful to me on many occasions. Today he made an obscene gesture in my direction in response to a question I asked him. When I asked for an apology, he just smiled and said nothing. I reported this to Dr. Mace and recommended a five-day suspension. This is a hard punishment, but these are exceptional times."

A wave of whispers rolled across the class. There had been no suspensions that year except for Rolfe Gerhardt and Virgi Prewitt.

"Who was it?" said Harriet.

"That's not our business here," said Mrs. Leibolt.

"Was it someone on the basketball team?"

"No."

"Was it Sonny Vacca or Stan Pignatari or Freddy Cucinelli?"

"No. And I don't want any more questions about this. I want to get on to your essay outlines. Let me remind you that you have less than three weeks before your papers are due—"

When the bell rang, Mrs. Leibolt came to his desk and touched his shoulder. She looked down at him and smiled. "Roger, I need to talk with you for just a minute before the next class comes in."

He could not remember that Mrs. Leibolt had ever touched him before. He sat in his seat, stiff and uneasy. He stared at her tight little breasts, and then at her stomach. The students from his class smiled and whispered, passed by on both sides as if he and Mrs. Leibolt were two rocks fixed in the middle of a stream. "I'll be late for History," he managed to say.

"Never mind that. This is very important. You're the only student in this class who hasn't turned in an outline for the final paper. I was wondering if you had an explanation."

"Not really."

"Well, are you working on your outline?"

"I was. For a while."

"When can I expect to see it?"

"I don't know."

"You don't know," she repeated.

"I had several topics, but I gave up on them."

"Why?"

"Mrs. Leibolt, I thought you said I wasn't supposed to talk in this class for the rest of the term."

"You'll answer me when I ask you a question," she said calmly. "Besides, this is not class. Class is over. Now what's the problem? Are you simply refusing to do the work, or is it something else? Something I can help you with?"

"It's something else," said Roger. He tried to meet her gaze calmly, hoping to exasperate her, make her ask *what else?* When she did not answer and did not look away, he lost his nerve and went on, trying to explain himself. "I didn't think you would like any of my subjects," he said hurriedly, "and I didn't want to have to read my paper out loud and have everybody in the class laughing at things they don't understand."

Mrs. Leibolt sat down at the desk next to his and crossed her legs. Then she raised her eyebrows and put a finger to her mouth as if she were about to shush someone. "You think you're a superior person, don't you? You think you stand out above and beyond everyone else."

Roger stared at her in amazement. "No."

"You think you're a genius. You think you don't need to abide by the rules and regulations that everyone else abides by."

"Mrs. Leibolt, I don't think that at all."

She leaned forward and her eyes narrowed. "There is something you need to know about yourself," she whispered. "Something you have never been able to face. I don't like to be the one to tell you, but do you know—do you have any idea—how *ordinary* you are? Have you ever seen your aptitude scores and your achievement scores? Roger, you are not one of the chosen few who, for better or worse, are going to change the world. Can you understand that?"

As she leaned forward, rigid and breathless and intense in a way he had never seen her, he knew the terrible import of what she had said. He felt his face turn scarlet. It came to him, suddenly, that all his life he had feared being ordinary more than anything in the world, and that this truth was the cruelest of all. It was the thing he feared, the thing that haunted him. He could stand forever with his arms raised in the night sky and nothing would ever happen. He had hoped, he had half believed, that he was infinite, that there was no end to what he might imagine and feel and understand. But he knew in his heart that this was not so. That much was clear from the way Mrs. Leibolt had arranged the seating in English class: he had once been first in the second row; that was the highest he had ever gone. Her purpose, he knew, was to find out how much everyone was worth, and she had done that. He had reached his high-water mark and now he was falling.

As she leaned toward him he realized that he no longer wanted to smell her perfume or look down the front of her dress. He wanted to get away.

"Roger, I don't mean to make you cry."

"I'm not crying."

"I just want you to see the truth. There is nothing wrong with being average. Average people have their lives too. They have their triumphs and their moments of happiness—"

"I don't have to listen to this," said Roger. "You're just—"

He had no words to fight her with. He felt empty. He stood up and turned away from her and then ran out of the room. Halfway down the hall he realized that he was late for History and that he had left all his books and papers behind in Mrs. Leibolt's class. He stopped, thinking that perhaps he should go back. But the longer he stood there in the hallway, the less it seemed to matter. He would be no more prepared with his books and papers than he would be without them.

An hour later he found himself standing in the lunch line with his metal tray and his carton of milk. The fat ladies dumped mashed potatoes and meat loaf and canned peas and apple dumpling on his plate, and he turned, almost blind with despair, into the huge and shapeless beast that was everybody eating and laughing and talking. He found an empty place and sat down, wondering what to do with all the food on his plate.

After a while he noticed that a hush had fallen over the whole south end of the cafeteria. Then loud whispers and a burst of voices. Then another silence and another rising of whispers. Finally he looked up and saw that dozens of students had left their trays to stand in small circles near the doorway. It came to him, finally, that something unusual must have happened.

As he turned back to his own tray, thinking that whatever

it was was not worth knowing, he happened to glance at the tray across from his. There on the other side of the table were two smooth hands and a bracelet of German silver.

"Hi, Roger."

"Ruth? Ruth! Have you—I mean, have you been sitting there all the time? I didn't see you. I guess I never even looked up—"

As he began to stumble over words he caught himself, swallowed down his panic, and just looked at her face. He had tried so hard not to think about her, and now, looking into her sad, quiet eyes, it was all he could do not to wince. But then she pushed away her tray and closed her eyes and he sensed that she was not even thinking about him. Something was wrong.

"Ruth? Are you sick?"

"No."

"Aren't you hungry? You look like you have a headache or something."

"I don't know how to say it. It's something awful."

"Something about me? What more could happen? Did I get suspended? Listen, you probably shouldn't be sitting with me—"

"It's not you. It's Harry Fisher. He's a friend of yours, didn't you say?"

"Sort of. Is he the one who got suspended?"

"Yes. Mrs. Leibolt reported him and he got a five-day suspension."

"That's not so terrible. Harry doesn't really need to go to school."

"He went home at noontime," said Ruth. "He shot himself."

Roger heard the words clearly enough, but for a few seconds they did not connect to anything that was real. He could not help but smile. Why would anyone want to say a thing like that?

"You're talking about Harry? Harry Fisher?"

"He shot himself in the head with a German pistol. He's dead."

"Dead," said Roger.

"The principal heard the gun go off over the telephone when he called Mrs. Fisher. He called the police ambulance. Harry was dead before they got there."

Roger stared at her. "Harry built a time machine. Did you know that?"

"No, I didn't know that."

"I saw it. I went inside. It really works. At least I think it does. Harry builds lots of things. He's a genius, but hardly anybody knew that. Harry—he never brought his good stuff to school. Or anywhere else."

"It's such an awful thing," said Ruth. "There's no words for it. The teachers—I guess all the teachers just pushed him and pushed him for not doing his work. He just smiled and made jokes about it until—until he couldn't make jokes about it anymore. I heard one of the teachers say—"

"Where's Mrs. Leibolt?"

"She's in her room. Dr. Mace is with her, and I think one of the other English teachers. Mr. Figge is standing outside the door telling all her homeroom students that they have to go to fifth period without their books."

Roger stood up. "I have to see Mrs. Leibolt."

"They won't let you in."

"I have to see Mrs. Leibolt. I have a few things I have to tell her."

"Roger, you better not. You're in enough trouble already."

"I'll see you later. Can you wait for me here? Never mind, I'll see you later. I'll call you. I'll—"

He walked out of the cafeteria and across the stone driveway that separated it from the main building. The sunlight blinded him. He closed his eyes and saw the bright sun disk looming above the maze of Amenhotep IV, the bright cotton clouds drifting across the vaulted ceiling, and the beautiful paper city. As he thought of the painted circle, he felt the real sun somewhere above him. It made things turn green, it made steam rise above the Watchung swamp, and it was now turning spring into summer.

But the sun was too bright for Harry. He lived in the dark, where he made his own light. He must have known there was no future in that, but perhaps it seemed like the safest thing, the only way he could win every time. Harry had no connections, nowhere to go, and so he took a trip on his own time machine and found that it worked. *Sashi sugi*. Enough is enough. That was the secret that Harry Fisher carried around with him from one season to the next. Mrs. Leibolt had given him the occasion for what he had always known would happen.

Roger pushed open one of the double doors to the school, took three bounding steps, and then pulled open the inner door so hard that something snapped inside the hissing air cylinder above his head. He realized that Mrs. Leibolt had also given *him* the occasion. She and Mrs. Daniel S. Treet and Dr. Mace and the Christian Alliance and Parents for Better Schools and Nuns and God and Patriotism and Jesus and Concerned Mothers and the Flag and Anti-Communists Everywhere and every slogan and march and jingle he could think of. *Sashi sugi*, he thought to himself. *Sashi* goddamn *sugi*.

Nothing seemed quite real as he walked down the dim hallway toward the small crowd of students milling outside Mrs. Leibolt's homeroom—nothing except his feeling of outrage and horror.

He knew that he was going to talk to Emma Leibolt. By God, he would talk to her here and now like nobody in the tenth grade had ever talked to any English teacher anywhere in the whole world.

Harry, he thought. *My God, you were a genius. Here you are dead and gone almost two hours and here I am still alive and so ordinary.*

32 What Tragedy Does

He was standing now in front of Mr. Figge. He was content for the moment just to stare at him, to watch his mouth move and see how his Adam's apple jerked up and down like a trapped sparrow when he talked. With his thin yellow hair and the pathetic little mustache that he had tried for three years to cultivate, he looked like a worried Russian clerk, or a failed dictator.

"This means you too, Roger," he was saying. "Especially you. Yes. Most especially."

"What?"

"How many times do I have to say it? You're not allowed in here. Please, would everyone go about his and her business? Dr. Mace doesn't want people congregating here. We have—you might say we have a problem. Yes. That would be a fair statement."

"I have to talk with Mrs. Leibolt," said Roger as the others began to drift away.

"Now look, Roger. I don't want any trouble. You be a good boy."

"Mr. Figge, let me put it this way. I'm only fifteen going on sixteen in about two weeks and I'm about a foot shorter than you but I'm going to smash your face in if you don't move over and let me in there."

Mr. Figge backed against the door and clutched the knob. "You're crazy. You wouldn't dare. You'd be expelled for the year."

"But it wouldn't look too good on your record either, would it, Mr. Figge? I can see it in the papers. High school teacher gets in fistfight while teachers drive student to suicide."

Mr. Figge's eyes went wide. He raised his hands in front of him when Roger stepped forward. "You don't know what you're doing," he said. "You'll wind up in prison."

"Just let me in there."

Mr. Figge moved just enough to one side so that Roger could get his hand on the knob. "It's your funeral," said the vice-principal. "Don't say I didn't warn you."

Roger pushed the door open. Inside it was like the Christmas tableau the seniors did every December. People standing around the manger trying to look very serious and trying very hard not to move.

From the far wall, sunlight flooded in through the six long windows over the shelves that housed paper and cardboard models of the Globe Theatre, crinkled tinfoil crowns, and student facsimiles of quartos rolled into scrolls. But no one sat in the phalanx of metal desks screwed to the floor. Mrs. Leibolt sat at her desk at the front of the room with her hands folded. Dr. Mace stood to one side, with the tips of his fingers touching her green blotter. He leaned over and whispered something to her. Mrs. Griffith, an older woman who taught senior English, sat in a chair in front of the desk, clutching at her purse and staring at the floor. Miss Mozart, the blond woman who was head secretary in the principal's office, sat next to Mrs. Leibolt. She was pressed forward so as to hear what Dr. Mace was whispering, and in her left hand she held a wad of Kleenex.

When Dr. Mace saw Roger standing in the open doorway, he straightened abruptly, removed his glasses, and took three quick strides toward him. "Get out," he said. "Get out this second. You have no business here. I told Mr. Figge—"

Roger slammed the door. "I was Harry's best friend," he said. "I was the only one he talked to. You and Mrs. Leibolt—you're the ones who killed him. You get out."

Dr. Mace made a sudden guttural sound, a snarl of pure hatred, and seized Roger by the wrist. Roger pulled away with such violence that he fell heavily against the blackboard and smeared his shirt with chalk dust. He heard Mrs. Griffith gasp.

"Don't touch me!" said Roger. "Don't any of you touch me!"

Dr. Mace hesitated. He glanced at Mrs. Griffith and Miss Mozart, and then at Mrs. Leibolt, who did not seem to be aware of what had happened. Roger walked to Mrs. Leibolt's desk and looked down so that his shadow fell across her face. He had no idea what he wanted to say to her, but he felt a rage shaking him, choking him, roaring inside his head. He knew that everyone in the room was watching him, waiting for him to say something, or do something.

He saw tears on Mrs. Leibolt's cheeks. The face itself seemed calm, impersonal, like a stone edifice. But behind the windows of her eyes he saw something terrible, and he remembered that once when he was very small he had seen a department store burn down. The place had held its shape for what seemed like hours and hours, but behind the windows he saw that a bright dance of fire was gutting the building.

"Mrs. Leibolt, I came to talk to you."

It was only then that she looked up at him. She smiled in her quick, abrupt way, and drew her dignity around her like a cloak. "Yes," she said. "I thought you might come. You were a friend of—the boy. I've forgotten his name. Isn't that strange?"

Dr. Mace pressed his hands together. "Roger, I think you can see that Mrs. Leibolt is distraught. She's in no condition—"

"You were supposed to know," said Roger. "You're a teacher, for God's sake, and you were supposed to know."

Mrs. Leibolt was still looking up at him. She smiled again, this time more faintly. "What was I supposed to know, Roger?"

Miss Mozart stood up very suddenly and then took a step away from the desk. It was clear that she did not want Roger towering over her. She began to cry. "Don't let him go on, for heaven's sake! She can't take this! She was like this last summer—"

"You were supposed to know about Shakespeare," said Roger, who still did not know what he was going to say. "The play's the thing, right? Then way over on the other side of your desk there's all of us. You wanted us to be all the same so you could give us all some Shakespeare and we could all get it in the same way, like when they pass out M&Ms in grammar school. But Shakespeare died a long time ago. His bones are lying over there in England someplace and his plays just sit there in books. But maybe he comes alive in us once in a while. And maybe you were supposed to know the difference between life and death."

"The difference between life and death," said Mrs. Leibolt.

"Stop it!" said Miss Mozart. "Stop it! Stop it! Stop it! Dr. Mace, will you please do something!"

"You wanted Shakespeare to be very specific and you wanted all of us to be very general," said Roger. "Just like Mrs. Treet wants us all to be patriotic and just like Senator McCarthy wants us all to hate Communists and just like all the Concerned Mothers want us to be like the Hardy Boys. But we can't do that because we're losing too much already when we get to be fifteen, and everything is getting far apart, and Mr. Heisenberg says that everything changes if we even look at it, and nobody knows just what's what, and we know it was real important what the Donkey said to the Cat, but we were never sure what that was in the first place. So we try to have a little faith, like Mr. Lowell did when he looked at Mars. We don't want to give up and just slash our arms because we all live in the Palace of Bad Luck, like the Arabs. That's why we can't all be general. Do you see now why we can't be general?"

"Listen to him!" cried Miss Mozart. "He's insane! And Emma's been so sick! And she tries so hard! And last summer there was that terrible business with her father and then she missed the first weeks of school—"

"Death is very general," said Mrs. Leibolt. "It covers everything."

"Dr. Mace? Are you going to stop this?" Miss Mozart took a step toward Roger.

"Harry won't be back on Monday, will he?" asked Mrs. Leibolt.

"No," said Roger. "He's not coming back because you didn't want him to come back. You wanted order and peace and respect, and you wanted us all to be the same. You wanted us all to die a little."

"I wanted Shakespeare," said Mrs. Leibolt. Her voice was dry now, and distant. "But my father—well—my father was an archaeologist. He was a genius, and I was so ordinary. I loved Melville and Twain and Emerson, but I could never—I just couldn't seem to—"

She was trying to get the words out, but she couldn't. For a moment it seemed to amuse her that she couldn't speak. She smiled at Dr. Mace, who seemed frozen in horror. It was the sudden smile that Roger had seen her make so many times, and he saw now that it was not a smile at all: it was a convulsion, a spasm of pain.

She stood up and looked vaguely around the room as if wondering where all her students had gone. No one moved. Miss Mozart was crying softly. Dr. Mace stood with his hands against his cheeks, and seemed about to say something. Mrs. Leibolt turned and went to the blackboard. "I do have standards," she finally managed to say. "If you have standards, why then you can all see what is fine and beautiful even if you can't—even if you don't have—"

She took a piece of chalk in her right hand and pressed her left hand against the blackboard for support. Then she stumbled. She clutched at the eraser rack and then with a little sob she fell to her knees, the chalk falling from her hand and breaking on the floor. She had tried to write something, but instead had left only a small, star-shaped mark in the middle of the empty blackboard.

Miss Mozart ran over to where she had fallen. Mrs. Griffith and Dr. Mace took Roger by his arms and led him out of the room. This time he did not resist. When they had pushed through the semicircle of students outside the door, they released him. Roger looked up at Dr. Mace. He anticipated anger but instead saw something closer to fear on the lean, bony face that had always, absurdly, reminded him of Abraham Lincoln.

"Roger—what are you going to do now?"

"Nothing. I'm going home. I'm not going to do anything."

The principal seemed to think about this. "That's good," he said after a moment. "You must be very tired."

"Yes."

"And what about tomorrow?"

"Tomorrow I'm just coming to school. I don't have any plans."

Dr. Mace rubbed his eyes. "Roger, I do hope that this tragedy—this terrible tragedy—will lead to a new understanding for all of us."

Roger was silent for another moment. "Is that what tragedy does?"

He remembered Romeo and Juliet, and how their double suicide brought the two warring houses together. No, he thought. That was Shakespeare. That was hundreds of years ago, if ever.

He walked out of the school and felt the cool wind blow against his face. He saw that Dennis and Frank were waiting for him on the other side of Paris Avenue. *Let it go*, he thought. *Let it all go. The school year is nearly over and Harry is right where he wants to be. Just let it go and everything will be all right again.*

33 | Thoughts Have Wings

Things happened quickly after the death of Harry Fisher. On Monday morning a round of letters, mostly from women, appeared in the *Greencastle Herald* demanding to know what was happening in their high school. Were academic pressures so intense and was discipline so strict that students were going to pieces? Killing themselves? On Tuesday morning two representatives from the town council spent the day at the high school talking to students in the hallway and observing classes. The next afternoon William R. Mace was summoned to a three-hour meeting of the county board of education. Later, when questioned by Truman Greenwood, he indicated that he and the board had had a frank and very useful exchange of views. That same day, PBS president Mrs. Daniel S. Treet reported to the *Herald* that their yearly funding for school improvements would be withheld pending a full investigation of policies and practices regarding suspension and expulsion. She added that rumors concerning certain vigilante activities at PBS were patently untrue and that she herself never went out after five without her husband.

When school let out that afternoon, Harry Fisher, Sr., a man Roger had seen only once, appeared at the door of the principal's office, demanding to see Dr. Mace. According to Miss Mozart, he forced his way into the office and after a brief scuffle was subdued by the combined efforts of Dr. Mace and Mr. Figge. According to Dr. Mace, Mr. Fisher had shouted obscenities and then run out of the office and fallen down the steps leading to the south entrance. According to Mr. Fisher, Mace and Figge had called him a filthy Jew Communist and tried to murder him right there in the principal's office. The one verifiable fact seemed to be that Harry Fisher, Sr., did receive emergency treatment at the local hospital that afternoon for a broken arm and a bruised elbow.

Two days later the whole incident was reported in the back pages of a New York City tabloid. HIGH SCHOOL STUDENT EXPELLED, COMMITS SUICIDE, PRINCIPAL SENDS FATHER TO HOSPITAL, the headline read. The next morning the school was full of people in gray suits and black briefcases, people Roger had never seen before.

"Do they think Dr. Mace and Mr. Figge are Communists?" said Marilyn Sord.

"I guess there's an awful lot of them around," said Buck Moore.

"Somebody said yesterday that the Communists are going to burn down Pangborn's bookstore," said Larry Norcross.

"That's 'cause the Communists don't want us to read," said Eddie McQueen.

The next day Roger saw in the *Newark Evening News* that Virgi Prewitt, who had been expelled for drawing bugs, had just won first prize in the junior division of the Newark Arts Festival, and that her painting was on display along with several dozen others at a Newark department store. Again there came a flurry of letters to the *Greencastle Herald*: Was Dr. Mace systematically getting rid of all the talented students, driving them into Jewish and Catholic schools? Didn't this kind of Nazi emphasis on repression and conformity go against everything our boys had fought and died for for five years? One angry mother wrote that if American high schools didn't improve, everyone would be driven to the Monteverdi method, which was full of Italian ideas. The following day someone replied that he did not see what Italian church music had to do with education, and just what did the lady think she was talking about anyway?

Near midnight on Saturday evening, person or persons unknown smashed all the rest of the windows in Pangborn's Used Book and Magazine Store. The next morning Larry Norcross and the entire basketball team were brought to the police station for questioning. No one bothered Roger or the other Denizens. It was clear now that they and Norman Pangborn had been the victims of a malicious stupidity that no one had a name for. By the following Monday, a kind of stunned quietude had fallen over the school. No one spoke in the hallways, the men with the black briefcases roamed the building, and classes were dismissed in the early afternoon for "administrative consolidation" and "pedagogy workshops." As Roger left for the day he saw Virgi Prewitt, flanked by her mother and father, entering the school. Dennis remarked to the other Denizens that the three of them looked grim but victorious, like Russian soldiers before the gates of Berlin.

Dr. Mace announced on the second Tuesday after Harry's death that Mrs. Leibolt, who had not appeared in school since that tragic day, would be on sick leave for the rest of the semester and that Mrs. Budge, a retired junior high school teacher, would substitute. There were unconfirmed rumors that Mrs. Leibolt had arisen one morning, smiled at herself in the mirror, and then attempted suicide. It was then Roger realized that falling in love was not the only reason people slashed their wrists. Yes, that was perfectly clear now. Harry Fisher, after all, had never fallen in love with anyone.

"Mrs. Leibolt would never do a thing like that," said Harriet Emerick.

"I heard three people say she did," said Melissa Van Ghent.

"But that's just a rumor," said Marilyn Sord.

"But where there's smoke there must be fire," said Mary John Grodner, who was finally getting into the spirit of things.

Although it was clear to him that various people were finally getting just a little of what they deserved, Roger took almost no satisfaction in this. He knew that in the very hour of Harry's death he had used the occasion as a weapon against his enemies, and when reporters questioned him he had replied that school officials had imposed a ban of silence on him and that he would thus be in serious trouble if he said anything to the press, or anyone else. That had been clever, he thought. But also vengeful, and perhaps dishonest. He had made the school look bad even as he pretended to say nothing, to bow to its authority. He was no longer the boy who said exactly what he thought, who was willing to die for his friends, who took girls to operettas, and who rose above the various war games that adults loved to play. Now he was a soldier like everyone else. Harry had been right about that. No, he thought. Harry had been wrong about everything. *Let it go,* he thought. *Let it all go. Summer is nearly here.*

On the way home from school he passed Harry's house. He had not meant to go that way, but Dennis and Frank had gone downtown for haircuts and so, as he walked alone, his mind had drifted. He had taken Recognition Street down the dark hill, and there he was.

And there in the backyard just in front of the garage, Roger saw something that made him shudder. A mountain of refuse—sticks and bits of colored paper, shattered glass, rubber tubing, lumps of plaster, splinters of wood, wheels, gears, radio tubes, light bulbs, bottles—everything broken, smashed, thrown into a terrible heap. All the delicate little houses and roads, and all the tiny automobiles and trees from Harry's paper city. The illuminated clouds of cotton moving on invisible pulleys. Roger had read a story somewhere about a daughter who had died, and the father and mother had kept everything unchanged in the girl's bedroom as a kind of memorial. But Harry's mother and father had destroyed everything. It was a terrible thing. Perhaps, he thought, they had torn up the whole house. Or perhaps there was something in the attic that Harry's father hated, something he thought was responsible for what had happened.

He heard something jingle, and then he saw Harry's dog chained to the porch. The dog sat on his haunches and stared at him mournfully, and then, suddenly, he pointed his nose to the sky like a wolf, and howled. The sound seemed to alter everything, changing the neighborhood into a kind of wilderness.

Roger dropped his books on the sidewalk and ran up onto the porch. He knelt down and hugged the dog, who whimpered when he touched him, as if love were painful.

"No Name Dog," said Roger. "Sweet No Name Dog. Harry loved you, did you know that? I was wrong about Harry not loving anything. Harry loved you. He loved you more than anything in the world—"

The dog whimpered again, and Roger pressed his face into the animal's neck. His throat tightened, and he felt tears in his eyes. Then he looked up and saw, through the dark porch screen, the shadow of a woman.

"Oh! Mrs. Fisher! I didn't know—I mean, I'm sorry if I—"

"Don't go away," said the Gray Lady. "Please, could you stay for just a minute? I have some chocolate cake. Nice boy like you. Such nice manners. Just like a private school boy. Stay and pet Nunnug for a spell. Poor dog, he gets so lonesome. He doesn't understand—you know—"

Mrs. Fisher let her fingers go down the screen. The sound of it was like someone screaming very far away.

The details of Harry's suicide came out in bits and pieces. Roger read about it in the paper, heard rumors from his mother when she came home from church on Sunday, and overheard other details from Melissa Van Ghent, who in turn overheard Miss Mozart talking about it while she was on office duty during study hall. Harry had shot himself in the mouth with an American army pistol, not a German Lüger as was first reported. His mother had been on the phone talking to the principal when she heard the shot, went upstairs, and found him in a large cardboard wardrobe that Harry had painted black. The bullet had blown the back of his head off, and fragments of his skull and brain had made a gray mosaic on the inside of the time machine. Harry's mother went back downstairs and screamed into the telephone that the school had murdered her son. Then she fainted. She later told reporters that she was surprised by all the things she found in the attic. Harry never had any money, she said, and she had no idea where it all came from. She added that she had not been up in the attic for over a year.

It never occurred to Roger that he should attend the open-casket service at the Morrison Funeral Home. He did not know Harry's parents, he was not a friend of the family, and he wanted nothing to do with Harry's death, or anyone else's. Besides, he did not want to see Harry. He had heard that the undertaker had worked for two days rebuilding Harry's lips and teeth and jaw with wax and porcelain and food coloring and nylon thread. Instead, he lit a candle in his room and let it burn through the night. He had seen that once in a movie, and it was all he could think to do for Harry Fisher.

Just after midnight he awakened. He sat up instantly and looked about the room. It was as if someone had put a hand on his cheek. Twice he saw the candle flicker, and he wondered what could cause that, since both of his windows were closed. Then he saw the beautiful Boy Scout knife sitting on his table in the corner. He had left it there unsheathed, and the blade gleamed a little in the diffused yellow candlelight.

During the last week of school the police quietly informed Norman Pangborn that he was free to open, Truman Greenwood was fired from the *Greencastle Herald*, Mrs. Daniel S. Treet resigned as president of Parents for Better Schools, and Dr. William R. Mace left every morning for a meeting somewhere downtown. By the end of the week shadows appeared under his eyes. Two FBI agents hiked through the Watchung Reservation and talked to students after school at Roosevelt Memorial Field. They looked very much out of place in their brown seersucker suits.

On Monday he spent his lunch hour in the cafeteria, a place he had avoided since Harry's death. Inside, things seemed normal enough except that people were unusually quiet and a uniformed policeman was inspecting the steam trays. The three fat ladies stood back against the stoves, whispered to each other, and murdered him with their eyes. Roger had always hated the cafeteria. He hated the smell of gymnasium wax, the stench of fried food and spilt milk, and the invisible clouds of heat and perspiration that made him not want to touch anything or sit anywhere.

Across the room he saw Ruth sitting with a new girl who had just moved from Iowa a month earlier. She wore a new jumper, a purple one with a white blouse underneath, and cuffs that burst from her wrists like white flowers. She was talking about something, smiling, moving her right hand in a little circle. The other girl nodded and smiled, and all at once he felt unhappy seeing her like that. So far away across the room, so perfectly occupied with someone else. He had seen her follow him with her eyes for weeks when nearly everyone else despised him, but he had let her drift away. She had asked for nothing, and so he had given her nothing. And now the school year was nearly over, and he had heard from Frank that Harriet Emerick had overheard Ruth's mother tell someone at church that the Jahntoffs would be moving to Cincinnati at the end of the summer. Time was passing, like wind. Time was passing and soon Ruth would be married to someone, raising children, and working as a secretary somewhere. She would forget him. It was not just the thought of losing her—it was the utter stupidity of it. He had never told her how he felt. He had not walked her home since Christmas vacation, which now seemed a thousand years ago.

He saw a free space at a table occupied by Curtiss Baylor, Larry Norcross, Buck Moore, Marilyn Sord, Melissa Van Ghent, and Harriet Emerick. On an impulse he sat down with them, something he had never even thought of doing before. Apart from brief and muted gasps from the girls, there were no repercussions, and Roger attacked his spinach cube, his beans, and his franks without looking up. Soon the conversations resumed.

Marilyn was the first to leave. She waved at everyone, smiled, and fairly danced out of the cafeteria, followed immediately by Harriet and then, more slowly, by Melissa. The boys sat for a while and leaned back in their chairs, like uncles without cigars. Finally Buck and Curtiss got up, mumbled something about the playground. Without looking, Roger saw the shapes of their bodies rising, moving, disappearing. Then he glanced up and saw, to his surprise, that Larry was still sitting in his place, his lunch only half eaten. He sat with his arms crossed in front of him. He stared at Roger.

"Well," said Roger.

"Well, well," said Larry.

"Well, well, well," said Roger.

Larry smiled his acid smile and put his feet up on the table. "Your face is all back together," he said. "After all the fuss you made."

"Didn't your mother ever tell you not to put your feet on the table?" said Roger.

"Lots of times. I tell her to go straight to hell."

"That's terrific," said Roger. "You're captain of the basketball team and you wrestle and you punch people in the face and you tell your mother to go straight to hell. You're just tough as nails, aren't you?"

"That's about it."

Roger stared at his enemy. There was something very odd about this, he thought. Why would he stay behind without his audience? Was there something he wanted to say?

"Aren't you going to run after your friends?"

Larry did not answer. He put his feet back on the floor and leaned forward in his chair. The malicious smile faded. "I know you," he said. "I know you real well."

"You don't know a thing about me," said Roger. "You don't know anything about anybody."

"I know you better than anyone," said Larry. "You and all

your books and your smart remarks and your father being an engineer and all. I know you real well."

"Jesus, is that supposed to make sense?"

"You know what I mean."

"I don't have the slightest idea what you mean."

"You can't catch as well as my baby brother," said Larry. "And you look like a grasshopper."

"Well, we can't all be beautiful like you," said Roger. "I mean, with all your pretty muscles and all that curly hair, you must stand in front of the mirror naked for about an hour every morning and just love yourself to death."

"You're just full of it, aren't you? Such a bright boy. I bet you read *The Atlantic Monthly*. I bet you do crossword puzzles. Well, let me tell you something. This is my time. Don't you ever forget it."

"You told me that once. It still doesn't make any sense—"

"For the next two years," said Larry, "you're the grasshopper and I'm the tiger in Technicolor. You're just damn lucky your crazy buddy blew his head off. That's the only thing—I mean the only thing in this whole world—that ever could have got you off the hook this year—"

"Larry, you're sick, you know that?"

"—and let me tell you, you're really gonna to get it next year. The whole school is gonna laugh its ass off every time you open your mouth. I don't give a damn about later on, you hear me?"

"What do you mean, later on?"

"You know what I mean. Don't pretend you don't know what I mean, you little bastard."

"You mean after graduation?"

Larry looked down at his hands. "You know just exactly what I mean," he said. His voice suddenly seemed very careful.

"You mean after graduation when we all go off to college? Is that it?"

"That's a million miles away. Right now I'm the captain of

the varsity basketball team—did you know I'm the only sophomore who ever made captain?—and you're the grasshopper with tobacco spit all over his face."

Roger stared at him. "You think that afterwards—" And then he remembered something about Larry not getting along with his father, not wanting to go to college and major in business administration or engineering. For the first time he wondered just what the future held for Larry Norcross, who now had everything. He could not imagine him going on to college and working at it. Larry hated books. Nor could he imagine him going into his father's business, wearing a gray suit, taking orders. He thought about the Japanese at Midway, the Japanese who had everything and lost it because their time had passed. They had come too far across the Pacific and had run out of luck.

"I guess you're not looking forward to graduation," said Roger.

The boy laughed. It was a cold mirthless laugh that reminded him a little of Harry. "I guess you could say that."

Larry wiped his mouth with his napkin and threw it on the metal tray. Abruptly he got up. He stood there for a moment, looking around the room, blinking, as if he had forgotten where he was. Then he picked up his tray and went the long way around the table so that he passed Roger on his way to the tray wash.

"There's only one way things can be," said Larry. "It doesn't—you know—it doesn't do any good to wish things could be different."

As he brushed by, he punched Roger very lightly on the back of his shoulder. "Listen," he said. "Take care of yourself."

Roger did enough studying during the last week of school to get through his exams, and after a day in the library he wrote an eight-page term paper for English class on "Senator McCarthy and the Death of American Democracy." Roger knew that he had, as usual, overstated his case, but Mrs. Budge gave him a C-plus. Across the top of his manila folder she wrote, "Interesting but confusing. Don't use semicolons until you get to college. Don't begin sentences with *but* or *and*." On his semester report card he received a C in all subjects except Latin. Miss Simic, in spite of his weak finish, gave him an A-minus.

On Friday afternoon William R. Mace held the final assembly for the year and passed out the annual prizes. Wilbur Frankey won the American Legion Essay Contest on "What the American Flag Means to Me." Curtiss Baylor won the Sophomore Scholar's Trophy. Harriet Emerick won the Latin Prize. Sidney Fitz, the boy who had the largest paper route in the high school and who had saved Piggy Munsen from drowning at the quarry pool on the north side of town, won the Good Citizenship Award from the Rotary Club. Johnny Chance, a boy Roger had never even heard of, was Sophomore Athlete of the Year, beating out Larry and Buck by six votes.

Roger was very happy not to have won anything. He was happy that everyone seemed to have forgotten him. He was happy that the little X in the *yes* box at the bottom of his report card indicated that he had passed on into the eleventh grade. He was happy that no one bothered him anymore, not even the Italians. He was even happy when his birthday came and went almost without incident: his mother left a card on his desk with a five-dollar bill in it and a promise that they would all celebrate when his father came home at the end of the month.

At seven-fifteen the following morning, Roger shut off his alarm, rolled onto his side, and gave himself one more minute of blissful sleep before the agony of getting up. An alarm clock in the morning, Dennis had once remarked, was like a screech owl perched on your skull. Roger took a deep breath and felt the morning cloud of misery gathering in his forehead. Then, with a rush of unreasonable happiness that comes only once a year, he remembered. A green door opened somewhere in his mind, and the light of summer filled his room. School was out. The summer stretched before him, infinite and various and full of mystery. He lay at the center of everything that was bright and beautiful. He opened his eyes and listened to the morning wind blow past his open window.

He could run through the woods. Take in the matinee at the Strand with Dennis and Frank. Spend cool hours under the slow, wooden fan at the library. Go down to Roosevelt Memorial Field and watch semipro softball in the afternoon or get lost in the pulpy pages of his science-fiction magazines. The world was suddenly and wonderfully crowded with possibilities. At eight-thirty he had agreed to meet with the other Denizens at Pangborn's and plan the whole summer.

He began to think of women. Marilyn Sord lay next to him, impatient because they had not *done it* for nearly twelve hours. He watched her lift up her cotton dress, the one with the little blue flowers all over it, to expose her long white legs. Instantly he was ready for her. He turned and began to move against his pillow, whispering beautiful obscenities, things that shocked and delighted her. In two minutes he spent himself. He noticed, when his breathing had quieted, that the breeze outside his window had gone away and left the morning warm and yellow and utterly silent.

Ythn reached down from the bedsprings in the upper bunk, where he had woven himself into a kind of tapestry, and curled one green finger around Roger's ear. "Well," he said, "if you're *quite* finished, I think we ought to have a little talk."

"I'm resting. I don't want to talk."

"This is a very important day," said Ythn. "This is the end of bondage and the beginning of freedom. The war is over."

"So?"

"So we need to have our First Day of Summer Vacation Colloquy."

"Ythn, go back to sleep. This is my quiet time."

"I wonder," said Ythn, "why you never think of Ruth when you do that."

"When I do what?"

"That. What you were just doing ninety seconds ago."

"Oh. You mean *that*. Well, Ruth is just not that kind of

girl. She's more the operetta type. You know, the kind of girl you take to dances and give roses to and sing songs about."

"Because she's beautiful she fails to inspire lust. How curious."

"Well, I did think about it a couple of times with Ruth if you have to know everything," said Roger. "Mostly in dancing class. When you hold her hand she kind of comes off on you, and then when you dance close when Miss Dot isn't looking, you can feel her eyelashes and her nipples and I'm telling you it's almost more than a man can stand. But I think with a girl like Ruth you shouldn't think about that stuff too much until you get married."

"Are you going to marry Ruth?"

"I can't. She's moving to Cincinnati. You can't marry a girl who moves to Cincinnati. Ythn, I really don't want to talk about all this stuff—"

"It will be sad when Ruth is gone," said Ythn.

"But she'll still be here for ages and ages, maybe even for the whole summer—"

Roger got out of bed, dressed, and then sat for a while on the floor in front of a pile of pulp magazines that he had been too tired to put away the previous evening. Three collapsed piles had fallen together, reminding him in a vague way of a ruined Aztec temple. He had gotten behind in his reading in recent weeks, but he had looked through some of the older issues in his collection, which seemed rarer to him, and more precious. He always began with the letter columns and then went on to the advertisements, which never failed to fascinate him. Now he turned to the back of an old issue of *Fantastic Adventures* and saw a blurb for the U.S. Rocket Society, an ad for a book of police jiujitsu strangleholds (only 25¢), information on how to build a celestial instrument that made music through the power of nature (no musical training required), and more ads for books on hypnotism and *illustrated* comic books (the kind adults like!). And finally: *Become a Mental Superman Overnight! Floor Everybody! No Studying! Rev-*

olutionary Memo-Prop does all your Thinking! It's Uncanny! Unprecedented! Free Money-Back Guarantee! Write: Bijou Hollywood Studio, Hollywood 28, California.

"All these things are sort of the same," said Roger. He ran his thumb along the ragged edge and the pages turned quickly.

"How do you mean?" Ythn made little circles with his suction cups over his mouth filament, a sure sign that he was either thinking deep thoughts or was about to do so.

"All that stuff is for people who can't think. They all promise you great power or the secret of life or something like that, and then when the stuff comes in the mail it's just this little mimeographed pamphlet that says you should practice mental discipline by thinking about your belly button for fifteen minutes every day, or it's this little celluloid whistle with a tweeter inside, and on top it says 'Music of the Spheres.' And then you can send for a free booklet that only costs two dollars. You know, like the Rosicrucians."

"Thoughts have wings," said Ythn.

"Don't give me that stuff," said Roger. "My thoughts are like owl pellets. My brain chews on all this stuff and spits it out and then it lies all over the place and no one else ever has anything to do with it. I hate thinking. Thinking spoils everything."

Ythn oscillated. "You know that's absurd," he said. "And you don't believe it for a minute. Not anymore. You dislike non-thinkers. You just said yourself that all the magazine ads are for people who can't think."

"Never mind what I said."

Roger flipped to the back cover of the September issue of *Fantastic Adventures* and saw the ad: *Thoughts have wings*. "The Secret Mastery of Life," said Roger. "God, I wish it was all true."

"You don't seem to care much for the American dream," said Ythn. "A really good cigar, a twelve-inch TV screen, a house in the suburbs, a passionate wife, two beautiful children, a country club membership, a two-car garage, and a three-week vacation every summer in Bermuda."

"Is that the American dream? I didn't know."
"You don't seem to find it terribly interesting."
"I like the part about the passionate wife."
"And the rest?"
"I hate it. I just hate it. I hate it like I hate television."
"You want a different kind of dream."
"Right."
"You want a whole symphony orchestra to burst forth every time God makes a sunset."
"Right."
"Nothing means anything without violins."
"Right."
"You want Mars. You want to live for a thousand years. You want wings. You want everything to be music."
Roger thought for a moment. "I guess so. But nothing you ever really want to believe in ever turns out to be true. That's why all this thinking is just not terrific. Not terrific at all."
"You are at the stage when everything seems to be coming apart. Everything is losing its essence. Everything is getting distinct from everything else because your sense of the uniqueness and complexity of human experience is so much greater than what it used to be."
"Ythn, I hate it when you talk like this. I never understand a word you say. You sound like one of those Unitarian ministers."
"Then let me show you." Ythn crawled toward him in his spidery way, and then reached out with all four of his arms.
"Ythn, what are you doing? You're getting too serious—"
"I want you to close your eyes," said Ythn. "I want you to think about where you are."
"Where I am? What you do mean, where I am?"
"I want to show you the thing you are most afraid of. You are afraid that you too have lost your essence. You are afraid that you don't exist."
Roger closed his eyes and felt the Martian's fingers on his cheeks. "Make sense, will you? Is this face music?"

"No, this is not face music. I am trying to help you locate the seat of your consciousness, as you humans call it."

"I still don't get it."

"I'm talking about where you really are. You're not in your foot, isn't that correct? Now keep your eyes closed and sit up straight and cross your legs. That's it. Now think where you are. Your brain is a great house, and somewhere inside there is a sacred place, a temple between your temples. Where are you? Can you find yourself?"

Roger knew that the bed was on his right and that on the other side was the window. He knew that if he leaned back he would fall over a pile of magazines. But where was *he*? He believed—he knew—that he was crouching somewhere behind his eyes. His fingers seemed far away now, and his toes. His hair grew a hundred feet above him, like grass on the surface of a small planet. But down here in the dark he was hiding somewhere.

He could feel Ythn touching him. The soft cups touched his ears, his brows, and wove in and out of strands of his hair and listened to the arteries pulsing at his throat. Ythn's fingers were stars in the darkness; they illuminated the great dome of blind sensations that was his awareness of the world when his eyes were closed.

"Roger? Have you found yourself?" Ythn's voice came from the outside, from far away, like someone shouting across a lake.

Roger reached into the place just behind his eyes, but he could not find himself. Odd. Only a moment ago he had been so sure that he was there. He felt further back. Nothing. The more he tried to stop thinking so that he could feel that central, pure awareness that was where everything began and ended, the less of it there seemed to be.

"It's like looking at a star, isn't it?" said Ythn. "One looks at a star and the star disappears. You look away and there it is again."

"This is scary," said Roger. "It's like there's no one home up here."

"It's frightening to look at anything closely when you're barely sixteen," said Ythn. "The thing you look at divides into parts and pieces. The ghost vanishes. The essence disappears. Even passion is that way. You think about sex too much and all you have is parts. You can't do anything."

"Nothing is real," said Roger. "That's what Harry Fisher found out. Everything is just facts. The great war is over and now there's just a whole bunch of aftermath."

"You must understand," said Ythn, "that the ghost still lives. But it's not something you can put in your pocket or someone you can meet for lunch. You must have faith. You must believe that the universe is like a rose and that it flowers out in all directions and that at the center of the rose there is a heart, a seed, something from which the ghost emanates. You must believe that it's there, and that it has always been there."

Roger opened his eyes. "I can't find myself," he said.

"You will," said Ythn. "Remember that to understand the labyrinth you must first become lost in it."

"Ythn, you never tell me anything practical. Like how to keep Ruth from going to Cincinnati."

Ythn looked at him, his gray eyes soft and lustrous, his arms and legs all crooked in concentration so that he looked like a jumble of coat hangers. Very gently Roger drew various parts of Ythn together and then held him against his chest. "You old fuzzy," he said. "You're all over the place. You have too many arms and too many fingers."

Ythn rested his furry, triangular head against the crook of Roger's arm. Roger felt a surge of electricity, a cold pleasant feeling that was vaguely like the taste of peanut butter.

By eight o'clock his room was clean, his teeth brushed, and he was on his way down Stone Hill Road toward Pangborn's Used Book and Magazine Store. The trees and lawns and houses moved by slowly, gliding along the edges of his vision, like green mirages. The air was thick with summer heat. A bright blue Hudson sedan passed by him on its way from somewhere to somewhere. He turned back once and saw

Ythn's faint outline behind his window, like a shadow, or a tracing of dust.

He was troubled by the strange thing that Ythn had taught him, and he wondered now if the reason that he could not find his consciousness was that not all of it was inside him. Perhaps consciousness was not a thing, but a meeting place. Somewhere between the stars—which were the brain of heaven in that awful poem that Mrs. Leibolt had forced the whole class to read—and the soft gray brain inside the dark cave of his own skull. It was like Pangborn's bookstore. You wandered through the Forest of Symbols. You reached out to the books and the books reached out to you, and the meeting place was a magic space somewhere in between. The mind was a part of everything and so the world was just not a string of pictures. It was not a comic book that you could read through and understand. It did not run on names, and it did not move through the grooves of slogans and clichés. And all the air-brush posters taped in the hallways of junior high schools all over America about hard work and success and opportunity and the American way had nothing to do with the real world.

He was surprised to see that all the windows at Pangborn's had already been replaced. A fresh gray wedge of putty along the edges showed the work had been done yesterday, or the day before. Nothing else had changed.

The bells jingled when he entered. The bright windows showing pictures of the world outside, the dim room with its rows of books, the iron radiators squatting like Chinese dragons, the ancient bronze cash register, the long table at the end of the room with its pitcher and glasses and chairs—all these things were like friends who had waited for him through the long weeks. Outside the back window Roger saw that Pangborn had cut the grass and raked all the cuttings into the far corner. Pale green leaves had curled around the grape arbor, and roses bloomed like dreams along the walkway.

Dennis Kirk had lost a little weight, and the shadow of a mustache lurked beneath his nose. Frank was still short and round and yellow. He saw from their puffing and their quick chatter that they had arrived only a minute or two before him.

Pangborn turned around the moment he heard the bell. His long nose, his narrow face, the soft hollows in his cheeks, his thin hair combed straight back—all these things looked so familiar they hurt. "Roger! Goddamn, you finally made it! Dennis and Frank have been here since five this morning—"

Dennis waved to him as though he were a mile away. "Hey, Roger! We thought maybe you got sick—"

"Roger?" Frank's voice was tentative, almost plaintive.

"Take a gander at my new windows," said Pangborn.

"They must have cost you."

"The city did it for free," said Pangborn. "One of the town councilmen, this big guy with a gray face, came over last week and said that in the interests of smoothing over relations the town had decided to fix the windows providing I would agree not to dwell upon the events of the last few weeks. I told him I would damn well dwell upon whatever I wanted to dwell upon, and that the freedom to dwell was one of my inalienable rights as an American citizen."

"Wow! That's telling him!"

"What did he say then?"

"He said I was a troublemaker and that he knew my kind, and then I simply reiterated that neither he nor the mayor nor the police were going to tell me what to dwell upon, think about, or meditate concerning. I added that if he did not fix my goddamn windows I would do a lot more than dwell, and that he and the whole damn town were already in enough trouble without my calling the governor, the FBI, and the Jewish Defense League. The next day the windows were fixed."

"Wow!" said Frank. "Did you really say all that? You didn't. Did you really?"

"I suppose all this has been terrible for business," said Roger. "I mean, business must be even worse than usual."

"On the contrary," said Pangborn, "business has been wonderful."

Pangborn led them to their table at the back of the store. As they sat down he opened a white box full of cream-filled delights and poured orange juice into cups, and the Denizens knew they were home. "I was losing my shirt all year long," Pangborn was saying, "and now I can't keep anything in stock. People ask for the damndest things. Apparently my reputation precedes me."

Dennis smiled. "So what do they ask for?"

"You remember the nun? Well, she came in again. I told her welcome back, but she swore up and down she'd never been here in her life. She asked me if I carried nudist magazines and if I had something called *The Garden of Love*. Said she had to be prepared to fight the Devil's work with foreknowledge. This other guy wanted a copy of *Mein Kampf*, and someone else wanted Polish magazines and someone else, this very old lady with flowers stuck in her hat, wanted an aphrodisiac cookbook she read about in a French magazine, if you can imagine that."

"What a switch," said Roger. "I mean from last month."

Pangborn leaned back in his chair and smiled. He looked tired. "Last month is such an old story," he said. "I call it Patriotism with Fangs. People get together around the campfire and sing ugly songs and make up stories about all the people who are not around the campfire. Their eyeteeth get very long. Pretty soon they see things that just aren't there."

"Like what?"

"They think the Communist-Negro-Jewish Conspiracy once again threatens the American Way of Life. They think the Flying Saucers have landed. God knows what they think. It's like something out of a comic book."

"It makes me think of Harry Fisher," said Roger. "I don't know why, but it does."

They sat together for a while without speaking. Soon the cream-filled doughnuts were gone and the pitcher of orange juice was half empty. Outside, three blue jays landed on the cement birdbath, ruffled their feathers, cocked their heads three ways, and then hopped over the rim, all in less than a second. Roger believed he had a clear impression of what it must be like to be a bird, to fly and sing and live everything so quickly, and always in the present tense.

"He came in here one day," said Pangborn. "Did you know that?"

"Harry? Harry Fisher came in here?"

"He sort of walked around for a few minutes. Pulled out a few books and looked at the covers. After he sniffed around for a while he asked if this was where the Denizens met, and I said yes and then I told him about how we sat around in the afternoon and talked and drank OJ and looked out the window. He gave me this funny little smile with his lips all pursed together and then made this bark that I guess was supposed to pass as laughter. And then he said, 'Sure sounds cozy. Like sardines packed in fish grease.' I guess that was his way of saying he didn't care much for intimacy."

"That's Harry," said Roger. "That's Harry all over."

"And then he did a very funny thing."

"What was that?"

"He pulled this package out of his shirt and unwrapped it. Said his mother forced him to buy a present for someone's birthday, and he asked me if it was the kind of thing a kid would like. Such a crazy thing to say. As if he were from the planet Venus and didn't quite know what a kid was."

"What was the present?"

"It was a hunting knife."

"In a leather sheath?"

"Right. A Boy Scout knife. He told me he heard that the birthday boy was a very unusual and very special kid, but then he added that this was only a rumor and that mostly when you hear that sort of thing about people it means that they either love Shakespeare or they eat owl shit. Does that make any sense?"

"It's rococo," said Dennis. "*Very* rococo."

"I hate it when people poke over things that dead people

said," said Frank. "People should be dead a lot longer before you start up with all that stuff. Like maybe at least five hundred years."

"God," said Roger. "God, I don't believe it."

"What?"

"He gave *me* a hunting knife. Just the day before—before he did the deed. Said it was something his father gave him, and I would be doing him a favor if I took it. Said it was a garbage knife. He was just about to throw it away, he said. And then when I thanked him and said it was a really great knife and that I never really had a good knife in my whole life, he got real mad. Why would he get mad? And why would he buy it for me and then pretend he didn't?"

"Some people can't stand to be thanked for anything," said Pangborn. "They can't stand it when they feel sympathetic or charitable. They can't stand it when someone finds some trace of human feeling in them."

"My father told me a story once about a prostitute named Evelyn Casablanca, only that wasn't her real name. Anyway, she used to cut herself in the arm every time she fell in love. She just hated herself when she loved anyone."

Frank got up and began to pace around the table. He hugged himself and shook his head and closed his eyes. "Why do we hafta talk about all this stuff?" he said, his voice rising almost to a screech. "Why do we hafta talk about bleeding prostitutes and smashed-up windows and what dead people said? Don't you guys know that we don't hafta give ourselves the willies anymore? All that's over with."

"You know, Frank's right about that," said Dennis. "We're being *very* rococo."

"Well then, let's forget about everything," said Pangborn. "Let's go for a ride."

"A ride?"

"Where?"

"In what?"

"I have a car," said Pangborn.

"A car?" said Frank. "You mean you drive? You go places?"

"You think I'm part of the bookstore," said Pangborn. "You think all I ever do is stack books and drink orange juice and talk to you guys."

Roger blushed. "Well, sort of. We thought maybe you had a room upstairs and had your meals sent in."

"This place has no upstairs," said Pangborn. "I'm here to tell you I have an apartment across town with two cats, a car, and an aunt who cooks like an angel. This summer I may even have a girlfriend. That is, if business continues to improve."

"God," said Roger.

"You're kidding," said Frank.

"Reality totters," said Dennis.

Their morning ride out into the Watchung Reservation in Pangborn's ancient Buick ("Old Whale Mouth," he called it) ended with a swing around Horseshoe Valley Road. As they counted the shadows in the sunken forest, they talked about their adventure in the Watchung, their encounter with the police, and the almost supernatural response of the citizens of Greencastle to their various activities. They all laughed into the wind. They knew their strings had snapped and they were free to float across the first perfect, clear day of summer. They agreed that within the week they would return to the Henrietta Mackelroy Swamp, this time with an army-surplus rubber raft, a box camera, a slingshot, and a whole pocketful of steel ball bearings.

Dennis and Frank had to be home early—their mothers were taking them shopping for summer clothes—and so Pangborn let them all off at Roosevelt Memorial Field. They shouted their goodbyes, agreeing to meet for lunch at Dennis's house at one o'clock sharp.

Roger began to run. He felt his tennis shoes dig into the green summer and the wind stream past his ears and between his fingers. He knew that he could run halfway across town without stopping. And he knew, as he had always known, that no one could catch him. Not the housewives who fumbled fruit in the outdoor market downtown, or the black man who polished shoes at the corner of Springfield and Maple, or the smiling pink-faced lady who sold tickets at the Strand (that stale, sweet, dusty popcorn paradise of Westerns and serials and detective thrillers that left your head buzzing after four hours in the flickering dark), not the milkman, all in white, who came like a ghost at six in the morning and left milk bottles and cartons of cottage cheese on doorsteps, not anyone anywhere, not even in Newark or East Orange, could catch him when he ran through the summer.

He took a half turn at the athletic house without breaking stride and passed the swings, the monkey bars, the concrete tunnels and painted pink castles, until he came to the point of the L where the two huge squares of the field came together. He looked up, and then he knew why he had come this way. Playground Joe had come back.

"Hi!" Roger shouted across the green grass. "Hi! It's me!"

Joe, dressed as always in his absurd black business suit, looked away from his strings for a moment and waved. Behind him, his pushcart, piled high with games, leaned at a dangerous angle. Joe did not seem surprised to see him. It was as if they had said goodbye only a moment earlier, and winter had passed in the wink of an eye.

Joe was eight months older, but he looked the same. It was not conceivable that he would ever change. He leaned from side to side as he walked. The scar ran down his neck. His paunch bulged under his buttoned suit coat. Roger had forgotten how ugly he was.

"Hi yourself," said Playground Joe.

Roger slowed to a walk and put his hands in his pockets. He squinted up at the three kites. "I'm Roger Cornell. You probably don't remember me."

"Course I do. That's my business. You're Roger Cornell. Course you are."

"Wind's up."

"Not too much," said Joe. "But I got three kites up, as you can see. Thought maybe I'd try one more. Glad you came along, Roger Cornell. Have to get my caroms and chess and croquet set up tomorrow. Time to get things going."

"Is this your first day back?" said Roger.

"Came back yesterday," said Joe. "Been watching the sky."

"Should be a good summer," said Roger.

"Should be," said Joe.

He saw that Joe still had two kites on the ground. He had painted a silver zeppelin on one, and a red clown on the other. "All hand-painted," said Joe. "Pretty good, don't you think? For an old veteran?"

"Real good, Joe. Do you still have the Flying Man?"

"Flying man?"

"You had a kite last September with a Flying Man painted on it. I think it was the first one you did."

"Never painted a flying man," said Joe. "Would have remembered that."

"But I saw it on the ground right here. I remembered it all winter. The Flying Man."

"You're thinking of something else," said Playground Joe. "I never painted a flying man. Just started up painting again this April."

"You just forgot," said Roger.

Roger peered up at the three kites, which now stretched far over the town. Joe was the only man alive, he thought, who could get a kite up and out over a thousand yards. Today it was two blue and one red. At that distance they were bright and tiny, like bits of costume jewelry pinned to eternity.

"The wind is steady when you really get up there," said Joe. "That's why they don't seem to move. Everything is steady when you get up high. 'Cept, of course, when it isn't."

"I guess you been up in airplanes a lot," said Roger. "I mean, during the war."

"During the war," said Joe.

"I think my dad flies sometimes," said Roger. "His company makes him go different places on business."

Joe was looking out into the sky past his kites. His eyes lost their focus.

"Was it a bad time, Joe? I mean, when you got hurt?"

"Got hurt," said Joe.

"It must have been a long time ago."

"We got shot up over Stuttgart," said Joe. "Everyone in the plane was dead but me and the copilot. We came through the flak and the fighters and then everything got real quiet going home. All those clouds rolling underneath us. After I lost all that blood I got to feeling real peaceful and light as a feather, and then I saw something."

"You saw something in the sky?"

"Something very big. Off on the left side about three o'clock. Sort of thought maybe it came to keep me company."

"But what did it look like?"

"I got hurt," said Joe. "I don't remember. It was something."

"You mean like a flying saucer?"

"Don't know. But ever since then I been thinking there's stuff up there in the sky we don't know about. Stuff hiding in the nooks and crannies."

Roger followed the long curving lines of nylon thread, hanging in the sky like enormous parentheses, until he found once more the diamond-shaped kites, two blue and one red. "I think you're right, Joe," he said. "In fact, I'm absolutely sure you're right. You can quote me on that." Somewhere, he knew, there would have to be a place in eternity for Playground Joe and his kites. Joe and his kites and games and the dome of blue that always hung over his part of the summer.

"Well, Joe, what's new? What's in the papers?"

"Ten months of truce talks in Korea," said Joe. "F. Batista set up a 'disciplined democracy' in Cuba, know what that is? W. C. Handy says he hates the NAACP. Ike is gaining in the primaries. The King of Jordan went crazy. Robert Merrill and Roberta Peters got married in March and divorced in June. A nigger wrote a novel. Can you imagine a nigger writing a novel?"

"Don't say nigger, Joe."

"Well, that's what they are, aren't they? Anyway, that's the news."

"The news is tough to understand," said Roger.

"The news doesn't make any sense," said Joe. "Never has."

Joe laughed. He laughed loud and hard, and then he jerked one of his kite strings. A thousand yards away Roger saw the red kite tilt from side to side like a jitterbugger keeping time with her shoulders.

"I got to go now, Joe. I got to run."

"Where you going? You just got here."

"We all have to meet at Dennis's house for lunch. We're going to make all kinds of plans for the summer and play checkers and listen to the Ritual Dance of Fire on Dennis's phonograph."

"Well, okay then. See you tomorrow. We'll get something going tomorrow."

"Right. See you tomorrow, Joe."

In less time than it took to say it, he was gone from the field. He ran past Harry Fisher's dark house and made his way up the long, shadowy hill where Recognition Street met High Point Avenue. Here he made a right turn into the sunlight.

It made him laugh with joy to think that it was still morning and still the first day of summer. There was so much new to think about now that things had turned out all right. He knew that he had heard the words of the Donkey spoken to the Cat, and that he and the Denizens had all been delivered from He Who Lived upon the Intestines of Princes, and that he could rest now in the Flowering Field north of the Grasshoppers. It all made perfect sense even though he had no idea what it meant. And then, as he ran, he stretched his arms to the sky, reaching for Mars as he had done on so many summer nights that last year, and the year before. And as he thought of Ythn and the Rosicrucians, he realized that he could always and forever leap from star to star, no matter how many light-years lay between. Thoughts (he thought) have wings.